A FATED EMBRACE

LaRaine opened her mouth to speak, but no sound came forth. She knew that she should protest, turn her head away, do something. Instead, her feet, of their own volition, rose on tiptoes to make her open lips more accessible to his mouth, which descended slowly, hypnotically, as if in a dream, to within a fraction of her own. She could feel his warm breath, coming more rapidly now, blowing sweetly across her face.

Brand reveled in the delicious fragrance of her perfume. He pulled her closer against his rangy length, and his lips hovered above hers, so close she could feel the quivering electricity charging wildly through her body, leaving her weak with a hunger she had never felt before—desire . . .

FORTUNE'S CHOICE

MICHALANN PERRY

ZEBRA BOOKS
KENSINGTON PUBLISHING CORP.

ZEBRA BOOKS

are published by

Kensington Publishing Corp.
475 Park Avenue South
New York, NY 10016

First printing: October, 1988

Printed in the United States of America

To Maura Seger and Victoria "Vicki" Thompson who encouraged me to stick with LaRaine and Flame;

To Joyce Smith at Books N' Stuff for her "advance promotion" on this book;

And to my agent, Ruth Cohen, who always believed in my "twin story."

Prologue

Gordonville, Virginia — March 1848

Clutching the blanket-wrapped bundle closer against his muscular chest, Thomas Ashby urged his horse forward into the angry, driving rain. He knew he should have brought the buggy, but there had been no time for rational thought — only quick action.

"It won't be long now, little daughter. You'll be in your mother's arms before the hour is out!" he encouraged, patting his burden reassuringly after checking to see that it was still dry under his warm coat. "You'll have the most beautiful, loving mother in the world."

A pang of guilt jerked violently through Thomas's conscience. He hadn't wanted to leave the baby's twin sister behind — not in that filthy, drafty shack with the drunken father and emaciated mother, who already had more children than she could care for, all bruised and hungry. But how could he have explained twins to Amanda? She would have known they weren't hers. Would she have accepted another woman's children? She had been so adamant about wanting her *own*.

7

It was a chance Thomas hadn't been willing to take, so he had paid Cutter Doyle a hundred dollars, more money than the Doyle family had ever seen; and he had taken only one of the newborns, knowing he would always be haunted by the other child's hungry cries as it suckled at its mother's dry breast.

Even now, he thought about going back for the other baby. But it was too late. He was almost home and he couldn't risk having Amanda waken before he returned. He had left orders for secrecy with the midwife and doctor, telling them to keep his wife drugged if necessary until he came back. And under no circumstances was anyone to know of the Ashby baby's death!

Thomas Ashby was met at the back entrance of his large home by the midwife, who only a few hours before had told him about the newborn twins. Not waiting for explanations, the old woman snatched the wiggling, wailing infant from the rain-drenched man, and dashed up the stairs with a spryness that belied her age by twenty years.

By the time Thomas had changed out of his wet clothing and entered his wife's room, the baby had been bathed, dressed in a soft flannel bunting, and ensconced in a satin-lined bassinet. Amanda had not awakened.

"How long is she going to sleep?" Thomas bellowed, his weary voice falsely gay. "She was in such a hurry to have a child, and now that she's got one, she doesn't wake up long enough to see her! Just like a woman," he laughed, the strain evident in his handsome face making him seem older than his forty-six years, despite his lean, hard body and head of thick blond hair.

"I think I saw her eyes flutter a few minutes ago," the old woman answered in a whisper. "It won't be

8

long now. Not with you makin' all that noise!" she scolded.

"It certainly is hard to get any rest around here," Amanda mumbled with a sleepy smile, extending her hand toward her husband. "Where is it? I want to hold my baby."

"I'll git her for you, missy," the old midwife said excitedly, happy to see that Amanda looked none the worse for wear. "She's been hollerin' for her ma!"

"No," Amanda answered urgently, trying to raise up and stop the woman. "Let Thomas bring her to me. She's our gift to each other. I want to be alone with my husband and little girl," she insisted, lying back on the pillow, her words still thick with the drug she'd been given. "You understand, don't you, Madie?" she asked the midwife, who made no secret of the fact that she didn't understand at all.

"Are you sure?" the woman asked hesitantly, trying not to let the disappointment show in her expression.

Thomas smiled his gratitude. "It's all right, Madie. Everything will be fine now—thanks to you. I don't know how we'll ever repay you."

"Yes, sir," she answered, making certain they were aware of her disapproval.

When they were finally alone, Thomas gingerly picked up the squirming infant and carried her to his wife's bed. "My darling wife, may I present your daughter."

"Oh, Thomas!" Amanda sighed, bringing the infant to her breast. "She's so beautiful!" She giggled happily as the tiny mouth clamped onto a swollen nipple and sucked noisily. "Look, Thomas! Her hair red! Your light hair and my dark hair have made our daughter's hair the color of copper. Isn't she the loveliest thing you've ever seen in your whole life?"

She lifted her eyes to meet her husband's loving gaze. "Thank you, Thomas," she said with feeling, unembarrassed by the tears that welled in her blue eyes.

"Thank you? For what?" he answered, his own eyes watering suspiciously at the vision before him.

"For this wonderful gift you've given me. For making me whole with your love and for this miraculous life our love has created. I promise you I'll be a good mother. You'll see."

"Sweet girl, I never had any doubt about your mothering capabilities." Relief flooded wildly over him, leaving him weak with exhaustion. "What shall we call her? The way she's going after her dinner—or is this breakfast?—maybe we should call her Voracious!"

"I think not." Amanda's happy laughter filled the room with music. "I'd like to name her after the rain, the spring rain. That way we'll never forget the glorious miracle God sent us this rainy night. Is LaRaine all right with you?" she asked timidly, knowing Thomas would accept any name she chose, but still wanting him to feel he had a part in the decision.

"LaRaine is perfect, my sweet," he said, stifling a yawn.

"Then LaRaine it is! Whenever we hear or see the rain, we'll be reminded of our gift to each other. No matter how others berate the rain, you and I will think only of the wonder it brings!"

Noticing her husband's weary face, Amanda patted the bed beside her and said, "Why don't you lie down with us, Papa? You're part of this family too!" she teased, pulling her tired husband down beside her to rest his head on the pillow. He offered no resistance and readily buried his face in the clou f black hair that fanned out beside her.

"I love you, my sweet Amanda," he sighed, drifting off to sleep, the first real sleep he had had in three days.

"I know you do, Thomas. And I love you," she whispered to his unhearing ears before she slept, too, secure with her husband by her side and their baby, the product of their love, slumbering peacefully between them at her breast.

Part One - The Search

"There is no disguise which can for long conceal love where it exists or stimulate it where it does not."

— La Rochefoucauld

Chapter One

LaRaine Ashby moved uncomfortably in her seat, rtain there had to be a more pleasant way to travel an by train. Of course, if she could have afforded ride in one of the new sleeping cars that the Ohio d Mississippi Railroad offered its first class pas- ngers, it might have been a different story. But she ew she had to watch her limited funds carefully, the crowded day coach would have to do.

Resolving to think of things other than her own scomfort, LaRaine held a scented handkerchief up her nose and tried to close her eyes and ears to e harsh sights and sounds made by the mixture of ople and foreign languages that occupied the car th her. But her effort was futile. There was no way block out the wretched odors that filled the air. nfortunately, the smell of unwashed bodies and ul breath, combined with the reek of alcohol, stale bacco, and greasy foods, was overwhelming — not mention the ever-present stench that assaulted her ises from the curtained toilet at the back of the r. How could she stand another hour of this? uch less another day and night.

15

Leaning her bonneted head against the dirty windowpane, LaRaine stared absently at the landscape whizzing past in a colorful blur of autumn reds, oranges, browns, and golds. She wondered for the thousandth time if she would be able to find her twin sister—or if she was even still alive. From what her father had told her, it was possible the girl might not have even survived infancy.

Closing her eyes, LaRaine drifted off into a fitful slumber, only to be brought startlingly awake when the train jerked to a noisy, coughing halt, bouncing her forward, then back into her seat. Squinting to see the name of the town on the sign outside the station, she read aloud, "Dundee, Indiana."

"Don't you want to stretch a bit, miss?" the kind conductor asked. "We'll be here about thirty minutes," he added, then moved on toward the baggage car at the front of the train.

Nervously checking the safety of her money and jewelry in the hidden pocket under the first flounce of the rust-colored muslin dress she wore, LaRaine stood up eagerly. Unaware of the relieved sigh she breathed as she rose, she couldn't help smiling at the prospect of a few moments in the fresh air and out of the stuffy coach. It was an answer to her prayer. Just a few whiffs of clean air, and she knew she'd be able to make it the rest of the way to St. Louis.

She took a step toward the aisle, then paused, glancing back at the seat she was leaving unattended. She hated to chance losing her place next to the window. Not only did watching the scenery through the dirty window help the hours pass more quickly, but it would be a very long night if she had nowhere to lean her head. Still, the thought of breathing clean air was too inviting, too tempting, and quickly drove all thoughts of unpleasant conquences from her aching head. She would just have to hope the seat would remain vacant until she returned.

Having decided to take the risk, LaRaine smoothed her hands down the wrinkled flounces on her conservatively styled dress, again thankful she had left the extra petticoats and hoop in Gordonville—since she hadn't been on the train more than an hour when she had seen that current women's styles were definitely not conducive to train travel.

Making one last check to be certain her brown straw poke bonnet was secured by the ribbon tied in an attractive bow below her left ear, she stepped eagerly into the very narrow aisle.

Taller than the average woman, at five feet six, the slender girl hurried toward the rear exit from the dingy car, her lightly freckled face tinged pink with anticipation.

In her excitement, she was unaware of the cool blue eyes that studied her—had in fact observed her with seemingly idle interest since she had boarded the train at the start of her journey three days earlier.

Damn, thought Brand Colter, wearily unfolding his lanky frame from the uncomfortable bench, across the aisle and several seats behind the spot LaRaine had claimed as her own. He had been hopeful he would be able to follow his quarry to St. Louis without revealing himself to her. But that would be impossible now. He couldn't let her leave the train—at least not without him nearby. Everyone knew Dundee was an unquestionable crime center and a known haven for criminals, where armed bands of robbers freely roamed the countryside unchecked—stealing, raping, and murdering. No, he had better keep her on the train if he expected to get to Missouri with her.

Shaking his head irritably, Brand stepped into the aisle, deliberately placing his long, hard body in the path of the girl who was hurrying toward him.

Before she could stop herself, LaRaine slammed into the man blocking her way, her face actually touching his shirt front before she bounced back from the impact.

"Where're you going in such a hurry?" he drawled rudely, catching her upper arms with strong, tanned fingers to stop her from falling.

"I beg your pardon," LaRaine returned with an indignant huff, giving her shoulders a shrug to free herself from the man's familiar grasp. Aware that the top of her head didn't quite reach the height of the offensive man's shoulder, she was forced to tilt her head back to see his hard face—unless she wanted to speak into his broad chest, which she definitely refused to do. Her father had taught her that no matter how frightened she was, not looking a person directly in the eye would put her at a worse disadvantage. It would make her look afraid. Besides, she knew all too well that watching a man's eyes was the quickest way to assay any situation, be it dangerous or otherwise. So, gathering every modicum of bravery she could muster, she met the stranger's gaze boldly, effectively disguising the painful flutter of fear gnawing at her insides.

"I asked where you were going," the man repeated softly. He studied LaRaine's upturned face with obvious admiration and surprise, his tone having lost the gruffness it had displayed when he first spoke. Up close, the girl was nothing like he had expected. The way dark auburn curls framed her face, she looked young, almost angelic, to him.

Angelic? I'm going crazy! She's an angel all right

18

An angel straight from hell! he reminded himself, remembering all he knew about this woman.

Brand Colter's lip curled with disgust when he thought of the ugliness that lurked behind the glaring eyes of the girl. No one knew how many men she was credited with killing. Yet, here she was looking directly at him, showing no shame, no regret, so close he could smell the delicate scent of her perfume, could almost count the light, fashion-defying freckles on her nose. He knew he should loathe her—but for some reason he didn't! Couldn't!

Her eyes were unlike any he had ever seen. Strange, spirited, innocent eyes. Innocent eyes? Impossible! She'd been Quantrill's mistress when she was fourteen, and there was no way of knowing how many men there had been since then. No, there was nothing the least bit innocent about this girl.

Yet, those eyes! What color were they anyway? Green? Yellow? Blue? *I'll be damned! They're all three,* he realized, returning her direct gaze, refusing to back off as a lesser man would be inclined to do under that intrepid frown.

But Brand was hardly aware of the expression on her face. He was too engrossed with her strange eyes. Centered around sparkling pools of black, her irises had the exotic look of green and yellow mottled jewels, ringed with a vivid band of dark blue, as if nature had deemed any one color insufficient to compliment her loveliness. There was even a speck of brown pigment floating boldly in the marbled color of her left eye—as if the artist had splashed it there as a last-minute signature to his finest work.

Brand continued to search the upturned face, hoping to find what it was about this particular woman that had the power to hold him spellbound where he stood in the dirty, narrow aisle of the westbound train.

Though her physical appearance attracted him to her, that wasn't it. No, it was something else, something so obvious that it was almost tangible.

It was her spirit. Never had he seen such undauntable spirit.

What in the hell are you thinking about? You know what this woman is, and you're standing here like a love-starved pup admiring her spirit! Suddenly Brand was overwhelmed with the desire to shake the girl, to make her be anybody but who she was.

"I said, where are you going?" he repeated through teeth clamped tight with anger.

"Where I'm going is none of your concern, sir!" LaRaine said scathingly, her husky voice unwavering, confident — exactly what Brand would have expected. "However, if it will remove your hands from my person, and you from my path, I shall be more than happy to tell you. I'm stepping off the train for some fresh air!" she said, praying her false bravado would convince the man who blocked her way that she was unafraid of him.

Pretending to believe her act, Brand backed down, removing his hands from her arms, his expression almost apologetic. "That's not a very good idea." He gave her a cool smile. "This is a rough town," he went on, his tone derisive. "A sweet, innocent lady like you wouldn't be in the station two minutes before someone would have dragged you off to steal more than your money. Abusing pretty young things is a way of life in this town!"

Doing her best to cover her shock, LaRaine tried to rally. "I don't know why you're trying to frighten me, but you're not succeeding," she stammered. "I can take care of myself." She grew light-headed under the knowing smirk he leveled at her.

"Somehow, I thought you'd say that," he grumbled under his breath, wondering how many weapons she had hidden on her person. Several, no doubt. He chastised himself inwardly for looking forward to the pleasure of searching her for the secreted pistols and knives. "Go on back to your seat."

"I must get some fresh air. Before I faint." She was no longer pretending. "Please allow me to pass," she insisted breathlessly, giving up the hope that he hadn't heard the tremble in her tone.

You're good, he told her silently as he shifted his weight and crossed his arms over his chest. *You could almost convince me you're as naive as you pretend to be. Almost, but not quite. I'm afraid I've seen your pretty face too many times to fall for your act.*

Losing patience with the charade—and with his faltering resolve—Brand blew out an exasperated sigh and gripped LaRaine's arm. He gave her a rough shove toward the end of the car. "Then, I'll come with you! You really shouldn't be alone—in case you faint."

"Take your hands off me," she spat angrily, struggling against his hold on her arm. "I don't want you to accompany me!"

Without warning, Brand became embarrassingly aware of an uncomfortable tightening in his trousers. He hurried her along with more urgency than necessary. "Right now I'm all that stands between you and that fresh air you prize so highly! So if you want to go outside, you don't have any choice but to go with me," he snarled, angry with himself for the unprofessional feelings he was having about the situation.

"You have no right to do this," LaRaine protested,

running to keep up with the man's long-legged stride. "I don't want you to come with me."

"Then get back to your seat."

As he had said, LaRaine had no choice if she wanted to get off the train. Besides, what could he do to her in the crowded station? If he tried to hurt her, she would scream and there would be someone nearby to assist. So she didn't resist when he guided her out of the rail car; and when they reached the platform at the back of the car, she hesitated only an instant before she started to step down from the train ahead of the rude stranger.

"Hold it right there," he growled, tightening his grip on her arm and yanking her to a halt. "Breathe fast, and then get back to your seat!" he ordered, his icy blue eyes searching the crowd of people milling in the depot. Since the arrival of a train in town was still a large event, they had drawn quite a crowd, and Brand Colter had no intention of allowing his determined companion to set one foot off the train to get lost in it.

"But I thought . . ." LaRaine started, dangerously close to tears, at last losing control of the facade she'd been able to maintain until then. Feeling the tears welling behind her eyes, she scolded herself for being so weak. Well, she might be weak, but she wouldn't let this bully see that weakness—not if it took every ounce of strength she had to hide it.

She bit her lip to stop her words, and screwed her face into a tight expression of resolve. She was not going to cry.

Despite all he knew about this woman, to Brand she seemed like a confused child—a child who could burst into tears at any moment. And he actually felt guilty for not believing her performance. In fact, for an instant, he was convinced the girl could not be who he knew she was. And he was momentarily undone by the realization of the girl's ability to make him think so foolishly.

Of course it was her! Who else could she be? There couldn't be two women like her. Two so lovely. Two with such red hair. Two with eyes so large. Damn! What was he doing here? Why did he have to be the one to spot her on the train? Why hadn't he taken an earlier—or a later—train? If only he could contact someone before they reached St. Louis, he could have her taken care of and be done with her for good. But as it was, it would be necessary to get her to Missouri before anything could be done about her. If she just didn't seem so vulnerable

"I know what you thought." His bitter answer made him sound much older than his twenty-seven years, even to himself. With great effort, he dragged his gaze away from her face to scrutinize the crowd with exaggerated thoroughness.

Drawing on strength she hadn't known she had, LaRaine swallowed back her tears, vowing she'd stay in the stuffy day coach another week before she would let this boor see that he had frightened her.

"Look here! I've had about enough of this," she lashed out angrily, the yellow in her eyes shooting piercing shards of fire at the man who had stepped into her life so abruptly. "If you don't leave me alone, I'll . . ."

An insolent leer on his face, he shifted his weight and narrowed his eyes threateningly. Pushing aside the front pieces of his black, thigh-length coat, he hooked his thumbs in his gun belt. "You'll what?"

LaRaine's panicked gaze dropped to the ivory-handled revolvers he wore low on his lean hips, the holsters tied to muscular black-cloth-encased thighs the way she'd heard gunfighters wore their guns.

And her bravado faltered again.

"Who are you?" she hissed, her stare held prisoner by the dangerous-looking weapons. "What do you want with me?"

"Who I am doesn't matter," he answered, letting his coat fall back over the guns, his voice raspy. "I'm just a man doing his job."

The peculiar answer, and the note of sadness LaRaine detected in the man's tone, brought her eyes back up to his face. Frowning her confusion, she studied him. His bronzed skin had the look of finely grained leather, with faint lines etched in his face evidently caused by long hours in the open. And she had to admit he was quite handsome—in a rough unorthodox sort of way.

His black hair was longer than was currently stylish, brushing the top of his black shirt collar and covering the tops of his ears. Worn with no part or hair oil, it was wavy and unruly, falling on his forehead in a manner that seemed appealingly little boyish and curling where it willed from under the wide-brimmed black hat he had shoved back on his head.

Clean shaven, with no customary mustache or bushy side whiskers, his strong chin, square jawline, broad forehead, and prominent cheekbones gave the overall impression of strength and honesty, for some odd reason making LaRaine instinctively want to trust him. Straight eyebrows and curling eyelashes of black emphasized the light color of his eyes that sparkled the brightest blue she had ever seen. His mouth was well shaped, if a little crooked, and his nose looked as if it had once been broken, but that too, only added to his look of strength; and all in all, LaRaine had to admit he was the handsomest man she had ever met.

Suddenly chagrined by her open appraisal of him, and realizing she hadn't responded to his last remark, LaRaine turned her face to the side. "And I'm part of your job?"

He nodded his head, his attention again focused on the people in the train station.

LaRaine's gaze followed the direction his was taking, stopping on a group of holstered men conversing furtively on the depot platform. "Do you know them?" she asked, her natural curiosity overcoming her confused anger for the moment.

"They're not important," Brand answered absently, his eyes still intent on the throng of people. "Are you ready to go back inside now?" Without waiting for her answer, he took her arm and started her toward the interior of the car.

Catching him off guard, she jerked her arm from his grip, but kept her back toward him. "I'll scream if you touch me again!"

Realizing her raised voice was calling attention to their presence, Brand decided it would be best to answer her questions. "The name's Brand Colter, and I guess you can say I just want to look out for your safety."

His low voice ghosted over her, sending disturbing chills throughout her entire being, embracing her, paralyzing her, and LaRaine could feel his warm breath on the back of her neck moving the tiny tendrils of dark auburn hair curling out from under her bonnet.

"I don't need anyone to look out for me," she breathed, embarrassed by the reaction she was having to his nearness. Thinking to put some distance between them, she spun to face him.

However, he was closer than she had calculated, and for the first time since she had encountered him, she was truly frightened — frightened of his virility, of the wonderfully clean smell of him, of the blueness of his eyes, of the strength in his large hands, of his intensity, of his immense height, of his broad chest and shoulders — and of the hot sting radiating, wildly, mortifyingly, from the pit of her stomach to her every extremity.

"I wouldn't say that," Brand laughed, showing even white teeth unstained by the use of tobacco. "Any woman foolish enough to travel without an escort needs someone to look out for her. You can't imagine what all could happen to you out here in this part of the country. Especially in a place like this town," he emphasized, slanting his head toward the throng of rough-looking citizens of Dundee. "But then, maybe you prefer the company of that type," he smiled knowingly.

Determined to disguise her surprise, LaRaine tilted her chin defiantly. "What is it you really want, Mr. Colter? And don't for one minute think I believe you have any desire to protect me."

"I'm tired of discussing it. Get back to your seat and keep the one beside you empty for me. You're going to have a companion for the rest of the trip to St. Louis — whether you like it or not!"

"This is ridiculous!" she sputtered. "I'm not saving you a place, and you're not going to be my companion or anything else!"

"You'll do what I say — if you know what's good for you," he said with a harsh laugh, giving LaRaine a rough nudge back into the rail car.

Deciding anything was better than continuing to talk to Brand Colter, LaRaine shook off his hold and stomped back into the foul-smelling train car. At least no one had taken her seat in her absence.

With a less than gentle shove, he forced her down

nto the uncomfortable bench. "Don't get up until I
ome back!"

Before she could respond with an order of her
wn, Brand chuckled. "And try to keep from check-
g whatever you've got in that hidden pocket of
our dress!"

"What?" LaRaine gasped incredulously. How did
e know? She'd been so positive no one would be
ble to detect the secret pocket she had sewn into her
ress! Was that what he meant by a job to do? Was
e planning to steal her money at the first opportu-
ity?

LaRaine shivered at the thought. She couldn't be
bbed! Everything she had of value was in that
ocket! When it was gone, she would have to stop
r search for her sister.

Seeing the look of genuine panic rise in the girl's
llow-green eyes, Brand gave her a knowing grin —
if he enjoyed her fear. But the feelings Brand
olter was having were anything but enjoyable as he
rew a waterproof canvas overcoat on the seat be-
de her, where she sat looking lost and alone, not
owing which way to turn. *She's really just a kid*,
 thought, a wave of guilt rocking over him.

Overwhelmed with a sudden need to defend him-
lf from wasting his sympathy on the likes of this
man, he twisted around and strode back out of
e car.

Feeling only slightly relieved as she watched Brand
olter's broad shoulders disappear through the
orway, LaRaine slumped down in her seat. For the
st time, she wondered if this whole trip was a
stake.

Allowing her tears to go unchecked now that she
s alone, she stared blindly out the train window,
nembering how excited she had been when she

had received William Pinkerton's letter from New York informing her there was a woman in southern Missouri who had a description almost identical to her own. No one knew for certain where the mysterious young woman came from, or what her real name was; but it was rumored that she was the daughter of a certain Cutter Doyle, the same man Thomas Ashby had named on his deathbed as being LaRaine's natural parent.

Pinkerton had said he felt it was his duty to warn LaRaine that there was a warrant out for the arrest of the other woman, who was supposed to have been a Confederate irregular fighter during the war. In fact, he had suggested that LaRaine forget contacting the woman and let him keep looking for another woman. But LaRaine knew in her heart that there was no need to search further. It was her sister. It had to be. Though the photograph William had sent was blurred and faded, it was impossible for LaRaine to deny the uncanny likeness to her own picture, so she had made immediate arrangements to close her house in Virginia and leave for Missouri despite William Pinkerton's warning.

And I'm not going to turn back, she told herself, straightening her posture and shooting a defiant glare over her shoulder at the rear door of the train. *I'll not be frightened by someone like Brand Colter.*

Turning back toward the window, she slipped her hand inside her reticule, feeling for the secure harness of steel. Her fingers closed over the small pistol within, and the strength of the metal rushed into her veins. *No one's going to stop me from finding my sister,* she sniffed decisively, still unable to stop the flow of tears that had been held back all the months since her father's funeral.

Crying as she was, LaRaine was unaware when the

ain slowly pulled out of the Dundee station; and though her head was turned toward the window, he didn't notice the view quickly go from the crowded depot, to the wide, unpaved main street, lined with tents, wooden shacks, saloons, and brothels, to the forest again.

Well, this is getting me nowhere, LaRaine finally thought, when at last her tears were spent, leaving her feeling surprisingly strong again. *I'll just stay on the train and ask the conductor to purchase my meals for me. No one can hurt me if I stay on my guard. We'll be in St. Louis tomorrow. The Pinkerton agent will meet me at the station, and he'll take care of Brand Colter if he persists in bothering me.*

She glanced down at the canvas coat crumpled in the seat next to hers. Without thinking, she rubbed the sensitive area on her upper arm where Brand had gripped her. She flinched when she touched a particularly tender spot. *I'll have bruises where his fingers dug into my arm,* she grumbled silently, determined to erase the odd feeling of sadness that enveloped her at the thought of never seeing Brand Colter again.

Chapter Two

Catching sight in the window glass of a sudde
movement behind her, LaRaine's thoughts were to
from the darkening landscape outside the train.
shudder of apprehension tripping up her spine, s
raised her glance.

There, above the reflection of her own face w
another face. Covering her open mouth with h
hand, she gaped in horror at the bizarre, expressio
less mask staring down at her.

Fighting the scream building in her throat, s
sucked in a deep breath, trying desperately to st
her rapid breathing.

"There you are," the frightening apparition sa
through the mouth hole in his feed sack mask.
been lookin' all over the train fer ya. What're y
doin' in this here car? I'd 'a figgered you fer travel
first class! Not in here with all this foreign scun

Through the eyeholes in the mask, LaRaine s
small eyes dart about derisively to take in all t
immigrants who occupied the day coach with h

"Are you speaking to me, sir?" she asked, assu
ing her most confident manner as she turned to fa
the man, as though she found nothing unusual
the fact that he was wearing a mask.

"Ya don't see no other fine-lookin' lady 'round ere, do ya?" he sniggered, again raking his glance ver the other passengers, who were all cringing in heir seats, hoping the bandit wouldn't see them and hoose them for his next victim.

LaRaine shot a desperate look at the man across he aisle from her, but he pretended not to notice hat was transpiring between her and the gun-toting uffian. She straightened her posture and glared directly at the bandit.

"Well, you must have mistaken me for someone lse," she offered, her voice politely condescending. he prayed the man wouldn't notice the quiver of er lower lip or her shaking hands as they twisted ne strings of her reticule with knuckle-whitening orce. Her posture stiff, she turned back toward the indow, hoping the outlaw would take her action as dismissal and leave.

"Oh, yer the one, awright. There ain't no doubt out that! I saw ya standin' on the platform back in undee — lookin' all snooty 'n actin' like you didn't now what you was doin' to the poor blokes who ouldn't never have no chance with a filly like you. Vell, it don't matter. I like my women high'n ighty! Makes bringin' 'em down that much better." e gave a loud laugh. " 'Course, on yer backs, none you's too high'n mighty!"

Stunned, LaRaine didn't speak. Her mouth falling pen, she stared numbly at the man who was begin-ing to fill her heart with a terror she had never efore experienced — not even during the war when oldiers from both sides had ravaged her home while ne had hidden in a secret cellar her father had built or that purpose.

Remembering Brand Colter as a spark of hope, aRaine cast a hopeful glance over her shoulder toward the rear exit from which she had expected him to return momentarily. But he wasn't there. No one was!

"Yer boyfriend ain't gonna be comin' to help y[sweetie!" the man said with a sneer, obviously enjoing her panic. "He's out fer a while." He paused laugh, then went on. "Yer my woman now. But I b[he broke ya in real good. I'll have to thank him if ever meet up with him again. Now, let's you'n me g[goin'."

He reached out and ran a black-gloved hand (LaRaine's arm and over her shoulder.

Shrinking back from his touch, she narrowed h[eyes threateningly. "Get your filthy hands off me[

With the speed of a striking snake, the bandi[hand grabbed the neckline of her bodice and ripp[it open, revealing the beginning swell of her f[breasts. "I'll put my hands on you any time I wa[to! Now, let's go!"

There was a collected gasp of surprise from t[passengers, but LaRaine barely heard it. Clutchi[at her bodice, she pressed herself against the wood[wall of the day coach she'd been so anxious to lea[only a short while before. "I'm not going with you[she said with the last fragment of her courage.

"Whit, what the hell're you doin' in here?" a voi[interrupted from the front of the car.

Everyone in the coach, the robber and LaRai[included, looked up to see another masked gunm[standing at the front entrance.

"I had to git somethin' I saw back in Dundee," t[man with LaRaine answered, never lifting his ga[from her heaving, hastily covered bosom.

"Well, git it 'n let's go. We're all finished up fr['n need to vamoose!" the other man ordered, turni[to leave.

"Ya heard Jake, Red. Better not keep my big rother waitin'. He gits right ugly when folks make im wait." He took LaRaine's arm and forced her to er feet. "Let's go."

"No!" she shrilled defiantly. Gripping the back of seat, she planted her feet.

Two woman nearby screamed, leaning forward as they were going to help. The bandit leveled a hard-yed glare at them and, moving as one, they sagged ack into their seats.

"I'm likin' you better'n better, Red," Whit rooned, swinging her easily over his shoulder and ubbing her rounded buttocks happily. "Mmm, ice," he chuckled to the accompaniment of her indless, frantic screams. "The wilder ya are, the ore I'm gonna like tamin' ya!"

"Somebody help me!" LaRaine cried desperately, ooking from one frozen passenger to another, her ves pleading. Her fists flailed uselessly at the man's ard back, while her feet kicked in mid-air.

The other travelers just watched, seeming to be ypnotized by what was happening, all obviously fraid to take action, no doubt praying the gunman ould not hurt them, as well as the girl! Only one nall man moved as if he might do something to elp LaRaine, and her heart leaped with an instant f relief.

The robber narrowed his eyes at the would-be vior, and the man froze in an awkward half-stand-g, half-sitting position. Shrugging his shoulders, e gave LaRaine an apologetic glance and fell back to his seat.

As though her struggles were no more annoying an a mosquito would have been, Whit carried aRaine to the front exit. Turning at the doorway to ave his gun at the dumbfounded travelers, he laughed. "You folks jest stay put. No one's gonna git hurt—'less one o' you tries somethin' crazy lik tryin to stop me 'n the little woman here." With that he backed out of the car carrying the wriggling yelling girl with him.

Her pistol! The pistol in her reticule. If she coul just get to it. However, LaRaine quickly realized th futility of that plan. The way the crude man wa holding her, the reticule was trapped between he body and the man's shoulder.

When a blast of cool evening air hit LaRaine i the face, the full comprehension of what was hap pening assaulted her with tornado force. This ma actually intended to take her away with him—to Go knows what fate!

Knowing she had no chance of physically fightin for her freedom, she took a deep breath and tried t reason with him. "Please let me go. I have to be i St. Louis. People will worry about me if I don arrive when I'm expected," she said sensibly.

"Sugar, the only way yer goin' to St. Louie is if'n take ya there!" he promised, running a hand u under her skirts to roughly knead her bottom.

An audible gasp wrenched from LaRaine's throa Horrified by the revolting probing and stroking her defenseless body and helpless to stop the viola tion, she renewed her fight with a strength she didn know she possessed. With bile rising chokingly her mouth, she kicked, she bit, she scratched every spot she could reach. Her screams rose to ea shattering volume.

But Whit was deaf to her cries, as well as numb her struggles, and continued to fondle and explo her through her thin undergarment.

It's a nightmare. It's not real, she told hersel closing her eyes tight in an attempt to blot out t

34

degrading feel of the man's rough, searching fingers.

"The way you feel, I might not never git tired o' you. You might not never git to St. Louie!"

How could this be happening to her? Where was the man who had insisted on appointing himself her protector? Where was Brand Colter.

At that moment, three other men joined LaRaine and her captor on the end of the rail car.

"What in the hell've you got, Whit?" one laughed, examining LaRaine in much the same way he would look over a sack of produce.

"What's it look like, Slidell? With winter comin' on, I got me a little somethin' to keep my bed warm!" Whit answered proudly, taking a hard, cruel pinch of LaRaine's bruised flesh. "If the rest o' her looks as good as her face, she's a real prize!" he said cockily.

LaRaine lifted her throbbing head and looked pleadingly at the other men. "Please help me," she begged weakly, her head spinning, her vision blurring from being held upside down for so long.

"Well, I'm shore glad you found some female company, Whit," another man said disgustedly, ignoring LaRaine's pleas. "How long's it been now? 'Bout a hour?"

"I don't need none o' yer wisecracks, Flint," Whit blurted to the other man. "I can't help it if'n the ladies all want me to bed 'em. I guess they jest know a man when they see one," he bragged, using his free hand to rub his crotch.

"Yer likin' fer stickin' the ladies is gonna be what does us in," Jake snarled. "I b'lieve next time we'll leave ya with the horses."

"Better not, 'less you wanna find the mares all knocked up when we git back," Flint said out of the side of his mouth.

"I ain't seen neither o' you turnin' down too many rolls in the hay," Whit laughed.

"What you do in yer free time is yore business, Whit, but when it starts interferin' with our work, it's my business," Jake, the obvious leader of the gang, said, his impatience with his brother evident.

"What's the matter, big brother? You 'fraid I won't share? Don't worry, 'cause soon as I git her broke, I'll give ya all a piece o' the action. I always do. Don't I, little brother?" he laughed, nudging Slidell who was eyeing LaRaine hungrily.

"Looks like this one's gonna take a lot o' breakin'," Slidell told him snidely, finally acknowledging the screaming girl's futile attempts to be free. "Ya jest might need some help, 'n I'm jest the feller fer the job!"

"That'll be the day! Don't ya worry none 'bout ol' Whit Ruston. 'Member that little blonde last summer? She shore was a fighter, but b'fore I's through with her I had her beggin' fer more. She couldn't git enough." Whit took a final squeeze of LaRaine's bottom and removed his intruding hand from under her skirt, sending a tiny whiff of relief flowing into her dazed brain. "That's jest to give ya a little taste o' the good times you'n me're gonna have when I git ya off this train," he said loudly enough for the others to hear—making certain they knew that nothing they said had bothered him a bit.

"Please let me go," LaRaine mouthed, the blood pounding in her head with deafening force.

"There's Tom with the horses," Flint shouted. He had removed himself from the conversation to watch for the signal. "Let's go." He rolled a small safe off the slow-moving train before turning to help the others shove a larger safe to the ground. "You ain't really gonna take that gal with ya, are ya?" he

36

grunted, exerting extra effort to move the heavy safe.

"I sure as hell am." Whit followed the tumbling safe and leaped from the train in one easy motion — taking his prize with him into the darkness.

Brand Colter lifted his throbbing head with agonizing effort. But the exertion was too grueling, and he couldn't summon the strength to keep it up. *What the hell happened?* he wondered, dropping his head back down. He concentrated on remembering as he steadily grew more aware of the rumble of the train wheels moving on the tracks beneath his ear.

He felt as if he'd been under the train, not on it!

Bent on ignoring his light-headedness, he hauled himself laboriously to a sitting position. In spite of the pain, he forced his eyes to focus on the darkness that whizzed past the moving train. Propping his elbows on his bent knees, he held his head in his hands, gathering a semblance of strength as the cool air hit him full force.

He remembered leaving the puzzled, copper-haired girl in her seat in the day coach. He had reasoned at the time that as long as the train was in motion, she wasn't going anywhere. Had he underestimated her? Had she known she'd been recognized, and been the one who hit him? Brand shook his head and frowned. No, it couldn't have been her. He would have recognized the scent of her perfume, the rustle of her dress. It had to have been someone else. Maybe a partner of hers or a member of her gang.

He knew now he shouldn't have let her out of his sight, but he'd had to get away before his desire became evident to everyone in the train. So he had headed for the open end of the coach, certain the ache in his loins would go away if he removed himself from her disarming nearness.

Placing his hand on the tender lump already forming at the back of his head, he winced when his fingers touched the sticky evidence of his assault, already clotting in his black hair. Hell, he couldn't remember the last time somebody had been able to come up behind him without being heard. And it wouldn't have happened this time—if he hadn't been so consumed with thoughts of what it would be like to kiss her sensuous lips, that creamy white neck, those full breasts that couldn't be disguised by the prim bodice she wore.

"This is getting me nowhere!" he muttered, claiming his black felt Stetson and staggering to his feet. Finding it necessary to lean on the railing to keep from falling again, he cursed his stupidity. He needed to rid himself of his crazy thoughts and concentrate on what had brought him to this point, on who had hit him, on completing his job, *and* on washing his hands of Flame Rider.

"If I'm going to make it to St. Louis with her," Brand muttered aloud, "I guess I'd better see if she's still here."

His head had cleared some, and the refreshing air on his skin had helped him regain his equilibrium, but when something flew past his gaze, he couldn't be certain it was not his imagination. Out of the corner of his eye, he thought he had seen a box tumbling from the car just ahead of the one he was in.

Certain his mind was playing tricks on him, he started to turn away. Just then a second box flew past him from the same point—but this one was larger and made a discernible thud when it hit the ground. Before he could examine the events assaulting his still partially dazed mind, he realized some

38

thing else had jumped from the train. It was a man carrying a burden over his shoulder. Three more human figures followed the first man and the boxes. All four took off running.

"Safes!" Brand shouted, the realization that the train had been robbed blaring his alarm. But before he could react, his eyes caught on what the first robber had set on the ground before him. It was a woman! Her! Flame Rider!

The train seemed to pick up speed, leaving the robbers unaware that their escape had been observed by the stunned man on the platform.

"Dammit!" The pain in his head was forgotten. "It was a robbery!"

Tearing open the door to the car's interior, he rushed inside to confirm what he already had surmised. She was gone.

He stared at his own coat which still lay in the seat as a grim reminder of his failure to carry out his duty. *At least now I know why I was hit on the head,* he thought angrily.

Well, Flame, if you wanted me out of the picture, you should've made sure it was permanent. He snatched up his coat and strode toward the exit, all thoughts of turning Flame Rider's capture over to someone else driven from his mind. "I'm taking you in—if it's the last thing I ever do!"

The jolt as Whit's feet hit the ground exploded through LaRaine, destroying the last of her hope. Raising her head with her remaining bit of strength, she screamed a shrill note into her abductor's ear.

"You can stop all that screamin' now, girlie. It's startin' to git on my nerves. 'Sides, there ain't no one to hear ya. Anyhow, I don't want ya so tuckered out

39

ya ain't no good to me. I like the gals I poke to have some fight left in 'em," he said, setting LaRaine on her feet and snatching off his mask to expose his face for the first time.

About twenty-five, Whit Ruston had stringy brown hair and heavy brows that met at the bridge of his large nose, giving him an even more frightening appearance than the mask had. His small eyes seemed black in the moonlight, reminding LaRaine of a rat's eyes, and she gagged involuntarily at the thought of the man touching her. Though he was muscular, Whit was only slightly taller than LaRaine, making it impossible for her to escape the odor of his foul breath when he spoke to her. And the sight of his yellowed, decaying teeth under the heavy mustache was an equally repulsive sight.

Nausea rose in LaRaine's throat again, and she grew dizzy. Unable to stop herself from reeling slightly toward the man's offensive bulk, she braced her hands against his broad, heaving chest to keep her balance.

"Whoa there, honey!" Whit chuckled, placing two thick paws around her small waist and holding her against his burly body. "I know yer prob'ly real anxious. I am, too. But we're gonna have to wait till the boys 'n me finish our business here." To make certain the girl knew what he was talking about, he cupped her buttocks with his hands and pulled her lower body abusively against his manhood, which was already displaying his obvious arousal.

Arching her back, Whit slobbered wet kisses on her cheek, grinding his hips against her at the same time he moved his lips toward hers. Thinking she could bear anything but his foul mouth on hers, she twisted her face to the side, giving him her cheek. "Please," she whispered forlornly.

"I said we gotta wait," Whit snarled, hurling her to the ground, where she sprawled helplessly, afraid to move — even to cover her exposed legs and heaving breasts.

"What are you going to do with me?" she asked, her yellow-green eyes wide with terror. LaRaine only had a vague idea of what went on between men and women, but she had heard enough horror stories during the war to know that being raped was the worst thing that could happen to any woman. She felt for her reticule to make certain the pistol was still there. It was, and she sighed her relief. *One bullet for him. One for me if I'm raped,* she vowed.

"Yeah, what're you gonna do with the little lady, Whit?" Slidell laughed, approaching the place where LaRaine lay on the ground, her skirts raised to display a long, shapely leg, her bodice ripped to reveal almost all of the fullness of her white breasts. Standing over her with his feet spread wide apart, Slidell took off his own mask and said, "You want me to show you what we got in mind fer you?" He began to fumble with the fly of his striped cotton trousers.

LaRaine stared wide-eyed at the horror unfolding before her eyes.

"You jest keep yer pants on, mister," Whit ordered his brother. "We ain't got no time fer that right now. Anyhow, I ain't so sure I wanna share her!" He shoved the younger man, who was slightly taller and more slender than he was, and reached down and hauled LaRaine to a standing position. He prodded her forward, forcing her to walk in the direction from which the train had come. "One thing's fer sure. You ain't gonna git a go at her b'fore I git my fill."

"Aw, hell, Whit! You know I was jest funnin' her. I wouldn't try to go first. Not when you found her.

41

But ya ain't gonna make me wait till yer tired o' her, are ya? Hell, Whit, if I wait till you git tired o' doin' her, I'll be too old to git it up!" he whined, racing after his brother and LaRaine, who was only kept on her feet by the band of steel that gripped her arm in the form of Whit's hand.

When the three arrived at the spot where the larger Adams Express Company safe had landed on its side, LaRaine saw the other two robbers had been joined by a third, evidently the one who'd brought the horses. Set on prying open the safe and claiming whatever cash and gold was within, they were already working on it with crowbars.

"You boys go on 'n git to work on the other safe," Jake Ruston ordered Whit and Slidell.

"That is, if you can keep from fightin' over that gal long 'nuff to finish what we come here for," Flint spat in disgust.

The brothers continued their arguing as they walked toward the other safe, each man now grasping one of LaRaine's arms, forcing her to run to keep from stumbling or being dragged. "I still don't see why ya gotta be so stingy with everythin', Whit. You always been that way. Never wantin' to share nuthin' with nobody till it was too old 'n wore out to be worth anythin'!"

"You jest keep on naggin' at me, boy, 'n I'll shoot yer pecker off b'fore I let ya at this here female. She's mine, 'n I'll say when 'n if anybody else gits a go at her!"

LaRaine's thoughts were a blur of confusion, and when they reached the first safe, she barely noticed when the two released their hold on her to work on the metal box.

However, after taking a moment to catch her breath, she was able to survey the area. Not far behind where she sat, forgotten by the robbers, was a dense woods. Whit and Slidell had their backs to her as, continuing their bickering, they concentrated on opening the safe.

If she were going to escape, it had to be now. She knew her chances of making it were slim, if not impossible, but she had to try. She couldn't kill them all with the two bullets her pistol held.

She glanced over her shoulder again to measure the distance to the woods. Ten feet at the most. If she could just reach the brush before they noticed she was gone, she might be able to find a hiding place in the dark forest. Surely they wouldn't stay to look for her. They would be in too much of a hurry to take their spoils and leave before the law came for them.

LaRaine gave no thought to what she would do once she eluded the brothers. She only knew she must get away—or die trying!

Taking a deep breath, she carefully bunched her skirts up under her bent knees. Keeping her attention focused on Whit and Slidell, she lifted her hips off the ground and cautiously eased her way back toward the woods.

Inching her way slowly toward the brush, she concentrated on everything the two were doing and saying, how many more feet to the edge of the woods, the crunch of twigs breaking as she moved over them, even the rustle of her dress material as it slid along the ground, ripping and snagging. But still she moved toward her goal, never allowing her eyes to leave the brothers at the safe they were working on.

"Sonovabitch!" an angry voice boomed, causing Whit and Slidell to look up from the safe.

LaRaine froze where she was, certain she had been discovered. Beads of sweat popping out on her forehead, she waited.

The sound of metal against metal rang through the air, jarring LaRaine's attention to the men at the larger safe. She could see Jake taking out his frustration on it with his crowbar. "This goddamn safe won't open."

"Yippee!" Slidell called to the others. "We sure got this'n open. Look't all that money 'n gold!"

"Wonder how much there is?" Whit pondered, delving greedily into the contents of the safe. "Come on, boys. Leave that'n. There's plenty here fer us all!"

Relief and understanding exploded into action inside LaRaine. Leaping to a crouch, she whirled away from the celebrating robbers and raced for the safety of the woods.

She ignored the sounds of her dress tearing as it caught on protruding branches and thorns; she paid no heed to the mud that covered her best pair of boots; and she was unaware of the blood trickling down her cheek where she had been scratched by a thorny vine. She had only one thought, which pounded over and over in her head in rhythm with her desperate footsteps. *Run . . . run . . . run . . .*

The pain in her side grew to agonizing proportions. But she kept running. Her surroundings became darker with each step she took away from the tracks. One foot in front of the other, she ran. Tears coursed down her cheeks to mingle with the dirt and sting the bloody scratches on her skin. Still, she ran. Her lungs expanding to the point of bursting, she fled deeper into the woods. *Run . . . run . . . run . . . run . . .*

Clutching at her side, she staggered to a halt, her chest rising and falling with labored pants. She couldn't go any farther. She had to find a place to hide before she fell down.

Spotting a gigantic fir tree, with broad, sweeping branches that dipped down to scrape the ground, LaRaine glanced back the way she had come, tilting her head to listen for sounds that indicated she was being followed. Convinced no one was there, she dropped to her hands and knees and scurried beneath the drooping tree boughs, which quickly enveloped her slight figure in their midst.

Burrowing into the thick cushion of dry needles covering the ground, she drew herself into a ball. Hugging her knees, she concentrated on quieting her breathing, stopping her sobs.

Resting her chin on her knees, she shifted her frightened gaze from side to side. In the distance she could still hear the train robbers celebrating their success. She squeezed her legs more tightly and rocked back and forth, willing her heartbeat to relax to a more normal rate.

Embraced in the quiet protection of the tree, her breathing became soft shuddering gasps. Slowly her eyes became accustomed to the intense darkness of her sanctuary, and her ears told her that the eerie night sounds of the forest were not to be feared—not like the shouts of the train robbers.

As the moments dragged by and still no one came for her, she began to believe again that she would survive. *In the morning, I'll make my way back to the tracks and follow them west until I come to the next town. If I have to, I'll walk all the way to St. Louis.*

Chapter Three

Standing on the metal step on the side of the coach, possibly three miles west of the spot where Flame and her men had disembarked, Brand hesitated only an instant before rolling to the ground. *You're going to pay for this, Flame. Not only for interfering with my vacation, or for robbing a train right under the nose of a Pinkerton detective. But you're going to pay for this goddamn lump on my head!* he thought angrily as his long legs loped at a steady pace toward the spot he had last seen the train robbers and Flame.

Brand quickly covered the distance to where the larger safe stood abandoned. An ironic smile curled across his face. For all their cleverness, the robbers had been unable to break open the sturdy Adams safe. *Sounds like they had better luck with the other one,* he thought, his expression sobering as he stepped into the woods. Moving cautiously, he crept toward the celebrating group of men gathered around the second safe.

Guns drawn, Brand Colter observed the four train robbers, who'd been joined by a fifth. They were eagerly dividing the contents of the smaller safe. Sweeping his gaze over the area, he was assaulted by the realization that something was wrong with the scene at the safe. Flame Rider wasn't a part of the revelry and money counting.

An instant of confusion halted his forward motion. He took another cursory glance around the clearing widening the span of his view. No Flame Rider. An annoying concern suddenly filled him with dread.

"Where's the girl?" he asked in a menacing, almost casual voice, despite the unexpected apprehension that was making his heart beat faster.

The five thieves whirled around in time to see Brand, dressed in the ominous black of a professional gunfighter, emerge from the darkness of the trees into the moonlit clearing. He was almost invisible against the black backdrop of the forest — with the exception of his teeth, which were bared in a frightening, satanic snarl.

"Where the hell'd you come from?" Jake Ruston stammered, unable to believe the fact that they were caught. He was the only man who spoke, however. The others just stared incredulously at the barrels of Brand's Remington .44 revolvers, uncertain if they were seeing a live man ofra ghost — maybe the devil himself.

Ignoring Ruston's question, Brand leveled one of the deadly pistols at a spot between the man's eyes and said through gritted teeth, "I asked you where the girl is."

The men all shifted their panic-stricken gazes to where they had last seen LaRaine — before they had found something more interesting to hold their attention. "She's gone, Whit!" Slidell blurted out, his eyes frantically searching the area.

"That's crazy," Whit gasped in alarmed terror. His eyes bulging with panic, he pointed a shaking finger

47

to where he had expected to find the girl. "She was right there. She musta run off into the woods, mister. We didn't hurt her. Honest, we didn't!"

So she wasn't part of their gang after all. They didn't even seem to know who she was. They thought she belonged to him. Well, they were right on that count. Flame Rider was his.

Brand didn't speak. There was no need. He told them all it was necessary for them to hear with the foreboding sound of two revolver hammers being cocked.

"Look, mister . . ." Jake Ruston began, taking half a step toward Brand.

"No, you look!" Brand came back, stopping Jake in his tracks, his voice obviously showing the restraint he was using to keep from gunning them all down at once. Always the professional, Colter quickly invented a ruse to disguise his true identity. "I've followed those safes all the way from Baltimore. They would've been ours in the next seventy-five miles. I have people and horses waiting for me up ahead. But now you've screwed up our plans with your clumsiness. I'd say you owe us. What do you think?"

"Hell, man," Frank stuttered. "If that's all what's gotcha so riled up . . ."

"We'll jest cut you in. You 'n yer girlfriend. There's plenty for us all," Jake added, feigning friendliness.

"It's too late for that, boys," Brand said, his voice a threatening monotone. "Now, where's my partner?"

"That little chit's your partner?" Slidell asked, astounded.

"Don't let that *little chit* fool you. You're lucky she didn't want to chance giving away our plans, or she'd have taken care of all five of you bastards! Now, where is she?"

"Hell, mister, she was right there," Whit whined. "I don't know what happened to her. I swear we didn't hurt her. Honest we didn't," he repeated.

"That remains to be seen." Brand motioned with one gun and kept the other aimed at the gang's leader. "Drop those gun belts, one at a time, and throw them over here to me. One stupid move, and your boss here gets the first bullet."

"Do what he says, boys," Jake Ruston ordered. The men, their faces shining with sweat, scrambled to follow Brand's orders. "Now get your loot and start walking back to town. If I ever see your faces again, you'll wish I hadn't!"

"Ain't ya gonna take our money?" Slidell asked stupidly.

"Since we're in the same business, I won't take your whole haul," Brand sneered, using one revolver to signal the men on their way. "I'll keep your horses, guns, and the other safe. That sound like a fair split to you boys?"

"But the other safe won't . . ." Slidell started.

"Shut up! Jus' git the hell outta here b'fore he changes his mind," Jake yelled at his brother, snatching up a satchel and scurrying along the tracks toward town.

"I'm warning you boys," Brand called after them as he vaulted into the saddle of a black horse. "If I don't find the lady, or if she's hurt, I'm coming looking for you; and I won't be so generous the next time we meet!"

Brand chuckled to himself as the five robbers made their frightened dash in the direction of Dundee. None dared to look back to see if he was still there.

49

When the scared robbers were out of sight, he dismounted and gathered up their discarded weapons, which he threw into a blanket and tied to the back of one of the other horses. Thus outfitted, he led the horses to the spot where the outlaws had indicated they had left the girl.

Stooping down to examine the trampled, dried grasses, he was able to see the trail of crushed weeds that led to the edge of the woods, determining that she had managed to scoot herself backwards into the trees. He wasn't surprised she'd had the courage and calm to carry out an escape, but he was amazed that she had left such an obvious trail. However, he was glad she had and led the horses into the forest at the same place LaRaine had entered not long before.

The light from the full moon, now at its zenith, filtered through the leafless trees, making it a simple task for an experienced detective like Brand to follow the trail left by a frightened girl. Discovering a bit of rust-colored muslin caught on a bush, a lost velvet reticule in a clearing, and the brown poke bonnet that had covered LaRaine's coppery hair, Brand proceeded quickly through the denseness.

Squatting to pick up a perfumed handkerchief from the carpet of dead leaves blanketing the forest floor, Brand grinned bitterly at the familiar scent which rose from the lacy flash of white in his hand. Again, he was astounded—and disgusted—by his overwhelming attraction to her.

"Damn!" He stuffed the handkerchief into his pocket and concentrated on following the blatant signs that marked the way the girl had fled. *If it weren't for her, I'd be halfway to St. Louis by now—instead of in this godforsaken woods!*

Well, that may be, but Brand Colter had never let down the law before, had never shirked his duty, no matter how unpleasant the task; and he had no intention of doing so now. So despite the uneasy feelings that plagued him, he moved on—even though instinct told him that each step he took toward Flame Rider led him deeper into a trap he might never be free of.

LaRaine sat up as straight as the low-growing branches of the tree would permit, her hearing alert to sudden danger. She had heard something! Something different from the night sounds of the forest that she'd already grown accustomed to.

There it was again! The cracking of a twig, the rustle of dead leaves crunching under heavy boots, the soft nicker of a horse. Someone was definitely out there. And he was coming toward her hiding place.

Watching the direction the footsteps were coming from, she patted the ground at her side. She would feel better with her derringer in her hand. When she didn't immediately find her purse, a fresh jolt of panic squeezed at her heart.

Certain it had to be there, she extended her hands in a wider arc, her taps on the forest floor growing more frantic by the instant. Nothing. The purse was gone. She must have dropped it in the woods when she was running. *No! I can't have dropped it!* She eased her knees up under her shaking body and stretched her search even farther out from where she was, burrowing and sifting her fingers through the brittle needles that covered the ground.

Oh, please, Lord, don't let them find me, she prayed silently, her eyes riveted in the direction of the footsteps, which grew louder with each step the stalker took in her direction.

"I know you're under there," a soft masculine voice called in a strong whisper.

Every muscle in LaRaine's body tensed and froze as she made ready to crawl out from under the tree on the opposite side.

"Come on out. It's Brand Colter—from the train. You're safe now. I won't hurt you. The others are gone."

Brand Colter? No, it can't be. How did he know where to find me? It's a trick. Unless he was with the robbers all along. . . .

"Come on out. Nobody's going to hurt you now!" he coaxed, his voice hypnotically gentle, as if he were talking to a frightened child. Watching the large fir tree where his search had led him, Brand leaned against the trunk of another tree, arms crossed on his chest. "I told you I was going to watch over you, didn't I? I sent those boys packing. You might as well come on out. I'm not leaving until you do."

He kept up the steady stream of words, though he was beginning to wonder if she were actually under the tree or had managed to exit on the other side of the huge spruce when she had heard him coming. "Do you want to stay here and wait for the Rustons to come after you? That's what's going to happen if you don't let me help you."

Not caring for the idea of working his long frame in through the low-growing, sharp branches, he decided to walk on, hoping his actions would disarm the girl and force her to show herself. If she would run into the open, he could easily overtake her, and that was definitely preferable to crawling on his belly under the boughs that grew less than two feet off the ground. Besides, on his stomach, it would be almost impossible to defend himself, should she decide to

52

attack with a knife or gun. "You're going to get awfully hungry," he called out over his shoulder.

LaRaine finally allowed herself to release an audible sigh of relief when she heard the man walking on — still calling to her, still telling her he would take care of her. *Just like you kept that man from taking me off the train in the first place. Thanks anyway, Mr. Colter, but I don't trust you any more now than I did before.*

The muscles in her legs cried out their protest as cramps seized them simultaneously. Biting her bottom lip, she forced back the scream that leaped into her mouth. Never had she been so frightened. But still she didn't move.

When at last Brand's voice had faded into the distance, LaRaine dared to shift her position and straighten her cramped muscles, so long frozen in a crouch. The action sent waves of frightening reality pounding cruelly into her brain, reminding her with a mind-clearing blow just how truly alone she was. And her alternatives narrowed to just one. She had to take a chance that Brand Colter was what he said he was, and nothing more.

"Come back," LaRaine pleaded, scrambling on all fours from under the drooping branches of her tree hideaway. "Please, come back!" She hit her knee on a protruding root. And the branches that had been her friends now turned on her, seeming to reach out and grab at her clothing and hair.

"Don't leave me here," she pleaded, escaping into the clearing beside the tree.

Able to stand erect for the first time in what seemed like an eternity, she dragged herself to her feet. Torturous needles shot into her legs and feet with the return of her circulation, and her legs folded beneath her. Crawling to a bare tree trunk, she hauled herself to her feet again, this time prepared for the prickly agony. Determined not to be left behind, she pushed herself away from the tree trunk.

Staggering, she took one step, then paused. Suddenly, the woods seemed to be closing in on her. There was no path. Nothing looked familiar. Maybe she had come out on the opposite side of the tree. No, she was certain he had been on this side, and he had gone that way. Her confused gaze shifted to her left. Or was it that way? Her eyes darted to the right.

She knew she was going nowhere, but merely circling in one spot, but she couldn't make her feet obey the command to start walking. She was no longer crying out, no longer trying to catch Brand Colter, no longer holding out any hope of ever reaching her destination. She couldn't even decide which direction the railroad tracks were.

Brand couldn't believe what he saw. *I'll be damned. She's scared to death!* Flame Rider scared! The woman he'd heard of wouldn't have been standing there whimpering like a frightened child—wouldn't have let the Rustons take her in the first place.

Brand shook his head in confusion, amazed to realize that no matter how tough a person seems, everyone has a breaking point, a weakness. Evidently, he'd found Flame Rider's. *Where's your breaking point, Colter?* he asked himself, the gut-knotting thought that he was closer to his own than he'd ever been in his life crossing his mind.

LaRaine heard the horses first—not loudly, just a soft snort, but it was not far ahead. Her immediate instinct was to step into the protection of a thick bush, but before she could react, she heard the

54

runch of footsteps in the dry leaves behind her. She
was trapped! "Who's there?"

"It's just me," Brand said softly, gently.

LaRaine whirled around to find Brand Colter
standing only a few feet away. Relief flooded over
her, lifting the unbearable weight of despair from
her shoulders. Without thinking, she threw herself
across the space that separated them and into his
powerful, protective arms. "I thought you had left
me." Pressing her wet cheek against his broad chest,
she clung to his waist, her words almost incoherent.

"There, there, it's all right now. I'll take care of
you," he soothed, his strong hands gliding over her
back and shoulders. She seemed so small, so defenseless; and for that moment, Brand didn't remember that she was a criminal wanted for murder
and robbery. He only knew he wanted to take care of
her, protect her. "I won't let anything happen to
you."

"They were going to . . ." she stuttered weakly. "I
didn't know what to do."

"You did the right thing. They didn't even see you
go."

"What if they come looking for me?" she asked,
the panic rising again in her trembling voice as she
lifted her head from his chest and cast a nervous
glance over her shoulder.

"We'll be long gone by then," Brand assured her,
growing more nervous and tense by the minute. But
it wasn't from fear of returning robbers! In fact, he
would have welcomed an interruption right then. At
least fighting with the Rustons would take his mind
off the beautiful girl in his arms—and off the pain
she caused in his groin. He wondered if she had any
idea what she was doing to him, all pushed against
his hardness, as if she couldn't get close enough, her

55

softness seeming to fit perfectly against his body, a if they were matching pieces of a puzzle that coul interlock in just one way. *Of course she knows That's why she's doing it.*

"I don't know what I would have done," she wen on. "I don't know how to thank you."

Brand cleared his throat. "No need for thanks." His hoarse voice revealed the inner turmoil he wa feeling. "I'm just doing my job."

"I don't understand," LaRaine started, lifting he head from the softly rising wall of his chest t examine his face. She still could not let go of th strength of him as her tear-filled eyes searched hi intense expression for the answers to her questions "Who are you? Why did you come looking for me?"

However, looking into the light-blue eyes, LaRain knew, in that instant, the answers didn't matter, wer of no consequence. LaRaine Ashby, who had neve in her life been alone with any man other than he father, knew the answers were of no importance a all. She had a staggering, mind-shattering sense o being safe and warm in the special place on eartl that had been created for her alone—in the arms o Brand Colter. It was where she belonged, woul always belong.

Her rapt gaze, still glistening gold with recentl shed tears, searched his for an explanation of wha was happening.

LaRaine opened her mouth to speak, but n sound came forth. She knew she should protest, tur her head away, do something. Instead, her feet, o their own volition, rose on tiptoes to make her ope lips more accessible to his mouth, which descende slowly, hypnotically, as if in a dream, to within fraction of her own. She could feel his warm breath coming more rapidly now, blowing sweetly acros

56

her face.

He reveled in the delicious fragrance of her perfume. She sighed. He pulled her even closer against his rangy length, and his lips hovered above hers, so close she could feel the quivering electricity charging wildly through her body, leaving her weak with a hunger she had never felt before—desire. Yet, still their mouths did not meet. Neither closed their eyes, as if to do so would break the spell that held them bound together at the brink of something too complex for either of them to comprehend.

Using every fragment of stoic denial he could muster at the moment, when all he could think of was how much he wanted the girl, Brand managed to regain control of his priorities and of the precarious situation. His hands slid to her trembling upper arms and he pulled her brusquely away from his painful need. "We'd better go. I want to cover some distance before the moon sets."

Without looking back, he dropped his grip on her arms and walked toward the spot where he had tethered the five horses, leaving LaRaine to follow behind him, more confused than ever.

The mesmerizing trance created by their physical contact cracked apart, freeing LaRaine's clouded thinking slightly. No longer under the scrutiny of the gripping ocean-blue eyes that went so easily from icy coldness to blazing infernos, then back to cold again, she was able to look at what had happened from a different perspective.

Thank heavens, Brand Colter was evidently the man of honor he claimed to be. If he had been going to rape and rob her, as the train robbers had been planning on doing, surely he would have done it then.

Embarrassment washed over her as she admitted

to herself that she had been saved through no action of her own. Instead, she had stood there, pressing herself against him, practically begging for his kiss. Disgust rocked through her as she remembered the sinking disappointment she'd felt when he had turned away from her.

Well, I won't make that mistake again, she vowed, shooting Brand a hate-filled glance. *I'll just follow behind him and let him lead me back to the tracks and to St. Louis. But I definitely won't get close enough to make that kind of a fool of myself again.*

When they reached the place Brand had tied the horses so he could silently double back and watch for LaRaine, he finally spoke. "Do you think you can walk until we get out of the woods?" Without waiting for her answer, he went on, taking care not to look at her as he checked the gear on each of the horses. "The brush is too dense in here, and I don't want to be slowed down by having one of us hit in the head with a low-hanging limb!"

He had said, "one of us," but he had meant her! As if he had no doubt that she would slow him down—just because she was a female. LaRaine's temper boiled. "Of course I can walk out! I walked in, didn't I?"

LaRaine's energy was returning in spurts. Her anger at herself, the strange man, her situation, had created an adrenaline flow that made her forget the cuts and scrapes on her face and arms, the weakness in her legs, and the ache in her back. All she could think of was showing the arrogant Brand Colter that she could take care of herself. "Are we going to wait for the next train?" she asked, leaving him standing where he was and taking off in the direction she hoped would lead her to the tracks.

He caught up to her in a couple of easy strides.

"Not unless you want to meet up with the Rustons again. Is that what you want?"

"Of course that's not what I want!" she hissed, taking two steps to match each of his. "How do you know those horrible men's names anyway? Are you part of their gang?"

"I thought you were!" he laughed bitterly.

"Me!" she shrieked. "How could you think that? Who are they?"

"Their daddy pretty much runs things in this part of the country."

"But they robbed the train! Won't the sheriff arrest them if we report it? Even if their father is important?" Her question was asked with all the righteousness of the very innocent.

Who're you trying to kid, Flame? "Their daddy *is* the law in these parts."

"I can't believe those vile men are allowed to run free, robbing trains and abducting innocent, law-abiding citizens. Surely someone is going to do something about it."

Brand didn't speak, didn't tell her that the Pinkerton Agency would definitely do something about the Rustons—but at a later date. Right now, he was interested in only one outlaw.

He studied her in the annoying way he had, making her feel as if he could look inside her head. His lips curled and he looked as if he wanted to say something. But evidently he decided against whatever it was, because he pressed his lips together and quickened his pace, forcing LaRaine to drop back—or run to keep up with him.

Following his example, LaRaine also grew quiet. If he didn't want to talk, it was fine with her. Besides, she needed all her strength to keep up with the long-legged man. If he were a gentleman. . . . *But of course he isn't. He's rude. Unfeeling. Cold. Not a gentleman, that's for certain!*

On the other hand—he hadn't taken advantage of her when she had thrown herself at him. A fresh wave of hurt washed over her as she remembered his rejection. She told herself again that she was relieved he had found her unappealing and unattractive.

But she wasn't relieved. Instead, her thoughts kept returning to the feel of Brand's arms around her waist, caressing her back, holding her against him. She had felt so safe. Watching his silent, forbidding form move ahead of her, she allowed herself to remember the solid feel of this chest when she laid her cheek against its strength. She recalled the exciting nearness of his mouth to hers, the feel of his breath on her face, the glint of desire in his eyes. She had thought he was going to kiss her.

Horrified, she admitted to herself that she had wanted him to kiss her. Had actually craved it!

The realization of her body's wanton betrayal stabbed LaRaine in the stomach with a deathlike blow, causing her to gasp aloud, loud enough for Brand to hear her and turn around.

"Are you all right?"

"Of course I'm all right," she spat irritably. "I'm just fine." She dropped her gaze downward, thankful for the darkness and for the fact that Brand couldn't see the guilty flush which had risen to her burning cheeks.

Chapter Four

Brand glanced up at the black sky that showed through the leafless branches over their heads. "The moon's set," he said offhandedly. He wasn't sure how long they'd been walking—three or four hours he decided—but he was anxious to mount up and put this Indiana woods behind him. He looked over his shoulder at his prisoner, his expression goading. "It should be safe to ride along the track easement now. You're not going to pretend you're too much of a lady to ride a horse, are you?"

LaRaine straightened her aching shoulders and stuck out her chin defiantly. Oh, how she'd love to slap that smirk off his face. "As a matter of fact, I ride quite well, thank you!"

Brand's lip curled bitterly. *The actress down to the last, aren't you, Flame? Let's see how far you'll carry your act.* "Astride?" he asked.

LaRaine glanced down at her skirt, then at the saddled horses. "I can, but I'm not dressed to ride astride. What will people think?"

An unexpected twinge of respect jerked through Brand's body. Never had he seen a woman—or man or that matter—with the ability to stick to a story so convincingly. His anger tightened in his gut. *She's a criminal!* he scolded himself for the hundredth time that night. But no matter how many times he reminded himself who and what she was, he couldn't erase the image of her trudging dauntlessly behind him during the past few hours. No matter how rough the trail had become, she had put one muddied boot in front of the other, over and over, refusing to ask him to slow down — even though it was easy to see everything that had happened had begun to take its toll on her strength.

Speaking of strength, his was dipping to an all-time low. "Come off it!" he bit out, giving the reins in his hand a jerk to bring the horses forward. "Don't you think you're carrying this too far?"

LaRaine's mouth dropped open to hurl an angry retort at him. But when she started to speak, she realized she had no words to deny what he'd said. Here she was, dirty from head to foot, wearing a dress that was ruined beyond recognition, and with hair that must look like it belonged to a witch. She had been kidnapped by train robbers and had narrowly escaped being raped. Then to top it off, she had spent the night tramping through the woods behind a man she didn't even know. And now she was worrying about what people would think if she rode astride wearing a dress — or what was left of a dress.

She sliced a glance up at Brand Colter to determine if he saw the humor in the situation as she did. His expression darkened and he shifted his weight crossing his arms over his chest as he made a deliberate show of waiting for her answer. But instead of having the effect on her he had obviously intended, his threatening glower just made the situation seem funnier to LaRaine.

Pressing her lips together to stifle the chuckle

building in her chest, she looked down at her boots. *What's wrong with you?* she asked herself sternly. *This is no laughing matter. You're in serious trouble. Serious! Didn't you see that look on his face? You might not even make it to St. Louis alive!*

She nodded her head and wiped her open hand down her mouth to erase the smile that still insisted on forming there despite her harsh self-reprimand. But her action was useless. The whole situation was just too laughable, too ludicrous: Brand Colter with his dour expressions and terse remarks, her with her silly worries about what people would think when she might not even live through the night.

Pursing her lips and forcing a frown, she sneaked another peek at Brand. If anything, his expression was more serious than before. She compressed her lips harder together, but it did no good. An unlady-like snort exploded from her throat.

Too late, she slapped her hand over her mouth as her shocked glance jerked back to Brand's solemn face.

At first it was just a snicker. But it quickly turned to giggles, which in turn became full-fledged guffaws that shook her whole body.

Unaware of the look of alarm that transformed Brand's face, LaRaine laughed harder and harder, oblivious to the tears that streamed down her smudged face, making muddy trails on her skin. It just felt so good to laugh again, something she hadn't done in months.

Panic thrashed in Brand's chest. He had pushed her too far and now she had broken. He grabbed her shoulders, fully expecting to look into the wild stare of a lunatic.

But instead of the insanity he had anticipated, he was given an insight into a quick, capable mind that was able to laugh at its own foolishness, able to admit the game was over, the charade at an end. Relief flooding through his strong body, he narrowed his eyes in puzzled amazement. Then he threw back his head and released a laugh that originated deep in his chest to mingle in the darkness with her higher, feminine giggles.

"You must think I'm crazy," she protested between hiccoughs.

"It crossed my mind." He hated the fact that he was actually beginning to like Flame Rider, and he tried to stop laughing. But he couldn't erase the smile that curved his mouth. There was just something about the way she looked at him. Her glance touched a spot deep within his soul—a spot he hadn't known existed in him. "Actually, I admire a person who's able to admit defeat."

LaRaine stopped laughing instantly. Her eyebrows arched quizzically. "Defeat? I wasn't under the impression there was a battle."

"You really do that well," he said, his tone admiring.

"Do what well?" Her voice rose in confusion.

"The indignant lady act. If I hadn't recognized you right away, you could have had me totally fooled."

"Recognized me? What are you talking about?"

Brand's expression sobered. "Come off it, Flame. The game's up."

"Flame? Who's Flame? My name's LaRaine, not Flame!"

"Give it up, Flame. It's over. I know who you are!"

She closed her eyes and inhaled a large gulp of oxygen, willing this craziness to end. Clenching her fists at her sides, she opened her eyes and forced a

64

patient smile. "Perhaps if we begin again. My name is LaRaine Ashby. Yours is Brand Colter. Who is Flame?"

He flashed her a conspiratorial wink and grabbed her arm. "Whatever you say." Starting toward the horses, he gave her a tug.

Rage and frustration exploded in LaRaine's head. Planting her feet, she wrenched her arm free of his grip. "Get your hands off me! I'm not going anywhere until you tell me what this is all about!" She brought her fist down, punching him on the shoulder.

He didn't blame her. He wanted to lash out at something, too. A vision of her body dangling from a rope flashed across his mind. *They can't hang her!* he protested. But another inner voice reminded him they not only could, but probably would.

He knew Flame Rider's outlook wouldn't be so bad if she only had to answer to the crimes committed in the name of the Confederacy during the war. He had read of cases where wartime guerrillas who had been denied amnesty at the end of the war, unlike the regular Confederate soldiers, were paroled after spending a minimum amount of time—or no time at all—in prison.

But Flame Rider would not be so fortunate. And it was her own fault. She had determined her fate when she had continued to use her guerrilla tactics after the war to lead her outlaw gang on a bank-robbing rampage all over Missouri. No, there would be no parole or amnesty for this woman.

A crushing temptation suddenly gripped him. It would be so easy to take her in his arms and run with her—run away from the Missouri border, away from the law, and away from the past!

His face twisted with anguish at the shock of what

65

he was thinking. *I'm getting soft in the head. It's just been too long since I was with a woman that it's got me thinking crazy. Yeah, that's all that's wrong with me. I'd be feeling this way over any female right now.*

Yet he was unable to tear his gaze away from the frustrated, angry face that shot daggers up at him, so mad, so afraid; and he was no longer able to think. His hands slid tentatively, tenderly down La-Raine's arms and around her small waist to rest hesitantly, almost shyly, on her back.

"I have to take you in," he whispered, the anguish of her nearness evident in his husky voice.

"Are you going to hurt me?" she asked softly, wondering even as she spoke why she was asking that particular question when she should have insisted on knowing where he was planning to take her.

"I don't want to." His lips descended to brush hers lightly.

A wild, agonizing delight coursed through La-Raine's body to the pit of her stomach. Without thinking, she closed her eyes and raised up on her toes, her need for more of his kiss evident in her tightly puckered lips.

Under any other circumstances, Brand would have smiled at the comical picture she made—dirty face, disheveled hair, and pursed lips. Unfortunately, her feigned naïveté brought Brand to his senses. He dropped his hold on her abruptly.

"Still going to play the dumb virgin, are you? It's no use, Flame. Your reputation precedes you. How many poor, unsuspecting souls have you pulled that sweet never-been-kissed act on? It's probably pretty effective on the men who prefer innocents. I bet it brought in plenty of customers before you got so famous. Is that how you got Quantrill to take you with him? Did you have him convinced he was the first man to have you? But you're wasting your act on me, honey. I prefer my whores with experience and honest enough to admit it."

Brand's words hit LaRaine like a stinging slap across the face. She was too hurt and shocked to even deny them. He thought she was a . . . a . . . She couldn't bring herself to think the offensive word, though it continued to pound cruelly in her mind until it was all she could hear: *Whore . . . Whore . . . Whore . . .*

What had she done to deserve such an unfair judgment from him? Had it been the way she had made it obvious she wanted him to kiss her? She tried to tell herself it didn't matter what he thought of her. But it did, and she hated herself for the fact that it did.

"Before we got distracted, we were discussing mounting these horses," he said, his tone biting. "We've wasted enough time. Are you going to ride astride, or not?"

"Yes, I'll ride astride." Her bruised and battered spirit conceded defeat. "Where did you get the horses?"

"Compliments of the Ruston brothers of Dundee, Indiana," he answered bitterly, wishing right that moment he could be anyone but himself, be anywhere but where he was, and doing any job but this one.

"I have only one request," LaRaine said. "Then I won't bother you again."

"Go ahead!"

"Who am I supposed to be? And what is it I'm supposed to have done to you?"

Unwillingly admiring her determination to stick to

her story, despite the fact that she had no control over the situation anymore, Brand thought what a good undercover detective she would have made—if she hadn't chosen another direction for her life to take.

Digging into his coat pocket, he lifted out a folded poster and extended it to her. As she opened it, he struck a sulphur match so she could see the printed words and picture.

"But that's not me!" she exclaimed, her eyes wide with surprise and recognition of the same picture William Pinkerton had sent her. He had said the woman had a bad reputation, but this poster said Flame Rider, who was also known as Mary Doyle, Barbara Doyle, and Lil Pepper, was wanted for robbery, murder, and treason. There was a reward of two thousand dollars for her capture. DEAD OR ALIVE!

And she had thought Brand Colter wanted to rob her! What a joke! If her predicament hadn't been so terrible, she would have laughed at herself. Her paltry belongings were nothing compared to two thousand dollars.

"You can't think this is me!" she pleaded desperately, her heart crashing against her rib cage with fear. "My name's LaRaine Ashby!"

For an instant, he actually allowed himself to believe that the girl hadn't known what to expect when he unfolded the wanted poster that bore her picture. But only for an instant. His mouth stretched into a sarcastic grin, and he raised his black eyebrows as he gave a doubting tilt to his head. "I've got to hand it to you, Flame. You don't give up."

"It's true! You've got to believe me. That woman on the poster must be my twin sister. She's why I'm traveling to Missouri. To find her! We were separated at birth. I just found out about her a few months ago. You've got to believe me!" she went on nervously, though she could see in his expression that her pleas were falling on deaf ears. But she had to keep trying. "Look, it says one of her names is Doyle! I was told my natural father's name was supposed to be Doyle — Cutter Doyle. I was adopted when I was only a few hours old, but they didn't take her. Don't you see? That has to be her on that poster. Not me!"

"You'd better give me your weapons, Flame!"

"Will you stop this!" she seethed, her words rife with frustration. "I told you I'm not Flame. And I have no weapons!"

"You won't mind if I find out for myself, will you?" he said. Without ceremony, he stooped before her and lifted her skirt.

"What are you doing?" she squealed, kicking out at him.

Wrapping his strong fingers around her ankle, Brand lifted upward, easily throwing her off balance and causing her to fall to the ground. "You could make this easier on yourself." His voice grating and angry, he straddled her hips and held her hands above her head.

"Please don't," she whimpered breathlessly, the fall having knocked the fight out of her. "I don't have any weapons," she insisted, her head turned to the side so she wouldn't have to see Brand's face leaning over hers, his eyes bright.

"I have to make sure," he said, his voice strained.

Moving off her, he reached for her boots again, slipping his fingers inside one in search of a knife.

LaRaine opened her mouth to protest further, then bit down on her bottom lip to stop herself. She'd done all the begging she would do.

Forcing her breathing to remain even, she stopped struggling. "Go on and search me. But I'm warning you, Brand Colter. If it takes me until I'm a hundred years old, I'll make you pay for the way you've treated me."

"I'm trembling all over," he said, circling a slender calf with his hands and gliding them upward in his search for weapons.

LaRaine sucked in a gasp of air, trapping it in her lungs as his fingers wrapped around her hips and patted them before traveling to the other thigh. Not even Whit Ruston's vile groping had been any more degrading. At least Whit's touch hadn't ignited this humiliating excitement riveting through her. She wanted to scream, she wanted to cry, and she wished she could die. But she refused to let him know how he was affecting her. So she did nothing.

When Brand finally finished his systematic and intimate search and realized she had been telling the truth, he sat back on his heels, more shaken than he would admit even to himself.

LaRaine finally gathered the temerity to look at him. And despite the humiliation she had just suffered, she found a strange satisfaction in his confusion. "Well, Mr. Colter, do you believe me now?" she asked maliciously.

"Yes," he said through his teeth. He sprang to his feet. "I should have realized the Rustons would have taken care of that already!"

LaRaine rolled to her knees and gave him her most scathing look. "Will you get it through that thick head of yours? I had no weapons, and I'm not Flame Rider," she seethed through her teeth, her eyes burning like a cat's in the darkness.

"Yeah," he said, thinking about the reticule with the derringer the Rustons had missed. He pointed at

70

a gray horse. "You ride that one. He seems gentle enough."

She scrambled to her feet. "Which is more than I can say for you!" Giving him a withering stare, she snatched the reins up from where he'd dropped them on the ground and placed a foot in the stirrup.

Acting automatically, Brand stepped forward to help her up.

"Get away from me!"

"I was just going to help."

"I'd rather be helped by a snake!" She stood up in the stirrup and swung her leg over the gelding's back, settling herself in the saddle. Her posture stiff, she looked straight ahead, determined to ignore the bulky skirts that hiked up to show her calves. Why should she care if he saw her legs?

"If you give me your word to behave, I won't tie your wrists."

"My word? Do you really think you can trust such an unsavory character as you've painted me to be?" she asked sarcastically, her tone chilling.

"You'll be good," Brand said, and mounted the black horse. "Or you'll be sorry." Without waiting for her to respond, he made a clicking sound and urged his horse forward, leading LaRaine's gray and the extra horses west along the railroad tracks at a brisk pace. He didn't look back to see if she was still on her horse, nor did he speak. Of course, what else was there to say? Besides, the less he said, the less chance there would be that he would start to believe her preposterous story. She was Flame Rider and his prisoner. That was all there was to it. And the sooner he got her to Missouri, the better.

Lost in her own purgatory of fear and confusion, LaRaine vowed to stop trying to convince Brand Colter that he was making a monumental error. *I'll let him take me to St. Louis and then I'll find a way to contact the Pinkerton agent. He'll straighten this out.*

Through the long night, that one thought kept LaRaine awake and upright in the saddle—that and the growing pain in her back and legs.

"I'm sorry, but I must stop," she finally had to admit. She was certain she would fall off the tall horse if she didn't dismount soon.

"You're right. I'll find a place to rest," Brand answered, his voice strangely sympathetic. "I bet you're hungry, too," he said with a smile, remembering neither of them had eaten since the afternoon before.

How dare he act as though they were on a social outing? After the way he had treated her! Mauled her! LaRaine knew she hated the smiling man more than she had ever hated anyone in her life.

In the gray light of the predawn, she was able to see his face clearly for the first time since the evening before in the train. The day's growth of black beard made his expression all the more frightening, his blue eyes even more deadly, his smile more cruel. Her fatigue screamed out her doubts. *What are you doing going along with him like a fool? He's not going to let you live all the way to St. Louis. He's going to turn you in dead. Probably after he rapes me. My God! If I don't do something, I'm not going to get out of this alive!*

She suddenly remembered that Brand had mentioned a town not too far in the distance, and a spark of hope flickered inside her. *If I can get to that town first, I can wire the Pinkerton office and they can vouch for me,* she thought.

Drawing on her fear for new energy, she leaned forward in her saddle and kicked her horse in the ides. Lying low on the horse's neck, she urged him nto a full gallop. *It's the only chance I have.*

"Watch out!" Brand shouted frantically.

But she didn't hear him. Concentrating all of her fforts on her escape, the only sounds she was aware f were the beat of her horse's hooves on the cinder-overed railroad siding and the pounding of her own eart as she sped away from her captor.

Her auburn hair whipped wildly around her face, tinging her sensitive skin mercilessly, blinding and hoking her. Gripping the reins and saddle horn ightly with one hand, LaRaine tried to wipe the angled mass of hair out of her face so she could ee. But the gesture did her no good. No sooner did he get one blinding strand out of the way, than nother snapped across her eyes to obscure her vi-ion again.

Brand watched in horror as LaRaine, fighting her air, rode her horse at breakneck speed toward a mall gully that crossed under the railroad tracks nd over her path. "Stop!" But his warning came too ate.

As if in a dream, he saw the galloping horse sit ack on his haunches, bringing himself to an abrupt alt on the brink of the ditch.

As though she'd been snatched out of the saddle y a giant hand, LaRaine was pitched forward over e gray's head and into the watery, weed-filled ench.

Coughing and sputtering, she lifted her face out f the water and peered through her wet hair at the rea round her. She took a mental inventory of her ody parts and determined that the water grasses rowing in the stream had cushioned her fall and at nothing seemed to be hurt seriously. Weighted own by her wet dress, she dragged herself up to her hands and knees.

"Don't move," a low, menacing voice warned, bringing her motions up short.

Startled by the intensity in the man's tone, LaRaine froze. But she was unable to stop her frightened eyes from traveling toward the source of the deadly whisper.

Brand Colter stood on the edge of the ditch, his black clothing and serious expression even more evil than before, his size more immense. Her gaze focused on his drawn guns, and a tremor of fear vaulted violently through her defenseless body, bounding off her ribs and into her throat. He was going to kill her, and there was nothing she could do. She couldn't have moved if she had wanted to. She was completely paralyzed.

LaRaine heard the click of the pistol hammer and bit her lip to keep from crying for his mercy. She squeezed her eyes shut to await his deathblow. She wasn't going to beg.

A soft movement slithered past her forearms, which held her upper body out of the shallow water. But LaRaine didn't feel it.

"Don't move," Brand repeated softly, his hoarse voice a command, a plea. "Shh, easy now," he lulled.

Was he talking to her or to himself? What kind of man soothed his victim before he killed her? If he was going to kill her, why didn't he just go on and get it over with?

Unable to stand the suspense any longer, LaRaine slitted her eyes in time to see the silent tail of a large brown-and-black snake glide past, only a foot away from her face. Her eyes widened in horror as the snake silently disappeared into the reedy cattails growing in the boggy ditch.

Before she could give voice to her fear, a shot rang out, cutting into the morning stillness. Paralyzed on her hands and knees, she gaped as the water was churned up in front of her. She stared in frozen alarm as the separated halves of the cottonmouth water moccasin exploded into the air. Her head rose in time to see the twitching tail land at Brand's feet with a soft thud, followed by a second thump on the opposite bank.

Her yellow-green eyes alive with terror, she shifted her gaze to the right, where the triangular snake head continued to writhe and hiss as though it was still attached to its body. She gaped at the white interior of the snake's open mouth, its fangs still moving and deadly, less than three feet from her face.

Somewhere in the distance, LaRaine heard primitive screams reverberating savagely in the early-morning silence, seeming to echo long after they had subsided; and somewhere in the depths of her hysteria, she felt herself being gently lifted by strong, masculine arms, to be carried to a resting place on the bank.

Chapter Five

When she awoke several hours later, LaRaine glanced around at her surroundings, wondering in her pleasant, half-awake state where she could be. The hours leading up to and including her fall had been momentarily erased from her mind.

The first flash of memory came to her as her sleepy gaze focused on a low branch to the side of the clearing. There, draped over the leafless limb, was the dress she had been wearing. With a violent explosion, the full meaning of her situation cascaded into her consciousness. If her dress was on the tree, then she must not be wear—She bolted upright, protectively slapping her arms over her chest.

Relief washed over her as the feel of Brand Colter's familiar canvas overcoat greeted her searching hands. Then a new thought pelted into her awareness. She didn't remember taking her dress off and putting the coat on. And if she didn't do it, then someone else must ha—

Her hands flew to her mouth to stop the shocked gasp that gathered there. Frantically, she swung her head around in a search for the truth. And there it was, the dreadful, awful truth—all around her everywhere she looked.

Appalled, LaRaine stared at the bushes edging the small clearing where she sat. There, blatantly displayed for all the world to see, was the rest of her clothing. All of it! Petticoats! Corset! Drawers! Stockings!

Gaping at the flagrant pageant of white surrounding her, she no longer had to wonder what she was wearing under the coat — or how she got undressed — and she gagged on the distasteful bile that rose in her throat.

"How do you feel?" Brand's low baritone cut into her panicked thinking. "I was beginning to think you'd sleep all day."

He actually had the audacity to smile as he approached her! "Get away from me, you monster!" she shrieked, drawing her exposed calves and bare feet up under the coat to cover herself more completely.

Brand's expression darkened. "I see you're feeling better. Well, that's good. We can get going. Your escapade has already cost me enough time. What the hell were you trying to prove anyway? How stupid you are!"

"Stupid, am I?" she shrilled, her face nearly as red as her hair. "I suppose I am stupid — for not killing myself when I fell. But I'm not so stupid that I'm going anywhere with you. Not after what you've done. I'd rather die. In fact, I wish I had!"

"After what I've done?" Brand bellowed. "Who was it that rode off helter-skelter with no thought of the consequences? I guess I should've left you in that ditch with that damned cottonmouth. It sure as hell would have made my job easier."

"But then you wouldn't have been able to rape me, would you?" she sneered. If it was the last thing she ever did, she would find a way to kill Brand Colter

77

for what he had done to her.

He chuckled. "Is that what you're claiming I did?
Rape *you?* The notorious Flame Rider who's known
how to make men happy since she was twelve or
thirteen years old? The same Flame Rider who could
probably give lessons to the greatest whores in Europe? The Flame Rider who couldn't begin to count
all the men she's been with? Raped? Don't make me
laugh, lady. Just who do you think would believe
such a dumb story? I can't think of a soul who'd
rush forward to defend the honor of a whore!"

"I told you! I'm not Flame Rider," she screamed.
"But even if I were, it would give you no right to
take me against my will, no matter how many men
there might have been!"

"Well, as long as you continue to make this ludicrous claim, I'd be interested to know how I compared with your previous experiences. Did you enjoy
it? Do you have any suggestions as to how I could
improve my technique?" he asked with a smirk, his
dark eyebrows raised questioningly. He wondered
with perverse curiosity how far she would go.

His face took on the expression of a cat toying
with a mouse before the final kill, and his blue eyes
sparked splinters of steel so ferociously that LaRaine
could almost feel the sting on her skin.

"Tell me the truth, Flame. Was it as good for you
as it was for me?"

LaRaine gasped at the inference. As if she could
or would enjoy an animal coupling with such a man.
"I wouldn't put it past you to have drugged me so I
wouldn't put up a fight!"

Walking over to check the drying progress of La
Raine's clothing, Brand chuckled softly, but there
was no humor in his expression. Did she really think
she could make him fall for her performance? The

78

an absurd thought occurred to him. Maybe she really thought she was someone other than Flame Rider and actually believed that she'd been raped. That would explain how diligently she was able to stick to her story.

He shook his head. No, he couldn't believe that. She knew exactly who she was and what was happening.

Brand closed his eyes in an effort to block out the pain Flame was causing him. Surely taking her in wasn't worth his own destruction. And that's what it was going to be if he had to spend much more time with her. He ought to just take her to the next town and turn her over to the local authorities. Let someone else get her to Missouri. Someone who wouldn't allow himself to become so emotionally involved with his prisoner. Someone who'd just take her in and collect the reward for her. Nothing more. Or if there were, it wouldn't be his problem anymore.

Even now, several hours after he had held her in his arms and undressed her, he still ached to caress her full breasts. He grimaced with the memory of the self-restraint it had taken not to touch or even look at any more of her flesh than was absolutely necessary when he'd removed her wet clothes. It had been ten times the agony he had suffered when he had searched her for hidden weapons earlier.

Cringing with the memory of her lying naked in his arms, so perfect, so desirable, so meant for a man's touch, for his kisses, Brand groaned. Never had he wanted a woman so much. Over and over he told himself she was a criminal, a murderess, a whore. But he couldn't erase the memory of the golden-red triangle guarding the portal to her femininity, or the feel of her womanly curves that still burned his fingers.

Yes, that was what he would do. He'd let someone else turn her in. But first, he had some straightening out to do.

When he turned to face LaRaine, his humorless smile was no longer in evidence on his scowling countenance. Instead, the look that replaced it was hard and cruel. "In the first place, *Flame*," he ground out, emphasizing the name, his voice seductive, threatening, as he strode with deliberate and menacing steps to where she sat huddled on the ground. "I don't rape, I make love. And I promise you that if I made love to you, you would remember. Have no doubt of that."

Bending down, he clamped his hands on her stooped shoulders and hauled her to her feet with a furious yank.

Before LaRaine could protest, Brand's mouth came down on hers with a crushing, burning force that took her breath away. Puzzling chills broke out over her skin at the same time flashes of white heat throbbed acid through her veins.

His tongue was savage as it raked the inside of her mouth, leaving no spot untouched by his plundering. LaRaine tried to resist, twisting her head to the side. But his mouth followed hers, refusing to give up its possession.

Her senses whirling in a violent confusion, she was hardly aware of the coppery taste of her own blood where her lips had been assaulted. Suddenly, she could fight no more, had even lost the desire to do so.

The pressure against her mouth eased and the kiss changed. It grew gentle, and the iron grip on her arms became a tender caress. Brand's hands slid to her back to span her narrow waist.

Giving herself over to feeling, she melted into his

embrace. She was only aware of the wonder of his warm lips as they burned a trail along her cheek to her ear. Her body seemed to have a will of its own, and she pressed herself closer to him.

Again she tried to muster the strength to stop what was happening. But she couldn't gather a shred of resistance. Nothing was happening that she didn't want with every particle of her existence. His kisses and his arms were the most wonderful things she'd ever experienced. And she could no more stop herself than she could have given up breathing. She was filled with feeling. Glorious, wondrous feeling. Strong, sensuous feeling. Desire! Agony!

The realization that her body was reacting in direct disobedience and denial of every standard and moral she had ever been taught brought LaRaine to her senses for a brief instant. She fought to emerge from the sensuous fog his kisses had driven her into.

"Please don't," she begged, even as she lolled her head back to give his mouth and tongue better access to her neck's pale softness.

"Don't do what?" He dug his fingers into the roundness of her bottom and pulled her toward the burgeoning hardness that was pressing against her middle. "Don't do this?" He ran his burning tongue around the outer shell of her ear. "Or this?" he asked, caressing her back and buttocks through the heavy coat while his teeth and tongue lingered playfully on her small earlobe. "Or do you want me to stop doing this?" he murmured, nibbling his way back to her open, waiting mouth.

"Yes," LaRaine sighed against his lips, vaguely aware that his hands had moved to her sides and were now under her arms, their heels pressing and circling along the sides of her heaving breasts.

"Yes, what?" Brand asked against her mouth,

parting his lips over hers.

She tried not to respond to his sensuous caresses, but she might as well have asked the sun not to shine, the wind not to blow. It was useless to deny what she was feeling. Her senses had taken over.

She was in a whirlpool, unable to fight the current, unable to keep from being suctioned farther into the vortex of desire that had drained her of her strength, consumed her totally. She was drowning, and she knew it. Yet she had neither the will nor the ability to save herself. She wrapped her arms around Brand's neck, drawing herself deeper into his embrace.

He used his tongue expertly to trace the outline of her mouth before moving it softly along the crease that separated her lips. Back and forth, round and round, the searing tip roved over her lips until they opened, shyly at first, and she accepted his entrance into her mouth eagerly.

This must stop. It's not right, LaRaine told herself through the warm haze of yearning Brand's kisses had awakened in her trembling body. Still she did nothing to prevent herself from being lowered to the ground, clinging desperately and hopelessly to his strength. Neither the shock of the hard earth beneath her nor the feel of his weight pressing her into it brought her to her senses. All she could do was luxuriate in his arousing embrace, glory in it, want more of it. She was lost.

Having leisurely searched out the sweet hollows of her mouth until he knew it as his own, Brand raised up on one elbow, his lip curling as he looked deep into her rapt gaze. How could she still seem so innocent when she was so sensual? But of course, she wasn't innocent. Just the way she moved her body against his could have told him that.

Studying her face, red and chafed by his rough beard, her lips, bruised and swollen by his kisses, Brand was unable to repress a low, agonizing groan of frustration. No matter who she was or what she'd done, he wanted her. *Well, why the hell don't you have her, Colter?* he asked himself angrily. *Why should you go the rest of the way to St. Louis with a pain in your gut when you've got a whore right here who's obviously willing to relieve it?*

In one deft motion, Brand ripped open the coat covering LaRaine's nude body. The breeze on her heated skin sent a chill of reason and fear into her passion-dazed mind. Her senses returning, she gasped and rolled to her side in an attempt to escape his voracious gaze.

Brand dug his fingers into her shoulder and brought her to her back again, openly devouring her exposed flesh with his eyes.

His gaze scorching her skin, she felt a flush of red tinge her fairness. Covering her bosom with one arm and her most private parts with the other hand, she made a desperate try at hiding herself. But it was useless.

Brand grabbed her hands and pulled them behind her to be held in his strong grip under her hips. Then, with taunting accuracy, his lips clamped onto a nerect nipple and sucked it into his mouth while his free hand kneaded and massaged the other breast.

A storm of reaction thundered through her veins. "No, please don't," she tried to protest, unable to stop herself from arching her breasts against his mouth and hand as she spoke, uncomfortably aware of a growing moistness between her legs.

Lying as she was, on her hands, her hips thrust upward, LaRaine knew she was helpless. Helpless to stop Brand. Helpless to stop herself. And, may God forgive her, she didn't care. She was glad.

Her thighs fell apart and her hips began to rotate and grind at the air above them, instinctively inviting him to appease the hunger in her loins. "Oh, Brand," she moaned, suddenly aware he was no longer holding her hands together beneath her. Working them out from under her bottom, she wound them around his neck to clutch him to her breast.

Brand suddenly raised his head and looked down into her eyes. "Well?"

She opened her eyes languidly, unable to bear having him leave her breast. The steel in his blue eyes sent a shiver of dread through her, but she was too far under his power to heed the warning. She reached for him, trying to bring his mouth back down to hers.

Brand started to give in, but brought himself to an abrupt halt. What was he doing here? Was this what his desire had driven him to? Making love to a criminal? *For God's sake, she's a killer, a whore!* She disgusted him. She stood for everything he hated, everything he had spent his life fighting against. How could he even think of wanting her? He didn't know the answer, but he knew that once he'd had her, he would only want her more. He had to get away before she pulled him any deeper into the deadly web she had spun with her desirability.

With a rough shrug, he shook off her hands and rolled away from her, springing to his feet. "Do you still claim you could have forgotten if I had raped you?" he snarled, unable to look at her.

Shocked by his words, LaRaine couldn't move.

As the realization of what he had done to prove his point sank in, she came to her senses. Pulling the coat closed over her nudity, she staggered to her feet. It had been a trick. He had deliberately seduced and humiliated her. And she had played right into his hands, responding like the whore he had accused her of being. He might as well have killed her.

Unable to look at him, she stumbled toward the tree where her dress hung. She had to get away. But before she reached her dress, her steps were brought up short.

Brand grabbed a handful of tangled, copper-colored hair and dragged her back against him. Holding her to his chest, he wrapped his hands around her and tore open the coat again. Catching a bared breast in each hand, he rubbed her tender nipples with his thumbs, laughing tauntingly as he felt them respond to his touch. "You didn't answer my question, Flame. Do you still think that if I had made love to you, you could have forgotten it?"

The knowledge that only a minute before she had practically begged him to take her, twisted in her stomach. She managed to form the word no, but she could produce no sound.

"I didn't hear you."

"I said no," she rasped, certain her degradation was now complete.

"No, what?" He massaged her breasts, emphasizing his control over her, over her surrender.

"No, you didn't rape me!" she admitted, her voice choked by tears. She was nauseated by her actions and by her body's immoral response to his touch. Even now, when she knew how he hated her, she felt her body moving instinctively toward the warmth of his hands.

LaRaine's stomach cramped violently. She was going to be sick. Shoving her fist against her mouth, she freed herself from Brand's grasp and ran toward the bushes, praying she would at least be spared the humiliation of having him see the weak, sniveling wretch he had made of her.

Please be a bad dream. Let me wake up in my own bed at home. There won't be any Brand Colter. No train robbers. Papa won't be dead, she prayed, retching up the sparse contents of her empty belly again and again. *Let this nightmare end.*

"You need to hurry," Brand called out, bringing LaRaine fully back to the realization that she wasn't sleeping, but was still his prisoner—in every sense of the word. "We need to be on our way. We've been here too long!" He sounded as if the past few minutes had never happened! As though they were on a friendly basis! Casual traveling companions!

Well, she would show him, she vowed, feeling slightly better now that her stomach had settled some. If Brand Colter could ignore his cruelty so easily, so could LaRaine Ashby. She would pretend it had never happened. She wouldn't let him know how he had degraded her. She'd do as he ordered, be completely passive—until they reached civilization and she could get help. Then she would have her revenge! She didn't know how or when, but she would get even for the way she had been treated by Brand Colter.

Fortified by her need for vengeance, LaRaine washed her face in a nearby brook and straightened her snarled hair by running her fingers through it.

Clinging to her plans for retaliation as a lifeline, she rejoined Brand, confident she could shove what had happened into the back of her mind. After all, if he didn't plan to ravage or molest her, then she should be able to survive anything he did until they reached a town and she could have her revenge.

She tilted her chin defiantly, tightened her hold on

the coat around her, and marched on bare feet back into the clearing. Determined not to look at him, she whisked her underthings off the bushes, dry or not. When she came to where her dress should have been, she didn't find it. Confused, she roved her glance over the other bushes and trees. "Where's my dre — ?"

Her gaze zeroed on the spot where Brand sat cross-legged on the ground, intent on the rust-colored material draped across his lap. Forgetting her vow to ignore him, she ran at him. "What are you doing to my dress?" she shrieked in surprise as he drew a needle and thread out of the material, then stuck it in the fabric again.

"Don't worry, your money's still there!" He didn't look up from his work. He inserted the needle into the dress with a jab. "I'm making it into a riding habit," he bragged.

She noticed he chewed his lower lip as he gave his full attention to the stitching he was attempting to do. And she experienced a brief moment of tenderness at the unlikely scene — a moment for which she chastised herself severely. There was nothing endearing about him. He was a cruel animal and she loathed him.

"We can't go all the way to St. Louis with your dress hiked up around your bottom and showing off your legs, can we?" he asked. "And I thought it would be a good idea to close up the bodice. I wouldn't want you to catch a chest cold," he said facetiously, making rude reference to what Whit Ruston had done to the front of her dress. "Though I did enjoy the view!"

"What!" She unconsciously gripped the overcoat tighter across her breasts.

"It was easy," Brand went on proudly, as if he had

not made his last comment, and as if she weren't standing over him sputtering with anger. "I used my knife to slit the front and back of your skirt up the middle!"

"You cut my skirt in half?" LaRaine choked. *Why don't you give me that knife and let me cut your pants in half—especially if you're still wearing them!*

"Now, all we have to do is sew the front to the back on each side. Then you'll have a riding habit fit for a queen," he announced, pleased with himself. He reminded her of a little boy showing off his handiwork and expecting praise. Well, he'd get none from her—even though she had to admit his idea was really very good. She probably would have thought of it before long, she assured herself.

"I found your reticule in the woods where you dropped it," he said casually, indicating the purse on the ground beside him.

LaRaine's eyes shifted hopefully to her lost purse.

"It's not in there anymore!" he announced matter-of-factly. "Not that an insignificant little pistol like that would do you much good. But it's lucky you were carrying a needle and thread," he said with intense concentration as he poked his needle purposefully into the muslin dress again. "Damn!" he yelled, quickly sticking his injured digit into his mouth in an attempt to suck away the pain.

Despite her humiliation and anger, LaRaine found welcome happiness in his distress, and she couldn't hide it. "Ha!" she blurted out spitefully. She wished blood poisoning would set in immediately. "Give me that. I'll sew it myself," she managed to say indignantly, snatching at the dress. "Men can't sew anyway. I'm surprised you even know how to thread the needle. You've probably ruined the dress!"

"I'll admit sewing's not one of my greatest talents," he grumbled, his finger still in his mouth, as he handed her the garment. "But sometimes a fellow who spends most of his time on the road has to do a little bit of everything if he wants to survive. There's not always a seamstress handy when I get a rip in my pants!" he laughed easily, finding it hard to disguise his admiration for the courage his fiery prisoner displayed.

Most women would be sniveling, pouting, or trembling pitifully if he had treated them the way he had treated her. Yet, she was acting as if it had never happened. He felt another twinge of guilt that he had let her bring out such an ugly streak in his personality, but he tried to tell himself she had deserved it. However, he wasn't quite convinced he hadn't been wrong. *Well, it won't happen again. I'll keep my hands off her. I'll treat her like I would any other prisoner,* he told himself resolutely, looking at her head already bent over the dress. But even as he was making his resolution, he had to fight to keep from reaching out and caressing a red curl that hung in her face. *Easier said than done,* he regretted inwardly and turned away from her. *It's going to be a very long four days to St. Louis!*

"What is it exactly that you do when you're on the road?" LaRaine asked, her curiosity overcoming her vow to remain silent until she could catch him off guard. He looked like some sort of gunfighter, she decided.

"Whatever I need to do," he sidestepped tersely.

"Are you a sheriff?"

"No," he quickly answered. No one needed to know about his connection with Pinkerton or the law. One person with Flame Rider's connections could spread the word like wildfire, and his job infiltrating outlaw gangs would be at an end. "I work for whoever pays me!"

"Who's going to pay you for me? I'm not worth anything to anybody."

Brand studied her serious face, his own expression incredulous. Damn, after all he'd put her through she was still hanging on to her story. "Two thousand dollars may not be anything to you," he spit out angrily. "Not with some of the hauls you've made. But I can think of lots of ways to use that kind of money!"

"What will you do when you discover I've been telling the truth? What will you do when you find out I'm not Flame Rider and that no one will pay you anything for me?" LaRaine spoke softly, her attention back on the dainty stitches her trembling hands were trying to negotiate.

"Would you believe me if I told you I'd be happy to find out you were anybody but Flame Rider?"

"No, I wouldn't."

Brand watched her for a long time. Damn! She made him feel like a no-good son-of-a—"Look, I'm sorry about what happened. No one deserves to be treated that way. You just made me so damn mad. But I give you my word that if you promise to behave I won't hurt you again."

"Whatever you say," LaRaine said, and kept on sewing, her martyred air making it obvious she expected to be abused by him again.

"Do you want some beef jerky?" he offered contritely. "You must be pretty hungry by now!"

LaRaine reached for the unappealing food he offered. "Thank you." Taking a bite of the tough meat, she chewed thoughtfully and returned to her sewing with the same lack of notice one gives a serving person in a restaurant.

Obviously her plan was already working. Brand

Colter didn't know how to react to her innocent victim act. Well, he hadn't seen the half of it yet. She would make him suffer, and there wouldn't be anything he could do about it because she would no longer try to defend herself. And if he tried to force himself on her again, she would treat it with the same lack of notice. She had no doubt Brand Colter would prefer a kicking, clawing, screaming female to a cold, indifferent one. She smiled to herself, satisfied that she had a plan which would keep her alive until she could get help.

"Look, I told you I'm sorry!" he said. "I didn't mean for that to happen. What do you want me to say?"

She glanced up as if she were looking right through him. "There," she said to herself. "All done!"

He frowned. Well, he wasn't fooled. She could act as innocent as a newborn babe, but he knew differently. And one way or another, he was taking her to jail, and nothing she did was going to stop him.

LaRaine looked at Brand as if she had just noticed his presence and then dismissed it as unimportant. She snatched up her drawers, chemise, stockings, and boots and headed back to the stream to dress for the remainder of the trip.

After a few minutes in the privacy of the bushes, she stepped back into the clearing, her improvised habit in place. "Shall we go?" she asked sweetly. "I know you're very anxious to reach your destination." *And I can't wait to see your face when I prove who I am and have you arrested for what you've done.*

91

Chapter Six

"We'll stay in Easterly tonight," Brand threw out with an offhanded grunt. LaRaine jumped at the sound of his voice. He had rarely spoken to her since they had gotten back on their horses that first morning; and because he had taken care to skirt all evidence of habitation during the four days of travel, his words were the first human communication she'd heard in several hours. She twisted in her saddle and stared blankly at him.

"I said we'll stay in Easterly tonight," he repeated, his tone annoyed. "We'll take the ferry across the river in the morning."

Immediately her mind whirled with thoughts of an end to her ordeal. Remembering that Easterly was just south of East St. Louis on the Illinois side of the Mississippi River, she forced her eyes straight ahead to disguise the flurry of excitement that lit them. *This will all be over by tomorrow!* her heart sang out. *Maybe even tonight, if he's going to take me into town instead of sleeping on the outskirts. I'll find someone to send a wire to the Pinkerton detective for me and he'll straighten this out. And then Mr. Brand Colter will get his just reward!* She shifted in her saddle, the telegraph she would send taking shape in her racing mind.

"I hope you're not making any plans to try anything stupid again," he said out of the corner of his mouth, his voice threatening. "I'd hate to bring you all this way and then have to shoot you while you were trying to make an escape."

"I have no intention of trying to escape. There's no need now. As soon as we reach civilization, I'll prove I'm not guilty of any of the things you've accused me of. In fact, if I were you, I'd be thinking of a way to avoid being arrested for kidnapping."

"I've got to hand it to you, Flame." Brand put emphasis on the name. "You keep up the act right to the very end. You'll probably still be acting like the wronged maiden when they string you up."

LaRaine gasped, instinctively grasping her throat, her yellow-green eyes so wide with terror that they bulged unattractively. "When they what?!"

Even the great Flame Rider is afraid of dying. Can't say I blame her. She's got plenty to be afraid of, he thought, not finding any pleasure in his prisoner's prospects. "String you up," he repeated softly, not bothering to disguise the regret in his expression. "What did you think your punishment was going to be? A hand slap?" Brand felt a twinge of pleasure at the fright he saw in her eyes. At least, he had found a way to force her to experience some of the anguish he'd been enduring since their first meeting.

He thought about how angry she had made him as they had traveled across Indiana and Illinois. Stoically sitting up straight in the saddle, she hadn't complained once, had never asked to stop to rest, or for food. She'd never even fought the rope on her wrists at night. He had thought he would break her, but, instead, their trip seemed to have made her stronger. He was the one breaking. He grew irate

93

just thinking about it. "Did you think you could kill people, rob banks, burn towns, and get off scot-free? All in the name of the Confederacy? Or were you planning on using your sex as your security? Well, I hate to be the one to tell you, but being a woman won't keep you from being hung for murder."

"I told you, I haven't killed anyone!" *But the idea is getting more tempting by the minute,* she thought, giving him a piercing stare, the fear in her face now masked by loathing. "But if you really believe I have, what's stopping you from 'stringing me up' right now?" The instant the words were out of her mouth she regretted them. Whose side was she on anyway?

"Believe me, I've considered it," he returned with equal venom. "But even you're entitled to a trial. You know, innocent until proven guilty and all that stuff." He said the word "innocent" as if it left a nasty taste in his mouth.

"Innocent until proven guilty? Is that what this is all about?" she shrilled, forgetting her resolve and self-control altogether. "Don't make me laugh. Haven't you already tried and convicted me?"

Her eyes widened with surprise as the screech of her own voice sent a stab of reason zigzagging through her. She was on the verge of losing control. *Just a little while longer, LaRaine,* she reminded herself. *Hold on just a few hours more and you can lambaste him with all he deserves. But for now don't ruin everything.*

Her rational inner voice overcoming her urge to panic and make a grab for Brand's revolver, LaRaine sat back in her saddle and sucked in a deep breath through her nostrils. Her lips compressed in an unrelenting line, she stared straight ahead and released the breath slowly. She was too close to the end of this ordeal to risk her salvation with a childish display of temper. She bit down on the inside of her cheek and tightened her grip on the saddle horn. *But once we get to Easterly, you're going to be very sorry, Brand Colter. Just you wait and see.*

Brand cursed under his breath and prodded her horse along. He would break Flame Rider if it was the last thing he did.

Entering Easterly an hour later, LaRaine felt a surge of relief. Now, she would have her revenge! Unfortunately, her relief was quickly replaced by confusion.

She stared at the rough wooden building Brand had halted the horses in front of. The only windows were small, barred rectangles, one on each side, and there was a solid door held shut with a heavy iron bar. The crudely painted sign announced it was the "City Jail."

Understanding exploded in LaRaine's mind, and her heart lurched in her chest, then sank to the pit of her stomach.

"You aren't going to leave me in there, are you?" Her pulse pounded mercilessly in her ears.

"Aren't I?" he returned quickly, his eyes roving expertly over the sturdy building. "Seems solid enough."

"Can't we stay on the outskirts of town and sleep on the ground like we've been doing?" she suggested helplessly, her vision mesmerized by the jail. Though she knew sleeping outside meant sleeping with her hands tied, she found that arrangement far superior to the jail. "You could even tie my feet!" she added. "Tie me to a tree!"

"I don't think so, Flame. I need a decent night's sleep, and the only way I'm going to get it is if I know you're not going to find a way to sneak up on me and put a knife between my shoulder blades."

"Come on, fella. We'll take care o' her fer ya!" a deep voice proposed from inside the jail. "We won't let 'er git away!"

LaRaine's gaze jerked up to one of the dark jail windows. The only thing she could see were dirty fingers gripping the bars. But she could hear the voices and her fear grew tenfold.

"What'd she do, buddy? Did ya already search 'er? Do ya need any help? We'll make shore she don't have nuthin' tucked away someplace warm. I seen gals hide things some mighty clever places."

Their vile suggestions echoing in her ears, La-Raine tightened her grip on her reins. She wasn't going to be put inside that building with those men. Brand Colter would have to shoot her first. Wheeling her horse around, she kicked his sides with desperate energy.

She covered only a few yards before Brand's horse drew alongside hers, so close the other horse's shoulder brushed her leg. "Get away from me!" she ordered, kicking out at Brand's shins. "I won't go in there! I'd rather be dead!" She slapped her hand on her horse's rump to speed him on.

With whipping surprise, a hard band of bone and muscle lashed out and wrapped around her waist whisking her out of her saddle.

A chorus of cheers sounded from the jailhouse as the riderless horse ran on.

"Please," LaRaine appealed from where she sat in Brand's lap. Her frightened eyes were filled with tears, and all the fight was gone from them. "Don' leave me in there."

A muscle twitched in his jaw, and his eyes narrowed with more anger than she'd ever seen him display. He turned his horse back toward the jail. He rode a few feet and brought his horse to another halt. "Why'd you do that, Flame? You knew you couldn't get away."

LaRaine searched his steely glare, looking for the tiniest bit of compassion in his eyes. She did her best to straighten her posture. "Because I'd rather have you shoot me in the back than spend one minute in that jail with those animals."

"Come on, mister. Bring 'er back," a man called from the jail. "We'll take real good care o' her."

Brand looked up at the source of the ribald comments, then back down to LaRaine. The muscle in his jaw bunched and jerked. "Damn!"

Without looking at the jail again, he tightened his hold on his prisoner and rode to the center of town, stopping in front of one of the town's few two-story buildings. His expression fierce, he dismounted and handed a coin to a boy with instructions for him to take care of the horses.

Minutes later, Brand shoved LaRaine into the small hotel room. Numb with fear that he would change his mind and make her spend the night in the jail after all, she no longer had the desire to resist him.

She vaguely remembered coming into the hotel, her feet running to keep step with Brand's long, angry stride; and she had a fuzzy picture of the desk clerk who had asked no questions when he had handed Brand the room key in exchange for the coin that had been slapped loudly on the scarred wooden counter in the rundown lobby. But it quickly faded from her memory like a dream upon waking.

Over the wheeze of her own ragged breathing and the furious pounding of her heart, all she could think of was that Brand had not condemned her to spend the night in that awful jail, and how grateful she was.

The scraping of the metal key in the door lock clamored through her consciousness in an ear-splitting throb. Her head filled with what sounded like a thousand cell doors being slammed shut at the same time. And with that sound the truth pummeled back into her consciousness. Brand Colter wasn't her savior! He was her enemy. And as far as being grateful to him, well, she'd show him her gratitude when they locked him up in jail.

Ignoring the weakness that gripped her, LaRaine swung around to face Brand. With catlike grace, she leaped across the space that separated them, her claws poised to scratch at the piercing blue eyes. "You were going to leave me in there with those monsters!" she screamed loudly, the high screech bearing no resemblance to her usual melodic voice. "How dare you treat me like an animal?"

He caught her striking hands in mid-air. "I can still take you back." The smile on his face was cold and sinister as he clamped his steely fingers around her delicate wrists. Though he held her so tightly the circulation in her hands was immediately cut off, her fingers remained curved in the attack position she had assumed, ready to draw blood. "Is that what you want me to do, wildcat?" he asked, looking hard into the yellow feline eyes glistening with the feral determination of a trapped animal. "Well, is it?" he whispered when LaRaine refused to respond or to back down. His thumbs slid around her wrists to exert pressure that could easily crack the bones should he choose to do so.

LaRaine's anger, held in check for so many hours, so many days, was beyond her control now. Unleashed in a blind torrential fury, her wrath drove every sensible thought of consequences from her mind, every sensation of pain from her body. Kicking at his shins, she strained uselessly against his grip. "I don't care what you do with me!" she spat hostilely.

Brand's cold blue eyes narrowed visibly. "Oh?"

But LaRaine took no heed of the challenge in his tone. She repeated her angry words. "I don't care what you do!"

His dark brows arched surreptitiously. His lip crooked in a threatening snarl.

"Well, what are you waiting for? Take me back! But the day will come when the tables will be turned. There isn't a jail large enough or strong enough to keep me from seeing you pay for what you've put me through!"

Looking into her angry face, red and flushed with exertion and fear, and still smudged with the dirt of their travels, Brand felt the now familiar ache in his groin tense painfully, agonizingly.

His trousers were stretched across his straining manhood, but LaRaine didn't notice. She was too far removed from rational thought to consider how he would act on her suggestion to do whatever he wanted with her. "Well? What are you going to do?" she goaded daringly, unaware of the forbidding change in Brand's expression, or the fact that the hard pressure on her slender wrists had let up ever so slightly. "Well?" she persisted, the venom dripping from her mouth, her lips curled in a sneer.

"What do you think I'm going to do?" he ground out through clenched teeth. He released her numb hands and hauled her by the shoulders against his chest, trapping her hands against the wall of steel. The air swooshed from her lungs in a loud gasp of surprise.

Brand's sudden embrace had all the effect of a

jaw-breaking, head-reeling slap across the face, and LaRaine was brought back to her senses with the force of an earthquake. What had she done? Brand Colter had left her alone as long as she had held her tongue, controlled her temper, and done as he had said. He had even seen fit to treat her with a bit of respect and consideration.

But she hadn't been able to hold her temper for just one more day—just until they reached St. Louis. Her father had warned about what a curse her bad temper would be if she didn't learn to control it. Now, it was too late.

LaRaine's helpless gaze lifted to Brand's mouth as it descended toward hers. He was going to kiss her, and her will to resist completely evaporated. But she had to resist, had to stop him. She couldn't let herself be swayed by his kiss again.

Managing one final burst of courage, she tossed back her head and laughed. The sound cut into the moment like a soldier's sabre slicing through the still air.

Brand's eyes snapped open wide.

"I thought you said you didn't rape women," she hissed. The muscle in his jaw knotted nervously, and her boldness grew when she saw the effect her words had on him. "Well, what are you waiting for?" she taunted, gambling he wouldn't want her if she didn't resist. "Here I am. Rape me!" she dared, forcing her look to be bored, her breathing regular. "Show me you're no better than the scum in that jail!"

Frozen in that embrace, his lips only inches from hers, ice-blue eyes searching fiery yellow embers, Brand blew out a frustrated puff of air.

His warm breath ruffled the wisps of auburn hair curling around her face, and LaRaine had to draw on the last of her strength to keep from leaning into his embrace. She shifted her gaze away from his and concentrated on a spot over his shoulder.

"It wouldn't be rape. And you and I both know it," he answered with resignation, his hands sliding down her arms to release her.

The desire to pull him back to her and apologize seized her. Stunned, she didn't move.

Apologize? I must be losing my mind. He's treated me like a criminal, dragged me across two states against my will, let me believe he was going to leave me in that jail, threatened me, called me names. And I'm thinking about apologizing for defending myself? I'll die first!

"What are you going to do?" she asked, the shakiness in her voice barely discernible.

"We'll stay here tonight and cross the river in the morning. I guess another night without sleep won't kill me." Walking to the door, he added offhandedly, "I'll have a bathtub brought up."

Surprised by his consideration after what had just transpired, LaRaine couldn't help showing her relief. Then a new worry occurred to her. "But the room's so small! Where—" she started, unable to stop the hot blush that crept to her cheeks at the thought of bathing in a room with a man, especially a man like Brand Colter. No matter how much she wanted a bath, she wouldn't even consider it.

"You forget I've seen everything you have to offer, Flame. But don't worry, I'll wait outside the door," Brand said quickly, fully aware he was making the concession with his own protection in mind. He was still feeling the agony of his most recent brush with temptation, and he wanted to avoid taking any further chances. Tearing open the door, Brand rushed out of the room as if he were narrowly escaping death.

LaRaine stared at the door, pondering his sudden change of attitude. Then she leaped into action. *I'm not going to dwell on thoughts of Brand Colter. He said I can have a bath. And that's all I'm going to think about now. That and finding someone to send my wire for me.*

It was only a short time before LaRaine heard the key turn in the lock again. Though he didn't speak, she saw Brand's hand and black shirt-sleeve as he opened the door for the scrawny, grizzled hotel clerk and his corpulent, white-haired wife to bring in a wooden washtub for her bath. Though the tub was old and rough, LaRaine couldn't suppress a smile at the thought of lowering her weary body into the tub once it was filled with steaming water.

The silent man and wife made several trips into the room with hot water, each time being allowed to enter and depart by Brand Colter, who she knew continued to stand his silent vigil outside the door. When the clerk left for the last time, his wife remained, and LaRaine's hopes soared. This was her chance. Surely another woman would have sympathy for her plight and be willing to help.

"You need anythin' else, gal?" the woman asked with unfriendly disdain. LaRaine's hopes plummeted. But she had no choice. *It's got to be her. There might not be another opportunity. She's the one I've got to ask to send my wire if I want it sent!*

But LaRaine's intentions were cut short by the woman's gruff voice. "Gimme yer clothes."

"What did you say?" she gasped, automatically clutching her dress, all ideas of asking the landlady to help her smashed abruptly out of her thoughts.

"I said gimme yer clothes," the haggard matron repeated impatiently, moving toward LaRaine as if she intended to strip her by force if she didn't comply with the older.

LaRaine took an instinctive step back to escape the woman's reaching hands. "Why do you want my clothes?"

"Yer man told me ta take yer clothes 'n wash 'em," the woman said sourly. "He paid me good money ta do the job, and I ain't 'bout ta leave this here room without 'em."

"But I have nothing else to put on," LaRaine whispered, embarrassed by what the woman must be thinking of her—checking into a hotel with a man and no luggage. "My clothing was lost in a train holdup," she guiltily explained.

"Look, dearie, it don't make me no never mind where yer clothes are. Jest give me what's on yer back 'n I'll have it back ta ya in the mornin'. Yer man said ya'd be jest fine in a sheet tonight."

"But you don't understand!"

"Come on, girlie. I done wasted 'nuff time on you. Are ya gonna give me the stuff, or do ya want me ta call yer ol' man 'n have him undress ya? Somehow, I don't think he's the kind o' feller a gal would wanna make mad," she threatened, unaware her own puffy face had taken on a ludicrous look of rapture when she had thought of having the tall man in the hall undress her and touch her own portly flesh. "Hey, mister," the woman hollered in the direction of the door.

"Don't call him," LaRaine pleaded urgently. "I'll give you my things, but you must promise to have them back to me as soon as possible. I won't be able to leave this room until I have something to wear!" Turning her back, she removed her dress hurriedly, taking care the woman didn't see her take the valuables from the pocket.

"Somehow, I don't 'spect that feller's got no idea

o' lettin' ya outta that there bed afore mornin' anyhow, so ya got nuthin' ta worry 'bout," she laughed lewdly as she accepted the rust-colored dress-turned-habit from LaRaine. "The drawers 'n chemmy, too," she ordered. "Ya ain't got no use fer 'em flat on yer back with a man on top o' ya!" she chuckled, watching LaRaine turn her back and step modestly out of her remaining clothing. "Don't know what yer actin' so shy 'bout. Ya ain't got nuthin' I ain't got. I jest got more o' it!" she bragged, proudly jutting her large, sagging breasts as she stepped through the door, leaving LaRaine modestly holding a sheet in front of her until she heard the lock in the door turn.

Outside the room in the hallway, Brand cringed when the old woman triumphantly held up LaRaine's clothing for him to see. In spite of the fact that her things were dirty, they still carried her familiar scent and he ached anew.

"She'll be all sweet-smellin' and ready fer ya pretty quick," the termagant promised sarcastically, her grin showing gums and three jagged teeth. "Don't know what a good-lookin' feller like you would want with a skinny little floozy like her though!"

The woman eyed Brand's crotch purposefully. Without warning, she slammed her huge, gyrating girth against him, forcing him back against the wall. She smiled up at him. "But if she don't treat ya right, ya come see me 'n I'll give ya a turn fer yer money! I can show ya all sorts o' ways ya pro'bly never thought o' ta use this." She grabbed at Brand's manhood, still rigid with desire for the girl in the room. The landlady arched her eyebrows in surprise and gave a triumphant laugh. "Why, yer already hard, honey. Ain't no man kin resist ol' Birdie's lovin'," she crowed.

"Get away from me, you pitiful old crone." He gave the woman an angry shove, torn between pity for the depths to which she had sunk, and disgust with the entire human race.

"Jest 'member what I said," Birdie laughed as she made her exit, her lumbering step just a bit lighter than it had been when he had first seen her. "I'll show ya a real good time," she promised over her shoulder and disappeared.

Brand waited in the hall for thirty minutes. It took him that long to get over his experience with the aggressive landlady. Then, once he no longer heard the sounds of LaRaine moving about inside the room, he ventured a tentative tap on the door. Receiving no answer, he turned the key and cracked the door open. Cocking his head to listen, he still heard nothing, so he opened the door and stepped into the dimly lit room.

He immediately spotted LaRaine wrapped tightly in a sheet and curled up on the bed, sound asleep. His heart raced unexpectedly. She looked so small, so defenseless. Unable to stifle a groan of anguish, he turned to lock the door behind him.

Unbuttoning his shirt, he continued to study the sleeping girl while he walked to the tub. Absently, he felt the tepid water, then peeled off his dusty clothing. *Just as well it's almost cold. Maybe if there were a few chunks of ice floating in it I'd be able to think of something besides her.*

But he knew there was only one way to slake his obsessive hunger for the girl sleeping so innocently, only a few feet away. *Damn her!* he thought, lowering himself into the water to bathe away the dirt and grime of their exhausting journey. But all the soap and water in the world wouldn't remove the pain he was suffering.

To hell with it! he decided, exploding out of the water with a vengeance. *She's a whore and that's what I need right now. A whore's a whore. It doesn't matter who she is. I won't be making a pact with an outlaw. It's not selling out. It's just relieving my "tension." That's all it is. Hell, I don't have to take her by force. No one rapes a whore. She wants me. She's just so good at her act that she's not going to admit it. Not if she still thinks there's a chance her masquerade might save her.*

His towel slipped from his hands to the wooden floor and he started, as if in a trance, toward the bed.

He had the sense of walking into thick mud. Each step he took sucked him deeper into the mire, yet he was unable to stop himself from moving on. He knew that standing still and doing nothing would result in his slow, suffocating death. And he couldn't go back to when he had never seen her, to when he had only thought of her as a criminal, a killer. That was the past, never again to be recaptured. Now the face on the poster had taken on another compelling dimension, and he could no longer deny himself access to her feminine softness.

Easing his naked body down on the edge of the bed, he studied the girl who slept with her red hair fanned out on the pillow beneath her head. So beautiful, so soft, so young. How could he have become so preoccupied with having her? Would once be enough? Twice? Would there ever be enough of her? He was afraid not. God help him, he was afraid not!

Chapter Seven

Knowing what he was doing could very well destroy him, Brand lowered his mouth to LaRaine's sleeping face. Almost shyly, he brushed his lips lightly over her closed eyelids.

She stirred in her sleep and he lifted his head to gaze down at her once more. The flickering candlelight made her exquisite features glow, and he choked back a knot of regret. *If I could only kiss away the past. If only we could begin our lives now, tonight, here in this room. But we can't, can we? You're a criminal, Flame. There's no way to undo the wrong you've done. No way to make it right.*

Anger and frustration driving him, he seized fistfuls of fragrant auburn hair, still damp from her bath, and fell on her, claiming her slightly parted lips in a hard, brutal kiss, willing her to wake up and give herself to him.

Jolted out of her pleasant dream, LaRaine was hurled into a nightmare. Struggling to free herself, she realized she couldn't move. There was a restricting weight on her chest. She couldn't even breathe. She was being smothered.

Panic rising in her chest, she opened her eyes and tried to protest the pressure against her mouth. But it was no use. Her attacker was unrelenting, filling her mouth with his tongue. She twisted to move her head away from the invasion. But she immediately realized her face was held in a vise between large palms. She attempted to raise her arms to fight him off, but she had wrapped herself so securely in the sheet that her arms were a useless defense. Still she continued to squirm and squeal.

"Don't fight me, Flame," he said, raising his head from her mouth to look into her eyes. "For tonight, let's forget everything else. Don't fight me anymore!" Burrowing his fingers deeper into the hair at her temples to hold her head still, he kissed her again. Only this kiss was different. Instead of forceful and degrading, it was gentle, almost loving.

A current of desire coursed defiantly through LaRaine's stiff body. And already she could feel the agonizing restlessness churning in her belly.

"You want me, too," he said against her lips. "Admit it, Flame. You want me!"

"No," LaRaine insisted, her protest a pleading whimper against the truth of his words. "Please don't do this to me. I'm not Flame."

"The actress to the end, huh?" Brand straightened and released a humorless chuckle. "Well, since you like games so much, we'll play the one you've been trying to get me to play ever since we met on that train!"

"What game?" LaRaine whispered, afraid to hear the answer, and uncomfortably aware of the rising heat in her bloodstream.

Standing up to unabashedly display his nakedness before her shocked gaze, he grinned sadistically. "Why, the game where the *sweet maiden* is ravaged by the *big bad man!*"

Reaching down, he grabbed her shoulders and

hauled her to her feet. With a rough jerk, he snatched the end of the sheet she had wrapped herself in. Then with a swift, angry motion, he sent her twirling out of the sheet and tumbling back onto the bed, naked and defenseless. Paralyzed with fear, she stared at him. This couldn't be real. It had to be part of the nightmare.

Held captive by his avid gaze, she trembled under the searing heat of his blue eyes as they crawled over her exposed flesh. But she could not move. She couldn't even tear her own curious stare away from the naked man who loomed over her.

There was a golden sheen of moisture on his lean, muscled body. He glistened in the light of the single candle that burned on the table; and the play of powerful sinew on his broad chest and arms seemed to ripple magically though he stood still to allow her time to study his body as he did hers.

The aura of strength, the blatant sexuality, the flat, corded stomach, the wide shoulders, the forest of curling, black hair that covered his chest, arrowing down his limber torso to . . .

LaRaine gasped aloud when her gaze fell below Brand's narrow waistline to the dark triangle that sprouted the seat of his desire. She jerked her gaze upward, trying to blot out the memory of what she had seen—and the knowledge of her own rising desire.

Smiling, he placed one knee on the bed beside her.

Oh, Lord. What was she going to do? She had to get away! She glanced from side to side in a desperate search for help.

Moving with the deliberate actions of a cat with its prey in sight, Brand lowered himself onto her.

As if he had dropped hot coals on her flesh, her belly contracted with the feel of his skin against hers. Squeezing her thighs together, she tried to twist away from the heat. "No! Get away from me. Don't touch me!" she cried, clawing at his shoulders. "I don't want you to . . ."

Moving his hips seductively against her, he grabbed her wrists and held them over her head. "Yes, you do. You want it every bit as much as I do." He dipped his head to kiss her mouth. "This is what we've both wanted from the first moment we met!" He kissed her again, this time more deeply.

Horrified to realize she was returning his kiss, she wrenched her mouth free. "No!"

"Yes," he argued, cupping her chin with his free hand and forcing her to look at him. "It's inevitable, Flame. And there's nothing either of us can do to stop it."

Moving his hand down her neck to catch a breast, Brand blazed a trail of fiery kisses along the base of her throat.

All the fight to be free suddenly evaporated. She was unable to stop herself. Hating herself for being so weak, she rolled her head back, arching her neck to give his mouth better access.

First, there was only the subtle desire to stop struggling against him. Then she was openly luxuriating in his caresses. And finally there was the instinctive movement of her own hips against his as his kisses sent waves of bubbling acid flooding through her veins.

Knowing the battle was won, that he would be given no more resistance, Brand released his hold on her hands and rolled to his side. He propped himself up on one elbow and looked down into her face. Studying her reactions, he brushed his fingertips in circular patterns over the silky skin between the base of her neck and the beginning swell of her lush breasts. He smiled as he watched her lift her swollen nipples toward his hand, and he delighted in seeing them tighten into hard, erect buds. "You're not playing the game," he teased huskily. "You're not fighting me."

Tears trickled from the corners of her closed eyes. Tears of degradation for what was happening. Tears of self-revulsion because she couldn't muster the desire to stop. "I know," was all she managed to say.

"Why not?"

"I won't fight you anymore. I've done and said all I can to convince you I'm not who or what you think I am."

Sensing that her fear was genuine, Brand didn't question why he felt the need to reassure her. Trapping her head between his hands, he looked intently into her eyes. His voice was a gentle pledge in her ear as he bent his head to kiss the telltale pulse at her temple. "I don't want to hurt you." He was confused by his promise even as the words fell from his lips. Why was he promising not to hurt her? She'd probably eat him for breakfast if he gave her half a chance. But he couldn't stop. Not now, when his entire body was on fire for her.

His lips burned across her face, taking care to kiss her eyelids, the length of her nose, her jawline, her ears, her chin, the corners of her mouth.

Unable to lie to herself any longer about what she wanted, LaRaine stopped thinking and slipped into a state of total feeling. All her doubts and fears were forced to the back of her mind. The only thing she was aware of was Brand's gentle, exploring mouth — a mouth she couldn't get enough of, a mouth she wanted to feel on her own again, a mouth that was driving her wild as it traveled leisurely over her face.

"You know I never would have left you in that jail

with those men, don't you?" he whispered, his mouth continuing its lazy and sensual investigation of the contours of her face.

Her only response was a low moan filled with yearning. Giving herself over to the power deep inside that was guiding her actions now, she ruffled her fingers into his thick hair and dragged him closer to her.

Brand slid a hand down LaRaine's back to draw her over on her side against his hard, virile length, molding her pliable flesh against his own. She could feel his manhood against her stomach, but instead of being frightened as she had been at first, she moved closer to its unique masculine feel.

At last his mouth found its way to LaRaine's open lips for the fervent kiss they both had dreamed of, fought against, and finally succumbed to. His tongue caressed hers with gentle urgency, and she no longer tried to stop herself from returning his kiss with a passion that matched his in kind. She was totally consumed with the moment. Only the glorious moment.

When they had drunk their fill at each other's lips, and when their caresses and kisses were no longer enough for either of them, Brand gently pushed LaRaine over onto her back again. Cupping a breast in each hand, he watched enchanted as her nipples grew even more erect and hard under his circling thumbs.

"I've thought of doing this since the first moment I saw you." He lowered his head to take a succulent nipple into his mouth. "So lovely, so good," he said against her skin, his tongue and lips nibbling their way across to her other breast.

Her insides boiling at inferno temperatures, LaRaine was aware of the moisture between her legs before she felt the pressure of Brand's hand as it traveled down her flat stomach to stop only a fraction of an inch from the golden-red treasure that guarded her innocence. There was no turning back, and at that moment, she knew what her newly awakened passion was telling her she needed—and what it would take to assuage the unbearable ache in her womb.

Tugging at Brand's damp curls, she brought his mouth back up to hers to kiss him. The kiss was deep and long, each telling the other what they were not able to say with words, would probably never be able to say. And when it ended this time, Brand began his final, sensual assault on her sanity.

With nerve-shattering kisses, he bathed her neck, her shoulders, her breasts, and her stomach. When her entire body was quivering with rapture, he slid his fingers deep into the silken delta at the top of her long legs. At his intimate touch, LaRaine flinched with surprise and grabbed at his wrist. But his purposeful strokes quickly ended her sudden flash of modesty. Lifting her hips toward the pressure of his hand, she cried out her ecstasy as every shred of her concentration focused on the point of her pleasure.

Her passion twisted beyond endurance, her world burst in a mind-boggling rainbow of color, setting her body jerking spasmodically against his hand.

"Please," she whimpered helplessly. Her head tossed from side to side and her nails raked across the broad expanse of his shoulders. But he kept massaging her, all the time kissing his way closer to the downy portal to her body.

Moving his tongue slowly along the satiny folds where his hand had given such rapturous pleasure an instant before, he brought LaRaine to new zeniths of passion over and over until she was weak with ex-

113

haustion and lay whimpering helplessly.

Kneeling between her open thighs, Brand licked and nibbled his way back up her body, now covered with glowing perspiration. Her hips lifted up to meet him, their gentle movement telling him it was time to make his long-awaited entry into the paradise of her body.

His turgid manhood hovered precariously above its moist, thrusting target for only an instant. Then, as he bent to kiss her mouth, he plunged deep into the center of her sexuality.

"Oooh," she cried aloud, tearing her mouth away from his as the surprising pain shot from between her legs to ricochet throughout her body.

"Aw, dammit!" Brand cursed, gathering her into his arms. "You're a virgin! I thought . . . Everyone says . . . Why didn't you tell me?"

"I tried to," she whispered, already aware that the pain was subsiding and that she was finding it difficult not to move closer against him. She couldn't believe she had the compelling desire to cover his face with kisses as he had hers. She wanted to wrap her legs around his strong thighs, and to run her fingers through the wiry black hair on his chest. She craved the feel of him deep inside her, filling the void his lovemaking had created.

Slowly, simultaneously, as he kissed away the hurt expression on her face, their bodies began to move in the age-old, undeniable rhythm of love. As their united tempo increased, so did LaRaine's upward invitation to Brand's downward thrusts. Soon, the only sounds in the room were their ragged breathing, and the squeak of the lumpy old bed that seemed to them as soft and silent as a billowy cloud created expressly for their lovemaking.

Together they climbed to magnificent, starry

heights, higher and higher, until both knew the fall to earth was imminent. Clinging to each other with all the desperation that leads a drowning man to grab for a single thread as a lifeline, LaRaine and Brand were flung helplessly into the great void of space. Then together, they were pitched convulsively back to the earth's atmosphere, to float down to the room their spirits had left only moments before.

Brand collapsed his full weight on her. "Are you all right?"

"Yes," she answered huskily. Fighting her tears, she squeezed her eyes closed in a vain effort to block out the reality of what had happened as it rushed back into her thoughts. Everything had changed, yet nothing had. No matter what had just happened.

They were both silent for a long time, each lost in painful thought. Finally, when he could no longer bear the doubts that tore at his conscience, Brand spoke. "I don't get it, Flame. How could you have lived the life you've lived and still be a virgin?"

Anger overcame the depression threatening to control her. Sucking in a deep breath of frustration, LaRaine hit him on the shoulders, shoving him off her. "When are you going to get it through your thick skull? I'm *not* Flame!" she yelled. "I'm LaRaine Ashby from Gordonville, Virginia, and I'm looking for my lost twin sister, who I believe is your Flame Rider!"

Heaving a disgusted sigh, Brand dropped his head back on the pillow and raked his fingers through his hair. "And when are you going to get it through that stubborn brain of yours that you're in deep trouble and lying isn't going to get you out of it?"

"I'm not lying, I tell you!" Clutching the sheet to her bosom, she sat up and swung her feet off the side of the bed. With an angry rip, she whipped the

115

sheet around her and stood up. "And if you weren't so stupid you'd . . ." She spun around to face him. "Doesn't the fact that I'm—" An expression of sorrow flashed across her angry face. "Was," she corrected herself. "—the fact that I *was* a . . . uh . . . inexperienced, prove to you that I'm telling the truth? You said yourself that Flame Rider is . . . uh . . . experienced."

Brand's gaze rose to her tear-streaked face. God, how he wished it did prove it. Even now she was the most desirable woman he'd ever known, and he could feel his body responding to her again. "Unfortunately, the only thing your virginity proved—" A spasm of guilt knotted in his midsection and he winced "—is that the rumors about your love life have been greatly exaggerated, not that you aren't guilty of robbery."

A spark of hope flickered in her eyes. "If stories about . . . uh . . . *that* . . . could be exaggerated, then what makes you think the other stories about Flame Rider couldn't be magnified, too?"

"Nice try, Flame." He sat up on the bed and reached for his pants. "But your crimes are all substantiated by evidence and witnesses. Only your love life is hearsay." Standing, he drew the trousers over his slim hips. "So why don't you stop fighting it and go back to bed. We're going to leave early in the morning."

Her fists balled on her hips and her bare feet spread apart in a defiant stance, LaRaine stared at his back as he shrugged into his shirt. "What are you doing?"

He flopped back down on the edge of the bed and picked up a worn black boot. "I'm going out. I need a drink."

"You mean you're going to leave me here alone

116

while you go out carousing?"

His boots tugged on, he stood and faced her, his mouth twisted in a sardonic grin. "Don't tell me you're going to miss me."

"Miss you? Don't make me laugh. I loathe you. You're a kidnapper and a rapist, and the sooner you're gone, the safer I'll feel!"

Brand crossed the scant space between them and clamped his fingers on her shoulders, hauling her hard against his chest. "I told you not to call me a rapist again," he warned through his teeth. "Or so help me, I'll—"

"Or you'll what? *Rape* me again? Do you think that frightens me now? After what you've already done?"

His expression darkening, he squinted his eyes into menacing slits and expelled a low growl.

Apprehension pounded in LaRaine's ears and her vision blurred under his arctic blue stare. But no matter what he did, she vowed not to let him see her fear again. Her hands trapped between them, she gripped the sheet tighter in her fingers and narrowed her eyes, too, returning his look glare for glare.

Their gazes locked in a standoff, neither of them moved for a full minute. Then, as if it were washed from his face, Brand's expression altered, changing from tightly controlled anger to disdain. He dropped his hold on her and shoved her away from him. "To hell with it. You're not worth it." spinning on his heels, he snatched up his hat and holster and wrenched open the door.

Frozen to the spot where he had left her, LaRaine stared at the locked door. Then a frightening thought broke into her trance. Now that he'd used her, he had no reason to take her to St. Louis. He was probably already on his way to see the Easterly sheriff to turn her in and collect his reward here. And in this small town, they would believe him and have her tried and hung before anyone knew the difference.

She rushed over to the window and ripped back the window shade to study her alternatives. Poking her head outside, she was immediately rewarded with the discovery of the front porch roof directly beneath her window. Her optimism soared. A jump of three feet at the most. Then she could climb down and make her way to the river where she would hire a ferry operator to take her across. Once in Missouri, it would be a simple matter to get to St Louis and to the Pinkerton Agency. At last, she would be safe.

Inadvertently checking to be certain she was still alone, she tossed a cursory look around the room. Then she caught sight of her reflection in the cheval mirror in the corner, and her heart sank with sickening understanding. The landlady had taken her clothes, and she couldn't leave dressed in nothing but a sheet.

Her frustration and disappointment forming a heavy lump in the pit of her stomach, she raked another glance over the room. There had to be something she could . . .

Spying the Rustons' saddlebags where Brand had dropped them by the door when they had first come into the room, her breath caught in her chest. "There must be clothes I can wear in there!" she exclaimed, her words a prayer as she dashed to the saddlebags.

Inside, she found a wool shirt and a long raincoat. "Well, this will have to do," she told herself. Dropping her hold on her sheet, she slid her arms into the shirt. Dismayed to see that it only covered

118

er to her knees, she grimaced. Hopefully, the coat would reach to the ground, but she would feel better if she had something under the coat besides skin. Then an idea occurred to her and her mouth split in grin.

Grabbing up the discarded sheet, she folded it in half and held it up in front of her. "Perfect," she old herself as she ripped a strip of muslin from the dge of the sheet. Pleased with her inventiveness, he refolded the sheet over the improvised belt and athered the bulky material on it and tied it at her waist. Giving the slit where the sheet edges came ogether a nervous glance, she adjusted the gap to he side for a bit more protection. "There, that ught to help." Donning the shirt over her skirt, she urned to finish dressing.

Her costume complete with the addition of her own muddy boots, as well as the long raincoat and a resser scarf tied over her hair, LaRaine retrieved her money and jewelry from under her pillow and eaded for the window.

Just as she was about to make good her escape, er attention fell on the chair where Brand had ossed his clothing before his bath. Excitement hrummed in her veins. There, on the floor under he chair, was his money belt, which he had evidently overlooked in his hurry to leave.

"Well, that's too bad," she said with a triumphant iggle as she made a dash for it.

Stooping to retrieve the belt, she hesitated. *It's tealing,* a tiny voice reminded her.

"He deserves much worse," she argued. "Besides, f he treated me like a prostitute, he should have een prepared to pay me!" Ignoring her conscience, he snatched up the belt, added her own valuables to ts contents, and hurriedly secured it around her

119

waist. Satisfied that the belt would stay in place, she dropped the loose-fitting shirt over it and buttoned the ankle-length coat. Checking herself in the mirror a final time, her mouth curved in a malicious grin. "Too bad, Mr. Colter, but it looks like your luck's about to reverse in my favor."

Brand curved his fingers around his whiskey glass and squeezed. Dammit! Why'd she have to complicate things by being a virgin? He tossed down the brown liquid in his glass, his mouth stretching in an expression of distaste as the liquor burned its way down his throat. He held up his glass, signaling to the bartender that he needed another shot. He would get rid of these ridiculous feelings of guilt where Flame Rider was concerned—if it took every drop of whiskey in Easterly to do it.

"Leave the bottle," he said, catching the bartender's wrist as the burly man finished pouring the refill and turned away from Brand's table in the corner. The bartender shrugged and released his hold on the bottle.

Quickly swallowing the fresh serving, Brand poured himself another slug of the numbing whiskey.

But it was useless. For at least the hundredth time since he'd left her fifteen minutes before, her words flashed across his thoughts: "If stories about . . . uh . . . *that* . . . could be exaggerated, then what makes you think the other stories about Flame Rider couldn't be magnified, too?" Against his will, his mouth turned up in a half smile as he remembered how she'd talked around it rather than use the word virgin.

God dammit! Gritting his teeth, he forced the

accidental grin into a frown. The muscles in his cheeks bunched and jerked with resolve as he fought to obliterate the doubts her statement had caused him to have. *It's all part of her act!* he reminded himself, bringing the glass to his lips.

But what if she was telling the truth? He shook his head and finished off another swallow of whiskey. *She's not. And no one in his right mind would be sitting here wondering if she was!* The fingers of both hands interlaced around his drink, he absently rocked it back and forth on the scarred table, sloshing the whiskey against the sides of the glass. Still, what if . . . ?"

"Enough!" he shouted, grabbing for the bottle again.

The bartender and the two men at the end of the bar looked up at him, their expressions puzzled.

Brand twisted his face in an embarrassed grin and brought the bottle closer. Angling it over his glass, he hesitated, thoughtful concentration darkening his blue eyes. What would it cost him to at least listen to her story one more time?

Methodically, he righted the bottle and answered his own question. *Probably not a hellova a lot more than my sanity.* He stared at his hands for a moment, then pounded the table with his fists and stood up. "What the hell! I can't very well lose what I've already lost, can I?"

Scraping his chair back on the plank floor, he dug into his pocket and brought out a handful of coins, which he pitched down beside the bottle.

Moments later, he stood outside the door to the room where he'd left his prisoner. "Everything okay?" he asked the landlord who sat in a straight-back chair balanced against the wall on two legs.

Shaking his head, the old man let the front legs of

the chair fall back to the floor. "Not a peep. She musta gone ta sleep right after ya left."

Brand gave a solemn nod and pulled a ten-dollar gold piece from his pocket. Pressing the coin into the man's hand, he said, "Thanks. I appreciate your help."

The man eyed the coin appreciatively. "Any time."

Waiting until the landlord had made his way to the back stairs, Brand used the time to compose his thoughts. When several minutes had passed, he took the key from his pocket and inserted it in the lock — though he still had no idea what he was going to say.

He drew in a long, steadying breath and turned the key. The click of the lock jolted up his arm and he froze. *This is crazy. I'm just asking for trouble.* He eyed the chair the old man had vacated. *If I had a lick of sense, I'd forget this whole thing and stay out here tonight. The less I have to do with her, the less chance I have of falling for her tricks.* He dropped his hand from the key and dragged the chair over in front of the door. Starting to sit down, his back to the door, he glanced over his shoulder at the lock again.

"Damn!" he muttered, standing up and pushing the chair out of his way. "I've come this far. I might as well go the whole way."

He ripped open the door and stepped inside the dark room. "All right. Tell me again how you're Flame Rider's twin sister . . ."

Chapter Eight

LaRaine stood in the shadows of a riverfront shed and watched as the operator of what appeared to be Easterly's only ferryboat doused his lamps for the night. Digging her hand deep into her coat pocket, she fingered the one hundred dollars in gold pieces and paper money she had removed from Brand's money belt while she'd waited for the ferryman to say good night to his friends. She hoped the trip across the river wouldn't cost anywhere near that much. But if she had to, she would pay it all if it meant putting Easterly and Brand Colter behind her tonight.

Taking a deep breath, she started toward the ferry. With a quick glance over her shoulder, she broke into a run, determined to get across the river before Brand Colter discovered she was gone.

"Hello?" she called out timidly as she approached where the ferry was tied to its narrow wooden dock.

Her greeting was immediately answered by a snarling black dog that came bounding around the side of a small shack in the center of the ferry, his fangs bared and glistening an evil white in the dark.

Clutching at her throat protectively, she froze in unmitigated horror as the huge dog lunged toward

123

her. Her heart felt as though it would burst with fear, but she couldn't move. All she could do was close her eyes and await the attack. When it didn't come, she slitted her eyes and peeked at the growling dog.

Only a few feet from where she was standing, her feet rooted to the bank, the mongrel reared up on his hind legs, but he advanced no farther. Surprised, she squinted, her gaze zeroing in on the tautly pulled chain that held the dog back. Unfortunately, seeing the chain only brought LaRaine minimal relief. The dog looked to be nearly as tall as she was—and perfectly capable of breaking the chain. "N-n-ice dog," she stammered, inching back from the ferry.

"Who's there?" a gruff voice asked from inside the shack as LaRaine tried to think of another way to get to St. Louis besides the ferry. She couldn't think of even one.

"S-S-Sir," she stuttered, forcing herself to speak. Her voice was shaking audibly, and at its sound, the dog increased the volume of his bark. "Nice dog," she pleaded, taking another step back. "I want to hire your ferry to take me across the river," she managed to call out over the dog.

"We leave at first light," the voice grumbled. "Come back then."

She looked back toward Easterly, then at the snarling dog who continued to strain against the chain. "I can't. Tomorrow will be too late. It's imperative that I get to the other side tonight. I'm willing to pay more than your usual fee."

The hinges on the door to the shack creaked and the barrel of a shotgun was poked through the crack in it. "River's dangerous at night. Don't nobody cross it after dark—less'n they're wantin' ta leave Illinois awful bad. That it, gal? You runnin' from

124

the law?"

Stunned by how close he was to the truth, La-Raine responded with an emphatic, "No! Of course not! It's just that—uh—my—uh—husband! I got a wire saying my husband's been injured in St. Louis. They don't expect him to live through the night." The tears in her voice didn't need to be faked. They were quite genuine. "I just want to see him one last time before he dies."

The crack in the door widened slightly. "How many o' ya wantin' ta go?"

She glanced up the levee nervously. "Just me."

The door opened a bit more. "I dunno. 'S awful dangerous crossin' in the dark. It's gonna cost ya."

"I'll pay you fifty dollars!" she offered over the dog's piercing bark.

A burly man in long underwear, boots, and baggy trousers held up with suspenders stepped outside. "It ain't worth the risk for no fifty dollars."

LaRaine looked up the levee again. She couldn't escape the feeling that Brand Colter would be appearing over the rise any second now. He could have easily already discovered she was gone and be looking for her. She returned her desperate gaze to the ferryman. There was no time for haggling. "A hundred dollars! If we leave in the next five minutes," she suggested.

The ferry operator hesitated, studying her. He was obviously trying to determine if he could get still a higher fare.

"It's all the money I have," she told him, anticipating his next words. "Please help me."

"A hundert it is, little lady," he agreed, stepping to the edge of the ferry and holding out his hand to help her on board.

Slipping her fine-boned hand into the thick paw,

LaRaine hesitated. What in the world was she doing? This man could rob her and dump her in the river and no one would ever know. And the dog. Did she really want to get to Missouri enough to share the crossing with that vicious dog? "Is he going, too?" she asked, eyeing the dog suspiciously.

Puzzled, the man looked at the dog as though he'd just noticed him. "Sure, but you don't need to be scart o' this mangy ol' cur." He scratched the dog's head and grinned. "He jest likes ta lissen ta hisself — like a lotta people I knowed."

Still not fully confident the man could be trusted, LaRaine looked indecisively in the direction of the town. There must be a safer way to get out of Easterly. But no matter how she tried to think of a better plan, she couldn't. It was the ferryman and his vicious dog or Brand — and at least the dog was on a chain. "Nice doggie," she said, and stepped off the wharf.

The instant she was on the ferry, the dog stopped barking, and his tail broke into a friendly wag, setting the entire rear half of his gangly body wiggling excitedly. He lowered his head and bared his teeth. But now that his master had accepted their passenger, his fearsome snarl looked more like a sheepish grin.

Relief flooded through LaRaine's blood, and her shaky smile broke into a laugh. Of course, the ferryman might still be planning to rob her and dump her in the river, but at least she wouldn't be chewed up by a dog first. And that gave her some consolation. "Oh, thank you. Can we leave right away?"

"Jes as soon as I see the color o' yer money." He held out his hand.

"Yes, of course, the money," she prattled, making another nervous survey of the levee as she emptied

126

the coat pocket of its contents.

Puzzled, Brand stared at the corral where the train robbers' horses lazily chewed on hay. He couldn't get over the fact that they were all still there. He shoved his hat to the back of his head and scratched his chin. He would have bet any amount of money—if he had any more than the few dollars in his pocket—that Flame would have taken the horses as well as his money belt. Not only to help her escape, but to slow down his pursuit. But she hadn't even taken one of them. Why not?

"Face it, Colter. Since this whole thing began, she hasn't done what you expected. And this time she outwitted you." He grimaced as he recalled his discovery of the empty hotel room a short while before.

It had been easy to determine how she had escaped. And it had been even easier to upbraid himself for his stupidity. How could he have been dumb enough to leave a prisoner alone without checking and securing every avenue of escape first? It certainly didn't say much for his experience and intelligence. Had he really thought that taking her clothes and leaving a guard at the door would hold someone like Flame Rider?

At least she was gone before I had a chance to make a complete ass of myself by admitting I might be beginning to believe her story about not being Flame Rider. "She would have still been laughing," he said aloud, his mouth twisted into a bitter grin. *But now I know the truth. Because only Flame would have gone out that window wrapped in a sheet.* "A 'lady,' like she wanted me to believe she was, would 'die first.' "

Now he had to figure out where she was and how

127

far she had gotten. It couldn't have been far without a horse and dressed in a sheet, unless . . .

With a flash of inspiration, the thought crossed his mind that she could be hiding somewhere in town waiting for him to leave. Once he was gone, it would be a simple matter for her to come out, buy some new clothes — with his money! — and to continue on to wherever she'd been going when he'd met her.

"Dammit! That's it! She's going to cross the river into Missouri." He tilted the brim of his hat low on his forehead and picked his watch out of his pocket.

Figuring he'd been in the saloon for thirty minutes, then adding another half hour for the time he'd spent looking for her, he concluded she couldn't have gone far. In fact, she was probably holed up somewhere near the Easterly ferry pier.

All she would have to do would be to watch from her hiding place until everyone was on board in the morning before boarding the ferry. That way, if he was among the passengers, she would simply wait for the next ferry. If he wasn't, she would take that one.

"Well, I've got news for you, Flame. This time, you've tricked yourself right into a corner. Because I'm going to find you if I have to search every packing crate and freight wagon on the levee." He took off running toward the river.

"Please hurry," LaRaine pleaded, her gaze zigzagging nervously between the sloping levee and the ferry operator as he worked at loosening the ropes that secured the craft to the pier. "There's no time to lose. He could be here . . . I mean *dying* right now."

"Hold your horses, little lady. I'm movin' fast as I

can. These ol' eyes o' mine cain't rightly see too good in the dark. I need some light. Bring me that lantern an' the tin o' matches on the table inside the cabin."

LaRaine's eyes widened in alarm. "A lantern?" She shot a furtive glance up the levee. "We don't need a lantern," she exclaimed, hurrying to his side. The dog, his tail still wagging, followed on her heels. She pushed the old man's hands aside and went to work on the stubborn knot. "Let me do it. I can see just fine in the moonlight."

The ferryman eyed her suspiciously. "Why don't you wanna use no light?"

LaRaine's head snapped up, her expression trapped. "It's not that—exactly." She checked the levee again. "It's just that—uh—"

"You sure yer not runnin' from the law, gal?"

She released a breathless laugh. "No! Of course not. It's just that—uh—I don't want to draw any unnecessary attention to us because—uh—"

"Yeah?"

"Because if anyone realizes you're making a trip across the river tonight, they might want to go with us rather than wait until morning! And we don't have time to wait for them to board!"

The man looked at the wagons lined up on the riverbank and nodded his understanding. "You might be right, but soon's we get out a ways, I'll have to light the lanterns."

"That'll be fine," she said on a relieved sigh, lifting her gaze to the levee, then directing it back to the rope. "There! It's untied." She slapped the rope into the old man's hand, keeping it wrapped around the post of the pier. "I'll get the other one and we can leave."

Her attention moved back and forth between the

rope and the horizon of the riverbank as she struggled with the second knot. "The way you tie up your ferry, there's certainly not much chance you would drift off in the ni—"

She stopped speaking and her back stiffened. She wasn't sure, but she thought she had seen something moving over the top of the hill that sloped down to the river from the town. Holding her breath, she squinted, her hands paralyzed on the knot.

The full silhouette of a wide-brimmed hat, broad shoulders, slim hips, and long legs crested the horizon, and LaRaine immediately recognized to whom it belonged. She would know that walk anywhere. "Oh, no!" she cried, tugging harder on the knot.

Fear thundering in her ears, she drew on strength she didn't know she possessed. Her fingers bleeding and raw from the rough rope, she burrowed them into the knot. "Let's go!" she rasped as she finally freed the ferry from the pier. "And for God's sake, please hurry!"

Brand jerked to attention at the sound of a woman's voice. Ignoring the packing crate he'd been examining for signs that Flame had been there, he moved his gaze carefully over the levee. It had sounded very close to the water. Maybe even on the water. Surely not. No one with any sense would go out in the river at night.

Probably just one of the women from those wagons over there, he decided, his attention on the western-bound emigrants' camp where they waited to cross the Mississippi River in the morning.

Brand had heard that ever since the end of the war there had been a steady stream of wagons leaving the States for the West, especially out of the southern states where so many men had come back from the fighting to find their ancestral homes leveled by the ravages of the war. However, he was surprised by the number of wagons this late in the year. There was no way they could get to California or Oregon before the snow.

He shrugged his shoulders. *They're probably planning on wintering in Missouri or Kansas so they can be among the first on the trail in the spring before the grass is all gone on the prairie.*

Heaving a wistful sigh, Brand tore his gaze away from the flickering campfires and wagons. Maybe one of these days he'd just quit his job at Pinkerton and do the same thing. Maybe even get married and have a few kids. He had always liked his job, and had always felt he was contributing something important. But lately, the loneliness of being on the move all the time and of never being able to trust anyone but himself had started to get to him.

For a moment, he let himself imagine what it would be like if he decided to go west and settle down. He could picture returning home at the end of the day and being met by his kids, their faces full of happiness that "Daddy" was back. And from the fire, their mother would look up and smile her delight at the sight of him. She would quickly wipe her hands on her apron, pat her hair self-consciously, then run eagerly into his arms and lift her face to his to receive his kiss.

The pensive smile that had relaxed his features grew hard as he recognized the auburn-haired woman who smiled up at him in his reverie. *Flame!*

Giving his head a violent shake to erase the unwanted vision, Brand balled his fist and punched the packing crate. "Hell will freeze over first," he swore, striding further down the levee toward a freight wagon that would serve as a perfect hiding place. *Once she's behind bars, I don't plan to ever see Miss Flame Rider again!*

At just that moment, clouds that had obscured the moon for several minutes drifted past, suddenly leaving the riverbank bathed in bright moonlight. Surprised, Brand's head snapped up, his attention coming to rest on the narrow dock where the Easterly ferry tied up.

His stomach did a sickening flip in his belly. The ferry was gone!

Though he'd seen it from the hotel room window a short while ago, there was nothing in its place now except a stretch of river water, gleaming gold in the moonlight — and empty. Desperate to disprove what he suspected, he scanned the waterfront for the missing ferry.

Then he saw it. The thing he'd been afraid of had happened. She was escaping, already a hundred feet out into the river. His eyes narrowed with frustration as he recognized one of the two figures on board as a woman. Even though he couldn't make out her features at that distance, there was no doubt in his mind who she was.

Whipping out his revolver, he ran toward the water, his steely gaze leveled on the smaller of the two people who used long poles to move the unwieldy craft across the current toward the Missouri side.

"So help me, Flame . . ." he yelled, lifting his Colt and taking a bead on her. "You couldn't leave well enough alone, could you?" He eased back on the hammer. It would be an easy shot, but he'd better do it fast or they'd be out of range for an accurate shot.

As if his subconscious enjoyed torturing him, the impossible daydream he'd just had flashed across his thoughts, and he winced. Then the memory of making love to her vibrated through his entire body, and his hands began shake. Drops of perspiration trailed down his forehead into his eyes.

"Dammit," he muttered, dragging a sleeve across his eyes to clear his vision. *She's a criminal. It's your job to stop her even if it takes shooting her!* he commanded himself.

He covered the hand holding the gun with his other hand. But even as he tightened his hold on the butt of the gun, he angled the barrel upward.

Who was he trying to kid? He wasn't going to shoot her—because he couldn't shoot any woman, he tried to convince himself. And because no matter what she'd done, she had a right to a trial. And because . . .

Another picture of his future played across his mind. Only, this time, he was old and tired. And there were no children and no wife greeting him. He was totally alone.

Anger and self-disgust ruptured the last of his control. It had been bad enough when he hadn't been able to think of anything but getting into bed with her. But this was going too far. For God's sake! The woman was a murderess! It was crazy. And he had no intention of allowing it to go any further. He was going to get rid of these ridiculous fantasies about Flame Rider once and for all.

Gritting his teeth, he squeezed off a shot—into the air. "You'd better watch your back, lady!" he shouted over the gentle lapping of the water against the wooden dock where he stood. "You haven't seen the last of me!"

Trudging north along the river road, LaRaine

struggled to keep her eyes open. Her feet were blistered from walking in the wet shoes and without stockings, but she kept picking them up and putting one in front of the other. The muscles in her calves were stretched so tight that pain pulsed up and down her legs, but she kept walking. And her shoulders ached from helping the ferry operator pole, then paddle when the water got too deep for the poles, across the river. Never in her life had she worked so hard, and never had she been so exhausted.

She glanced woefully at a copse of trees by the side of the road, tempted to lie down for a few minutes—just to rest her eyes. But she couldn't stop. She had to get to St. Louis by dawn, because she had no doubt that since she had hired the only ferry in Easterly, Brand Colter would be on the first steam ferry that left East St. Louis in the morning—if he didn't find a way across the river sooner.

At the thought of Brand being right behind her, she cast a worried glance back down the road in the direction from which she'd come. Shaking her head stubbornly, she willed the idea from her thoughts. He would be on that first ferry out of East St. Louis in the morning. And she intended to have the law waiting with a warrant for his arrest when he disembarked on the Missouri side of the river. She managed a weak smile at the thought.

But she had to get there first. Raising her weary hands to her face, she smacked her cheeks in quick succession to wake herself up. It helped alert her somewhat, but it did nothing to make her forget her agony—or the man who'd been responsible for it.

Determination for revenge pumped in her heart with renewed vigor. It wasn't enough that he had kidnapped her, mistreated her, and raped her. He'd tried to kill her, too! Remembering the startled horror she'd felt when she'd looked up and seen him on the dock, his gun aimed directly at her, she found the energy to pick up her step slightly.

However, when the clatter of wagon wheels and horse's hooves broke into her thoughts, she stopped in mid-step. What if it was Brand Colter? Praying she would be hidden in the shadows, she stepped to the side of the road and waited for the horse and wagon to bump over the rutted road and pass her.

When she saw a bent old figure driving the wagon, relief swept over her and she had a saving idea. Moving into the middle of the road, she held up her hands. "Please!" she shouted. "Can you give me a ride?"

"Whar ya headed, missy?" the old man on the driver's seat asked.

"St. Louis!"

"Hop on," he said, indicating the back of the wagon with his thumb. "If ya don't mind ridin' in back with the chickens."

LaRaine clapped her filthy hands together and broke into a run before the man could change his mind. "With the chickens will be fine!" she answered gleefully, thinking she wouldn't have turned down the ride even if he'd been hauling manure!

Working her way into a tight space between the cages, she heaved a sigh of happiness.

"All set?" the driver asked.

"Yes, thank you," she answered, bending her arm and propping it on the cage closest beside her. "This is perfect."

The instant she was settled, the last of the strength that had kept her on her feet seeped from her limbs. Her eyelids opened and shut languidly, as if she'd been drugged, and she could barely hold her head up.

The driver clucked to his mules and flicked the whip over their backs. "Perfect," she repeated with a contented grin as the wagon started forward. Numb to any discomfort, she laid her head on the bend of her elbow. And before the mules had drawn the wagon ten feet, she was sound asleep.

"This is as far as I'm goin', missy," the driver announced a minute later, bringing the wagon to a jerking halt.

Certain she'd just gotten into the back of the wagon, LaRaine lifted her head slightly and tried to open one eye a fraction of an inch. "I don't understand," she said, her words slurred. "You said you'd take me to St. Louis?"

The old man laughed and eased down from his seat. "Wake up an' look 'round ya, missy. Two hours done passed since I picked ya up off the road. You're in St. Louis, sure as shootin'!" He began to work the ropes that held the stacked chicken crates in place.

LaRaine lifted her head a bit higher, propping it with her hand to keep it from falling again. Straining to pry her eyelids apart, she raised her eyebrows upward. One eye opened ever so slightly.

As the startling change in her whereabouts registered in her groggy brain, both eyes popped open and she bolted up straight, her head swiveling from side to side as she took in the new surroundings.

It was no longer night, and they were in a marketplace teeming with people instead of on the lonely river road. All around them were stalls and other wagons filled with produce, farm tools, and animals: ducks, goats, chickens, pigs—even cats to supply the need for constant rat control. The sellers and buyers were all shouting at the same time, and the cacophony of voices combined with yapping dogs

136

and giggling children to clear the last traces of sleep from LaRaine's head. Then her gaze fell on the one thing she wanted even more than breakfast — a stall with clothing for sale!

Unfolding her bent legs, she scrambled out of the wagon and smiled. "Thank you so much for your help," she said to the chicken farmer, pressing a coin into his hand.

The man looked at the money she'd given him and shook his head. "There's no need to pay me, missy."

LaRaine shooed his extended hand away from her. "Oh, yes there is. I owe you a lot more than money. You may have saved my life. I don't think I would have made it without your help."

He still looked uncertain, but put the money in his pocket. "You gonna be all right?"

"Oh, I'll be fine! Now that I'm finally here, everything's going to be just fine." And she set out toward the clothing stall to buy something presentable to wear.

Brand paced back and forth as he waited for the side rail of the ferry to drop so the gangplank could be put down. He had been the first passenger to board the earliest steam ferry out of East St. Louis that morning and had expected to be here shortly after dawn. However, the crossing, like everything else that had happened during the last twenty-four hours, had been a disaster. An irate fireman who'd been let go the week before had sneaked on board and knocked the current fireman unconscious, then doused the fire in the boiler furnace before anyone had noticed his presence. Consequently, the large ferry had been rendered powerless and had drifted downriver with its load of wagons, people, and animals, forcing the crew and passengers to paddle and pole up the river as well as across it. But now at last he was in St. Louis—only two hours late.

The rail crashed down and Brand bolted off the ferry, taking the steep levee at a run. "All right, Flame," he muttered, "you've made a fool of me for the last time. Now we both know the rules of the game, don't we?" *And it's a game I have no intention of losing!*

Chapter Nine

LaRaine read the gilt lettering on the window that proclaimed the location of "The Pinkerton National Detective Agency." She was glad now that the office had been closed when she'd come by just after dawn. It had given her a chance to find an inexpensive hotel nearby — and to wash away some of the evidence of her hard night on the river.

Taking an anxious breath, she glanced down at the brown calico dress she had purchased at the farmer's market and adjusted the waist of her bodice. Though she'd have preferred to arrive at the Pinkerton office dressed with more style, she had to admit the dress fit quite well. And it was infinitely better than what she'd been wearing earlier. She patted the bonnet on her head to check its placement, then reached for the doorknob.

As she stepped into the small, orderly office, a neatly dressed young man leaped out of his chair, his face splitting into a friendly grin. "Good morning. May I help you?"

"Mr. Murphy, please," LaRaine answered. "Please inform him that Miss LaRaine Ashby from Gordonville, Virginia, is here to see him."

The smile slid off the tall clerk's freckled face,

replaced with one of immediate concern. "Miss Ashby! Am I glad to see you! When you didn't arrive as expected, I didn't know what to think. I wired William in New York and Mr. Pinkerton in Chicago, and as far as they knew you had left Virginia on schedule and should have been here over a week ago."

LaRaine stared in puzzled silence at the boyish face as the man went on.

"Then when I learned that the train you were on was robbed and that a young woman—"

"Mr. *Murphy?*" she asked, her tone disbelieving.

"Oh! Please forgive me! I haven't introduced myself. I'm Mike Murphy, the manager of the St. Louis headquarters." He came around the desk and guided her to a chair.

"Aren't you a little young to be . . . ?" She clamped her mouth closed on her blunt observation. Sitting down, she removed her gloves. "I mean, I expected you to be a much older . . ."

Mike Murphy grinned and shrugged his shoulders. "I could say I'm just a boy genius. But the truth of the matter is that freckles are a young man's curse because he's always mistaken for a youngster." He paused for effect. "Actually, I'm thirty-two and a married man with three children of my own."

Finding it difficult to believe that Mike Murphy wasn't still in his teens, LaRaine didn't know what to say.

Sensing her unease, Mike sat down at his desk and assumed his most professional manner. "Now that we have that out of the way, shall we get down to why you've come to St. Louis, and why you didn't arrive when we expected you? We were very worried. Mr. Pinkerton would never forgive me if I let something happen to his old friend's daughter. For that matter, I wouldn't be able to forgive myself!"

Determined not to display the hysterics that boiled in her emotions, LaRaine took a deep, steadying breath, then told him everything that had happened to her, leaving out only the most personal details. She had no intention of sharing those with anyone.

His expression incredulous, Mike propped his elbows on the desk and leaned forward, his mouth and chin pressed thoughtfully against his folded hands, his forehead furrowed in a deep frown. When she was through relaying the events of the past week, he shook his head, his expression admiring. "I'm really astounded by your bravery and calm, Miss Ashby. You are truly an amazing young woman."

She smiled her thank you, though she didn't feel the least like smiling. Nor did she feel very brave or calm or amazing. "You will see that they are all arrested, won't you?" she asked anxiously.

Mike leaned back in his chair and clasped his hands over his lean middle, his mood serious. He couldn't help noticing the way her hands twisted nervously at the gloves she had draped neatly across her lap when she first sat down, and he knew she was not nearly as confident as she appeared. He wished with all his heart he could tell her what she wanted to hear. But unfortunately . . .

"As you may or may not know, Miss Ashby," he began, "Pinkerton detectives do not actually arrest people. In some cases, we're hired by private individuals to hunt down specific lawbreakers who've run afoul of the law. For instance, Wells Fargo might hire us to solve a stagecoach robbery. Or—as in your case—someone asks our help in finding a missing person. But we don't make the actual arrest. That's up to the public lawmen. So I can't guarantee their arrest, but I will report the train robbers' supposed identity and whereabouts to the railroad, and to the sheriff in Dundee, Indiana. Other than that, unless the railroad contacts us to go after them to retrieve their goods, I'm afraid there's not much more we can do."

"What about the bounty hunter? Surely you can do something about him! He took me prisoner and forced me to travel across two states with him. I want him in jail!"

Mike pursed his lips and tapped them with his thumbnail. "I have to be honest with you. Since this didn't happen in Missouri, and because he made what the police will probably see as a logical mistake about your identity, I don't think there's much chance of his arrest. Besides, since no one saw you, it's really your word against his."

LaRaine thought about the old couple in the hotel, but she couldn't use them — not if she wanted to keep what went on in the hotel room secret. Her shoulders slumped perceptibly. "You mean there's nothing I can do?"

Mike shook his head apologetically. "Not unless you have some proof."

"What if he comes after me again?"

Mike sat up straighter. "Now that you're under our protection, you don't need to worry about that happening. Until I have a detective available to take you on your quest to find your sister, I will assume personal responsibility to see that nothing like that occurs again."

"What do you mean, 'until a detective is available'?" LaRaine asked. "I assumed I'd be able to be on my way in the morning."

His mouth quirked in an embarrassed grin. "All the agents assigned to this office are out on cases right now. So all we can do is wait until one is

142

solved."

"Surely there's someone!"

Mike shook his head ruefully. "I'm afraid not. We are expecting a detective to transfer here in three weeks. But he's on the first leave he's had since before the war, and I don't expect him to show up here one day before that."

"Three weeks! I can't wait three weeks!" she exclaimed, mentally counting the money she had remaining, including the cash she had taken from Brand Colter's money belt. "I can't afford to live in a hotel that long and still be no closer to locating my sister at the end of that time. You must find someone to take me tomorrow!"

"I'm afraid that's impossible, Miss Ashby. But of course, you will be Mr. Pinkerton's guest until a man becomes available to act as your escort and to ensure that you're not mistaken for your twin again."

Before LaRaine could protest further, the front door burst open with an explosive bang. Mike's attention snapped toward the entrance, and LaRaine's head revolved around to see what the disturbance could be.

"I've decided I won't take my leave right now, Murphy," the intruder announced as he stormed into the office. "I'm going after the Flame Ri—"

"That's him!" LaRaine screamed, springing out of the chair and pointing an accusing finger. "That's the man who held me prisoner!"

"—der gang," Brand finished as she spoke, his blue eyes widening with shock as recognition penetrated his rage. "You!"

Volleying her frantic gaze from man to man, LaRaine waved her finger in Brand's direction. "Quick! Do something!" she shrieked at Mike Murphy. "Don't let him get away!"

The first to recover from the shock, Brand turned up his mouth in a bitter grin. "I've got to give you credit, Flame—"

"Once and for all, I'm not Flame! Tell him who I am, Mr. Murphy!" she ordered.

"—I never thought you'd carry it this far—"

"It would seem," Mike interrupted, "that we have a case of mistaken identity here. Perhaps if we all sit down, we can find a reasonable solution to this little—uh—problem."

"Little problem! Is that what you call what he did? Well, we'll just see what the police have to say about this!" She snatched up her purse and started for the door.

Brand's arm shot out in front of her and wrapped around her waist. "You're not going anywhere, Flame!" He shoved her back into the chair and stood over her, daring her to move.

She leaped out of the chair, issuing a challenge of her own.

Brand narrowed his eyes, and spoke between his teeth. "Take one step toward that door, lady, and I'll tie you to the chair!"

"You wouldn't dare!" she shrilled, pushing her face up to his. "This time I have a witness to your abuse! And we'll see that you spend the rest of your life in jail!" She planted her fists on her hips and spread her feet in a defiant stance. However, she didn't move from that spot.

"I think we can straighten this out if we all sit down and talk about it reasonably," Mike Murphy interjected, not certain whether this was a laughing or crying situation.

Brand and LaRaine, their faces red with anger, wheeled toward Mike Murphy and began speaking at once, their accusing words such a jumble that he

144

didn't really hear what they were saying. But it wasn't necessary to "hear" every detail to get the gist of what had happened. Brand Colter was convinced she was Flame Rider and LaRaine Ashby was convinced he was a kidnapper.

Mike opened his desk drawer and removed a large revolver. His face calm, he aimed the gun at the ceiling and fired it. Immediate silence filled the office. "Now, as I was saying," he started again, laying the Colt on his desk in plain sight. "Sit down!" When neither of them moved, he wrapped his hand around the butt of his gun. "Please," he said with a smile.

"Look, Murphy—" Brand began, taking a seat.

"Quiet, Colter, or I'll get you thrown in jail just on general principles. You'll have your chance to talk."

Fuming, Brand lazed back in his chair and crossed his arms over his chest.

LaRaine shot him a smug glance, and returned her attention to Mike Murphy. Giving the Pinkerton man her most charming smile, she said, "I know—"

"You'll have your turn, too, Miss Ashby," Mike told her. "But I'm going to talk first."

Her eyebrows arched with indignant surprise at the reprimand, but she sat back down and folded her hands primly in her lap.

"Now," Mike said when the opponents were properly subdued, "what we have here is clearly a simple misunderstanding."

LaRaine opened her mouth to protest his words, but one subtle look from Mike closed it again.

"A *misunderstanding* we're going to straighten out if we stay here all day." LaRaine and Brand exchanged angry glances, but both remained silent. "First of all, Brand, this is Miss LaRaine Ashby from Virginia—not Flame Rider."

Brand shook his head and blew out a disgusted snort.

Undaunted by Brand's obvious disbelief, Mike went on. "Miss Ashby is the daughter—or should I say the adopted daughter—of Mr. Thomas Ashby, a close, personal friend of Mr. Pinkerton's."

Brand rolled his eyes.

"Let me emphasize the word *close*," Mike added, the threat in his tone obvious. "For some months now, we've been corresponding with Miss Ashby in an attempt to locate her twin sister, whom we believe to be Flame Rider, the woman you mistook her for."

"You don't really believe this hoax, do you?" Brand blurted out, unable to remain silent any longer. "I don't know what she's trying to pull, but she's no more Flame's twin than . . ."

"What I believe is of no importance, Colter. But yes, I do believe her. And more important, Allan Pinkerton believes her. And he's the best judge of people I've ever known—not to mention my employer. Besides, we have proof."

Brand arched his brow skeptically. "What proof?"

Mike produced a large envelope from his desk drawer and removed its contents. "This is a letter written to Mr. Pinkerton by Thomas Ashby explaining the whole bizarre story."

Brand took the parchment and unfolded it, quickly scanning the words on it. When he was through, he refolded it carefully and handed it back to Mike. "This letter doesn't prove anything. It could easily be a forgery. If she's telling the truth, why didn't her father look for this missing 'twin' himself? Instead of allowing his 'daughter' to come alone?"

"Unfortunately, Mr. Ashby died just a short while after he wrote this letter asking Mr. Pinkerton for his help," Mike said, giving LaRaine a sympathetic glance.

"How convenient," Brand grunted under his breath.

"I beg your pardon," LaRaine said.

He directed a knowing glimpse at her and smiled sarcastically. "You thought of everything, didn't you? With the supposed author of that letter dead, there's no one to disprove your claim, is there? So I guess you win."

"For your information, Mr. Colter," she came back stiffly, her eyes glistening with tears at the mention of her father's death. "Mr. Pinkerton and my father corresponded for many years, and he would have known if the handwriting on the letter were a forgery or not. But it makes no difference to me what you believe. I'm not afraid of you anymore. From now on I will have a Pinkerton detective at my side to protect me from you—and from other animals like you and the Rustons!"

Mike cleared his throat loudly. "Uh—there's—uh—something I think you should know about Brand Colter, Miss Ashby."

"The only thing I want to hear you say about him is that he's been placed behind bars!"

Mike winced as he prepared for an explosion. "He's the Pinkerton detective I was telling you about," Mike announced in a dreading rush of words.

LaRaine's mouth dropped open unattractively. "You mean the one you were going to assign . . . ?"

His freckled face aging by the instant, Mike nodded his head. "The agent who was due to return from leave in three weeks."

"And the only detective available to help me if I want to leave tomorrow," she said, shaking her head at the irony of her plight.

With an uneasy grimace, Mike nodded again. "I'm afraid so."

A triumphant smile spread across Brand's face. "So it looks like we're stuck with each other after all!"

LaRaine released a frustrated hrumpf and shot to her feet. "I'd prefer to travel with a snake." She stomped across the wooden floor toward the door.

"You have to understand," Mike said, coming around the desk and following her. "He was only doing what he thought was his job when he captured you. After all, your resemblance to your sister is quite remarkable. Anyone could have made the same mistake if he'd ever seen a picture of her."

"He made a mistake all right!" she spit out as she trounced through the door and stepped into the street. "And so did I when I allowed myself to believe you would be able to help me!"

Mike Murphy dashed out the door after her. "Wait!"

Brand caught up to him, grabbing his arm. "Let her go," he said, as they watched her cross the street and enter the Wickersham Hotel. "She'll be back. Once she calms down, she'll remember the only chance she has of getting where she's going is with a Pinkerton man beside her. Otherwise, she's going to end up in jail before the day's over."

"Hmp, that's easy for you to say. Allan Pinkerton didn't *personally* entrust her care and safety to you! And what do you think my chances are of keeping this job if she gets arrested?"

An idea began to form in Brand's thoughts. He wasn't for one minute fooled by Flame Rider's game, whatever it was. But if he wanted to prove she was lying, he was going to have to stick to her like mud on a boot until she slipped up. And there was only one way to do that. "What if I apologized and said I believed her?" he asked Mike.

The office manager shook his head dejectedly. "I don't know. She's awful mad. I doubt anything short of seeing you in front of a firing squad would make her happy. In fact, I wouldn't be surprised if she's sending a wire to Mr. Pinkerton already."

Brand winked mischievously and gave Mike's shoulder a conciliatory pat. Shooting the worried manager a cocky grin, he thumped the brim of his hat and shoved it to a carefree angle on the back of his head. "Don't give up yet, Mike. You haven't seen what miracles the old Colter charm can perform."

Her chest rising and falling rapidly, LaRaine locked the door to her room and pressed her forehead against it. What was she supposed to do now? She couldn't afford to wait until another Pinkerton detective became available to escort her. And that could be weeks. But she couldn't bear the thought of going with Brand Colter. Even if he were willing to admit that she wasn't Flame—which he obviously wasn't; and if she could forgive him for the way he had treated her—which she couldn't, there was no escape from the fact that every moment she spent with him would be a reminder of her shameful behavior the night before.

She rocked her head in hopeless frustration and pounded the door with her fists. There had to be something she could do. But what? As if in answer to her question, she spotted a copy of the *Missouri Republican* newspaper that had been left on a small table by the door. Of course! That was the answer! She'd hire someone else to take her. Pinkerton wasn't the only detective agency in the world. Surely there was at least one more in a city the size of St. Louis.

Seizing on the idea, she grabbed up the newspaper and unfolded it excitedly. Her eyes quickly scanned the front page. When she saw nothing to help her, she opened it and hurriedly checked the next page for ads. When her perusal of those pages also revealed no answers to her dilemma, she ripped the next sheet aside.

Her gaze traveled up and down the columns of print, her frustration growing line by line. Then an article at the bottom of page five seemed to leap out at her, and she gaped in surprise. "Flame Rider Rides Again," she read aloud, her eyes moving swiftly over the words under the large-print heading. "Fenwick!" she exclaimed as she read the location of the Rider gang's latest robbery.

When she was through reading the story once, she shook her head in stunned horror and read it again. She'd been so certain that her sister was innocent of the charges Brand Colter had accused her of. But here it was in black and white, a detailed account of Flame Rider's crimes, all of them so much worse than LaRaine had imagined. The article even stated that Flame had been with William Clark Quantrill and his Confederate raiders when they had attacked the pro-Union town of Lawrence, Kansas, in 1863, killing every man and boy in the town.

LaRaine drew in a shaky breath and crumpled the newspaper. *Lies!* she thought fiercely, tossing the paper to the floor. Unfortunately, getting rid of the paper didn't block out the memory of the words in the article, and they continued to race through her mind. "On more than one occasion, it has been reported that Flame Rider was heard boasting that she hurled the first torch in the fire that burned

Lawrence to the ground that fateful night."

LaRaine slumped into a chair, her glazed stare unfocused. Was it possible Brand and the newspaper were telling the truth? Could Flame Rider be as bad as the rumors said she was? Could identical twins be so different? A saving possibility occurred to her. Maybe Flame wasn't her missing twin at all! Maybe it was just a coincidence that their pictures were so similar.

She shook her head hopelessly. No matter what the real Flame was like, she couldn't convince herself that they weren't twins.

She stiffened her spine defensively. If she and Flame were twins and twins could not be so different, then there had to be another answer. Could the newspaper have deliberately painted Flame in a bad light because she had been on the wrong side in the war?

Or . . . LaRaine thought, her forlorn expression growing indignant as she warmed to the idea of proving Flame's innocence, if only to herself. "I wouldn't put it past them to have elaborated on the facts just to make their story more sensational!"

As she bent to retrieve the wrinkled newspaper, a gentle rap sounded at the door, shattering her concentration. She looked up, her brow furrowed by questions. Forgetting the discarded newspaper, she rose from the chair slowly, her puzzled gaze on the door.

"It's Brand Colter," a deep voice called out. "I need to talk to you."

LaRaine's heartbeat accelerated, and her breathing became rapid and shallow. Chiding herself for her excited reaction to his voice, she stood perfectly still. Maybe he would go away if she didn't answer.

"I know you're in there," he said, his words

slightly muffled as if his lips were pressed against the door.

A rush of anticipation raced through her veins and her stomach did a somersault as the image of his lips touching the wood brought back erotic memories of the night before. Shame and self-disgust quivered through her. How could she feel like this after the way he had treated her? Determined not to give in to her desire to see him just one more time, she stared hypnotized at the doorknob.

"Look, I came to apologize," he pleaded from the other side. "The least you can do is hear me out. I want to help you find your sister."

Confused by his announcement, LaRaine took a step toward the door and reached for the latch. But she caught herself in time, dropping her hand to her side. *It's a trick. I know it's a trick.*

When she still didn't answer, his tone became anxious. "Look, I don't know what else I can say. Won't you give me another chance?"

Another chance? Apologize? Was she hearing things? Just a few minutes before he'd insinuated that she was a liar, and now he was offering to help her. She shook her head, positive this was another attempt to take advantage of her. *Well, whatever he's up to, he's not fooling me with his apology!*

She grabbed the edge of the bureau with the intention of shoving it against the door.

"Dammit! I know you're in there!" he announced, his tone no longer placating. "And if you don't open this door I'm coming through it."

The muscles in her back and arms straining, La-Raine tugged on the bureau, but the heavy piece of furniture wouldn't budge. She looked around the room frantically for something else to use to block the door.

But she was already too late. With a splintering sound, the flimsy hotel-room lock sprung open, and she was trapped.

She stared for a frightened instant at the giant form that filled the door frame. Then, reacting on instinct, she grabbed the edge of the door and tried to fling it shut. "Get out of here!" she ordered.

With a resounding whack, Brand slammed the heel of his hand into the door, ripping it from her grip and sending it banging against the bureau as he stepped inside the room.

Her frantic gaze zipped around the small room in a desperate search for an escape. But there was none.

LaRaine took a step back. "You'd better leave me alone," she gasped, her voice shaky.

"Not until you hear what I have to say." Without looking behind him, he kicked the door shut and took a purposeful step toward her.

Continuing to back away from him, she pointed a trembling finger at him. "I'm warning you! I'll scream!"

Smirking, Brand continued his advance. "It won't do you any good. I told the desk clerk you were my runaway wife and that I'd come to take you home to our babies. He'll just think you're—"

"You what?" Her face reddened with anger. "How dare you do such a thing?" She retreated farther into the room. The soft bump of her thighs against the bed as she backed into it brought her retreat up short. A frantic look over her shoulder confirmed the fact that she was truly trapped, and fresh panic shook her.

Taking another predatory step forward, Brand shrugged. "I didn't want to take the chance you wouldn't be reasonable."

"Reasonable!" She looked frantically around the room for something with which to defend herself. Spying the oil lamp on the table beside the bed, she snatched off the glass chimney and raised it over her head threateningly. "I'll show you reasonable."

154

Chapter Ten

LaRaine and Brand gaped at each other in paralyzed silence as the glass chimney sailed past his head and crashed against the door. Shards of glass exploded in every direction on impact.

Horrified, LaRaine's mouth dropped open as, before her eyes, tiny beads of blood popped to the surface along a thin line on Brand's cheek where he'd been hit by a flying sliver of glass.

His shock transformed into rage, Brand dove across the short space between them. Slamming into her, he propelled her onto the bed with the force of his body.

"Didn't anyone ever tell you it's dangerous to make threats you might not be able to follow through on?" he breathed rapidly, raising his head to examine her face. "Someone could get hurt."

Her glance darted to the wound on his cheek, and a pang of guilt stabbed at her. For an instant, she lay perfectly still beneath him, stunned by the need to reach up and caress his cheek as her nurturing instincts called out for her to do. But she had no intention of apologizing—or of taking care of his cut. He could bleed to death for all she cared!

She narrowed her eyes and averted them away

from his bleeding face. "Get off me!" she ordered, flailing her arms and legs to remove him.

"Not until we talk."

"We've already talked." She squirmed with energetic protest under his weight.

Brand grunted and shook his head. "Okay, if that's the way you want to play." Pressing her harder into the mattress, he rotated his hips suggestively in answer to her agitated movements.

Without warning, a rush of excitement flooded through her veins, settling deep in the pit of her belly and radiating out from between her thighs. Fighting the overwhelming desire to wrap her arms around his waist, she stilled her movements and, grinding her teeth together, dug her fingers into the cover beneath her.

"That's better," he said, his breathing more rapid than his exertion warranted. "Now, are you ready to listen?"

Not trusting her voice, she looked away and nodded her head.

"Good," he rasped, suddenly finding it difficult to concentrate on what he had to say. Clearing his throat, he shifted his weight in a vain attempt to ease the building pressure in his loins. "Uh . . . I've thought about it, and . . . uh . . . I guess I owe you an apology."

"Does that mean you've decided I've been telling the truth after all?" she snipped, still refusing to look at him.

He stiffened, his eyes darting nervously from left to right. He suddenly realized he couldn't lie to this woman. "Uh . . . I . . . uh . . ."

LaRaine rolled her head to look up at him. "Well? Is that it? Is that why you're here? To tell me you believe me now?"

"Yeah. Uh. I mean . . . well, uh . . . sort of. I mean . . ."

"Sort of?" she exclaimed, shocked by his answer. She resumed her struggles, even angrier now.

"Hold still, dammit, and I'll explain," he protested, his body's awareness of her beneath him growing to agonizing proportions.

"Explain what? Either you believe me or you don't."

"It's not that easy. Actually, I don't know what to believe. But since Allan Pinkerton and Mike believe you, I guess I owe it to you to give you the benefit of the doubt."

Her eyebrows arched in mock surprise. "Oh, do you now? That's very charitable of you," she spit out caustically. "But quite frankly, Mr. Colter, I don't want your charity. And if this is your idea of an apology, I don't want that, either! Now, please get off me and leave."

"This isn't charity," he said, ignoring her demand. "I came to tell you I'll take you to southern Missouri if you still want to go. We can leave in the morning."

She curled her lip in a sarcastic smile. "Why? Because Mike Murphy ordered you to do it?"

"No one ordered me to do anything!" he answered defensively.

"Then you must be planning to catch me off guard and turn me in as Flame the first chance you get."

His face grew red with impatience and guilt. "I don't suppose it would ever occur to you that I was doing this to give you the opportunity to prove you're Flame's twin, and not Flame herself?"

"Don't make me laugh. I don't need to prove anything to you. I've already proven it to your employer's satisfaction, and that's all I care about.

What you believe, one way or the other, means nothing to me. Now let me up, or so help me, I'm going to scream!" Sucking in a deep breath to follow through on her threat, she pushed at his bulk.

His nerves stretched to the limits by the warm body molded to his, Brand's resistance snapped. Dipping his head, he covered her mouth with his, smothering her scream.

"Mmm," she protested, pounding his back with her fists and moving her head from side to side in an effort to escape his forceful kiss. But it was useless. No matter how she twisted and turned, he didn't release her.

His lips melted into hers, forging their mouths into one as he swept the heat of hers with his tongue.

Then, as though she were a puppet controlled by strings, her hands stilled on his back and she stopped shaking her head. Though she no longer had the will to fight him, she held very still, valiantly trying not to respond. But her resistance was useless. She was no longer in control of her actions.

Slowly, like flowers opening, her fists relaxed, fanning her fingers on his back. His relentless kiss seared from her mouth to the very soles of her feet and back again. And she was lost.

Barely able to breathe, her toes curled in exquisite rapture, and the last thought of resistance dissipated. She wound her arms tighter around him.

His hands slid beneath her buttocks, lifting her toward his burgeoning desire. "Oh, God," he groaned as she moved against him, instinctively parting her thighs to settle him more securely between them. "You feel so good."

Forgetting his suspicions and intentions, he buried his face in the curve of her neck and shoulder, reveling in the delicate fragrance that lingered there.

The pupils of his blue eyes dark with passion, he brought his hands around to the front of her and worked them between their bodies to cup and caress her breasts. "I've been wanting to do this all morning," he moaned, sliding his mouth down to her breast. When he had thoroughly kissed one firm mound through the thin material of her dress and chemise, he left it, glistening and wet, its nipple prominent, and gave his full attention to her other breast.

Because he had knocked her back onto the bed from a standing position, her feet were still on the floor. And when Brand slid to his knees between her thighs, she made no move to sit up. With shaking hands, he raised her skirt and petticoats, catching the drawstring of her drawers and untying it with a frantic yank. He wrapped his fingers around her hips, and bent his head to kiss the juncture of her thighs through the white lawn drawers, then smoothed the pants downward.

Modesty and reason lost, LaRaine's hips rotated in a provocative invitation. Releasing a soft groan of relief, Brand separated the moist petals of her body with his thumbs, exposing the heart of her womanhood to his rapt gaze. "This is all I've thought of since last night," he sighed, ducking his head to gorge himself on the nectar of her.

"Oh!" LaRaine wailed, her hips jumping against his mouth as his lips clamped onto the swollen kernel of her desire and tugged. Sucking, releasing, sucking, releasing, he worked the bud into a pulsating bomb, which threatened to explode at any moment. "Please," she sobbed, threading her fingers into his dark hair and rocking her own head back and forth in agony. "Yes. Oh, yes."

When the explosion came, the spasm of ecstasy that shuddered through her shook her from head to foot, bucking her hips wildly against his kiss. The strength completely drained from her limbs, she went limp, her breathing loud and gasping.

Brand wasted no time removing her drawers the rest of the way and getting rid of his gunbelt and unbuttoning his trousers. Dipping his head for a last taste of her, he draped her legs over his shoulders and moved his body over hers again.

Taking her mouth with his, he plunged his tongue deep into its heat as he sank into the welcoming cove of her femininity.

This time there was no startling twinge of pain for LaRaine as he entered her, only a fathomless sense of fulfillment, and she released a happy sigh.

Because of the way he had positioned her, Brand's thrusts were deeper than the first time they had made love. The tight folds of her body molded around the entire length of him, holding him, squeezing him, caressing him. He pressed into her harder and faster with each descent, his passion roaring beyond control now. Soft moans and the gasping hiss of labored breathing combined with the sensuous sounds of flesh slapping against flesh when they came together, and with the gentle sucking sound of protest her body made when he drew back for his next stab. Harder, faster, deeper. Harder, faster, deeper.

LaRaine realized the explosion she had experienced before was going to happen again and she strained to put it off, wanting to hold on to the euphoria just a moment longer. But there was no stopping it now. The release was imminent, inevitable. Wrapping her arms around Brand's neck, she clung to him, calling his name over and over again as he took her over the edge.

As her climax overtook her, Brand tensed and reared back, his eyes squeezed shut in ecstasy as he pumped his soul into her.

When the muscles of her sex had contracted around him, and had greedily wrung the last of his passion from him, she dropped her head and flung a forearm up over her eyes. She couldn't move.

His breathing hard and fast, Brand levered himself up, separating them quickly and rolling to his back.

An overwhelming feeling of loss washed over her as she felt her body give up its precious possession. And with the sense of emptiness, reality came flooding back into her thoughts. He had used her again, and she hadn't even tried to stop him this time. All it had taken was one kiss and she had opened up to him. Disgust and revulsion for what he'd made of her formed in a hard knot in her belly.

Tears filling her eyes, she struggled to sit up, pushing her skirt down to cover her nakedness. She couldn't look at Brand.

"Well," she said at last, her voice quivering as she stood and walked away from the bed to the washstand. The evidence of what had just transpired was hot and sticky between her legs and her self-dislike grew—as well as her hate for the man who had shown her what she really was. "Is this why you said you'd escort me, even though you don't believe me."

Brand stood up and straightened his clothes, his expression filled with remorse. "I didn't want that to happen."

A pang of hurt pinched at her emotions, but she fought to stay calm. "You said you've thought about it all day."

"Yes, but I didn't mean for it to be this way," he said, standing behind her, lifting his hands to put

161

them on her upper arms. But he thought better of it and dropped them at his sides.

"Oh, didn't you?" she asked bitterly, catching sight of the damp circles on the front of her dress where he'd kissed her breasts, and hurting anew. "Why in heaven's name not? Isn't that what you do with a . . . a . . . the kind of woman you think I am? Just hold us down, toss up our skirts, and use us to relieve your male desires. Then throw us aside when you're through."

"Look, I don't know where you got your ideas about men, but you forget who you're talking to. I know you're not the 'kind of woman' you're so convinced I think you are. Remember me? I was there. You weren't a prostitute yesterday, and unless you spent the last few hours going into a new line of business, you're not one today."

Her hands hanging at her sides, she lowered her head. How she wished she could believe him! But she knew what she knew, and only a—one of "those" women—would have responded to a man like she had. "There's no need to be kind. I know that a lady would never have . . ."

Brand's face broke into a sympathetic smile. "So that's it," he said, bracketing her arms and turning her toward him.

Her chin touching her collarbone, she didn't resist.

"Someone told you a 'lady' doesn't enjoy making love, didn't they?"

Startled, she looked up. "Everyone knows a proper lady only . . . uh . . . submits . . . uh . . . out of duty to her husband. Only the most immoral of women would actually li—" Her eyes widened in surprise as the reality of what she'd almost admitted hit her. "I mean . . ."

"I know what you mean," he said with an understanding grin. He knew he shouldn't be letting her get under his skin like this. He knew it was all just part of her act, and it was bad enough that he continued to want her physically. But what he was feeling right now was quite another matter, and one that could only cause him trouble when he proved once and for all who she was.

Despite the inner voice chiding him, he gathered her into his arms and burrowed his fingers into her hair, bringing her head to rest on his chest.

LaRaine tensed, then shook her head in abject surrender as she dissolved into his embrace. Her revelations about herself had taken too much out of her. She didn't have any more fight left.

Unable to resist his need to console her, Brand drew her even closer. "Someone must have filled your head with a lot of foolishness when they told you how a lady's *supposed* to feel," he murmured into her hair. "But they were wrong. What you felt when we made love was right. You responded the way a woman was meant to respond."

"But—"

"Shh," he crooned, caressing her back and head. "It's all right."

Safe and comforted in his arms like this, LaRaine could temporarily forget her shame and embarassment. If only they could stay like this forever, his arms around her, his strength supporting them both.

Even though she knew the moment of closeness was an illusion, LaRaine couldn't bring herself to tear away from his embrace. Not quite yet. It had been so long since there'd been anybody she could lean on, so long since she'd felt safe. She would just stay here in the security of his arms for a moment more. Then she would make him leave.

Wrapping her arms around his waist, she moved closer, pressing her face in the curve of his neck and shoulder. She slid her hands up his back and clung desperately to his shoulders. "I wish we . . ." she started, catching herself before she revealed too much.

Lost in his own forlorn thoughts of helplessness, Brand sucked in a deep, regret-filled breath, then released it slowly. If only she would admit to him who she was, maybe he could help her get a lighter sentence. But as long as she continued her charade there wasn't much he could do.

Brand nodded his head dejectedly. "Yeah, me, too."

She pressed her forehead against the granite of his chest. "Please," she wept, the floodgate on her tears opening all the way. "Just hold me."

Overwhelmed by the desolation in her tone, Brand hugged her tighter against him, his mind racing frantically for a way out of the mess they were in. Then an idea occurred to him, and he held her away from him so he could look into her eyes. "Maybe things aren't as bad as they seem! You could turn yourself in and I could go with you to testify that you've changed and really want to start over. I know the judge would respect the opinion of a Pinkerton detective, and he'd probably give you a parole, or at the most a very light sentence! Then we . . ."

The expression on LaRaine's tear-stained face hardened, and her lip curled up with bitterness. Dropping her hands to her sides as if her hold on his waist had suddenly burned her, she twisted out of his grasp. Self-conscious and hurt by the truth that hung in the air between them, she spun away from him. All his sweet compassion and understanding assurances had been nothing more than another ruse to trick her into confessing that she was Flame rider. And she had actually been on the verge of believing he not only trusted her, but was beginning to feel something for her—besides lust.

"Is this your way of giving me 'the benefit of the doubt'?" she asked with deadly calm, her fists balling into the folds of her skirt. "I would appreciate it if you would leave now. I'm very tired and have some business to attend to. And please tell your employer that I will no longer require the services of Pinkerton National Detective Agency."

Aw, hell! He'd ruined everything now. He should have known better. She'd been on the verge of trusting him. But he'd let stupid sentiment *and* a big mouth get the better of him. Now, she would never open up to him willingly—or let him help her. But he couldn't give up now. One way or another, he was going to prove she was Flame Rider.

Wheeling around, he slapped on his hat and snatched up his gun belt. He wrenched open the door, then turned back to her for a parting remark.

"I'll tell him, but you're making a big mistake, *Miss LaRaine Ashby*," he warned with an amused grin. "Because the instant you step out of this hotel without someone from Pinkerton to protect you, you're going to be fair game for every bounty hunter and lawman in the state of Missouri—and none of them will give a fig about your 'proof'—or your life! Remember, the wanted poster for Flame Rider says dead or alive, so whoever spots you is probably going to shoot first and ask questions later!" He chuckled and stepped out into the hall, slamming the door behind him.

At a loss, LaRaine stared at the wooden door, her thoughts a riot of turmoil. Of course Brand was right. She needed protection. Her glance shifted distraughtly to the newspaper still on the floor where she had tossed it. But even if there was an advertisement for another detective agency, she knew she couldn't risk contacting one. She would be taken into custody before she could even tell her story. And even if she could find someone willing to listen, she had no real proof. Only Allan Pinkerton's letter to Mike Murphy, and that was at the Pinkerton office. Besides, no one other than a Pinkerton employee would take that letter as evidence. *Not even every Pinkerton man believes it.*

Admitting to herself for the first time that she was in serious trouble, she sank down in a chair and covered her mouth with her fingertips. Of course, she could tell Mike Murphy that she'd changed her mind and would wait for the next detective who was available. Or she could accept Brand Colter's offer. What difference did it make if he didn't believe her? As long as he adhered to the official Pinkerton opinion that she was telling the truth, it didn't matter what he believed.

A pang of disappointment twisted through her heart. It hurt terribly to know that he hadn't felt anything for her. All the time he'd been deliberately worming his way into her trust to try to trick her into betraying herself.

"Well, I won't give him another chance to make a fool out of me."

Of course, if I get myself shot by a bounty hunter, or thrown in jail by some sheriff, I won't be in much of a position to worry about being made a fool of, she thought sadly, remembering the old adage about, "cutting off your nose to spite your face."

I'd really like to be there to see his arrogant face when he finds out I've been telling the truth, she thought with a revengeful smile.

The true danger of what she was considering exploded in her head. She couldn't go on the trail with Brand Colter! Because of the scandalous way she had behaved, he would be expecting the same privileges. Just look how quickly she had given in to him—twice! She had permitted him liberties no decent woman would ever allow, and she had actually enjoyed it, wanted it, cried out for it. And even now, after all that had happened, she had to admit to herself that she might not have the willpower to turn him away if he came back through the door right that minute.

She buried her face in her hands, catching a new deluge of tears. It was no use. No matter how desperate she was for his help, she could never see Brand Colter again, not if she wanted to salvage even a tiny fragment of her self-respect. She would simply have to find another way.

"That'll be four bits," the ruddy-faced barber said, removing the towel from Brand's shoulders, then giving his clothes a final dusting with the whisk broom.

Brand levered himself out of the chair and ran his hand over his freshly shaved cheeks. "Thanks," he said, flipping a coin into the man's hand. He ran his fingers through his hair, then picked up his hat and dropped it into place on his head. "That feels better."

Stepping outside, he glanced in the direction of the Wickersham Hotel. He automatically focused on the third window from the left of the second floor, the room he had determined to be Flame's. Just as he started to step off the curb to cross the street, he noticed a woman exit the hotel. Though her bonnet was pulled very low on her head, covering all of her hair and obscuring her face, Brand recognized the brown calico dress Flame had been wearing earlier.

He moved quickly into the shadows of the doorway to watch her. Her head ducked, she peeked out from beneath the wide bonnet brim and looked furtively up and down the street, then took off toward the levee.

Giving his quarry time to reach the intersection, Brand ambled in the same direction, taking care to keep her in view. But his intent to be secretive was wasted. She was definitely a woman with a purpose and one with her mind elsewhere. Still, he kept his distance and his casual pace as he followed her three blocks to Trussel's Emporium, where she paused to survey the merchandise in the window.

Brand immediately stopped. "Give me a paper, kid," he said to the newsboy a few feet away.

"Yessir!" The youngster, his hands and face black with newsprint, ran over to where Brand stood beneath a shop awning and handed him the paper. "That'll be two cents."

Looking down in the young face, Brand was rocked with a wave of sadness. The boy couldn't be more than eight at the most, and he knew there was a good possibility this child was homeless, maybe living in a packing crate on the levee, or at least fatherless and supporting a mother and younger siblings with his paltry earnings. It was a scene he'd seen hundreds of times since the war. All over the country, families had been left without homes. And all too often, children without parents had been turned out into the streets where they were forced to fend for themselves or starve. "Here you go, kid. Buy yourself a peppermint stick or some chewing gum," he said, handing the boy two dollars.

The urchin's eyes widened in astonishment. "Thanks, mister!" He poked the coins deep into the pocket of his worn pants and dashed back to his newsstand—a small crate with a grimy toddler leashed to it.

Tearing his eyes away from the pitiful sight, Brand glanced up just as LaRaine disappeared into the store across the street.

"Hey, kid, you want to earn five dollars?" he asked the boy.

The newsboy looked at him, his expression a sad mingle of distrust and need. "Whadda I gotta do?"

Sensing the boy's reason for apprehension, Brand answered quickly. "Just go into the emporium over there and see what the lady wearing the brown calico dress and bonnet is doing in there."

"That's all?" The suspicion was still in his voice.

Brand smiled. "That's all. My word."

"I can't leave my stand. My little sister . . ."

"I'll watch them both till you get back. And, while you're in there, you might as well bring back a loaf of bread and some cheese—and maybe a pail of milk."

"Okay," the boy said, evidently deciding Brand was to be trusted. He took the shopping money from Brand and ran across the street.

The instant the eight-year-old was out of sight, his sister began to cry. Cursing the war again for what it had done to the country, Brand hunkered down beside the little girl and chucked her under the chin. "Shh, he'll be right back with something to eat. Doesn't that sound good?"

The boy was back with his purchases in less than five minutes. Glancing nervously at his stand to be sure his sister was safe, he handed the food to Brand.

Brand shook his head. "That's for you and your sister," he said, handing the boy the promised five dollars. "Now, what about the lady in the brown dress?"

Moving quickly, the boy dug in the sack and broke off a chunk of the cheese and handed it to his tiny ward. "She tole the storekeep she wanted ta outfit her brother with some jeans, a coupla shirts, a long coat, some boots 'n socks, a hat, some long underwear — an' a gun."

Frowning, Brand looked away from the happy baby who was now eagerly washing down the cheese with the milk her brother held up to her mouth. "Thanks, kid," he said, giving the boy's thin shoulders a pat and standing up. "You've been a big help. You be sure and eat some of that yourself. You need to put a little meat on your bones."

Chapter Eleven

"It looks like your 'client' is about to head out on her own, old pal," Brand announced as he entered the Pinkerton office.

Mike Murphy bolted up out of his chair, his eyes bugging. "What are you talking about? Didn't you straighten things out with her?"

Brand shrugged his shoulders. "I guess she's impervious to my charms."

"What makes you think she intends to go alone?"

"If she doesn't, she's made some mighty odd purchases this afternoon — especially for the proper eastern lady she's *supposed* to be." He pulled a chair up and nonchalantly propped his feet on Mike's desk. "But then, maybe she's not who she's supposed to be after all."

"What do you mean, odd?" Mike asked, his eyes shifting nervously from Brand Colter to his view of the Wickersham Hotel across the street. "What did she buy?"

Brand smiled secretively.

"Look, Colter, stop playing games. If anything happens to that girl . . ." He dragged in a deep, uneasy breath. "Just tell me what the hell's going on?"

Tired of teasing Mike, Brand swung his feet to the floor. "She spent the last few hours buying herself men's clothing, a gun, a horse and saddle, and enough hardtack and jerky for at least a week."

Mike winced. "Maybe she bought them for someone else."

"She told the shopkeeper she was buying the things for her brother—who, by the way, happens to be just her size. And she told the stable owner that her 'brother' would be by to pick up his horse before dawn tomorrow morning."

"Well, maybe she was telling the truth," Mike said, his tone wishful.

Brand arched his eyebrows and shot Mike a look of reproach. "You don't really believe that, do you, buddy?"

Mike shook his head regretfully. "No, I guess not. But she can't be planning to go alone. A lady with her upbringing wouldn't consider doing anything so foolish."

"Of course not," Brand agreed pointedly. "On the other hand, I don't think Flame Rider would hesitate to ride out alone, do you?"

"I'm warning you, Brand. Don't start on that again. I told you, as long as Mr. Pinkerton believes she's LaRaine Ashby, that's who she is. Have you got that?"

Brand shrugged and grinned benignly. "Sure, Mike. Whatever you say." He stood up and sauntered toward the door. "But that leaves you in the same old predicament, doesn't it? How're you going to protect your 'client' if she refuses your help?"

Mike smiled sadistically. "That's your problem, Colter."

"My problem? Sorry, pal. I've decided to wash my hands of this whole thing. From this moment on,

I'm on leave."

"You might want to reconsider that decision," Mike said. "I wired Mr. Pinkerton in Chicago and told him about the mix-up on the train, and how you had volunteered to give up your leave to go in search of Flame Rider . . ."

"And?" Brand asked suspiciously.

Mike's grin broadened. "He wired back and said that since you were the one who blundered, he wasn't the least surprised that you had insisted on doing whatever it takes to make things right."

"You're kidding."

Mike shook his head. "Looks like mine's not the only job on the line, doesn't it, 'pal'?"

Brand eyed Mike skeptically. What the hell was he supposed to do now? After a great deal of tortured soul searching, he had come to the conclusion that the only way to overcome his weakness for Flame Rider was to put her and Missouri as far behind him as possible. Let someone else bring her in. "She's made it very clear she doesn't want to have anything to do with me."

"Then don't tell her. Evidently, you followed her today without her knowing it. Just keep on following her and make sure she doesn't get into any serious trouble."

"I got news for you. That woman *is* trouble."

"Then, be there to get her out of it."

"What happens when it turns out there's no twin sister?"

"Bring me the proof and we'll present it to Mr. Pinkerton together. But unless your proof is *irrefutable,* you'll treat her like any other client we've been hired to protect. Agreed?"

Brand studied the window on the second floor of the hotel across the street. "And I have your word you'll back me up when I get the proof?" he reconfirmed thoughtfully.

"You have my word—*if* you get the proof."

The sun was a blazing ball of gold on the eastern horizon when LaRaine rode toward her destination two mornings later. There was a chill in the air, signaling the end of Indian summer. Seeing the misty puffs her breath formed in the air, she was glad she had bought the overcoat to protect her. Brand Colter's face flashed across her mind, and she wondered where he was right then. Had he spent the night sleeping on the cold ground like she had? Or had he been warm and snug in a bed with some woman?

Shaking her head to get rid of the thoughts that had plagued her since that morning in her hotel room, she nudged her mount forward. *I hope I never see him again.*

As she fought her memories of Brand Colter, LaRaine noticed the road seemed to look more traveled than it had before. Urging her horse over the hill in the road, she was excited to discover a town in the valley below. *That has to be Fenwick,* she decided, reviewing the directions the stable owner had given her before she left St. Louis.

She hauled her horse to a stop and studied the town, already alive with bustling morning activity. She blew on her hands and rubbed them together thoughtfully.

Now that Fenwick was actually in sight, she was feeling unsure of herself again. How was she going to find out what they knew about Flame without giving herself away?

She couldn't just ride into town and ask the sher-

174

iff. He would be too familiar with Flame's face and might not be fooled by her own disguise. Maybe she could talk to the newspaper editor. Surely he would have the latest knowledge on Flame's whereabouts. But he would also know what she looked like.

Then an idea struck her. Where did the paper get its out-of-town news? From the telegraph office, of course!

"And the telegraph operator might not be as likely to recognize Flame!" she said aloud, then added, "Though no one's going to mistake me for Flame in these clothes—as long as they don't get too close a look at my face."

The nagging voice in her head reminded her again that she should have accepted Brand Colter's offer. No matter how begrudgingly it had been offered, having a Pinkerton detective to vouch for her if she got caught would have certainly come in handy right now.

"But there's no use crying over spilt milk at this late date." She took off her hat and propped it on her lap. "As long as I keep my hair covered and don't let anyone see my face, I'll be fine." Working quickly, she rewound her thick auburn hair into a tight knot. Satisfied that it was as secure as possible, she replaced her hat, pulling it low on her forehead and over her ears. She gave the hair around the hatband a final check to be sure there were no stray wisps showing, then as an extra precaution, she turned up the collar of her coat.

She glanced down to make certain there were no telltale feminine curves showing under her bulky clothing, then whipped the gun from the holster she had buckled over her coat. Though she'd checked the revolver's load several times in the past twenty-four hours since she'd left St. Louis, she gave the gun's cylinder a spin to check it one more time.

When everything had been checked and rechecked, she admitted that she couldn't put off what she had to do any longer. Releasing an apprehensive sigh, she clicked her tongue and signaled her horse forward.

Riding into Fenwick, LaRaine kept her head down, but her eyes remained alert as they took in the scope of the small town. Everything seemed to be normal for a town just waking from a night's sleep, and she relaxed ever so slightly. But her eyes continued to zigzag from side to side, ready for anything the least out of the ordinary.

On the right she saw a white-aproned storekeeper sweeping his porch. *Like he's probably done every day for years.* On the left she heard music and a burst of laughter from a saloon. *Nothing unusual about that.* In the alley between the saloon and feed store, she saw a gaudily dressed woman being kissed by a cowboy. *They definitely aren't interested in a stranger riding down Main Street.* Upstairs, on the second story of the hotel, she saw a woman shaking linens out of the window. *No threat there.* Ahead, a large dog stepped off the boardwalk to follow two children across the street. *Couldn't be more ordinary than that.*

Spotting the telegraph office, she was seized by an idea. As long as she was going in there anyway, maybe she should send a wire to Mike Murphy to tell him where she was. Just so he and Mr. Pinkerton wouldn't worry, she told herself.

A familiar, blue-eyed face smiled in her mind, and she frowned angrily. She refused to consider the possibility that she harbored a secret hope that Mike Murphy would send Brand.

Still giving everything around her careful scrutiny, she tied her horse in front of the telegraph office.

Moving in what she hoped was a convincingly masculine saunter, she stepped inside the small office. Hooking a thumb in her holster belt she stood with her feet apart. Careful to keep looking around so the clerk wouldn't get a good look at her face, she spoke to the thin, baldheaded man who operated the transmitter. "I need ta send a wire ta St. Louie," she said in a voice that was falsely deep.

"Sure thing, mister," the man answered eagerly, thinking how the gunfighters got younger and younger every day. *This one don't even look old enough ta shave.* "Jest write down on that pad what ya want ta say and where ya want ta send it. Can ya write, young feller?"

LaRaine didn't answer, certain that the fewer words she used the less likely the possibility she would be recognized as a woman, or worse still, mistaken for Flame Rider!

She started to take off her glove to write, but thought better. Her small-boned hand would be a definite giveaway. Leaving the gloves on, she took the pad and scribbled in a large scrawl that looked as manly as she could manage: TO MIKE MURPHY. PINKERTON DETECTIVE AGENCY, ST. LOUIS. RIDING OUT OF FENWICK TODAY. L. ASHBY.

"That'll be two bits," the man behind the counter said, his eyes running curiously over the message she had handed him.

"Huh, oh sure." She dug into a coat pocket for coins. They were hard to handle with gloves, but she finally managed to produce the twenty-five cents the operator had asked for. "How long will that take to get there?" she asked, walking toward the door to look out on the street, her back to the clerk.

"It'll be there right away," he answered, already

sitting down to tap out the wire on his transmitter key. "You one o' them Pinkerton detectives?" he asked when he had finished.

LaRaine jumped. "What?"

"You're a might young for that kind o' job, ain't ya?" he asked conversationally.

Seizing the opportunity to get the information she needed, LaRaine rested her elbow on the counter. Keeping her head turned away from the clerk so she could survey the street, she lowered her voice. "Don't let my looks fool you," she rasped.

The man leaned forward. "I guess you're on some big case right now, huh?"

LaRaine nodded solemnly. "But that's between you and me. I don't want anyone to know I'm in town."

The telegraph operator put his finger to his mouth. "My lips're sealed," he promised. "I don't guess you could tell me who you're a-lookin' for? I might be able to help ya out. News 'bout everythin' what happens in these parts comes through here."

"You might be able to help me at that," LaRaine said, doing her best to keep her tone casual—and her voice deep. "What do you know about Flame Rider?"

The man's eyes lit up. "Flame—" he said loudly, then lowered his voice. "I mean Flame Rider," he whispered. "Is that who you're after?"

LaRaine nodded, still managing to keep her face averted under the guise of observing the street. "You know where she's been seen last?"

"She was here last week. Her an' her boys robbed the bank."

"Which direction did she head when she left?"

"South, I heard."

"Have you heard anything about her since then?

Have there been any other robberies?"

The clerk shook his head thoughtfully. "Nope. She jest rid inta town one day 'n robbed the bank, then disappeared inta the hills again. Some folks b'lieve she's got a hideout south o' here, but no one's never been able ta find it."

"Thanks," LaRaine said, straightening up. "I appreciate the information."

"Wish it coulda been more."

"That's okay. You've been a big help. I think I'll go on over and get a bite of breakfast at the hotel. Don't forget." She held a gloved finger to her lips.

The man held up his hand in the sign of an oath. "Ya can trust me, mister. I won't breathe a word."

With that, she stepped back out onto the street and breathed a sigh of relief.

Adjusting her collar around her neck and over her jaw and chin, LaRaine headed across the rutted street, leading her horse behind her. *What would Mama think if she could see me now? After all the times she insisted I walk like a lady. 'Always use small, dainty steps.' 'Don't run.' 'Don't swagger.' 'Toes pointed straight ahead.'* LaRaine smiled to herself and deliberately lengthened and widened her stride, bent on controlling the natural, feminine sway of her hips.

Aware that no one seemed to be giving her a second glance, she giggled inwardly. *This is sort of fun. Sort of an adventure. If I live long enough, won't I have tales to tell my children.*

It was a game she and her father had played whenever things were going wrong, whenever they were afraid, whenever the soldiers had come on their place during the war; and LaRaine was glad to see it still worked. She felt better already. Hadn't she fooled the telegraph operator? And hadn't she found out which direction Flame had gone?

Her confidence bolstered, she sauntered into the hotel dining room, glancing around to be certain there was no unexpected danger lurking at one of the tables. There were several men already eating, all dressed similarly to her, but none of them looked like a threat to her. Deciding it was safe to stay, she scraped out a chair and sat down in the corner where she could see everybody who came in or left the restaurant.

The minute she had seated herself, she was greeted by the buxom brunette she had seen shaking linens out the upstairs window. "Whatcha want, honey?"

LaRaine kept her eyes and face down. "Ham, eggs, and grits," she answered in her pseudomasculine voice. "And coffee."

"Comin' right up, sugar," the waitress answered and turned to wiggle her way back into the kitchen.

LaRaine sat with a gloved hand shading her eyes, hoping she looked like a cowboy who had had a rough night. Though she was sure no one had given her any notice, her left hand rested only inches from the handle of her revolver.

The serving woman was true to her word and was back in minutes with a heaping plate of food, the entire mound drenched in thick milk gravy. If she hadn't been so hungry, LaRaine was certain she would have been sick at the sight of the greasy glutton's delight. As it was, she hunched over her plate and attacked the food greedily—just the way she had seen the other customers do. She ate noisily, gulped her coffee, and even managed to release a particularly rude belch.

However, for all her assumed masculine mannerisms and actions, she couldn't eat like a man and soon realize she wouldn't be able to make a dent in the pile of food that seemed to be growing before her eyes. Shoving her plate away, she took a final swig of coffee and stood up, slapping a dollar on the table.

"What's the matter, honey?" the waitress asked from across the room, causing every customer in the place to direct his eyes toward the stranger who stood ready to leave the corner table.

LaRaine glanced up to meet the curious stares of half a dozen men. "Ya talkin' to me?" she asked, her voice as low as she could manage.

"I sure am. Didn't ya like the grub? Was there somethin' wrong with it?"

LaRaine felt the sweat trickle from under her hat and down her face. Her heart was pounding so hard she was surprised they couldn't all hear it. Maybe they did! Maybe that was why they were looking at her so strangely. "No, ma'am, it was just fine. Real good. But I had a rough night and my belly's not feelin' too good this mornin'."

"You sure that's all it is, mister?" a deep voice asked from the doorway. Everyone in the dining room looked in the direction of the voice.

LaRaine's frightened gaze fell on the glistening star on the town marshal's broad chest, and her heart sank sickeningly into the pit of her stomach.

"Yes, sir," LaRaine stuttered, certain every man in the dining room could tell she wasn't who she pretended to be. She wanted to run, but the only way out was blocked by the lawman. Her gaze shifted nervously toward the kitchen. No good. The waitress was inadvertently guarding that exit. There was no choice but to continue her masquerade until she was actually exposed.

"Yer new 'round here, ain't ya, young feller?" the marshal drawled, his words more a statement than a question. "I don't recall seein' ya b'fore. Where ya from?"

"St. Louie. I'm just passin' through." The words were harder and harder to articulate. Her mouth was dry and she was positive she was going to be sick — if she didn't faint from the heat first.

"St. Louie, huh? Somethin' 'bout ya strikes me real familiar. Ya been to Fenwick b'fore?"

"No, sir, I ain't been here before," LaRaine stuttered, her confidence deteriorating by the instant. "You don't know me."

"Take off yer hat an' lemme git a good look at yer face," the marshal ordered. "I never forgit a face."

He knows. He's just playing with me. Like a fish dangling on a line. Letting me think I might get away. And then reeling me in. "My h-h-hat, sir?"

"That's what I said."

"I don't understand, sir. I ain't done nuthin' wrong, have I?"

"I didn't say ya had, boy. I jest wanna see yer face better. See if I can place where I seen ya b'fore. I could swear I know ya," the man said, smiling as he walked toward LaRaine.

She was cornered like a helpless rat. Should she draw her gun? If she did, she wouldn't have a chance against someone like the tall, mustached man who approached her. She'd be dead in an instant. On the other hand, she reasoned, if she were discovered, what was the worst thing that could happen? She'd be identified as Flame Rider and arrested.

Someone from Pinkerton is bound to come looking for me when they get my wire. They'll be able to clear this up.

Her shoulders sagged in surrender, and she reached up to remove the sweat-soaked hat from her head. She heard the collective gasp of surprise from

182

the restaurant patrons as thick red hair tumbled down her back, free of the confining hat.

"It's her!" one of the men shouted, pointing a finger accusingly. "It's Flame Rider!"

"What's she doin' back in Fenwick?"

"I figgered she'd be long gone by now."

"What's the matter, Mizz Rider?" the marshal sneered. "Didn't you'n yer boys do 'nuff damage t'other day? Is Fenwick the only town in Missouri with a bank?"

"But I'm not Flame Rider," LaRaine started, even though she had told herself she wouldn't try to explain to this man. "I'm her twin sister. I didn't know she'd been here."

"Sure," he said, drawing his gun and stepping toward her.

"You've got to believe me!"

"Sure we do. But I doubt old Mizz Wigginton's goin' ta. Her husband, the late Mr. Wigginton, died durin' yer robbery t'other day. Ya skeered him so bad, he up and dropped dead right there in the middle o' the vault. Take off the gunbelt, Flame. Nice 'n easy," the steely voice ordered.

"But I didn't rob your bank! And I didn't kill anyone," she insisted, following the man's orders.

"That's fer a court ta decide," he said, shaking his head and gripping her arm to guide her out the door. He had expected her to put up a fight, but maybe it was like she had said—she'd had a rough night.

From where he stood on the hill, Brand had a perfect view of Fenwick. Through his binoculars, he had watched Pinkerton's "client" ride into town and tie up her horse and disappear into the telegraph

183

office, then cross the street and enter the hotel. *Probably to get something decent to eat,* he thought with irritation as he put the binoculars back into their case.

"Which is what I'd be doing right now if I could risk having her know I'm on her trail." He removed a strip of beef jerky from his saddlebags and leaned against a nearby tree. Tearing off a bite of the dry meat with his teeth, he slid down the trunk to sit, his gaze on the familiar roan horse tied outside the hotel.

As soon as she rode out of town, he would go and find out who she had sent the wire to. It could easily tell him where she was headed. He already had a couple of ideas. For one, he considered the probability that she was meeting up with her gang. But that seemed unlikely because she wouldn't have wanted to lead a Pinkerton detective to their hideout.

Another possibility he considered was that she had decided to get out of the bank-robbing business and had planned to use the Pinkerton Agency to establish her new identity. But why come back to Missouri, where she was so well known? Of course, as long as she had left her booty hidden here, she would have a reason to risk being recognized in her home state. Of course, if she had proof she was someone else and had a man of unquestionable honesty to support her claim, what was there to stop her?

"Guess I spoiled your little game by not going along with you, didn't I, Flame?" He bit off another bite of jerky in answer to his stomach's rumble. "Sorry about that."

Suddenly, a commotion at the hotel caught his attention and he sat up straight. Tossing the jerky aside, he reached for the binoculars.

"So, Flame," he said when he saw her walking toward the jail at gunpoint. "It didn't take you long to get in trouble, did it?"

He bounded to his feet and made a dash for his horse. Whipping the reins up from the ground, he stuck a boot in the stirrup and took hold of the pommel. Then he hesitated.

"On the other hand, there's not really any hurry, is there? A few hours in a cell might be just what she needs to scare some sense into that stubborn red head of hers."

A satisfied grin on his face, he stepped back down and dropped the reins to the ground. "And besides, as long as she's not going anywhere, I could sure stand a bath and a hot meal."

When they reached the small office that fronted the town jail, the marshal shoved LaRaine roughly ahead of him. Without speaking, he reached out for the buttons on her coat, managing to unfasten them in one swift motion. Grinning cruelly, he ripped open her coat and raked his gaze over her, making it obvious this was one job he was going to enjoy being very thorough about.

He grabbed her by the coat lapels and jerked her against him, his angry face only inches from hers. "Now, let's jest see what we got here," he growled.

"You hidin' any other weapons, Flame?" he asked, taking her coat and tossing it aside.

"No," she stuttered, closing her eyes to blot out the horror of what was happening.

"Well, I b'lieve I'll have ta find that out fer myself," He unbuttoned her flannel shirt, his big hands brushing the fullness of her breasts several times, each time lingering longer before moving on. He pulled her close to him, so close she could feel the hairs of his mustache tickling the skin on her face, while he slid first the suspenders, then the shirt from her shoulders. Running his hands up and down her back in pressing, circular motions, he grunted. "Nothin' back here."

Moving his hands around to the front, he cupped a breast in each hand and squeezed her hard, forcing a cry from her lips, which she had tried to keep sealed during the entire, degrading ordeal. "There's somethin' here. That's fer damned sure."

"Please don't," LaRaine said with tear-filled eyes, her voice sounding strangled and small.

"What's the matter, Mizz Flame Rider? Don't ya like bein' on the receivin' end?" he laughed. "Ya got a knife?" He didn't wait for her answer before his large hands slipped down into the waistband of the trousers she was no longer able to hold up without the suspenders. Sliding the breeches down over her hips, the marshal began to breathe heavily. "Ya got a real good body, Flame—even in them men's clothes," he hissed. "As a matter o' fact, I could probably be persuaded ta believe yer story 'bout bein' yer own twin sister," he hinted suggestively, gripping her buttocks and pulling her lower body against his trousers, stretched tight by his swollen member. His mouth came down to silence her protest, the taste of stale tobacco and coffee almost as offensive as the kiss itself.

It was the final blow. LaRaine could bear no more. Even when he had been convinced she was Flame Rider, Brand had never treated her with the disgusting lack of respect this supposed defender of the law was giving her.

Lifting her knee, hard and damaging, LaRaine gave the groping man a blow in the groin that

186

should have been enough to incapacitate any man. But to be certain, she bit his tongue and socked him in the flabby belly at the same time.

Doubled over in pain, the man fumbled for his gun, but he was too slow. LaRaine kicked it out of his hand with a speed born of desperation. They might arrest her. They might even try and convict her. But no one was going to rape her—not without a hell of a fight!

She looked around quickly for an escape, thinking to grab her gun and run. But before she could move, the marshal's balled fist came out of nowhere to crash blindingly into her jaw. Her head snapped back and her knees buckled under her.

"We'll talk when ya've had time ta think 'bout yer other choices," he threatened, his pain still evident in his gasping voice as he hurled her limp body into a small cell. He looked down on the crumpled, beaten heap on the dirt floor. "But ya better make up your mind how much you want me to b'lieve you right quick. Folks 'round here'll be 'spectin' a hangin'. Since they got yer thievin' hide under lock 'n key, they won't be in no mood to take a chance on you gettin' loose."

Part Two — The Meeting

"Fortune never seems so blind as to those upon whom she has bestowed no favors."
— La Rochefoucauld

Chapter Twelve

"It's true!" Jeff Crieger vowed excitedly. "I swear to God, if I ain't seen her with my own eyes, I wouldn't a b'lieved it. On my ma's grave, she's a dead ringer!"

"Slow down, boy," Roy Benton told the teenager who had come racing into the cave hideout south of Fenwick. "Why don't ya tell us exactly what happened. From the beginnin' this time."

Finding Roy's disbelieving tone demeaning, the blond youth shot the older man a dirty look and went on speaking to the redheaded woman who studied him thoughtfully.

"I did jest like ya tole me, Flame. I walked inta town 'n acted like I had all the right in the world ta be there. I was jest hangin' 'round outside the general store, keepin' my eyes 'n ears open, when the whole durn town started buzzin' 'bout havin' the famous Flame Rider under lock 'n key. Ya should hear how that marshal's braggin' 'bout bringin' you in," he went on, enjoying the attention his news was receiving from the beautiful gang leader.

"Skip all that, Jeffie," Flame said impatiently. "Did ya actually see her up close? Is she really my double? Or is she jest some gal with a bunch o' red hair?"

"It's more'n the red hair, Flame. I tell ya, she's a

dead ringer! 'Cept maybe fer bein' a little paler. An' her hair might be a tinge darker. But other'n that, you two couldn't be more alike if you was twins."

"But how close did ya git?" Roy insisted, certain the boy was elaborating on the tale to keep Flame's attention.

Adding a tone of suspense to his voice, Jeff said, "What would ya say if I tole ya I took her supper to 'er?"

"I'd say that's pretty damned close." Flame laughed at the boy's eagerness to tell his story. Though Jeff Crieger was only three years her junior, Flame felt decades older than the boy — as if she were old enough to be his mother. "How'd ya manage ta do that?"

"Well," Jeff went on, doing his best to make himself sound clever and brave for Flame, while continuing to exclude Roy from their conversation. "When I heard you was in jail, I hurried over ta the jail ta find out the truth. There was a big crowd there, an' they was yellin' fer a hangin', so I knew I had ta do somethin' fast. But I weren't sure what to do. Then I sez ta myself, 'Hell, Jeff-boy, why don't ya jest walk on in there'n see her?' So that's what I did."

"You didn't!?!" Flame choked, her bluish-yellow eyes wide with surprise.

"I did. I walked in there jest as cocky as ya please 'n asked fer a job — you know, sweepin' up the place, cleanin' out the cells, *feedin'* the prisoners. He hired me on the spot an' sent me over ta the hotel ta get a dinner tray for the prisoner." He paused for dramatic effect.

"Well, go on!" Roy yelled impatiently.

Giving the man another annoyed glance, Jeff went on. "So, I got the tray and took it over ta the jail," he said smugly. "Ya should o' seen it. Big as life, the marshal handed me the key ta the cell, an' I walked right in."

"Go on," Flame coaxed, her mind racing with possibilities.

"She was sleepin' an' didn't wake up when I tried to rouse her. But damned if it waddn't you layin' there. So I high-tailed it out o' there an' come back here ta get some help ta break you out."

"An' that's when you found out your eyes was playin' tricks on ya," Roy said with a sneer. "Are you sure you ain't jest makin' this up?"

Jeff narrowed his eyes at Roy. "You callin' me a liar, Benton?"

"Shut up, you two!" Flame ordered, walking away from them, deep in thought. "I gotta think." Was it possible that a twin sister actually existed outside her own childhood fantasies? After all these years of wondering if Cutter Doyle had been lying about the twin who had gone to live with the rich family, was she going to learn the truth at last?

Of course, this could just be a coincidence. The woman in the Fenwick jail probably didn't even look like her at all. Still, what if . . .

"Tell me, Jeffie," she said, wheeling around to face the two men. "What kind o' shape's that gal in? Does it look like she can ride?"

"I don't know. She didn't look too good, Flame," Jeff answered. "She's all weak 'n groggy. Hardly even looked up when I brought her dinner."

"What're ya thinkin' o' doin'?" Roy asked suspiciously.

When LaRaine awoke, she had a grueling, throbbing headache that drove all thought of anything else from her mind. Wincing, she tried to open her

193

eyes, but found the effort too painful, and she closed them again. Staying motionless, she waited for the pounding in her brain to subside.

As she became more alert, she noticed that the ache spread into her jaw as well. And everything that had happened came rushing back into her thoughts. Cautiously, she opened her eyes and looked around the jail cell, despite the pain the slight action caused.

Though it was dank and cold, she breathed a sigh of relief when she saw that the marshal had returned her clothing after locking her in the small cubicle. Determined to move even though her limbs felt like they were liquid, she dragged herself from the tattered cot and staggered toward the heap of clothing she recognized as hers.

Bending down to lift the trousers from the floor, she grew even more lightheaded. Swooning, she grabbed the iron bars. Clinging to the metal, she closed her eyes and waited for the wave of dizziness to pass.

When she felt a bit stronger, she supported herself against the bars and stepped cautiously into the jeans. Slowly, still fighting her vertigo, she donned the flannel shirt and fastened its two remaining buttons. *At least it's warm*, she thought sluggishly, forcing herself to push away from the security of the bars.

She weaved to the cot and fell down on it, promising herself she would be better if she rested just a few minutes more.

When she woke again, she felt stronger, more able to cope with her latest reversal. Sitting up on the edge of the cot, she noticed the tray of cold stew and dry bread on the floor beside her. She had a vague memory of speaking to the young boy who had

194

brought it. Studying the unappealing dish of questionable nourishment at her feet, she gagged at the sight of large globs of fat floating in the watery stew. She could swear a couple of them were alive.

Giving the tray a shove under the cot so she wouldn't have to look at it, she stood up and moved on unsteady legs to the cell bars. What she needed was a drink of water.

"Marsh—" she started to call out, but caught herself at the sound of men's voices in the outer office. They were talking in a low confidential tone and she couldn't quite make out what they were saying at first, but she listened anyway.

"What about the reward?" she heard the marshal ask in an anxious tone. "What about my two thousand dollars?"

"Take this voucher to the army depot and they'll give the money to you," the other man answered, though his voice was muffled, as if he had his back to her. Leaning into the corner closest to the front office, she put her ear between the bars and strained to hear better.

"Why not jest keep her here till the trial?" the marshal asked suspiciously. "After all, we're the ones who caught her. Ain't we got a right to see justice done?"

"I see your point, Marshal. But you know the Army. They won't rest until she's in a stockade on government premises. Anyway, you'd never be able to keep her secure in this matchbox jail. No, we need to transport her tonight—before her people get wind that she's been captured. They'd be here in a flash. And a lot of people could be killed if her boys came into town shooting," the other voice responded wisely.

"Yeah, I guess you're right . . ." the marshal

hemmed and hawed. "Still, it jest don't seem fair."

The marshal's visitor's voice rose impatiently, and LaRaine heard the thud of an angry fist slamming against a desktop. "Look, man, you've got your orders. Now give me the prisoner!"

"All right, all right. I'm jest bein' careful."

"And the Army appreciates that. But we're wasting valuable time."

LaRaine scrambled back to her cot when she heard the sound of keys in the heavy wooden door leading from the front office to the block of four cells, where she was the only prisoner.

Fear ran wild through her veins as she lay with her back turned to the bars, her face to the wall. A picture of herself dangling from an army gallows danced across her mind, replaced by Brand Colter's grinning face and his voice saying, "Didn't I tell you this would happen?"

"Here she is," the marshal sniggered rudely as he unlocked the door to the cell. "She don't look as pretty as her picture though. She put up a fight when I 'rested her. But it's her all right. Ain't no doubt 'bout that. Wake up, Flame. Ya got a visitor," he said, putting a hand on her shoulder.

Jerking rebelliously away from the marshal's offensive grip, LaRaine turned over to sit up, her eyes narrowed threateningly. In the dim light, she was able to make out the face of the marshal in detail. But all she could see of the other man was his large outline in the entrance of her cell, and the fact that he was wearing an army uniform.

Grabbing her by the shoulders, the marshal dragged LaRaine to her feet and whispered, for her ears only, "See? Ya shoulda been nicer ta me. Now it's too late. I can't do nuthin' ta make things easier fer ya anymore. Ya ain't my prisoner no more." He chuckled and turned her around to prod her toward the cell door by rubbing his hand over the rough material covering her bottom. He failed to see the officer's eyes narrow, or to notice the muscle that twitched imperceptibly beneath the man's tanned cheek.

"Here ya go, Major," the marshal announced. "Ya want me ta put the cuffs on 'er? Or do ya wanna do it yerself?"

"I can handle it, Marshal," the major responded gruffly, never letting his gaze shift from LaRaine's downcast eyes. "Do you have any property we need to collect before we leave, Miss Rider?" he asked impersonally.

"I had a .45 revolver, and a horse and saddle," she said, not looking up. "And some money," she added, lifting her gaze accusingly toward the marshal, who obviously hadn't intended to return her property to her. "I had about a hundred dollars, and some pieces of jewelry the marshal said he would lock up for safekeeping."

"Get her stuff, Marshal, and I'll write you another receipt," the major ordered coldly, his dislike for the man obvious.

"But what's she gonna do with them things, Major? She won't need 'em hangin' from the end o' no rope," he argued.

"Nevertheless, you may recall that in the United States a prisoner is considered innocent until proven guilty. Therefore, all of her property remains in tact—with her. Get her gear! Did she have a coat? It's cold out tonight."

"Yeah, she had a coat." The marshal stomped out of the cell block, leaving LaRaine with the major.

She had only been half listening to the conversation between the two men, so she was startled when the major spoke to her in a hoarse whisper. "Just don't give me any trouble, and I'll get you out of here," he said, holding his mouth close to her ear while he clicked the handcuffs onto her wrists.

LaRaine's head snapped up at the sound of the familiar voice, and her flabbergasted stare was impaled by warm blue eyes — Brand Colter's eyes!

She opened her mouth to say his name but was silenced by the look of caution and the subtle tilt of his head, indicating that the marshal wasn't out of earshot. "Just come along now, Miss Rider. I want to be in Lexington as soon as possible. Marshal! You got those things ready?" he hollered.

"Yeah," the lawman answered, obviously annoyed that he wasn't going to be able to gloat over the fact that he had Flame Rider in his jail for three weeks until the circuit judge came to town — or the fact that he had bedded her. Of course no one had to know that part. "You take care o' yerself, now, Mizz Flame. Shore wish ya coulda enjoyed our hospitality a bit longer. I ain't gonna fergit our little tumble earlier. Yer really somethin'," he added with a leer, already planning the embellishments he would put on the story when he told his friends about the time he had spent with the famous Flame Rider.

"How dare you?" LaRaine gasped, unable to voice the words she had for the marshal's blatant insinuations.

Brand studied the two for a minute, then turned on his heel, jerking his prisoner after him. He didn't speak as he forged the receipt for LaRaine's things and the voucher for the marshal's reward. Then he pushed LaRaine out the door of the jail, a little less gently than was necessary.

He came! He came for me! He must believe me a little bit, she thought excitedly, feeling warm and safe for the first time in what seemed like years.

Brand didn't speak until they were well out of town, but when he did, his cold, biting tone took LaRaine by surprise. "I guess it'll be okay to take off the handcuffs now," he said, stopping and reaching for her hands.

"Thank you," she answered, her face pinched with confusion.

"Did you sleep with him?" he blurted out suddenly.

"Did I what?!" she shrieked, not caring if anyone heard her or not. "How dare you ask me such a thing?"

"Well, did you?"

"For your information, Mr. Colter, the only man I ever, as you so delicately put it, 'slept with,' was a crude, uncaring cad who has tied me up, handcuffed me, called me a liar and a . . ." She took a swipe at her tear-stained face with the sleeve of her coat.

Brand was ashamed that he had voiced his question—and angry with himself for letting her answer make a difference to him. "I'm sorry. I shouldn't have asked you that."

"Sorry's not good enough, Brand Colter. What if my answer had been yes? What if the marshal had raped me as he planned to do? What if I hadn't been able to fight him off? What would you have done then? Branded me with a scarlet letter and thrown me back to him?" Openly sobbing now, the tears that had been building to flood proportions since the instant she had been unmasked in the hotel dining room splashed hotly down her anger-contorted face.

"I'd have gone back and killed the rotten bastard!" he answered, his voice so full of hate that it caught LaRaine off guard.

"You would?" she asked, frowning her puzzlement.

Unable to stand seeing her so miserable, Brand reached out and put his hand on her leg. "It's just that I .. "

"What?"

Brand drew back his hand and directed his gaze straight ahead. "When that pig of a marshal said what he did back there, I wanted to tear him apart with my bare hands," he admitted, the confession out of his mouth before he could stop himself. His eyes rounded with surprise. "I mean . . ."

"You did?" she asked, staring at him in stunned amazement.

Fighting his feelings, Brand faced her. "You know I should have left you in that jail, don't you?"

"Why didn't you?" he asked.

"It was your own fault you got arrested," he continued, ignoring her question.

"Why didn't you leave me in the jail, Brand?"

Searching her face for an answer, he opened his mouth to speak, then closed it again.

"Why, Brand?"

"Because it's my job to protect Mr. Pinkerton's clients, no matter what I think," he spit out defensively.

"That's the only reason?"

"Why else would I do it?"

"I don't know. Maybe because you aren't completely convinced I'm Flame."

"Don't be ridiculous."

LaRaine wiped her tears with the heels of her hands and shrugged. "I guess I was wrong." She gave him an I-know-what-I-know smile. "But I'm glad you came. No matter why you did it."

He stared at her long and hard, as though he were

weighing a life-threatening situation. Letting a low growl, he straightened in his saddle and kicked his horse forward, leaving her to fall in behind.

"And you're glad too," she said to his back. Though he didn't answer, she could tell by the way his posture stiffened that she had definitely struck a tender spot in his armor.

Brand and LaRaine rode into the night, each lost in deep thoughts, neither of them feeling the tiredness that should have plagued them.

About an hour before dawn, Brand stopped and pointed toward a crest on a nearby hill. "I know of an old shack over there where we can get some rest," he suggested, feeling sure they were far enough from Fenwick to be safe for the time being. "Or do you want to keep going?"

"I'd really like to stop," she answered. "Especially if that stream I see disappearing behind the hill goes anywhere near the shack," she added optimistically.

"Then let's go." Glancing over his shoulder to be certain no one was a witness to their detour, Brand led their horses over the rise in the land.

When they were hidden from the road, he brought the horses to a halt and dismounted. Reaching up, he caught her around the waist and lifted her down from her horse. Her hands on his shoulders, she looked up into his face. "Thanks."

Brand flinched, noticing the ugly bruise on her left cheek for the first time. He couldn't stop himself from gently covering it with his palm. "Did that sorry excuse for a marshal do that?" he asked, instantly blaming himself because he had left her in jail all day rather than getting her out right away.

LaRaine shrugged and gave him a conceding grin.

"I guess you were right about what would happen as soon as someone got a good look at me." She tilted her head, pressing her face against his hand. "It feels better already."

Brand glanced nervously at his hand, then jerked it back as if he'd been burned, clearing his throat as he did. "I'll go check the place to be sure no one's around."

"I want to go with you."

"No, just wait here until I get back," he told her harshly, not sure who he was angrier with: himself for letting that bastard marshal get his hands on her or at her for being so damned sweet, when more than ever he needed to stay angry with her.

Waiting nervously with the horses, LaRaine glanced around the heavily wooded area and wondered how Brand had ever found the shack. It was totally secluded and almost invisible against the backdrop of leafless trees.

She breathed a sigh of relief when she saw the blue soldier's uniform round the ramshackle building and wave an all clear to her.

"Looks like no one's been around here in months," he said, beckoning her to come forward. "You go on and look inside while I tie the horses in that grassy clearing over there."

Doing as he told her, LaRaine opened the door to the shack. Inside, it was worse than it was outside. There was a crumbling fireplace, two or three pieces of broken furniture, and discarded evidence of past visitors. A mouse dashed across the filthy room to disappear beneath a stack of rags. This was definitely not a place she intended to spend much time.

Stepping back outside, she closed the door behind her and dusted her hands back and forth against each other. "I think we'll be more comfortable out here," she announced as Brand came back.

He couldn't help smiling at the look of distaste on her face. Acting on impulse, he brushed a wisp of hair back from her face with the tips of his fingers. "Not as fancy as you're used to?"

Thinking of the dreary jail cell, she smiled, too. "The only way this place could be made habitable is if we burned it to the ground and started over."

"That bad, huh?"

Smirking mischievously, she nodded. "That bad."

His fingers lingered on her cheek, his expression sobering. He rubbed the edge of his thumb over the bruise. "Does it hurt?"

"Not now," she returned, the pupils of her eyes darkening.

"That's good." He reached up and plucked off her hat. Her hair tumbled free, its fiery color coming alive with the sunlight that filtered through the overhanging trees. Unable to stop himself, he burrowed the fingers of both hands into the coppery tresses on either side of her face.

LaRaine took a step closer to him, placing her hands lightly on his waist. "Where did you get the uniform?"

"A Pinkerton detective always has a disguise or two in his saddlebags. They come in pretty handy."

"Well, it certainly did last night. Did I tell you how relieved I was when I realized it was you?" she asked, lifting her mouth toward his.

"I find that hard to believe," he said hoarsely, despite the leap of excitement that jolted through him at her admission. "I didn't think you had much use for me."

"Maybe I was wrong." Her voice was a husky purr.

Brand swallowed uneasily. "You mean that?" He

203

smoothed his hands down to her shoulders.

She nodded.

"I still don't believe you're who you say you are," he warned.

"I know. But I'm going to prove it to you. That is, if you're still willing to give me the chance."

LaRaine snuggled more securely into Brand's embrace and laid her head on his chest. "Will you stay with me so I can find the real Flame Rider and prove to you who I am?"

"Yeah, I'll stay," he said with a defeated chuckle. Then he changed the subject. "Say, I thought you wanted to take a bath. Maybe I'll join you."

"Together?" LaRaine choked, flustered that the shocking idea sent a quiver of excitement racing through her veins.

"Why not? It's not as if we're strangers," he reminded her, his eyes twinkling bright blue as he slipped the heavy overcoat from her shoulders.

"But we can't bathe together! Not in broad daylight!"

"Oh? Are you saying if it were dark, you'd take a bath with me?"

"I'm not saying anything of the kind! Don't put words in my mouth." She tried to sound indignant, insulted. But she failed miserably.

"As long as we're both going to take a bath, we might as well scrub each other's backs," he coaxed.

LaRaine shook her head slowly from side to side.

Seeing that she wasn't going to change her mind, he asked, "Well, how do you propose to do this and maintain your privacy?"

Accepting his challenge, she turned out of his arms and retrieved her bedroll.

Minutes later, when she stepped into the cold brook, she smiled warmly at him. "Now, isn't this a good idea?" she giggled, looking at the brown blanket she had draped from a thick clump of bushes on one bank to a wall of green on the other. The gray blanket, about six feet downstream, was tied in the same fashion, completing the fourth wall on La-Raine's private bath.

"Yeah, just great." His expression sour, he watched unhappily as she slipped under the corner of the blanket before she removed her clothes.

"Isn't this nice? You can take your bath on that side, and I'll bathe in here," she said, snapping a thin bar of soap in half and handing Brand a piece under the blanket wall.

"Very clever," he agreed halfheartedly. Taking off his clothing, he stepped into the frigid water to the sounds of LaRaine splashing in the stream and humming contentedly to herself. "Brr, it's cold," he said conversationally, sudsing his skin enthusiastically.

"Yes, but clean, and just what I needed," she replied, exhilarated. "Actually, there's nothing like a bath to ease away all your worries," she said a few minutes later, after rinsing the soap from her long hair. "Don't you agree?"

When she received no answer, fear that she was alone rose suffocatingly into her throat.

"Brand?" she called. No answer. She stared helplessly at the blanket that had separated them, panic pounding in her heart. "Brand! Where are you?"

Afraid of what she would find on the other side, but knowing she had to look, she carefully pulled back the edge of the blanket.

"You looking for someone, lady?" a deep voice asked from behind her.

Chapter Thirteen

Whirling around angrily, LaRaine flew at the grinning man, unmindful of her nakedness, unmindful of his. "Don't you ever do anything like that to me again!" she screamed, beating her fists against his hard, hair-covered chest. "You scared me to death. I thought you were gone!"

"I thought you might need help getting all the soap out of your hair—or something," he smirked, refusing to let anything deter him from drinking in all of her glistening beauty.

A wave of color rushed to LaRaine's face with the realization that Brand was making love to her with his eyes—caressing her shimmering, apricot-tipped breasts, sliding along the narrow curve of her delicate waist to her softly rounded hips, skimming worshipfully over her belly to focus on the coppery delta of her sex, and finally gliding the length of her long, graceful legs to where they disappeared into the icy water. They studied each other for a long time, her yellow-green eyes bright with viridescent light, his countenance a study in urgent longing.

"You're beautiful," he whispered, his ragged breath a tribute to the work of art he was loving with his gaze. "I want you." It was a plea, a demand, a prayer.

"It's not right," LaRaine protested weakly, looking up into his hungry eyes and trying to remember why she shouldn't let Brand make love to her—anytime! Anywhere!

Taking a deliberate step closer to her, he circled the slender column of her neck to gently run his thumbs idly from her chin to the sensitive hollow beneath her ears. Breathing in deeply, he inhaled the sweet fragrance of her feminine scent into his nostrils and was immediately intoxicated with her power over him. "It feels right," he said.

He drew her unresisting body against his virile length, conquering the last minuscule fragment of her resistance with his kiss. Fusing his lips hungrily to hers, he plunged his tongue into her mouth, robbing it of its nectar, making it his own. "It can't be wrong."

Her breasts painfully swollen with desire, she relinquished all resistance and leaned into his embrace. One of her arms went around his neck to burrow into luxuriant black hair, while the fingers on her other hand splayed against the hard wall of his chest, ruffling her fingers through the damp curls thickly covering its breadth.

Spanning her slender waist with his hands, Brand caressed his way over the silken skin of her back and buttocks. His mouth moved lovingly over her face and neck, his kisses leaving a fiery imprint on her water-cooled flesh.

His lips claimed hers in a fierce kiss as he bent to scoop her trembling body into his strong arms. Lifting his mouth from hers, he searched deep in her changing eyes to confirm what her kiss had already told him. What he saw made his thudding heart skip a beat. He saw the reflection of his own desire shining hungrily at him from swirling pools of colored glass. "I'll make it right," he vowed, reclaiming her mouth, this time with a feral energy that took away the last of his ability to reason.

With tongues mating in the rhythm of love, with warm hands caressing cool flesh and turning it hot with their touch, and with fingers entangled in thick wet hair, they found their way to a mossy blanket of green where he lowered her with painstaking care.

Spreading her splendid hair around her to dry, Brand raised up on one elbow and looked down at the closed eyes of the woman who had come to occupy all of his thoughts, both waking and sleeping.

LaRaine sensed she was being watched and opened her eyes to smile. "What?" She trailed an index finger idly from the center of Brand's forehead, down his crooked nose, over his mouth, to the tip of his strong chin. "What are you looking at?" she sighed, not really needing an answer to her question. She could see it all in his loving blue eyes.

"You. I'm looking at you," he confirmed, gently tracing the outline of her mouth with his thumb while the rest of his hand gently brushed the dark bruise on her jaw. "I wasn't sure I'd ever be with you like this again," he confessed, unable to hide the pain he felt when he thought of living without her.

"I like your face," LaRaine said, memorizing his features with her hands. "I especially like your eyes. They remind me of a clear summer day. But they look so out of place in your dark face—especially when you scowl," she teased, frowning as she spoke.

"I like your eyes, too," he laughed. "They remind

me of a special marble I had when I was a kid. Swirls of blue and green and yellow. They never look the same way twice. Did you know they change color with your moods? When you're mad, they're yellow — like a cat's eyes; and when you're afraid they're a pale blue; but when you're being stubborn and determined, they're as green as this moss."

"What color are they now?" LaRaine asked, trembling with pleasure from his gentle massaging of her flat stomach.

"Black," he answered, looking into her desire-enlarged pupils. "They look like deep, dark pools of inky water that call out to a man. They're eyes a man could drown in and he wouldn't even care. He'd fight for the chance."

Brand's lips brushed each of LaRaine's eyelids closed before he laid his upper body over hers and covered her face with gentle butterfly kisses, working his way leisurely to one sensitive ear. Taking a soft, plump earlobe into his mouth, he tugged gently while his hand made its way around her throat where he stroked the silky flesh with adoration.

"Are you cold?" he asked into her ear, his hands roaming over her stomach and rib cage and warming her entire body as no fire could ever do.

"No," she purred, unconsciously stretching under his artful caressing.

Cupping a full breast in one palm, he used his thumb and forefinger to bring its rosy crest to a tight bud of longing as it raised upward to beg for more. And the pleading, pouting nipple wasn't disappointed. Brand quickly acquiesced to its demands and blazed a trail of fiery kisses from her earlobe, to her neck, to its lush fullness. Softly squeezing a firm globe of white flesh in his large hand, he was unable to suppress a small groan of appreciation as his

209

mouth closed hungrily over the engorged peak, sending alternating waves of hot and cold running rampantly over LaRaine's flesh.

Threading her slender fingers into his thick, dark hair, still wet from the stream, LaRaine clutched him to her breast and called out his name without knowing. "Yes, yes, yes," she moaned over and over. "That feels so good, I can't bear it," she panted softly as his tongue and teeth made their way to her other breast, before traveling along the flesh of her stomach.

LaRaine was hardly aware when Brand slid first one knee, then the other, between her thighs, because they were already relaxed and open in unmitigated anticipation.

Leaning back on his haunches, he looked down at her and smiled. She was beautiful beyond all expectation against the carpet of velvety green moss, and though he knew what he was doing would only make it harder to give her up when the time came, he couldn't stop.

Holding a breast in each hand, he bent to alternately kiss the twin peaks before he laved his way down the center of her body, paying particularly agonizing attention to the deep navel that stood out on her white belly as a mystery cave to be thoroughly explored.

Then, when he could no longer deny himself the knowledge of the treasure that lay hidden behind the coppery triangle at the entrance to his final destination, Brand slid his body downward and buried his face in the downy island to love the silken folds of her.

LaRaine's senses, already honed to the point of explosion, were driven beyond anything she could ever have imagined as he moved his tongue along the

210

length of her. He explored every secret recess, making love to her with his whole mouth—licking, sucking, and biting until she was hurled violently over a sensual precipice from which she fell, crying out her glorious agony.

Writhing and moaning, she was desperate to feel Brand inside her, and struggled to bring him back up over her body to kiss her mouth. Winding her arms around his broad back and holding him tight to her, she reveled in the feel of his weight on her, pressing her into the damp moss. Her hips moved upward, and he needed no further invitation to plunge into the moist depth of her body.

Brand started to raise up on his arms to take the burden of his weight off her slight body, but she drew him to her and clung to him with long, smooth legs wrapped around his sinewy, hair-roughened thighs. She used her grip to pull her own hips upward, ever upward, matching the primal beat of his lovemaking in the mating ritual that was as old as time.

Smoothing her palms over the corded muscles of his back, she kissed the perspiration-dampened skin of his shoulder and neck, certain she would never get enough of him. She squirmed beneath him in an attempt to get closer. She could feel him inside her, could feel the folds of her body enveloping him, holding him, drawing his seed from him, and still she realized her capacity for wanting him was untapped. Positive her pleasure could not be greater, her rapture still climbed as Brand dove deeper and deeper into the boiling interior of her soul. Deeper, deeper, faster, faster, until she had only one exquisite, primitive thought.

Jerking spasmodically against Brand's hips, she had her final release. She cried aloud with the beauty of it, only an instant before he, too, burst out of his sexual haven where nothing but the moment mattered.

Filling her with his strength, he relaxed on her as together they drifted back to earth to the sound of ragged breathing and joyful laughter. When he finally collected his composure, he started to roll away. "No, don't leave me," she begged, gripping him tighter with her arms and legs. "Don't leave me ever," she said, feeling happy for the first time in months. For the first time since her father had died, there was someone she could lean on, could depend on, could—love.

"Never?" he questioned with a quirked brow, resettling on her to kiss her face. "Never's a very long time," he said sadly, her words bringing the impossibility of their relationship back to mind. "We're going to have to get up sometime."

"No, never," she insisted, refusing to think about what might happen if she couldn't find Flame and prove her own identity to Brand. She would find her sister. She would convince Brand that she was La-Raine. And Brand would return her love.

"Aren't I heavy?"

"Dreadfully," she laughed.

"Are you cold?"

"Freezing," she replied, suddenly becoming aware there was a chill in the air that had been nonexistent during their lovemaking. She also realized Brand's exposed flesh was bearing the brunt of the cold.

"Hungry?"

"Now that you mention it, I'm starved." Taking him by surprise, she gave his shoulder a shove and rolled him onto his back. She leaped up and scrambled to her clothing.

"Hey, wait a minute," he shouted, reaching out to

grab a trim ankle and pull the fleeing girl to the ground. "One more kiss before you leave," he ordered.

"No more kisses until you feed me. I'm really hungry."

"So am I," he said, his voice husky as his mouth closed over hers.

"Whadda ya mean she's gone?" Flame Rider shouted at the news Jeff Crieger had brought her.

The teen took a step back. He had never seen his boss so angry. Her face was as red as her hair. "I'm sorry, Flame, but it's true. The Army musta got word 'bout the arrest 'n come ta git ya—er—her. The marshal said it was ta keep yer gang from gettin' wind 'bout where ya was 'n comin' ta bust ya out."

"How the hell'd they know 'bout it? Where's he takin' her?"

"That's jest it, Flame. The major tole Marshal Scott he was takin' ya—her straight ta the depot at Lexin'ton, but someone spotted 'em ridin' in the direction o' St. Louie."

"Whadda ya think?" Flame asked Roy and Jeff. "Did he take her ta Lexin'ton or ta St. Louie?"

Roy made an impatient face. "I think we oughta fergit the whole damned thing. I don't wanna mess with the Army no more'n I gotta. I say, let 'em have her 'n hang her. It'll take the heat off us fer a while. Might give us a chance ta git out 'n spend some o' the money we got."

"That's not what I asked ya, Roy," Flame said with a disgusted sneer. "An' ya might as well git it through that dense head o' yers. I'm gonna find that gal 'n git some use outta 'er 'fore she takes the blame fer me. Now, do ya think they went ta St. Louie or ta Lexin'ton?"

"I think St. Louie!" Jeff interrupted.

"Why do ya think that, Jeffie?"

" 'Cause it's closer 'n he'd be able ta git help there. I don't see the Army takin' someone as dangerous an' slippery as Flame Rider all the way 'cross the state with only one guard. I say St. Louie."

"Ya got a good head on yer shoulders, Jeffie boy. Ya keep usin' yer brains like that 'n you'll go a long way," she said with a meaningful smile, sending the boy's hopes soaring. "So, St. Louie it is!" she announced.

"Ya mean yer gonna waltz inta the city 'n chance gittin' spotted on the hunch o' some dumb kid who ain't even dry behind the ears?" Roy shouted indignantly, furious that Flame was planning to ignore his advice.

"I don't do nuthin' on nobody's hunches—'cept my own. But if the feller doin' the advisin' is a clever, thinkin' man, I listen."

"But—" Roy started.

Flame ignored his interruption. "What Jeffie says makes good sense. Anyhow, if she ain't in St. Louie, we'll be able ta find out where she is. I think capturin' 'me' is big 'nuff news ta be in the papers, don't you?"

"I still think we should fergit this whole crazy idea," Roy insisted.

"Then go on 'n fergit it, Roy. Jeffie'n me can handle this without yer help," Flame laughed. "In fact, I think that's the first smart thing I heard ya say. Git on back home where ya think yer safe, an' we'll meet up with ya when we're through with our business."

"I ain't leavin' without ya, Flame," Roy said.

"Git it through yer thick skull, Roy! I ain't got no

214

use fer no yellowbellies in my gang."

Roy looked indecisively from Flame to Jeff.

"Go on," she snarled, flexing the fingers of her right hand over the handle of the gun she wore strapped to her leg. "Git yer things 'n git goin'," she ordered through clenched teeth, the cold smile on her face frightening. "Git on back to the hideout with the rest o' the boys. We'll meet up later on."

Watching the interchange, Jeff promised himself he would never do anything to make Flame that angry with him. "Jeffie, git our gear 'n we'll leave right now. We done already wasted enough time."

Flame walked away from the two men, closing the subject to further discussion. Both knew that once Flame Rider had made a decision, there would be no change of plans. She was going to St. Louis with Jeff Crieger—and without Roy Benton.

Brand sat propped against a birch tree, his hat down over his forehead so LaRaine couldn't see if his eyes were open or closed.

"A penny for your thoughts," she said, standing over him.

"I was just thinking how complicated life can get," he mused, chewing a blade of grass thoughtfully.

"But there's always a way to work things out if you want to badly enough," she said optimistically, glancing around the grove of trees that hid their presence from the road. Who would have thought yesterday that today she would be here and with him?

He chuckled bitterly at her naïveté. "Maybe in fairy tales."

"You're awfully sour." She crouched on her haunches and peeked up under the brim of his hat.

Wishing this time together could last longer, he gave a half grin. But he knew that when they left here, it would be the beginning of the end of their relationship, and the thought hurt more than he cared to admit. But once she admitted who she was, he would have no choice but to take her in if she still refused to surrender herself. And that would mark the end of their relationship. Even if he could manage to get her a lighter sentence, it would be over.

"You know what you need?" she asked with a smile.

Brand shook his head and grinned, his mind on how desirable she was. "No. What do I need?"

"A hot meal! That'll make you feel better," she promised, crossing her heart solemnly and failing to notice the cloud of sadness that darkened his face. "I'll cook up some beans and bread."

"Sounds good." He drew her into his arms, tempted to put off the inevitable just a while longer. "But I guess we'd better get going."

"A few more hours won't make that much difference. Besides, I started soaking the beans this morning while you were sleeping. We might as well eat them."

"You've thought of everything, haven't you?" he said, knowing he was only making things more difficult for himself by not just refusing her outright.

"And wouldn't a cup of hot coffee taste good?" she teased, running her fingers up into his hair until she made his hat fall off.

Glancing around uneasily, Brand's gaze came back to LaRaine's expectant look and he laughed helplessly, his melancholy temporarily eased. "What the hell? We might as well. But I'm warning you, don't make the grub too fancy. I won't know how to act."

"It'll be wonderful," she squealed, jumping to her

216

feet with the enthusiasm of a child at the circus. "Papa taught me to cook on the trail. And if I start now I can have the fire out before dark!" She was already gathering dry tinder. "At night you can see the tiniest fire from very far away," she said, obviously quoting her father.

"I didn't realize cooking over open fires was something fathers taught their 'proper' daughters," he said, unable to hide his doubts.

LaRaine gave him a scolding look. "I thought we were going to drop that subject until one of us proved something—one way or the other."

"Yeah. I'm sorry. So, tell me, why did your father teach you to camp?"

"Actually, I've had lots of time to think about that the last few days," she said, carefully clearing dead leaves and debris out of the area where she planned to build her fire. "He always believed a woman should be as capable of surviving as a man should be, so my 'education' was more liberal than most— even considered scandalous by some. And with the uncertainty we lived with from day to day during the war, he felt more than ever that I should be able to take care of myself if anything happened to him. We never knew when the Yankees, or even our own troops, would descend on us and force us to hide out in the woods. And, too, I like to think he might have been preparing me for this trip to find my sister."

"Yeah, that's probably it," Brand answered absently, imagining what it would be like if she were telling the truth about being LaRaine Ashby.

"I wonder if Flame knows about me," she mused suddenly, biting her lip as she concentrated on making a tepee out of the small sticks she had gathered. "Dry leaves burn easily, but they don't make good

217

tinder because they smoke too much," she told him, obviously reciting a lesson learned long ago.

Brand watched her, grinning at her lesson in fire-building, despite the fact that his heart was bursting with unhappiness. He would always remember her this way—hunched over a pile of dry twigs and wearing the funny, baggy trousers, suspenders, and long johns. She looked like anything but the beautiful vision he had first encountered on that westbound train. Yet to him she was more lovely now than ever before.

"There," she announced, standing up to proudly admire the tiny fire she had started. "What do you think?"

"I'm impressed," Brand said. "I didn't realize I had found Daniel Boone that night in the woods."

"Don't make fun of me. You want to eat, don't you?"

"What exactly are you planning to cook on that little fire? Two or three beans each?"

"Of course not! I'm putting these bigger pieces of wood on it. They'll burn down to coals." She looked up smugly, and saw that he was still teasing her. "You just wait and see," she promised, shaking a stick of wood at him before adding it to her fire. "You'll be sorry."

I already am, he said to himself, miserable with his decision to stay, as well as ecstatic with the thought of a few more hours together before they had to face reality again. He coughed and turned away from her. "While you do that, I'll go take care of the horses."

A little later, she handed Brand a plate filled with bacon-flavored beans over a large chunk of cornmeal bread. Lowering herself down beside him and propping her own plate in her lap, she watched him

218

anxiously. "Well, what do you think? Aren't you going to eat?"

"Aren't you?" he returned, tentatively raising a spoonful of aromatic food to his mouth.

"Sure I am. I'm starving." She lifted her own spoon to her lips. But she continued to study him rather than eat. She waited while he chewed, first one bite, then another. She couldn't tell anything from the expression on his face. She watched him eat until she couldn't stand the suspense anymore. "Well? How is it? Am I a wonderful outdoor cook? Tell me! Did I work magic with those dried beans and cornmeal or not?"

Instead of answering, Brand took another bite and shook his head from side to side, seeming to be at a loss for words.

"Is it that bad? You hate it, don't you? What is it? Too much salt? Not enough salt? Say something!"

"Taste it," Brand ordered solemnly. "It's not too bad," he said, wolfing down a large spoonful.

LaRaine took a bite of her own food and chewed thoughtfully. "What do you mean, *not bad?* That's one of the best plates of beans and cornbread I've ever tasted in my life!" she protested indignantly.

"That's what *I* thought," Brand said, greedily shoveling another bite into his mouth. "I just wanted to be sure my epicurean taste buds hadn't been so abused and numbed by bad cooking that I was beginning to think just about anything was good," he went on somberly.

Then his face split into a broad, crooked grin. "Really, it's wonderful! You did work magic with those dried beans and cornmeal."

"And?"

"And what?"

"And after the way you frightened me, making me think it was awful, you'd better keep the compliments coming if you want seconds," she smiled spitefully, happily watching him empty his plate. "I expect raves!"

"You're a marvelous cook, an artist!" he said lavishly, sneaking his spoon over to steal a bite out of her plate. "Now, can I have some more of this delicious fare? Please?" he begged melodramatically.

"All right. But in the future, you'd better remember that the way to get me *not* to cook for you is to tell me that my cooking's 'not bad'! Is that understood, Mr. Colter?" She pointed the bean ladle at him threateningly, then dished up the remainder of the beans over the bread in his plate.

"Yes, ma'am," he saluted. "I swear on my life that I will never again say your cooking is not bad."

"That's better," she said, handing him his plate. Her heart was swelling with pleasure, and for an instant, she couldn't imagine ever wanting anything more than this wonderful moment. This feeling of happiness should be enough to last her a lifetime.

But a wave of regret swept over her face when she remembered that her time with Brand Colter was only temporary. Even if he suddenly believed her, she had no right to personal happiness — at least not until she had found her sister and made things right for her.

"Do you suppose she's happy?" she asked suddenly, her beaming face growing pensive.

Brand didn't need to ask who *she* was. "She must be, or she wouldn't keep doing the things she does," he answered noncommittally. Picking up both their plates, he started toward the creek. "Since you did the cooking, I'll clean up."

"Thanks. Now that I think of it, I am rather

tired." Thoughts of Flame had invaded her contentment, and she was unable to shake them off. Where was her sister right then? What was she doing? Was she as bad as everyone said? *She can't be. I know she's not. She's just never had a chance. No choice.*

"Do you want another cup of coffee?" Brand asked softly, interrupting LaRaine's reflective mood when he returned to the fire.

She shook her head to ward off the depressing thoughts she was having and forced a smile. "I thought you wanted to leave after we ate."

"It'll be dark pretty quick," he said, refilling her cup, then his own. Setting the pot aside, he lowered himself to the ground beside her. "I guess we could stay here until morning—if that's okay with you."

LaRaine's heart skipped an excited beat. "That's fine with me—if it's all right with you."

Brand released a relieved sigh. "It was a good meal," he said, changing the subject to safer ground. "One of the best I've ever had."

LaRaine grinned up at him, glowing under the compliment. "You were surprised, weren't you? You didn't believe I could do it, did you?"

"I wasn't sure," he admitted. "But you're full of surprises—as I'm just beginning to find out. I bet you can do just about anything you set your mind to," he chuckled admiringly, putting his arm around her and drawing her head to his shoulder.

Together, they watched the dying embers of the fire, and neither of them spoke as the final rays of the sun cast their last rosy glow on the peaceful idyll they had found in the clearing. Both Brand and LaRaine were lost in thoughts that could not be verbalized, neither of them daring to think past the moment. It was enough to just be together and share this moment of contentment.

When LaRaine finally spoke, it was about Flame, and she didn't notice the tightening of Brand's grip on her arm. "I wonder what she's doing right now," she said pensively.

Brand's hold on her tightened possessively. "Yeah, me too."

Chapter Fourteen

"Now, ain't that a cozy sight?" a voice drawled from the darkness.

Whipping his gun from its holster, Brand pushed LaRaine out of the way and leaped to an alert crouch, his gun barrel aimed at the bushes where their surprise visitor lurked. "Show yourself or I fire."

"That ain't no way to treat company," a second voice joined in from behind Brand.

"There are two of them!" LaRaine hissed as Brand wheeled around to confront the second person.

"That's right, little lady. I b'lieve you're caught in what folks call a 'cross fire.' Wouldn't you say that's what they're caught in, Slidell?"

"Sure looks that way ta me, Whit."

Brand swung his gun from side to side, trying to get an exact fix on each of the intruders. "Come out," he ordered.

"We'll do that, mister. Jest as soon as you drop your firearm an' grab fer the sky."

Brand hesitated.

"Or the gal gits it."

Brand laid the gun on the ground at his feet and unfolded his long legs to stand.

The invisible stranger laughed. "Ain't he clever now? Can't you jest see him thinkin' he'll make a grab for that pistol when he catches us off guard? Shove it over here, 'n be quick about it." The order was followed by the click of a hammer being cocked.

Giving the revolver a firm kick, Brand slid it across the ground toward the bush hiding one of the men.

"That's better," Whit Ruston said, stepping out of the shadows.

"It's the men from the train," LaRaine gasped, her fear intensifying. "What are you doing here?"

His gun on LaRaine, Slidell Ruston joined his brother. "We come fer what you stole from us back in Indiana."

Brand's eyes narrowed intently as he gauged his chances of overcoming the two of them. If he could get them to stand together, he might have a chance. "I left the horses and your gear in St. Louis, but you're welcome to these."

"Now, ain't that right friendly?"

"You think we come all this way fer a coupla horses? You ain't as smart as I took you fer if that's what you think."

"Then what?" LaRaine asked.

"Your boyfriend here made us look bad an' we don't take too kindly ta that."

Panic seized LaRaine. "What are you going to do?"

"First we're gonna give him a little o' his own medicine," Slidell said, coming up behind Brand and bringing his locked arms down over Brand's head and trapping his prisoner's arms against his own rib cage.

Acting as though they were following a prearranged plan, Whit brought up a booted foot and planted it squarely in the most vulnerable part of Brand's body.

"Stop!" LaRaine screamed, flying at Whit as Brand grunted and doubled forward despite the weight of Slidell on his back.

With the speed of a rattler, Whit backhanded LaRaine, sending her tumbling. A loud thunk cracked through the air as the back of her head slammed into a tree.

When she didn't move, Whit jerked his head in her direction. "Go check on her," he ordered his brother, keeping his gun pointed at Brand.

Gasping and gagging, Brand stumbled to the ground when Slidell released him. Shaking his head to clear his thoughts, he measured his distance from Whit. It would be dangerous, but while Slidell had his attention diverted, he might be able to kick the gun from his hand.

"Keep your gun on her. An' use it if either o' them tries anythin'. She might jest be playin' possum."

A new wave of dread washed over Brand. He couldn't do anything as long as LaRaine was in danger.

"She better be all right," he managed to choke out.

"She ain't dead," Slidell called out. "But she's liable ta be sleepin' fer a while. She's got a good-sized lump on the back o' her head."

"Let her go," Brand said, struggling to his feet. "Your fight's with me, not with her."

"Now, why would we wanna do that? She's the reason we come all this way. We aim ta have us a high ol' time with her. Then when we git tired o' her, we gonna turn her in 'n collect the reward."

"You bastard," Brand yelled, diving for Whit's gun. "If you lay one filthy hand on her, I'll . . ."

225

The point of Whit's boot caught Brand under the chin by surprise and sent him sprawling back on the ground. "You try that agin an' I'll kill her right on the spot," he threatened, stooping beside LaRaine and holding his gun to her temple. "Tie him up, Sli, an' let's git goin'."

Following Whit's orders, Slidell Ruston quickly divested the half-conscious Brand of his hat, shirt, and boots, then staked him spread-eagled on the ground. "There, that oughta keep him."

Satisfied that Brand wouldn't be going anywhere, Whit quickly tied LaRaine's wrists and ankles. Then he wrapped a blanket around her limp body and tossed her over the front of his saddle, mounting behind her. "Just in case you need somethin' to do while yer lyin' there waitin' fer the weather an' the varmints ta finish ya off, just think about what a good time we're havin' with your gal."

"Mornin', Mizz Flame," Slidell said, squatting down beside LaRaine. "How ya feelin'?"

"Where are we?" LaRaine rasped hoarsely, squinting her eyes to look up at the Cheshire-cat smile on Slidell's homely face. "What've you done with Brand?"

"You don't need to worry none 'bout him. We done took care o' him good. He won't be gittin' in our way agin."

Panic shot through LaRaine. "Is he dead?" she asked in shock.

"Maybe not yet, but the shape he was in when we left him last night, it won't be long."

If he was alive when they left him, he still is! she swore to herself, refusing to believe anything else. *I've got to get to him before it's too late.* "What are

226

you going to do with me?"

"I don't blame ya fer wonderin' 'bout that, but ya should o' knowed someone was gonna turn ya in sooner or later. Yer gonna have ta pay fer all them Union folks you'n Quantrill's boys done in durin' the war. It's our patriotic duty to turn ya in ta the 'thorities," he said proudly.

This was crazy. Here she was lying helpless on the ground and listening to a criminal talk about patriotic duty, while Brand could be dying. How could she defend herself against such insanity? But she had to. There had to be a way to escape and help Brand.

In the back of her mind, a plan of survival began to take form. It was only the tiniest seed of an idea, but it was all she had. She concentrated on it, encouraging it to grow until it was battling the pain in her head for attention.

What would Flame do if she were trapped by these two not-so-bright outlaws?

She definitely wouldn't snivel or cry or beg. She'd know that wouldn't be the way to deal with Whit and Slidell Ruston. And she would never act weak. No, she'd be strong. And smart. Smarter than they are—which shouldn't be very hard.

"What're you going to get out of this, Slidell?" LaRaine asked curiously, trying not to think about the uncomfortable deadness in her bound hands and feet, her aching head, or the remaining minutes of Brand's life as they ticked away.

"There's a thousand-dollar reward on yer head," Slidell answered, confused by LaRaine's conversational tone.

"Is that what Whit told you? A thousand dollars?" Her tone inferred knowledge of a lie.

"Sure it is! If ya don't believe me, ask him."

227

"How much of that do you think he's going to let you have?" LaRaine asked confidently, hoping the outlaw would think she knew something he didn't know.

"Half," he answered proudly.

"Half of a thousand is only five hundred, Slidell! That doesn't seem like much to me—not when he has you doing all the work," she said with a sympathetic smile.

"We're splittin' the work 'n the loot, like we always do," Slidell defended.

"Where's Whit now?"

"He's sleepin' while I do the first watch. We were up all night, ya know!"

She nodded. "I see. Well, if you're willing to settle for a measly five hundred dollars—if you're actually able to get him to give you your share—then—then I won't say anything else." She gave the man a long, understanding gaze and changed the subject. "When are you going to give me something to eat?"

"I'll feed ya when I'm good'n ready." His eyes narrowed accusingly. "What'd ya mean 'bout Whit not forkin' over my half o' the reward?"

"Is that what I said?" She feigned a nervous giggle. "It must have been the heat inside this blanket making me talk funny," she said, making an obvious play at hiding something. "Just forget I said anything."

"Look, lady! If ya got somethin' ta say, ya better tell it ta me if ya know!" Slidell rasped, his brow furrowed deeply. He jerked her to a sitting position and glared threateningly at her.

"Really, it was nothing," she stammered, growing excited with the success of her plan—so far.

"I'm warnin' ya, Flame," he said close to LaRaine's face.

Digging her nails into her clenched palms, she swallowed back the bile that rose in her throat.

"It's just that I heard your brother say something about collecting the reward and giving you five hundred while he kept fifteen hundred. He said you weren't smart enough to know what to do with any more than that anyway."

"Fifteen hundert fer him and five fer me! That's . . ." Slidell paused and counted on his fingers.

"Two thousand," LaRaine supplied him with the answer.

"Two thousand? Why that lyin' bastard!"

"He also told me I was his woman and that he wasn't going to share me with anyone else—not even you," LaRaine added, putting the final clincher on her story.

"Oh, yeah? Did he now?"

"I have to admit that bothered me, Slidell, because I like you. I really like you a whole lot. And you're a lot better looking than Whit is." She smiled suggestively, seductively.

"When he wakes up, Whit 'n me're gonna straighten out a few things!" Slidell swore softly. "He's gonna give me my share of everythin'—the money an' you!"

Better act now, LaRaine, or he's going to wake up his brother. And Whit won't be as easy to trick.

"Slidell, I was thinking," LaRaine started, her tone hinting at an intriguing conspiracy. "I know where there's a lot more than two thousand dollars. It could be ours—yours and mine. What do you say? It would be a chance for you to get out of your brother's shadow—do something on your own." LaRaine held her breath as she watched the play of emotions, from indignation to greed, cross Slidell's mustached face.

"Where?" he asked suspiciously, unaware of the nervous twitch in his right eye that made his eyebrow look like a live caterpillar dancing on his forehead.

"Come on, Slidell. You don't think I'm that dumb, do you?"

"How much money ya talkin' 'bout? Where is it?"

"Listen, Slidell, as much as I like you, I'm not about to tell you where I've got over forty thousand in gold and cash hidden away—not until you untie me and we have a deal, that is," LaRaine added, her expression flirting, asking Slidell if he was ready to talk partnership—in more ways than one.

"Where'd ya git forty thousand dollars? Who else knows 'bout it?"

"You forget, I've been a busy girl since the war," she bragged. "But don't you worry. It's all mine, and no one knows where I've got it hidden. No one but me. If you turn me in and I get hanged, which is likely, no one will ever know the pleasure of spending all that beautiful money." LaRaine shook her head regretfully as she continued to reel in the dangling bait on her line—together with her hooked mark.

"How long'll it take us ta git there?"

"That depends on where we are now and how long it takes you to get me untied."

"How do I know ya ain't lyin' ta me?" he asked dubiously.

"You don't. There's only one way to find out, Slidell. But what've you got to lose? If I'm lying, you can still turn me in. Only then, you won't have to share the reward, or me, with Whit."

"You'd better not be tryin' ta make a fool o' me." He peered furtively around the clearing where they had made camp. Assured by Whit's loud snoring several feet away, he quickly untied the rope wrapped around the quilt. When he had the rope free, he chuckled mischievously to himself. "Whit's gonna shit when he wakes up 'n we're not here!"

"Let him," she encouraged, careful not to display any discomfort with the man's choice of words. "There won't be anything he can do about it if we take all the horses. He'll be too busy trying to make his way back to Indiana."

Slidell hesitated before removing the confining blanket.

"You're not backing out, are you? I thought you wanted to be my partner?" Her tone was coaxing, teasing.

"That ain't the problem. I was jest thinkin' 'bout Pa 'n my brothers. They're gonna beller like new-made steers!"

"I bet they won't. In fact, I wouldn't be surprised to see that they were real impressed that you finally did something on your own. How many of them ever brought in so much money alone?"

"Hell, none ov 'em. But they was awful mad when you 'n that feller come inta our territory an' tried ta pull off that train holdup right under our noses. Everybody knows southern Indiana is Ruston territory, an' we don't 'low nobody else comin' 'round. 'Sides, we can't stand Rebs. My brothers 'n me all fought fer the Union!" he added proudly, failing to mention the fact that all four brothers had deserted within a year of their enlistment, and that Jake Ruston had been arrested for stealing his captain's wallet!

"Look, if you're afraid, we'll just forget the whole thing. But don't expect Whit to turn me down when I make him the same offer."

"Who said anythin' 'bout bein' 'fraid?" Slidell returned angrily, unwinding the blanket and going to

231

work on the ropes at her wrists and ankles.

"That's better," she said, clambering weakly to her feet, knowing there was no time to pamper herself with sympathy. She glanced uneasily at the sleeping Whit, but he continued to snore contentedly, totally unaware of the drama taking place only a few feet away.

To restore her circulation, LaRaine shook her hands, stamped her feet, and walked in small circles. She looked up to find Slidell watching her.

"What are you staring at?"

"I swear, Flame, you're 'bout the prettiest gal I ever seen."

She forced a smile. "Hush now. There's plenty of time for that sort of talk after we get away from here," she said, making her voice teasing and sweet. "Now, go on and get the horses so we can leave before Whit wakes up," she ordered.

"Hell, we got time," he said, moving toward her, a purposeful leer on his face. "He'll be out for hours."

LaRaine's heart pounded furiously. She was certain that any minute she would give away her scheme—or that Whit Ruston would awaken and stop them. "If we don't go before your brother wakes up, there isn't going to be any forty thousand dollars. And no you and me," she reminded the man with emphasis. He continued to grin at her with an idiotic look on his face.

"He ain't gonna wake up 'fore noon," Slidell assured her. "We got enough time fer at least one little kiss ta seal our deal," he said, reaching out for her as he spoke.

LaRaine felt her heart drop to the pit of her stomach. She had been hopeful she'd have more time before she'd be forced to deal with this. She had been certain the thought of such an exorbitant amount of money would be enough to drive other thoughts from Slidell's simple mind. She was wrong!

"All right, Slidell," she began impatiently. "If you're not smart enough to see how every minute we delay cuts into our chances of success, then I'm not going to waste any more time trying to convince you." She took a step toward him.

Stealing herself for the repulsive feel of Slidell's mouth on hers, she clenched her fists at her sides. "Well, go on and get it over with so we can be on our way."

All of her psychology was wasted on Slidell Ruston, and he grabbed her in his arms to pull her against his swollen lower body. Cupping his hands under her bottom, he bent her over and planted a slobbering kiss on her mouth. Running his large hands up and down her back and grinding his manhood against her, he forced his tongue between her teeth to fill her mouth with its vile, smothering presence, almost causing her to gag.

Moving her head breathlessly, LaRaine cried, "Slidell, please!" She wanted to scream out at him, kick him, bite him. But she knew she had to keep her self-control just a bit longer. "We've got to leave now. There's no time for this!" she insisted desperately. However, Slidell wasn't listening to anything but the primal beat of his own carnal lust.

In an obvious hurry, his hand slid around from her back to fumble with the buttons on her shirt and to press abusively on her left breast with its heel. It was almost more than she could bear, but she had to make one last try to stop him with words.

"Slidell, honey, you promised just one kiss," she said, her hands gripping his waist with the intention of pulling him away. But there was no way to cool his lascivious ardor with reason. Even the knowledge

233

of what his brother would do if he awakened and caught them was not enough to deter Slidell Ruston now.

Then LaRaine's answer came when her hands brushed the handles of the Starr double-action .44 caliber revolvers that hung low on Slidell's hips. At first, her fingers jerked back from the contact, as if she'd been burned.

Then, as reality seized her thoughts, she reacted with the gut instinct of self-preservation that had taken her this far.

Sliding her hands caressingly up and down the sides of Slidell's barrel chest, she groaned aloud, slipping first one gun, then the other, out of the enraptured man's holsters.

"Slidell," she said against the offensive mouth which had returned to kiss hers.

"Mmm," he moaned.

"Get your filthy hands off me or I'm going to blow a hole the size of Indiana through you." Her voice was hard and frightening, and Slidell dropped his hands immediately, to stare aghast. "Don't try anything. I can fill your belly with lead before you say hello. Now, just get over there with your brother."

"But, honey, I thought ya liked me. What 'bout our deal? What am I gonna tell Whit?"

"I'd say you've got a real problem, Slidell," she laughed. "Take off your boots and pants," she ordered, watching both men while Slidell tugged off his boots. "Pants, too! Toss them over here." She pointed to her right.

"Hey, what the hell's goin' on?" Whit asked sheepishly, waking to find his brother stripping.

"Whit, she got my guns!" Slidell whined childishly.

234

"Damn! How the hell'd that happen?" Whit asked, sitting up to draw his own gun.

But LaRaine was too quick for the unsuspecting man, his senses still dulled by sleep. She fired a pistol, hitting Whit Ruston square in the center of his hand, shattering its bones and sending his revolver flying. "Oh, my God! She shot me! She shot me in my gun hand! Shit, it's killin' me!"

"The next move you make, Whit, the bullet will be between your eyes, and you won't feel a thing from then on. Now, Slidell, take off his boots and pants and toss them in the pile," she ordered.

Slidell quickly did what she said, then looked at her for further instructions.

LaRaine wasn't certain what to do next. She couldn't risk getting close enough to them to chance being overpowered, yet she couldn't leave them without immobilizing them. As the two watched her, waiting for their opportunity to take her, they were surprised to see her face split in a malicious grin.

"Get the blanket, Slidell. Whit looks cold. You wrap him up nice and cozy like you did me—ropes and all. Then we'll talk about *us*," she told him. Let him think for the moment that she still might take him with her. "Go on, honey. I don't want to kill anybody—not unless it's really necessary." The tone in her voice left no room for doubt that she would not hesitate to pull the trigger if it *was* necessary.

"Go on! Do what she says, Slidell," Whit urged, his face white with the shock of seeing his own blood flowing from the painful wound in his hand.

Slidell quickly bound his brother in the blanket. Then, turning to LaRaine, he tried to charm his way back into her good graces. "What now, sugar?"

"Now, knot that rope around your neck." She pointed to a rope she spotted on one of the horses.

"You do know how to make a noose, don't you?"

"You're crazy!" Slidell stuttered. "I ain't gonna make my own noose. I ain't gonna help ya string me up!"

LaRaine raised her eyebrows in surprise and cocked the hammer on her revolver. "Would you rather bleed to death?"

"But, Flame!" he protested.

She aimed the gun in her left hand directly at his crotch.

"Okay, okay!" He was certain she'd never have the strength to actually hoist him up.

With trembling hands, Slidell tied a hangman's knot in the rope and held it up for LaRaine's approval. She nodded her head and indicated with a revolver that he should put it around his neck.

"Ya ain't really gonna try ta hang me, are ya?" At that moment, Slidell wasn't positive she couldn't carry out anything she set her mind to.

"Just put it on," she said, "and throw me the other end." Slidell hesitated, and a purposeful grin spread over LaRaine's face. "Don't test me."

His hands trembling, Slidell dropped the noose over his head.

"Now, get over there and toss the other end of the rope to me." She indicated a thick tree with a sturdy, low-hanging branch about eight feet above the ground. A perfect hanging tree.

"Please don't do this, Flame," he whined, moving toward the tree, then pitching the rope to her. "I thought ya liked me. We didn't mean no harm. We wouldn't 'a turned ya in."

LaRaine took up the rope and mounted a horse, giving the rope a jerk on his neck. "Unless you tell me right now where you left Brand, you're a dead man, Ruston."

236

Grabbing at the rope to pull it away from his neck some, he answered frantically. "Back where you was camped when we found you. We didn't kill him. Honest ta God, we didn't. Jest let us go and we'll get out o' your life forever!"

"What direction?"

Slidell raised his hand and pointed up the road. "That way."

"You'd better be telling the truth," she said, riding her horse around the tree with the end of the rope still in her hand. "Because if you're lying, or if he's dead, I'm coming back to kill you like the lowlife sniveling coward you are deserves," she threatened, making a second turn around the tree.

"But ya can't leave us here like this!" Slidell protested from where he stood against the tree, after she had finished wrapping him up like the lead in a string pencil. "Whit's pro'bly already dead. He ain't made a peep since I put him in that quilt. Do ya want more dead men on yer conscience?"

"I can live with it," she returned, bundling up their boots, guns, and gear and putting them on the back of one horse.

She strapped Slidell's holster around her hips, then did a last check to make certain the Rustons wouldn't be able to escape anytime soon.

Repeating her promise to come back for them if Brand wasn't where they said he was or if he was dead, LaRaine rode her horse away from the clearing, leading the other horses behind her.

As the distance between her and the spot where she had left the Rustons grew, she became more anxious. What if she was too late? What if Slidell had lied about where they had left Brand?

Glancing up at the sun, as her father had taught her to do, LaRaine determined that it must be about nine o'clock in the morning. That would mean that possibly twelve hours had passed since they had left Brand. A new current of fear shot a jagged path through her at the thought.

"He can't be dead," she swore aloud, kicking her horse to pick up his pace. From what Slidell had told her, they had managed to get about twenty miles southwest of the camp during the night. She calculated that if she kept up her speed, she should be able to make it back in about an hour—if the horses didn't play out. "He has to be alive!"

Please get me there in time. Don't let Brand die, she prayed. *I don't know what I'll do if he dies.*

Wiping her face with the sleeve of her shirt, she sniffed back the tears that had suddenly gathered in her eyes.

"Hold on, Brand. Don't stop fighting. I'm coming. Hold on just a little bit longer."

Chapter Fifteen

"Oh, no!" LaRaine hauled her panting horse to a stop and bounded to the ground at a run. "What have they done to you?"

Brand opened his eyes and smiled sluggishly. "Am I in heaven or hell?" he asked through parched lips as he looked up into the concerned green eyes of the woman who bent over him.

"You're alive!" Her gaze traveled hungrily over his broad, sweat-glistening chest as she swatted away the gnats and flies that buzzed around and crawled over his bared flesh.

"O-pen to debate," he rasped with difficulty.

"Are you shot?" she asked, not seeing any bullet wound.

He shook his head and smacked his lips in an effort to moisten the inside of his mouth. "I guess they decided to save the bullet and let the elements do it for them." He raised his head slightly and studied his surroundings. "Where'd you come from? How'd you get here?"

"We'll talk about it later," she said, already at work on the tight rope that held one of his wrists to a stake in the ground. There was no time to lose. His hands had already begun to swell and turn a bluish color.

The rope was bloody, and she winced as she exposed his raw wrist where he obviously had tried to wrench himself free, no doubt causing his wrists to swell and the ropes to tighten and cut off the circulation in his hands. 'I should have killed them," she mumbled as she freed that wrist and leaned across him to untie the second one.

With the sudden rush of blood into the veins of Brand's hand, white-hot light flashed behind his closed eyelids. He threw back his head and yowled his pain, unable to stop himself. It was excruciating. Never had he felt such agony.

His sanity at stake, he slammed the throbbing hand under his opposite arm, squeezing it to his chest with his biceps.

The pain from his torment in the one hand only slightly eased by the pressure of his arm, he was unprepared for the new wave of suffering that exploded in his other hand as LaRaine freed it from its binding. "Aagh!" he moaned, oblivious to the tears that gathered in the corners of his eyes.

"Oh, I'm sorry!" she wailed, her own eyes overflowing with tears. Not knowing what to do, she clamped his hand between hers and covered his pulsating fingers with kisses. "Just hold on to me. It'll go away."

As the pain in the hand under his arm subsided, he relaxed slightly and looked up at her. "Hey, are you crying for me?"

Releasing his hand and laying it across his midriff, she wiped her sleeve over her eyes and shook her head, going to work on freeing his bound ankles. "No," she lied with a self-conscious laugh. "I must have gotten something in my eyes."

240

Brand nodded his head and smiled. "That's not what it looks like to me."

When both his ankles were free, she examined his face, looking for signs that he really was feeling better. Convinced he wasn't just pretending, she suddenly lost the tenuous control on her emotions she'd fought to maintain and broke out into tears. "I was so scared," she wept, unable to look at him. "I thought they had killed you."

"Would it have made that much difference to you?" he asked, struggling to sit up.

Surprised by his question, her head bobbed up. "How can you ask me that? Of course it would make a difference. I lo—"

Unexpected joy surged through Brand. "What?"

Her expression startled, trapped, LaRaine said, "Um .. I ... I mean I don't like to see anyone suffer."

"Is that the only reason?"

"Yes ... no ... I mean ... Don't you know why?"

"Because you still need someone to support your claim that you're Flame Rider's sister?"

She bit her lip reluctantly, and shook her head. "I came because I—I care about you," she admitted in a nervous rush.

Never had any words affected him more. He knew he shouldn't believe her. After all, she was a criminal and a liar. But still he basked in the warmth of her admission. She cared about him and ... "Lord help us both, honey," he said, gathering her into his embrace. "I've tried to fight it, but the truth is, I care about you, too."

"Well, Jeff, whadda ya think we got here?" the

241

redheaded woman on the tall sorrel horse asked the young man shortly after dark.

"Hell, Flame," Jeff answered. "They just look like a coupla drifters who met up with some penny-ante highwaymen. Let's leave 'em fer the vultures."

Flame Rider smiled patiently, showing clean, even teeth. "That might be a mistake." She swung her right leg over the saddle and slid to the ground to walk closer to the gagged man tied to the tree. "You need to always check everythin' that's even the least little bit peculiar. You never can tell when you might learn somethin' that could save your neck."

Shoving her face up close to the face of the man tied to the tree she said, "For instance, this here feller jest might have somethin' to tell us. Maybe a new bunch is workin' around here. We'd sure want to know somethin' like that, wouldn't we?"

"Sure, Flame," Jeff agreed eagerly.

"Why don't you see who we got in that there blanket while I see what this feller's got to say?"

"Yes, ma'am," the boy said, dismounting with a jump.

"Now, that's the way I like my boys to take orders." She rewarded Jeff with a beaming smile. "I hope ya don't never get like Roy."

Vowing to stay in Flame's good graces, he quickly went to work unwrapping Whit Ruston. "I won't."

"Jest 'cause a piece o' paper says the war's over, don't mean it's over for us," Flame lectured, never losing the smile on her face as she examined the bound man in front of her. "And in war, there's gotta be discipline. Discipline! That's the secret to our success. Someone givin' the orders an' someone else follerin' them. There ain't no room in a outfit for two leaders. As long as you remember that, we're gonna get along fine."

"I'll remember. You can count on me, Flame."

"Yeah, I know I can," she returned, a satisfied smile on her lightly tanned face. "Now, let's us see what this here feller's got to say 'bout how he come to be tied up to this here tree."

Turning to Slidell, Flame quickly took the gag from his mouth and slapped him across the face to bring him out of his dazed lethargy. "Who done this to you, boy?" she asked the man who was at least four or five years her senior.

"I knew you'd come back fer me, Flame," Slidell said, his hoarse voice almost inaudible. "I knew ya wouldn't leave me here to die!"

"What the hell're you babblin' about, man?" Flame hollered. "Hand me the canteen, Jeffie," she ordered. "Maybe a sip o' water'll help him talk some sense."

She grabbed Slidell by his hair and tilted his head back, then poured the water into his open mouth and down his throat. "Stop," he sputtered helplessly. "You're killin' me."

"You jest might be right about that, mister, if ya don't do some quick talkin'," Flame snarled through clenched teeth held close to Slidell's face.

All the color drained from Slidell's ugly face. He had thought she was hard before, the way she had left them for the wolves and ridden away without a backward glance; but now she made his blood run cold.

"Whadda ya want me ta say?" he whimpered.

Flame's expression soured with disgust. She hated to see anyone snivel and whine.

"Tell me who left ya here? How many of them was there? An' what way'd they head in? That oughta do for starters."

Was it a test? Was she wanting him to pretend he

243

had never seen her before? That's how she was acting. Or did she want to impress her companion with what she had done without any assistance? That must be it! She was going to use him and Whit as an example to keep the kid in line — unless he had his own army with him.

"It was jest you, Flame," Slidell started, eager to say what she wanted him to say, and certain he had made the right decision.

"Ya better stop stallin' if ya know what's good fer ya," Jeff said, pinching Slidell's chin and cheeks in one strong hand.

"I'll handle this, Jeffie," Flame said. "You get on back an' see what's in the blanket." Returning her attention to Slidell, Flame took a knife out of her knee-high boot and held it below his ear, the point just short of puncturing the indented spot behind his earlobe. "Now, what were you sayin'?"

"I don't know what you want me to say, Mizz Rider." Slidell tried to shrink away from the knife's pressure. "Tell me what to say, and I'll say it."

"I wish to hell I knew what yer talkin' about! Jest tell me what happened, an' I'll be the judge o' what's important," she sighed, confusing Slidell even more.

"Like I said, ya got the drop on us 'n took our horses, guns, hats, boots — and our pants. The whole time I kept tellin' myself ya'd come back fer us. Ya jest wanted ta show us how ya was boss, and let us know that no one was gonna turn ya over to the law. Right?" Slidell spoke faster and faster, encouraged by the fact that Flame was listening to him, and not interrupting or denying what he was saying. "It was jest a lesson, huh?"

When he finished talking, Flame continued to stare at him aghast. "Are ya sayin' I'm the one who tied ya up like this?"

244

"Yes, ma'am, but I'll tell the boy somethin' diff'rent if that's what ya want."

"Shut up, you stupid bastard!" Flame hissed angrily. She had to think. Suppose, just suppose, he was telling the truth—from his point of view, of course. Suppose someone—someone who looked so much like Flame Rider that even Jeff couldn't tell the difference—had taken the two by surprise, robbed them, and left them. "What was I wearin' when ya saw me last? How good a look at my face did ya git? What did ya do to make me mad enough ta leave ya here all trussed up like a Thanksgivin' turkey?"

"Ya know all that," Slidell sniffed childishly.

"Yeah, well, tell me one more time."

"I really thought ya liked me. But when I kissed ya, ya went crazy."

"Yeah." She nodded her head in disgust as she looked at the pitiful excuse for a man. "That'd make me purty sick, all right. But there's gotta be more'n that to make me this mad," she insisted, running the tip of her knife along the crease of his neck at the jawline.

Flame listened in amazement to a bizarre tale of being taken against her will from a westbound train in Indiana, escaping, making her way to Missouri with her partner, only to be abducted again.

"Honest, Mizz Rider, it was Whit's idea to turn ya in to the 'thorities fer the reward once we figgered out who ya was. I never did think it was such a good idea! But my brothers was so mad 'bout yer partner takin' our guns 'n horses back there in Indiana, we had to git even. I'm awful sorry. My word on it!"

"Stop your blubberin', ya piece o' scum. Do ya think I want your life story? I only wanna hear 'bout this gal who's passin' herself off as me. Did she actually tell ya she was Flame Rider?"

Slidell thought back for a moment. "No, I don't guess ya did. But it was you all right. Who else's got yer long red hair 'n them funny cat eyes? I won't never fergit yer pretty face," he grinned, unaware that any man's charms were nonexistent as far as Flame Rider was concerned. "Ya gonna let us go now?"

"When I'm good'n ready, boy. When I'm good'n ready." She ran a gloved hand over her mouth in a thoughtful gesture, trying to sort out all he had told her. He was too stupid to make up such a far-fetched story.

She put her face up close to Slidell's. "Think real hard, mister. There must be somethin' diff'rent 'bout that gal 'n me. Look close," she ordered, her voice low and deadly.

"Well, I done noticed one thing," Slidell started hesitantly.

"Go on."

"It's yer mouth. It don't really look no diff'rent, but you sound diff'rent. You say yer words diff'rent now. B'fore, yer voice was softer, maybe a might higher—like a lady's. An' I don't recall ya usin' no cuss words when ya was here b'fore."

"There! That proves it ain't me! In the first place, I ain't no goddamn lady, 'n I sure as hell never talked like one!" she laughed proudly. "An' in the second place, if you done to me what you done to her, you'd be the ones talkin' higher. I'd a gelded you sons-o-bitches back in Indiana."

Slidell winced at the thought that she might still choose to do that.

Whit was just coming to and screamed when Jeff lifted his swollen gun hand to examine its injury curiously. "Looks like she had some help, Flame."

246

"Who shot him?" Flame asked Slidell, holding his head by the hair.

"You did," he stammered. "I mean she did. He tried to draw on her after she got the drop on me, an' she jest blew the gun outta his hand. Best shootin' I ever seen from a woman."

Flame bristled. She was known for her sharp-shooting and didn't care for the idea of anyone horning in on her reputation. She whipped out a revolver and emptied it into a branch fifty feet away, cutting it in half and causing it to fall to the ground. "She jest got lucky, 'n don't ferget it!"

"Yes, ma'am. Jest lucky. Not near as good as you!" Slidell agreed. "Ya goin' after her? Do you'n the boy need some help?" he offered anxiously, still not sure where he and his brother stood with the real Flame Rider, or how they would get back to Indiana.

Using her knife to cut him loose, Flame laughed at the offer. "Not from the likes o' you Yankee trash. You two'd better get your yeller asses back to Indiana b'fore ya run into that bad lady again. Next time, she might not be in such a good mood as she was this mornin'. An' if I ever hear o' you thinkin' 'bout takin' me in again, I'll hunt ya down an' kill ya myself. Ya got that?"

"Yes ma'am, Mizz Rider," he whined.

"Did ya get that, mister?" she asked Whit, who sat staring at his bloody hand, trying to figure out what had happened to him.

"Huh?"

"Jest tell her we won't get in her way no more, Whit!" Slidell coaxed urgently.

"Naw, we ain't gonna git in your way no more," Whit promised groggily.

"I'm countin' on it. The river's that way," she said,

247

pointing eastward and laughing. With that she sped away, red hair unfurled behind her.

Neither Jeff nor Flame spoke about what had happened. She was too deep in her own thoughts.

For as long as she could remember, she'd been told about a beautiful twin sister who had been adopted by a rich man back East, while she, who was too ugly and worthless to be taken, had been left behind to live in squalor with her natural family.

Flame's mother had died when she was only eight years old, leaving the skinny, malnourished child to fill a woman's role in a houseful of males.

She cringed at the unbidden thought of the first time Cutter Doyle had forced himself on her. It was the day they buried her mother, and he had taken his daughter to his bed to hold her while she cried. That had been the beginning of a life in hell for Flame. Only then she'd been known as Mary.

By the time she had reached the age of ten, she was not only used regularly by her father, but also by all three of her older brothers who enjoyed showing off their sexual prowess and imagination to each other, at her expense and humiliation. And all the time, she was told how fortunate she was to have a roof over her head, food in her belly, and a family who loved her in spite of her ugliness and worthlessness.

For five years Mary Doyle had been beaten, raped, molested, tortured, used like a slave—all in the name of her own unworthiness. The only thing that had kept her from killing herself had been the fantasy of her beautiful twin sister, the sister who would one day come for her and save her. So, when life had been too terrible for her young mind to bear, she had escaped over and over into her imagination to spend time with her twin, who lived in a huge house with a private room for everyone — and an indoor privy! There had been clean linens on the imaginary canopy beds, and hundreds of beautiful matching dresses for her and her sister to wear. And there'd been no one in her fantasies like Cutter Doyle and his crude sons.

However, as with most childhood fantasies, by the time Mary was thirteen, she had come to realize there was no sister in the East, and no one was coming for her. There were only two ways out of the hell in which she lived — and she wasn't ready to die. Not yet. Not without having a chance to live first.

Silently, stealthily, she had walked from pallet to pallet to make certain her brothers and father were truly asleep in their usual Saturday night drunken stupors. She still remembered the flood of excitement that had spread through her body as she threw straw over the dirt floor of the shack. Never again would they use her the way they had tonight.

When she was through, she slipped outside the door and picked up a kerosene lamp. "May you all rot in hell," she swore, tossing the lantern into the dry straw.

The room exploded into flame, and for the first time since her mother had died, she smiled. "There, Pa, you won't never again say I can't do nothin' right. I did this right, didn't I? Just this once, I did somethin' right!"

That had been five years ago. Five years since she had run screaming from her burning house to a nearby farm with her story of Yankee soldiers raping her and killing her brothers and father. Of course, the gentle family of Confederate sympathizers had believed the girl. Why wouldn't they? Hadn't the Union troops committed hundreds of atrocities since they had forced Missouri's Confederate troops to crumble early in the war?

It had been while she was staying with the gener
ous Samuels family that she had met the dashing
William Clarke Quantrill. The infamous ex-farmer
horse thief, schoolteacher, gambler, and desperado
was the head of an unofficial Confederate band of
guerrillas that was notorious for sacking Union
strongholds in the state of Missouri and the sur
rounding territories. He had been tall, exciting, deb
onair, and the closest thing to a gentleman Mary
Doyle had ever seen.

Knowing from an early age how to please a man,
Mary, who had blossomed into a shapely, red-haired
beauty under the wholesome cooking and nurturing
care of Maud Samuels, set out to seduce the hand
some guerrilla commander. After a brief affair with
the young girl, Quantrill had been easily convinced
to take her with him on his next raid, seeing the
convenience of having such an eager bed partner
with him.

Riding with Quantrill's band, Mary Doyle had
ceased to exist. With the tossing of the first torch in
Lawrence, Kansas, Flame Rider came into being.
From that day on, the reputation of the red-haired
woman on the tall sorrel horse had burgeoned. The
people of Missouri who stayed loyal to the Confed
eracy had loved her. The pro-Union citizens had
hated her, feared her. They still told their children
stories of the Woman of Fire who would come and
take them away if they misbehaved, while southern
ers told their youngsters tales of the Angel of Fire
who would come and rid their state of all the cursed
Yankee devils. Flame Rider would be the one to
restore their confiscated lands. Believed to be the
one to protect them from the Yankee soldiers, she
had soon been seen as the last unquenchable flame

of the Confederate cause.

When the war came to an end, Flame had ridden toward home with a loyal group of men, only to discover they were all to be denied the amnesty afforded regular Confederate soldiers. There were already warrants out for their arrests. And it was then that the small band had begun to use their techniques of guerrilla warfare to successfully wage war against the bankers and stagecoach lines—all owned and controlled by the Yankees. And her reputation had continued to flourish.

But now she had discovered there was a possibility that her long-forgotten childhood fantasy might be coming true.

But ya come too late, sis—if that's who ya are. I got no use for ya now. I got my own self out o' hell without no help from you. I hate the thought o' you now. Growin' up rich 'n spoilt. Leavin' me in that cesspool with them bastards. No, if that's who ya are, you're way too late. I don't need ya. Not one bit. Alls I want from ya now is to see if you're real or not.

" 'Less I find somethin' useful to do with ya," she said aloud as an idea of retribution and escape from a life she'd grown tired of began to form in her mind.

If you're really a lady from back East, 'n if you're really my identical twin sister, ya might not be too late, after all. "In fact, ya might be just in time."

LaRaine finished rewrapping Brand's wrists and lay back down beside him. "I think you're going to live," she said, snuggling up against his side and resting her head on his shoulder. She sifted her fingers idly through the forest of hair on his chest and

251

kissed the flesh next to her mouth.

"I think you're right," he said with a chuckle, trapping the fingers on his chest in his hand. "In fact . . ." He moved her hand down the middle of his body to the fly of his jeans.

Startled to find that the denim was pulled tight to accommodate his swelling desire, she rolled her head to a position where she could look at his face. "Now?" she asked, her chin propped on his shoulder. "You can't be serious."

"Believe me, sweetheart. It's serious." He pressed her open hand against himself and lifted his hips toward it.

"What about your wrists?" she protested, the familiar ache in her womb clenching in anticipation. "Are you sure you . . . ?" She inadvertently squeezed and rubbed the hardness beneath her fingers, thrilling to the realization that her touch was making him even larger.

"Believe me, what I need isn't going to hurt my wrists."

Freeing her hand from his, she played with the top button of his pants for a second, then undid it before moving to the second button. "Are you sure?"

He moved his hips against her hand in answer to her question.

She trailed her lips to a flat male nipple and flicked her tongue over it as she unbuttoned the second button and slid her fingers to the third. "I'd hate to make things worse," she teased against his chest as she skated her mouth to his other nipple.

Frantic for relief, Brand pushed her hand out of the way and finished the job, then lifted his hips and shrugged out of the jeans.

Suddenly as desperate as Brand, LaRaine removed her own jeans and shirt. When she was naked, she lay back down. Her upper body over his, she rubbed the sensitive tips of her breasts against his hair-roughened chest and resumed her seductive massage of his manhood.

Without warning, Brand clasped her waist in strong hands and positioned her in a straddle over him, holding her moist femininity above his straining desire. "I don't think I'll ever get enough of you," he said, dropping her hard onto himself as he bucked his hips and drove deep into her with the full force of his passion.

"Brand," she cried, splaying her hands on his chest as she matched his upward strokes with each of her descents. Then, much faster then she expected, she felt the tightening of her muscles as she was pitched into the glorious agony of her climax.

Brand followed right behind her, panting his happiness as he pumped the last of his strength into her.

"I was right," she sighed, collapsing her head onto his chest.

"Yeah? About what?" he asked hoarsely, cupping her bottom and pulling her closer on him.

"You're definitely alive."

"Only if you keep taking such good care of me," he teased without thinking. But as soon as the words were out of his mouth, he knew they were the truth. She had become part of him, as necessary to his life as air and water. She was his heart. And he wasn't sure he even wanted to try to survive without her.

Sensing the change in Brand, LaRaine started to roll away.

"Not yet," he said, unable to disguise the note of sadness in his voice. "Don't leave me yet."

Smiling, she relaxed on him again. "I'm not going anywhere."

"What if I told you we would forget the past and

asked you to go west with me right now? Tonight!"

Every nerve in LaRaine's body stretched taut. "Are you asking me to marry you?"

"I guess I am. What about it? We could put everything that's happened behind us and start a whole new life out West. You could call yourself LaRaine or whatever you want."

"But no matter what I called myself, *you* would always think of me as Flame, wouldn't you, Brand?" she asked accusingly.

"No! I wouldn't. We'll leave all of that here."

LaRaine pulled herself free and picked up her clothing. "Even if I were willing to spend the rest of my life with a man who believes I'm a liar—which I'm not—I can't leave Missouri. Not until I finish what I came for."

She stood up and hurried toward the creek for a bath—and to hide the fact that she was crying.

Chapter Sixteen

"I guess we oughta stop for the night an' give the horses a rest," Flame said begrudgingly, gauging the time to be about midnight by the position of the moon in the sky. Her disappointment at not having caught up with her double evident in her voice, she pointed to a copse of trees several yards off the road. "Over there looks like a good place to make camp."

Jeff, who had been struggling to keep from falling asleep in the saddle for the last two hours, nodded his head and turned his horse toward the grove Flame had indicated. "Anythin' looks good to me. I'm beat," he admitted, leaving her staring angrily up the road, as if she were still weighing the thought of going farther that night.

As Jeff neared the trees, he was so exhausted he didn't notice the warning swivel of his pony's ears. Nor did he hear the telltale rattle of a snake hidden in the tall brown grass—until it was too late.

Jeff's frightened pinto squealed, forcing Flame's attention away from her own distracted thoughts in time to see the pony rear and flail at the air with his front hooves. And before she could grasp what was happening and act, she saw Jeff fly through the air

255

as his mount took off running.

To her horror, Jeff landed headfirst with a soft thud that echoed in her ears as if it had been thunder. The sound sent a wave of nausea washing over her. Fighting the panic that threatened to overwhelm her, she kicked her horse into a gallop, screaming shrilly as she rode, "Jeffie!"

Drawing near the crumpled, motionless heap that was Jeff, she wailed, "Jeffie, are you all right?" though she could see by the distorted angle of his head to his shoulders that his neck had snapped on impact.

She swung her leg over the saddle before she had reined her horse to a complete halt—the same way she had dismounted at a run a hundred times before. But this time was different. Her boot caught in the stirrup, tripping her and sending her tumbling to the ground on her face.

"Dammit!" She flipped over onto her back and reached for her boot to free it from the stirrup.

It was then the snake that had frightened the pinto chose to make its presence known to her horse.

The sorrel reared, pitching Flame backward, her foot still caught. "Whoa, girl," she tried to soothe the mare. But the horse, round eyes bulging with terror, only heard the sound of her own fear and took off at a wild, uncontrolled gallop, dragging her rider alongside.

Using every bit of her concentration and instinct to escape the thundering hooves that pounded a tattoo of deadly beats in the earth beside her head, Flame managed to raise her upper body. She tried to reach her boot and pull her foot free. But it was useless. It had slipped all the way through the stirrup, which was around her ankle now, and the

ACCEPT YOUR **FREE GIFT** AND EXPERIENCE MORE OF THE PASSION AND ADVENTURE YOU LIKE IN A HISTORICAL ROMANCE

Zebra Romances are the finest novels of their kind and are written with the adult woman in mind. All of our books are written by authors who really know how to weave tales of romantic adventure in the historical settings you love.

Because our readers tell us these books sell out very fast in the stores, Zebra has made arrangements for you to receive at home the four newest titles published each month. You'll never miss a title and home delivery is so convenient. With your first shipment we'll even send you a **FREE** Zebra Historical Romance as our gift just for trying our home subscription service. No obligation.

BIG SAVINGS AND **FREE** HOME DELIVERY

Each month, the Zebra Home Subscription Service will send you the four newest titles as soon as they are published. (We ship these books to our subscribers even before we send them to the stores.) You may preview them *Free* for 10 days. If you like them as much as we think you will, you'll pay just $3.50 each and *save $1.80 each month* off the cover price. *AND you'll also get FREE HOME DELIVERY*. There is never a charge for shipping, handling or postage and there is no minimum you must buy. If you decide not to keep any shipment, simply return it within 10 days, no questions asked, and owe nothing.

MAIL IN THE COUPON BELOW TODAY

GET FREE GIFT

To get your Free ZEBRA HISTORICAL ROMANCE fill out the coupon below and send it in today. As soon as we receive the coupon, we'll send your first month's books to preview Free for 10 days along with your **FREE NOVEL**.

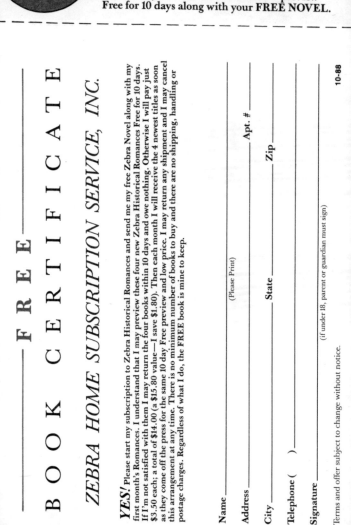

——— F R E E ———
B O O K   C E R T I F I C A T E

ZEBRA HOME SUBSCRIPTION SERVICE, INC.

YES! Please start my subscription to Zebra Historical Romances and send me my free Zebra Novel along with my first month's Romances. I understand that I may preview these four new Zebra Historical Romances Free for 10 days. If I'm not satisfied with them I may return the four books within 10 days and owe nothing. Otherwise I will pay just $3.50 each; a total of $14.00 (a $15.80 value—I save $1.80). Then each month I will receive the 4 newest titles as soon as they come off the press for the same 10 day Free preview and low price. I may return any shipment and I may cancel this arrangement at any time. There is no minimum number of books to buy and there are no shipping, handling or postage charges. Regardless of what I do, the FREE book is mine to keep.

Name _____

_____ (Please Print) _____

Address _____ Apt. # _____

City _____ State _____ Zip _____

Telephone ( ) _____

Signature _____

_____ (if under 18, parent or guardian must sign) _____

Terms and offer subject to change without notice.

10-88

Get a Free
Zebra
Historical
Romance

*a $3.95
value*

ZEBRA HOME SUBSCRIPTION SERVICES, INC.
P.O. BOX 5214
120 BRIGHTON ROAD
CLIFTON, NEW JERSEY 07015-5214

weight of her own body was forcing her heel and toe to act as a lock, securing her to the crazed animal's side. All she could do now was ride it out—and hopefully survive.

Protecting her head with her arms and doing her best to hold herself so that her buttocks would take the brunt of the grueling punishment, Flame tried again to talk to the horse. "Easy now, Red. Whoa, girl. Whoa, there." Although the horse showed no signs of slowing its pace, she forced her voice to remain calm.

Then, as suddenly as she had started running, the mare stopped, her barreled sides heaving laboriously.

"Are you all right, mister?" Flame heard a man call out from the darkness. She was vaguely aware of the sound of running footsteps, the sound of her own heart pounding in her breast and the sound of heavy breathing as the mare's inflamed nostrils flared to suck in large amounts of oxygen.

Then she heard nothing at all.

"Oh, my God! She was telling the truth!" Brand gasped, kneeling beside the unconscious rider on the ground beneath the winded horse.

LaRaine ran up behind him. "Is he dead?" she cried, starting to peek over Brand's view-blocking shoulder. "What do you suppose happened to him?"

Her action broke alarmingly into Brand's benumbed state, and he bolted up from the ground. Grabbing her shoulders, he spun her around so that she couldn't see what he had discovered. "Go back to camp!" he ordered harshly, his mind whirling into a kaleidoscope of panic and relief and questions and decisions to be made.

"But I want to help," LaRaine insisted stubbornly.

"You don't want to see this."

"What do you think you're protecting me from? I've seen wounded men before. During the war I took care of several," she explained, straining against his grip.

"Just take my word for it," he pleaded. "I need to do this alone. If the rider's dead, I'll have to bury the body. There's no need for you to see it." He choked, wondering how he would prepare her for the knowledge of who the rider was. "And if sh—he's alive, I'll . . ."

Flame moaned thickly, "What the hell're you standin' there for? Get me outta this goddamn stirrup!" she ordered.

"It's a woman, Brand!" LaRaine shouted, breaking from his grip to run toward the fallen rider.

"LaRaine, no!"

"She's alive. I've got to help her! You poor thing," she sympathized, kneeling beside the rider and carefully working her foot out of her boot. "What on earth happened to you? We were afraid you were dea—" She turned to look at the other woman's face for the first time.

Flame's mouth dropped open. "I'll be damned."

"It's you!" LaRaine gasped, recognizing the face that stared back at her with eyes like her own, wide with stunned amazement.

Frozen in mid-motion, the two sisters studied each other for what seemed an eternity. Flame recovered from the shock first and managed to drag herself to a sitting position. "So, it's like Jeffie said. We're dead ringers." She dusted herself off and stood up without assistance from LaRaine, who continued to watch her with spellbound curiosity.

Flame was uneasy about the way the man with her sister kept watching her, his hand resting alertly near the revolver he wore low on his right hip, but she pretended not to notice. "Well, what the hell're ya starin' at? Ya knew about me, didn't ya? Ain't that why you're here? To find me? What the hell'd you 'spect? Some snooty lady all gussied up in fancy clothes an' spoutin' fancy words?"

"I don't know what I expected." Then LaRaine's instincts took over. "I suppose I expected you to ride on the horse, not under it," she said with a nervous laugh, trying to think of even one of the things she had planned to say to her twin when they finally met. This was definitely not the way she'd imagined it would be. Instead of running into each other's arms, here they were, one sister tongue-tied and the other looking as if she would bolt and run at any instant. "Are you all right?" she finally thought to ask. "I mean, do you think you have any injuries we need to take care of?"

" 'Bout wore out the seat o' my britches," Flame laughed, realizing for the first time that by some quirk of fate, she wasn't seriously hurt. "Guess it'll take more'n bein' drug by a goddamn horse to do me in," she bragged.

"What happened? Where did you come from?" LaRaine asked, feeling foolish and self-conscious, but unable to say the other things that were on her mind—like how long she had prayed for this meeting.

"I heard talk you was in these parts, an' I just figgered to have me a look—ya know, see fer myself," Flame answered, her tone bored. "An' now I seen ya, so I guess I'd better be gettin' on my way," she added, turning to gather up her horse's reins.

259

Flame felt, more than saw, Brand's posture straighten perceptibly, but LaRaine stopped her before he drew the gun he had started for.

"You can't leave!" LaRaine protested, placing a restraining hand on Flame's arm. "Not after all this time. There are things we have to talk about. You've got to stay."

"The way I see it, 'sister,' you 'n me got nothin' to talk about. So I'm gettin'."

"No!" LaRaine demanded. "You're not going anywhere until you hear what I've come to say."

Brand smiled at the look of surprise on Flame's hard face. It was evident it had been a very long time since anyone had dared to use that tone of voice with Flame Rider. In fact, Brand was certain that if he hadn't been witnessing the reunion, Flame would have considered drawing on someone for such a transgression, but instead, she turned back to her sister and asked, "All right, what's so all-fired important that ya got to say?"

"Well, for one thing, don't you want to know what my name is? Aren't you curious about why I came looking for you after all this time? Don't you care where I've been?"

"No, but you might as well spit it out since you ain't gonna give me no peace till you do." Flame leaned against her horse's hip with exaggerated nonchalance and crossed her arms, making certain LaRaine could see how boring she was finding the entire conversation. "What's your name?" she asked dutifully.

"LaRaine. LaRaine Ashby."

"LaRaine? Now, ain't that pretty? Well, it's been real 'nice' meetin' you, 'LA-Raine,'" she said, turning her back and making ready to mount up. "Now, I gotta get goin'."

"Hold it right there, Flame," Brand said, speaking for the first time and moving with lightning speed toward LaRaine's twin sister. "You're not going anywhere."

"You better get yer friggin' hands off me, mister," she said through clenched teeth, glaring threateningly at the spot on her arm where Brand's strong fingers held her in an iron-tight grip. "Men 'a been killed for less," she sneered, the warning in her voice genuine.

"I don't doubt it, but tonight you're not going to be killing anyone," Brand said, his own voice every bit as intimidating and menacing as hers. "You're going to give me your weapons, and then the three of us are going to make a little trip back to our camp, where you're going to politely listen to what your sister has gone through hell to tell you. Do you understand?"

"Hell, yeah, I understand. I understand I'm s'posed to meet my boys a coupla miles down the road, 'n they'll be comin' fer me if I don't show up," she answered bitterly, staring boldly into Brand's deadly blue eyes with unmitigating hatred. "You're already a dead man," she laughed. "Do *you* understand that, you cocky bastard?"

"I understand that you'd better watch that filthy mouth of yours or I'm going to put a gag on it." He deftly removed the holster from around Flame's hips. No one spoke while Brand took a small pistol from the waistband of her tight-fitting trousers, another from her hat, and a long-bladed knife from each of her boots.

"Come on, let's go," he said when he was finished searching her. Pushing her ahead of him, he turned

261

to LaRaine who still hadn't recovered from the shock of finding her sister. "Bring her horse and things. We're going to get this whole thing over with tonight!" He prodded Flame forward.

"Don't be so rough," LaRaine pleaded, running to catch up with Brand and Flame. "She's had a nasty fall."

"Yeah, I had a nasty fall," Flame mimicked.

"Not nearly as nasty as the one you're going to have if you keep opening your mouth."

"Brand, stop it!" LaRaine insisted emotionally. "I won't have her talked to like that!"

So, it's already beginning, he thought sadly. "Well, you'd better get used to it, LaRaine—" His voice broke as he thought of her by her real name for the first time. What kind of demented irony was this to have the moment when he'd finally learned the wonderful truth about her identity mark the end of their relationship?

"Like I got used to the way you treated me when you thought I was Flame Rider?" she asked sarcastically.

"Face it, it's the only thing someone like her understands—or respects. Where she comes from, the biggest, meanest, and loudest animal gets to be the king of the hill—that is, until some bigger and louder animal comes along and takes away the hill. Isn't that right, Flame?"

"She's a human being, not an animal!" LaRaine defended, close to tears, torn between knowing what Brand said was true and her instinctive protectiveness and love of her sister, her own flesh and blood.

"He talks real tough, don't he?" Flame asked LaRaine with a bitter laugh. " 'Course what man wouldn't with a gun in the back o' a female half his

size. But ya can bet he won't be nothin' against one
'o my boys when they get here. Any one o' them
could chew him up 'n spit him out."

"Get a rope," Brand said to LaRaine as they approached the campsite.

"Rope?" LaRaine gulped, remembering Brand's
threat to see Flame "strung up." "What are you
going to do?"

"Relax. I'm not going to hang her." He looked at
Flame and added, "Yet. I'm just going to tie her up
so she doesn't get the urge to travel in the middle of
the night."

"No! I'm not going to stand by and let you tie my
sister up."

"She's trapped, LaRaine. There's nothing she
won't do to get free—even go against her own sister.
And I'm not going to give her the chance to hurt
you. Now get the rope."

"I won't do it!" She narrowed her eyes, openly
challenging him. "If you want the rope, then get it
yourself, Brand Colter."

Releasing a frustrated growl, he caught Flame's
arm and dragged her to where he had a hank of rope
looped over his saddle horn.

Wondering how she had ever allowed herself to
fall in love with such an unfeeling brute as Brand
Colter, LaRaine watched helplessly as he tied
Flame's hands and ankles and propped her against a
tree.

When he was through, he stood and walked wearily to where LaRaine watched. His heart tightened
in his chest as he saw her expression filled with
loathing, where he'd seen love only a few hours
before. "Promise me you won't untie her and I'll
leave you two alone to talk."

Her lips compressed in a thin line, LaRaine lifted her chin defiantly.

Brand shrugged, his resignation to the situation evident in his slumping posture. "You're not leaving me much choice."

He grabbed LaRaine's wrists and pulled them behind her.

"What do you think you're doing?"

"If you're not with me, you're against me," he spit out caustically, winding the rope around her wrists.

"I'll never forgive you for this, Brand," she vowed as he walked her to a second tree and sat her down facing Flame, who was eagerly taking in everything that was happening.

"I know," he said, his voice cracking. He quickly bound her ankles and stood up.

"I'll give you two some time alone," he said uneasily, not wanting to leave LaRaine with her vicious twin for even a moment, but knowing it was what he had to do. "But if I hear or see one thing that looks like either of you has moved, I'll be all over you like a fly on a manure pile. You got that, 'ladies'?" He leveled his gaze directly on Flame.

"Can't you see, I'm just a-tremblin'?" Flame returned.

"I'm sorry," LaRaine apologized to Flame as soon as Brand left. Her expression dark with regret, she did her best to block out the dislike she saw in her sister's eyes as they studied each other. *It's fear, no hate!* she tried to convince herself. *She can't hate me, any more than I could ever hate her.*

"So! Imagine you just appearing out of nowhere like that!" she started, making a desperate effort not to think about the horrible crimes her sister had supposedly committed. But it was no good. She could concentrate on little else.

"Why, Flame? Why have you chosen this life for yourself?"

Flame's eyes narrowed resentfully. "Who are you to ask me about my 'choices'? When in your whole life did ya have ta choose between anythin' more serious than what fancy dress to wear to what fancy ball, or what fork to eat with? Ya got a real nerve judgin' me, *LaRaine Ashby!*"

LaRaine detected a slight quiver in her twin's bottom lip as Flame tilted her head back and looked at her from the corner of her eye, which glistened suspiciously.

"I'm not judging you, Flame," she said, her heart twisting painfully. "I'm your sister. We're flesh and blood. I love you. I want to help you."

"All your sisterly love's a little late, ain't it? Where were you when I coulda used your help? Why are ya just now comin' 'round after all this time when I don't need ya no more."

"It's not too late!" LaRaine responded. "Not for us."

"Hmp."

"And as for my not coming sooner, I didn't know about you until a few months ago when my father was dying. He told me then. That was when I began my search for you. And I've never given up the dream that we would be together one day."

"Your pa the man who took ya when we was babies?"

"Yes, that's him. His name was Thomas Ashby and he was a wonderful, loving man."

"Yeah, that's real clear to see," Flame said with a sneer. "I guess that's why he took jest you an' left me behind."

265

"He didn't want to leave you there," LaRaine protested. "In fact, he never stopped feeling guilty for not taking you, too. His last thoughts before he died were of you!"

I jest bet. Skeered o' goin' to hell! Flame thought, determined to hold on to her hate for Thomas Ashby *and* his daughter, LaRaine. But her hurt was too deep and she had to know why she had been left behind to endure Cutter Doyle's abuse. "Then why'd he do it? Why'd he take you'n not me?" she asked in a small, little-girl voice that sounded out of place coming from the life-toughened criminal. But the pain she had suffered as a result of Cutter Doyle's cruelty was too near the surface to hide. "Cutter said it was 'cause I was scrawny 'n homely. He said the rich man only wanted the pretty twin."

"But that's not true! Papa said we were both scrawny and exactly alike, right down to the red fuzz on our heads. You have to understand, his own baby had died that night. He just wanted a baby."

"Then why didn't he take us both?"

LaRaine sighed and shook her head. "That's a question he never stopped asking himself until the day he died. But at the time, he did what he thought he had to do. You have to understand his wife had given birth to a stillborn baby that night, and he wanted to spare her the pain of knowing. So, when he heard about us, he went to see Cutter Doyle. He was tempted to take us both, but he was afraid my mother might not accept another baby if she knew it wasn't her own. So, he made the decision to take just one of us and not tell her the truth. But it wasn't because there was anything wrong with you. It was just by chance that he took me and not you. It could have just as easily been the other way around!"

"But it wasn't, was it? So, while you was livin' your wonderful, lovin' fairy tale life with your 'wonderful, lovin' fairy tale pa 'n ma, Cutter Doyle an' his boys was usin' me for boxin' practice — when they wasn't humpin' me or makin' me cook an' clean for them or passin' me around to their friends for whiskey money."

LaRaine's eyes bugged and her mouth fell open on a horrified intake of breath. "What did you say?"

Flame raised her watery gaze and gave LaRaine a malicious smile, obviously glad she had shocked her. But the smile lasted only an instant before she had to look away. Fighting the tears she had held in for so many years, she shook her head and laughed self-consciously. "Ya know what's really funny 'bout this? I used to dream . . ."

"What?" LaRaine asked, torn with guilt for what her sister had endured.

"Nuthin'," she spit out, struggling to resume her tough facade. "It was crazy."

"It's not crazy to dream. Tell me, please," LaRaine insisted softly.

Flame sniffed and ran the tip of her tongue along her upper lip. "I always used to dream that someday my rich, beautiful twin sister'd come 'n take me back to live with her in a great big palace. We were goin' to live happily ever after, like in a fairy tale. See, I told ya it was crazy." Flame hung her head disconcertedly.

"Maybe not so crazy," LaRaine soothed. "Though I'm not rich and I don't live in a palace, I still came to take you back with me if you want to go. I would've come sooner, but it took me this long to find you."

"You ain't rich?" Flame asked suspiciously, wondering if LaRaine were telling the truth.

"Actually, I should say *we're* not rich — since Papa's will left everything to the *two* of us. You and me together."

"Then, he musta been rich," Flame insisted. "Poor folks ain't got much use for wills."

"At one time, our family was well off, but after the war, there wasn't much left — just a big house on four hundred acres in Virginia, and in need of lots of repairs. And he left us the general store in town. It's not much now, but together, you and I could rebuild it to what it was before!" LaRaine said excitedly, wanting to instill her twin with her own enthusiasm.

Flame blurted out a loud derisive snort. "That's the dumbest idea I ever heard!"

"Why?" LaRaine asked, actually surprised Flame couldn't see the plan as a solution to her own problems.

"Well, for one thing, in case you ain't noticed, I ain't goin' nowhere. When you'n me are through talkin', your friend is gonna turn me over to the law, an' if he's got anythin' to say about it, I'm gonna get hung by the neck till I'm dead." With eyes crossed, Flame flopped her head to the side, contorted her mouth, stuck out her tongue, and made a strangling noise.

"Stop that this minute!" LaRaine scolded. "I'm not going to let that happen!"

"Yeah? Just how ya gonna stop it?" Flame asked, pointing her chin toward LaRaine's bound ankles. "From where I'm sittin', you're not in much better shape than me."

"But there's no warrant out for my arrest. He'll

release me in the morning, and I'll testify at your trial. I'll tell them how it wasn't your fault. Besides, Brand tells me most of the unofficial Confederate soldiers are being sentenced to almost no time in jail—a few months at the most."

"An' did he tell ya I'd only get a few months for the stuff I done since the war was over?"

"No, I must admit he said you could hang for those things. But I can't believe you've ever killed anyone. You haven't, have you? I mean killed anyone?"

"The law says I have," Flame sidestepped glibly. "So it don't make no diff'rence what's true. I'm gonna hang."

"No!" LaRaine cried out in frustration. "I'll never let them do that to you. There has to be something we can do. Some way to convince the authorities that you're not really bad."

"It'd be nice if I could wipe the slate clean an' start over again, but there ain't no way—'less maybe you'n me . . ." Flame stopped, deliberately manipulating her sister. "Unless, we could get on them horses 'n get as far away from here as we can. Somewheres they never heard o' Flame Rider."

"But they'd come after us, Flame. You would still be a wanted criminal. And I would be, too. No, the only answer is to clear your name."

"If we get outta the States, maybe go out West to the territories, folks in them parts have enough trouble just gettin' by. They ain't gonna pay attention to a coupla gals from the East who ain't done nothin' in their part o' the country."

"But it would still be wrong."

"Yeah," Flame said, looking doomed. "I shouldna said nothin'. Forget it. Ya just do what ya gotta do.

I'll be fine. No hard feelin's."

"But what about Brand? He would stop us," La-Raine said, thinking aloud about Flame's ludicrous proposal. She knew she owed her twin her allegiance, no matter what the personal cost, but to actually leave Brand, to willingly take up with a wanted criminal, to become an outlaw herself, to head for the wilds of the West — wasn't it too much too ask?

"You're in love with that no-good bounty hunter, ain't you?" Flame accused. "That's why ya won't help me get away. You're wastin' your time, ya know. He's just usin' you to get ta me. Once he collects his reward money, you ain't gonna see him no more. I've knowed his type plenty o' times b'fore. Tell ya they love ya till they get what they want. Then they're gone."

"That's not true," LaRaine protested weakly. "He's not like that at all." A sickening pain gripped her chest as she realized the possible truth in her sister's words. It wasn't as if they had known each other long enough for him to actually care about her. Had she been fooling herself, thinking she might have a future with a man like Brand Colter? "I don't believe it! He cares about me," she insisted, trying to convince herself even more than Flame.

"Sure he does," Flame laughed acridly, giving La-Raine a pitying look. "I could tell by the way he treated ya — tyin' ya up like he did."

"You're wrong. And I'll prove it! Brand," she called out. "Brand, can you come over here?" Her voice was surprisingly even. "You just go along with what I say, and I'll show you he cares," she told Flame defiantly.

"Yeah," the low masculine voice answered from

enough distance where he couldn't eavesdrop on the reunited sisters, but still close enough to hear if LaRaine needed him. "What is it?" he asked, approaching the two who studied him in a way that made him feel uneasy. He could have sworn he saw a glimmer of satisfaction flash spitefully in Flame's eyes. His gaze shifted anxiously to LaRaine. "Are you all right?"

"Of course I'm all right," she answered sharply. "Except for these ropes on my wrists and ankles."

"I'm sorry about that, but you didn't give me much choice."

"Yes . . . well, that aside, my sister and I have had a long talk and we have a proposition for you."

Chapter Seventeen

Brand arched a doubtful eyebrow and lounged back against a nearby tree. "A proposition?" He crossed one ankle over the other and folded his arms over his chest. "What kind of proposition?"

LaRaine shot Flame a tremulous glance, then spoke. "I think my sister will have the best chance for a parole if she turns herself in and stands trial voluntarily—rather than being taken in like a common criminal."

"She *is* a common criminal, LaRaine."

Ignoring his snide comment, she went on. "If she turns herself in and I testify on her behalf that she wants to reform, I feel she has a very good chance of being released—if not on her own recognizance, then on mine."

Brand threw back his head and laughed. "Let me guess. And you want me to go along with you and let her go."

"Of course it will be necessary for you to release us and let us ride into St. Louis on our own."

Nodding his head, Brand turned to Flame and asked, "Do you really expect me to believe you've seen the error of your ways and want to turn over a new leaf?"

"You heard the lady," Flame replied, shrugging her shoulders.

"And you actually believe her?" he asked LaRaine, the expression on his dark face incredulous.

"Of course I do!"

Suddenly there was nothing to laugh at, and his smile dissolved into a scowl. "Don't you see what she's doing to you, LaRaine? She's using the same trick on you that you used on the Ruston brothers. She's trying to split us up by making you think she's going along with you. And you're falling for it." He was so frustrated that he wanted to pick LaRaine up and run with her.

"I'm telling you, it's not a trick. She's promised not to cause any more trouble, haven't you, Flame?" LaRaine nodded toward her sister.

"Word o' honor," Flame promised smugly, knowing Brand could see through her guise but that he would be helpless to convince LaRaine that her sister was not to be trusted. *She feels so damned guilty about me she'll believe just about anythin' I want her to. Even when he points out exactly what I'm doin'.*

"Sorry to disappoint you, Flame, but it won't work. You might be able to convince LaRaine of your good intentions, because she's the type who always thinks the best of everyone, especially her no-good sister who she loves without even knowing her. But there's no way I'm buying it!"

"It's not an act!" LaRaine stressed. "She really wants to make amends and start fresh somewhere else."

"Well, she's going to have to convince a judge and jury—*after* I take her in."

"Can't blame him, Sis. That reward must look like pretty easy money right now. He ain't gonna give that up."

LaRaine looked at Brand, as if seeing him for the first time. "Is that it? Is that why? For the reward?"

"If that's what you believe, then I guess we don't know each other as well as I thought we did." His voice was tired and filled with pain. She would never believe that he had to do this for her. Until Flame was behind bars, LaRaine would never be safe again. "So I guess that ends the discussion. Do you need anything else?"

"Will you at least loosen the rope on our wrists so we can get some sleep?"

Brand shook his head sadly. God! This was destroying him. "I'm going to get some sleep," he said, pushing away from the tree he was leaning on. "And you girls would be smart to do the same. We're leaving for St. Louis at first light."

"Well," Flame gloated when she was certain Brand was out of earshot. "What'd I tell ya? He ain't about to let me turn myself in. He wants that reward money too much. So I guess that means I done reached the 'end o' my *rope.*'" She smiled inwardly at the effect her choice of words had on her sister.

"Not yet, you haven't," LaRaine whispered tersely, peering toward the place where Brand was already stretched out on the ground with his back to them. Satisfied that he wasn't able to see her, she used the tree trunk behind her to support herself and eased up to a standing position. Bracing her shoulders against the tree, she brought her bound wrists down under her bottom, then bent in half so she could step through the circle her arms formed at the back of her knees. "As long as I have a breath in my body, you haven't reached the end of anything," she said, bringing her hands to her mouth. "How dare he try to use me to destroy my own sister?" she complained, tearing at the knot with her teeth.

"What're ya plannin'?" Flame asked, standing up and copying LaRaine's actions.

"When we're sure he's sound asleep, we'll leave for St. Louis by ourselves. You can turn yourself in and prove your innocence. Then we can go back to Virginia and make a new life for ourselves," she said with determination, doing her best to ignore the wave of misery that swept over her at the thought of never seeing Brand again.

"But if I go to trial I could still get sent to prison or get hung," Flame protested, chewing at her ropes. "Even if I turn myself in."

"Nonsense, no one is going to believe you're a criminal—at least not when I get through fixing your hair and buying you some clothing that's a little more feminine than what either of us is wearing!" Just then she felt the knot on her wrists shift, and the rope loosened.

"What about him? He'll come after us the minute he finds us gone. He prob'bly ain't a real heavy sleeper—'specially when he's got him a prisoner worth some money."

"It won't matter," LaRaine said, concentrating all her effort on untying the rope. "We'll get enough head start to turn you in before he catches up with us."

"Just to make sure we get a good distance between us, there's a vial o' chloroform in the pocket o' my saddlebag. If we pour some o' that on a bandana and hold it over his mouth an' nose, we'll give ourselves some extra time b'fore he wakes up."

"No!" LaRaine hissed emphatically.

"It's the only way," Flame insisted. "An' it won't do nothin' to him but give him a extra good night's sleep." *Unless someone puts too much chloroform on the bandana. Then, it's so long Mr. Bounty Hunter!* "I thought ya wanted to help me."

"I do, but not like that," LaRaine said, freeing her hands at last and sitting back down to work on untying her ankles. "We'll simply give him a few more minutes to get fully asleep. He hasn't had much rest lately, so he's probaoly exhausted."

"All the more reason to help him get a good night's sleep. What the hell's wrong with that?"

"Flame," LaRaine said, releasing her own ankles and scooting across the ground to work on freeing her twin's wrists. "I said, no! Now, if you want me to help you, you're going to have to trust me."

Deciding against further arguing—for the time being, Flame shrugged her shoulders. She should have known LaRaine wouldn't have the stomach for doing what had to be done. But no matter, she would just do it herself, because one way or another, Brand Colter wasn't going to be in any shape to follow them. "What the hell, we'll do it your way."

LaRaine grinned and hurriedly pried the knot on Flame's wrist apart. "By the way, when we go to the authorities, I do hope you're not going to keep up the bad language and act so tough. I think it will work against you if we're trying to convince them that you couldn't have done anything wrong. Ladies don't talk like that, nor do they rob banks. Do you see what I mean?"

"Yeah, sure," Flame muttered thoughtfully, almost tempted to go along with LaRaine's ridiculous, optimistic scheme for starting a new life together. Almost, but not quite. No, she would stick to her original plan. She'd learn everything there was to know about her sister, and then she would become LaRaine Ashby, leaving the real LaRaine to take Flame Rider's place. It was about time life smiled on

276

her, instead of her sweet, do-gooder sister!

"We'll lie down as if we're sleeping and wait until he's completely asleep," LaRaine said, curling up on the ground.

"I still say it'd be better if we . . ."

LaRaine patted her sister's arm. "Just trust me, Flame. I won't let anyone hurt you ever again. Not even Brand Colter."

"I hope he sleeps at least until we get far enough away that he can't hear us," LaRaine told her sister as they stole away from the camp, leading their horses on foot.

Flame looked back over her shoulder and grinned. *Oh, he'll sleep, all right. With the dose of chloroform I left on that bandana under his nose, he'll be lucky if he wakes up at all!* she said to herself, thinking how easy it had been to fool LaRaine into thinking retrieving their weapons was the only reason she had gone back to the camp after they had gotten free.

"Damn, this feels good!" Flame exclaimed a few minutes later when LaRaine deemed it safe to mount their horses and ride.

LaRaine raised a disapproving eyebrow at her sister. "Remember what I said about the way ladies speak, and the way criminals speak."

"I mean, *goodness me,* this feels lovely," Flame corrected herself sarcastically.

LaRaine smiled, determined to forget the misgivings that were tearing at her heart. "That's much better." Gathering the reins in her hand, she sprang to the back of her roan gelding and dug her heels into the animal's sides. Her decision made, there was no turning back. Not now. Not ever.

"This isn't the way to St. Louis," LaRaine announced in shocked dismay when the first light of day appeared at her back instead of before her, as she had expected.

"It ain't?" Flame said, enjoying her sister's confusion. "Well, whadda ya make o' that?"

"You promised you'd turn yourself in in St. Louis."

"You were the one makin' all the promises, Sis. Not me."

"But our plan was to have you turn yourself in there!" The pitch in LaRaine's voice rose drastically, her frustration and surprise apparent.

"Your plans, not mine," Flame ground out vengefully, tempted to gloat over the fact that she had been able to make her stupid twin betray the man she was so obviously in love with. However, she wasn't ready to disclose her true intentions—not yet anyway. There was still a lot more she was going to take from LaRaine Ashby before that time came. So she controlled her desire and said, "Don't you see? I don't stand a chance if we go to St. Louie. Them city folks'll have me strung up b'fore I can say howdy."

"So, all along you knew you weren't going to turn yourself over to the authorities," LaRaine accused, her voice hurt and small. She felt foolish and angry—betrayed.

You're beginnin' to get the idea, Sis, Flame thought. But aloud she said, "I'm gonna turn myself in, like ya wanted. I swear I am. Just not in St. Louie, that's all." It would be a lot easier to force the gullible LaRaine to do her bidding if she didn't suspect she had walked into a trap.

"Then where?"

"Littleton. There's a army depot there."

"But isn't Lexington a long way from here?" LaRaine couldn't believe what Flame was suggesting they do. She knew she should just turn her horse around and try to get back to Brand before he woke up—if he hadn't already. She shuddered to think what he would do when he found her gone. No, she couldn't go back to him now. He would never forgive her.

"That'll give you'n me time to work on my manners 'n stuff. Ya know, make a lady outta me so they won't think the worst b'fore they even hear my story." *And by the time we get that far, I'll be so much like you that even that sonovabitch bounty hunter won't be able to tell us apart. Fact is, next time one o' us sees him, you'll be dead an' I'll be you!*

"I can see your point about needing more time," LaRaine admitted hesitantly. She felt as if she were being torn in half. She couldn't go back to Brand, and she knew she shouldn't go forward with Flame. "But how can we possibly ride very far and not be caught?"

"Easy as pie—'less one o' us gets careless," Flame laughed. "An' I ain't gonna let that happen. I got friends all over the state who'll hide us out if we need to be hid. B'lieve it or not, there's a lot o' folks who think o' me as a kind o' hero," she boasted.

"Heroine," LaRaine corrected. "A man is a hero, but a woman is a heroine."

"Huh?" Flame was puzzled that LaRaine hadn't acted impressed with what she had told her. Then her expression beamed in recognition of what LaRaine was doing. "Oh, I get it! You're already startin' with my learnin'. 'Heroine,' " she repeated, trying to give the word the same gentle, musical inflection LaRaine had used. "They think I'm a *heroine!*" she said triumphantly.

"That's better," LaRaine encouraged, touched by her sister's sincere efforts to improve herself. "Exactly how far is it to Littleton? How long do you think it will take us to get there?"

"Hell, it ain't fer. Not more'n two, three days." Flame slapped her sister heartily on the back, satisfied that LaRaine would remain her willing prisoner a while longer.

Though she smiled inwardly at Flame's enthusiasm, LaRaine raised her brows disparagingly. "It looks like we're going to need every bit of that two or three days," she groaned, shaking her head goodnaturedly.

Flame laughed easily, showing no trace of embarassment or resentment. "I mean, *goodness,* it ain't fer."

"It isn't *far,*" LaRaine pointed out.

"Nah, not fer a-tall!"

"I mean you should use the word *isn't* rather than *ain't,* and the pronunciation is *far,* not *fer,*" LaRaine giggled, loving the closeness she felt growing between her and her sister. She was more determined than ever to make Flame's future brighter than her past had been. In fact, she swore to herself, it would be her total reason for living. Everything she did and said from that moment on would be done and uttered with that single purpose in mind. No sacrifice on her part would be too great to ensure Flame's prospects.

The two sisters progressed slowly the next two days and nights, riding only after dark and keeping to the back roads. One taught, and the other thirstily drank in her new knowledge the way desert sand would welcome rain.

LaRaine was amazed at how quickly her sister learned, very rarely forgetting a lesson already taught; and by the end of the third day, she felt there might actually be a possibility that Flame could convince the courts she was a misunderstood "lady" who could never possibly have done anything wrong.

Deciding not to ride into the town of Littleton after dark, LaRaine and Flame opted to spend the final night on the trail reviewing point by point the story they would tell the authorities. And it would give them a chance to wash their dirty hair and bodies so they could look their best.

"Tell the truth," Flame said, toweling her hair dry with a blanket as they sat beside the fire at the entrance to a cave she had found for them to camp in. "When you shot that Wilt Ruston feller, did you have any idea you would hit him? Or were you just as surprised as he was?"

LaRaine smiled. During their days of travel, she'd been so busy teaching Flame how to speak and act like a lady that there had been no time to share the circumstances of her own upbringing with her sister. "It was no surprise or accident, Flame. I usually hit exactly what I aim at," she modestly confirmed, her face breaking into a laugh at the look of utter disbelief on her twin's face.

"You're kiddin'!" Flame gulped, slipping back into her old way of speaking. "Where in the hell, I mean where in *heaven's name* did you learn to shot a gun?" Until that moment, Flame had assumed that LaRaine had just been lucky and that the Rustons had just been slow. "I didn't think that was part of a lady's training," she said, taking special pains with her diction and using a voice that sounded strangely like LaRaine's, very aware of the softer, less grating tone she could affect now.

"My father thought a girl's training should be well rounded, so I started learning to shoot a pistol and rifle when I was about eight years old. He had me on a horse at age five, and by the time I was twelve, I could hunt and fish and ride with the best of the boys my age. If my father hadn't been so well liked, the way I was raised might have been considered quite scandalous. As it was, I think some of the local wives make it a special point that their delicate daughters didn't spend too much time around me. I could have influenced them in the wrong way, I guess." She smiled with resignation, still finding the memory of an occasional snub painful.

"What did your mother think?" Flame asked, still taking care to pronounce her words correctly.

"She thought it was a wonderful way for me to be brought up. She called it giving me 'the best of both worlds'—a man's and a woman's. You see, she was a very unhealthy child and was never given a moment of freedom. Her parents hovered over her constantly and she was never allowed to do anything. So, in effect, I suppose I was doing all the things she had always wished she'd been able to do."

"My ma never had any kind of freedom, either. She had her first baby when she was thirteen, and from then on, she was having babies and getting beat up by Pa. Never havin' enough to eat, workin' from mornin' to night, cookin', cleanin', carin' for sickly, hungry kids." Flame's lip curled in disgust at the sight she saw in her mind's eye, and correct diction was now the furthest thought from her mind.

Viewing the misery in her sister's expression, and hearing the bitterness in her tone, LaRaine ached anew with guilt. Somehow, she should have been there to help her mother and her sister. She should have known her natural mother. "What was she like?" she asked softly, both wanting and not wanting to know.

"I don't really remember. She died when I was eight. I just recall thinking that she didn't have to suffer no—I mean any—more. I missed her, her and her sad, washed-out face, her red hair turned gray before her thirtieth birthday, but I was glad she was dead. Glad she'd never have to do for or be beaten by Cutter Doyle again." There was a heartbreaking sheen of tears glistening in Flame's blue-green eyes, and she swiped at them angrily. "And I knew I didn't want to be like her," she added resentfully.

"Flame," LaRaine said, reaching out to touch her sister's arm compassionately, not bothering to suppress her own tears. "The other night you said something about . . ." She swallowed back the bile that rose in her throat. ". . . about how your father and brothers . . . uh . . . treated you. Was it . . . I mean . . . were you . . . ?"

"Tellin' the truth?" Flame finished for her, her laugh harsh and bitter. "Oh, I was tellin' the truth, all right. My own pa raped me the night o' my ma's funeral," Flame said bluntly, wanting her sister to feel all the hurt that had been inflicted on her by their father.

"How could he have done such a terrible thing? You were just a baby? And his own daughter!"

"Do you know I can still feel the pain?" Flame snarled, hugging her middle tightly and moving back and forth rhythmically where she sat on the ground. She looked defenseless and alone—not at all like the hardened criminal, Flame Rider.

"If only I could have been there," LaRaine wept, scooting over to wrap both arms around Flame. "Maybe together we could have stopped him."

283

"But you weren't, were you?" Flame accused, stopping her rocking to look at her sister through hate-filled eyes.

LaRaine would have been afraid if she had realized the meaning in Flame's expression, but she was too hurt, too shocked, too repulsed by what she had heard—and too full of love—to notice the danger lurking deep in her sister's eyes. "No, I wasn't there. And I'm so sorry. I would give my life to have been able to help you," she said urgently, pulling Flame's head to her shoulder.

That's just what I have in mind, Sis. You giving your life to help me, Flame thought, ignoring the small pang of remorse that gripped her. She refused to admit to herself how much she had liked the time she had spent with her sister.

"What about the others?" LaRaine asked softly. "Didn't they try to help you?"

"What others? You don't mean my brothers, do you? Oh, they helped all right. It wasn't long before they were helpin' themselves to a share o' what Cutter was takin'. It was real handy for all of them to have a live-in cook, housekeeper, and whore!"

"Don't say that about yourself! You weren't a whore! You were a vilely mistreated child!"

"They used to laugh when I would try to fight them. They even brought home friends to use me—for money, o' course. Money for their whiskey," she spat out, feeling a strange, euphoric relief to at last be telling someone the terrible secrets that had haunted her entire life. Maybe confession really was good for the soul. Maybe the hurt would go away, the guilt, the feeling of worthlessness, the nightmares. She prayed it would.

"But in the end, I had the last laugh," she went on, almost seeming to talk to herself. "I was the only one laughin' the last time I saw 'em."

"What happened?" LaRaine asked innocently, expecting to hear a tale of how the young girl had escaped the hell they had forced on her. A tale of running away, or maybe a tale of a gallant William Quantrill saving her. Anything but what came next!

Turning to look at LaRaine, Flame looked surprised to see her sister, surprised that she would ask such a stupid question. With eyes glassed over, she answered woodenly. "I killed them." She ignored LaRaine's sharp intake of breath and went on easily. "Everyone b'lieved it was the Yankees. That's what I told 'em. But there weren't any Yankees. Just me. It was just worthless little Mary Doyle all the time," she sang, seeming to be pleased with herself for fooling everyone, and for keeping her secret so long. "Just worthless little Mary Doyle," she hummed happily.

LaRaine choked, afraid to ask, but she had to know the answer. "How?"

"I set fire to them while they were passed out drunk," Flame answered confidentially. "I burned their filthy, whorin' bodies to a crisp."

Heaving violently, LaRaine dropped her hold on her sister and ran, half crawling, to the edge of the clearing. "No, no, no," she sobbed over and over as she repeatedly vomited the contents of her stomach onto the ground, fifty yards from where she had left her twin sister. Then, when there was nothing left in her belly, she curled into a tight ball and lay down on the cool forest floor, trying to understand how such a terrible thing could have happened to her sister.

At the cave, Flame rose and checked the horses, laid out her bedroll, washed her face, then sat down to await her sister's return. It never occurred to her that LaRaine would leave her or that she wouldn't understand. In fact, for the first time in her life, a kind of peace enveloped her, seeping through her, lifting her up and away from the past.

Flame's expression showed no evidence of the torture her admission had caused her. *It's like Cutter's poison was bottled up in me all this time. And now it's all outta me. I'll be new. I am new,* she rejoiced.

So lost in her newfound truce with her lifetime of nightmares, Flame failed to notice the nicker of the horses.

"Quick, get inside," LaRaine announced in a husky whisper as, her revelations about Flame forgotten for the moment, she led the horses into the cave. "Someone's coming."

"Probably just some wild animal looking for something to eat," Flame suggested, going along with LaRaine.

"Shh," LaRaine ordered. Fear pounding in her ears, she pulled a revolver and squinted her eyes, trying to catch sight of any movement that would give her a clue to who—or what was out there.

"The game's over, ladies," a hard male voice called from the darkness.

"Brand!" LaRaine rasped, panic exploding in her chest.

"Goddamn!" Flame cursed, leaping to attention, her head revolving from side to side in a search for a way out. "How'd he find us?"

"There's no way you can escape. Toss out your weapons and come out with your hands up," he ordered, his voice sounding very tired.

"Didn't you say you found a back way out of here?" LaRaine asked, an idea starting to form in her mind.

"Yeah, but a horse can't get through it."

286

"That's all right. Brand won't know that," she said. "Go out the back way—leave one of the horses in a back chamber when you go. He'll think you rode out."

"What are you going to do?"

"I'll give you time to get out. Then I'll go out and tell him that you left me here alone. That way, while I delay him, you can go to town and surrender yourself. When I think you've had enough time to get away, I'll tell him where you really are, and he'll bring me to town to be sure. Then I can testify for you."

"It'll never work."

"Have you got a better idea?"

Flame snatched up her holster and strapped it on. "I guess not."

"Don't worry. It'll work," LaRaine promised, crossing her fingers behind her back. "Just trust me."

Chapter Eighteen

"I know you're in there," Brand shouted. "I'm going to count to three and then I'm coming in! One . . ."

LaRaine checked over her shoulder to be sure the boulder in front of the narrow passageway completely hid the way to the back side of the hill. She wanted to give Flame as much time as possible before she surrendered.

"Two . . ."

Leaving the second horse in the back chamber of the cave, she held up a torch and walked backward toward the front of the cave, brushing away their footprints with a dead tree limb as she went.

"Three!"

"Don't shoot!" she called, glancing around the main room of the cave. "I'm coming out!"

"Throw out weapons first!" Brand ordered. "Then come out with your hands up."

Very slowly, LaRaine pitched her guns out of the cave one at a time.

"Everything."

She waited a full minute before she answered, her voice trembling. "Flame's gone, Brand. I'm here alone."

"No more lies, LaRaine."

Determined to give her sister every edge possible, she slowly inched her way out of the cave until she was beside the fire, her hands raised over her head. "I'm not lying. She left before you got here."

"You expect me to believe that?" he asked from the bushes, not crazy enough to show himself. "Get out here, Flame!"

"She's gone, I tell you."

Of course, LaRaine could be telling the truth. After all, once Flame got away from him, she probably had no more use for her gullible sister. Disgusted with himself for even thinking of trusting LaRaine after what she had done, Brand asked, "What happened, LaRaine? Did Flame decide she didn't need you anymore and dump you? What about your big plans for her to turn herself in and have you testify for her?"

LaRaine saw no reason not to tell him the truth now. Surely, Flame was nearly to town by this time. It shouldn't be more than a mile from here, and she didn't want to waste too much time before she and Brand got there to support her story. "She went to surrender herself at the army depot. I stayed behind to delay you—Can I put my hands down?"

Brand hesitated for a moment, thrown by the truthful tone of her voice and by the way she looked directly at the bush he stood behind as though she were looking him in the eye. "I don't believe it," he said, his gun still on her. "Now, where is she?"

"Right here, Colter," a hard female voice said from behind him. "And I got a .44 aimed square at your head. Now, drop that gun an' walk nice an' easy up to the cave!"

He let his gun fall to the ground and raised his hands, then walked slowly to where LaRaine stood, his eyes narrowed on her and his lip curled.

"Flame!" LaRaine cried, wincing under the betrayed look Brand gave her. "Why are you here? I thought you were going to town to turn yourself in!"

"That's 'cause you're a fool, LaRaine. I wasn't never gonna turn myself in."

"What about our plans?"

Flame shook her head and laughed. "Where do ya think you are, girl? We're not back East where everything goes accordin' to your fancy 'plans.' Out here, folks make plans as they go along. They shoot first an' make plans later."

"But I was going to be there to vouch for you!"

"For such a smart gal, you're sure dumb," Flame said. "Don't you know that as soon as they found out there's two of us, they'd figger we was both in on the robberies all along. We'd both be danglin' by sunrise."

"Unless there's someone to testify on LaRaine's behalf," Brand inserted.

"But there won't be." Flame leveled her gun at Brand's chest and pulled back on the hammer.

"No!" LaRaine shouted, jumping in front of Brand. "You'll have to shoot me first."

A flicker of uncertainty flashed across Flame's face, but she quickly hid it. "I was plannin' to let the law do it for me, but I guess it don't make no difference. As long as you're dead and they see your body, they'll quit lookin' for me."

"Get out of the way, LaRaine. She means it," Brand ordered, his heart pumping with fear for LaRaine's life. Yet, he didn't dare move, not with her in Flame's line of fire.

Her own heart shattering with disillusionment, LaRaine stood firm. "She doesn't mean it." Her posture stiff and unyielding, she held her tears at bay with unrelenting will. "She won't shoot me. She can't. She can't kill the one person on earth who cares for her and who's tied to her even more strongly than by blood. I'm part of her, and she won't be able to destroy the part of herself that's me." She smiled sympathetically. "You won't shoot me, will you, Flame? No more than I can stop loving you."

Flame's hand shook slightly and her eyes shifted uneasily. "I will if ya don't stand aside," she threatened. Suddenly she didn't sound so certain. She raised her gun slightly and tightened her finger on the trigger.

"No!" Brand yelled, knocking LaRaine aside with a blow to her shoulder, and presenting himself as a target. "Leave her alone. I'm the one you want!"

Biting her bottom lip in concentration, Flame steadied her gun with both hands. "Thanks, Colter," she sniffed, her vision blurring with unexpected tears.

Lying on the ground where she had fallen, LaRaine stared as her sister leveled her gun barrel on Brand. "Don't do it, Flame," she screamed.

Her posture tense, Flame hesitated for a long moment. Then there was an almost indiscernible relaxing at her shoulders. Slowly, her gun still on Brand, she backed away from the camp to where Brand had tied his horse. "Don't try to come after me, or next time I won't change my mind!" To the sound of horses' hooves, she disappeared into the night.

"LaRaine! Are you all right?" Brand asked, running to her. Stooping, he gathered her into his arms and clutched her to his chest. "God, you scared me! Why would you do such a stupid thing?"

"I couldn't let her shoot you," LaRaine said, wrapping her arms around his waist and burying her face against his shirt, unable to stop the flow of tears any longer. Lord, it felt good to have his arms around her again. She just wanted to curl up in the security of his embrace and forget the heartbreaking revelations of the last few minutes.

"She was going to kill you!" He tightened his hold on her shaking body and stroked her back "Dammit, Rainy!" His voice broke as he inadvertently called her by a loving nickname. "Don't you realize, she could have killed you?"

LaRaine felt his big chest shudder beneath her head. Drawing back to see his face, she was surprised to find tears trailing over the tanned surfaces of his cheeks from his misery-filled blue eyes.

Her heart exploding with love, she clasped his face between her palms and wiped the pads of her thumbs along the sunken hollows beneath his eyes. "Would it have made that much difference to you?"

The side of his mouth quirked up in a half-grin, and he brushed the backs of his fingers over her tear-dampened cheek. "Yeah, it would have made that much difference."

"Even after what I did?"

He sucked in a deep breath and let it out slowly. "Even after that. And I guess it all worked out for the best. At least now you finally know the truth about Flame Rider—and the kind of danger you're in until she's in jail."

"I still have to try to help her, Brand," she said firmly. "I just went about it the wrong way when I aided her escape from you."

"Help her? Are you out of your mind? She was ready to kill you!"

"But she didn't, did she? Or you! Don't you see? She could have killed us both, but she didn't. Under all that tough exterior of hers, I believe she's a frightened, lonely little girl who is fighting for survival the only way she knows how. And I know in my heart she *couldn't* kill anyone." The memory of what Flame had told her about her father and brothers flashed across LaRaine's mind. "Unless it was in self-defense," she added.

"Well, I'm not going to give her the chance to get to you again. I'm taking you back to St. Louis where you'll be safe. Then I'm going after Flame Rider alone. And this time I'm bringing her in."

"You're wrong. We're both going after her, and we're both going to bring her in."

"I won't let you do it."

"You can't stop me. She's my sister, Brand, and she's totally alone. Even if it means giving up everything, I can't turn my back on her. Not when she needs me now, more than ever."

"I can't believe you can forgive her after what she almost did."

LaRaine smiled. "But you're going to help me anyway, aren't you?"

"If I say no, I guess you'd do something dumb like trying to go alone again, wouldn't you?"

LaRaine nodded. "Besides, if we waste all that time going to St. Louis first, you might never find her. She told me these Ozark mountains are filled with caves and underground springs and streams where a person could hide out indefinitely. This way, we can go after her right now before her trail gets cold."

Brand shrugged in resignation. "It won't do any good to try to follow her tonight. Any signs she's left will be too hard to spot in the dark."

"As soon as it's light then?"

Brand hunched his shoulders and grimaced. "Yeah, I guess so."

"Thank you!" she exclaimed, throwing her arms around his neck and kissing him.

Both of them were startled by the electrical jolt that speared through their bodies with the innocent gesture. Without warning, sensuous desire preempted all thoughts of Flame or anything else.

Crushing her to him, Brand slanted his mouth over hers, taking a hungry sweep over its welcoming interior with his tongue.

"Rainy, Rainy," he moaned when at last he ended the kiss to catch a breath. He buried his face in the curve of her neck and shoulder. "You're so sweet and trusting," he murmured against her skin. "God help me, you've bewitched me," he sighed, his tone betraying the knowledge that he would do almost anything to have her. "I'll never get enough of you."

"I'm glad," she said. "Because I can't seem to get enough of you, either. And when I thought I'd never see you again . . ."

As if controlled by one brain, four hands tore frantically at the clothing that separated their yearning bodies, tossing shirts and pants and boots aside with wild abandon.

Their naked skin glistening in the golden light of the dying fire, Brand sat back on his calves and lifted her onto his lap to straddle him. With a relieved sigh, she impaled herself on him. Her feet on the ground on either side of his hips, she raised and lowered herself hungrily.

"Oh, God! It's so good," he wailed, digging his fingers into her hips and thrusting himself hard into her.

"Yes, yes," she cried, totally giving herself over to her ecstasy. Taking her by surprise, her passion stretched to the limit and exploded in a rainbow of color almost immediately, draining all the strength from her limbs. "I'm sorry," she panted. "I couldn't stop myself."

Burying his face between her breasts, Brand stilled his movements under her. "Don't be sorry. I love it when you respond like that to me," he murmured against a soft mound.

Their bodies still joined, he gently grasped her upper arms and lowered her back along his thighs, so that her head and shoulders were on the shirt one of them had tossed there. "You're beautiful," he sighed. "I love to look at you." Running his hands along her calves, he wrapped her legs around his waist and locked her ankles. Then, gripping her hips, he raised up on his knees so that the coals of the fire gave her exposed flesh a golden sheen.

"Noo," she wailed, fully recovered from her climax, yet feeling her desire start to grow in her belly again.

"Yes," he growled, slamming into her, his own need out of control now. "Now, and again and again. Until I end this hunger you've created inside me."

Then there was no more conversation, only concentrated groans and senseless murmurings of love and sex, until at last he poured himself into her, crying her name over and over again. "Rainy, Rainy, Rainy. I love you!"

"And I love you, Brand," she gasped, her own release pounding in her soul. "I'll never love another!"

After long moments, in the final wake of their rapture, LaRaine thought about the vows they had exchanged. Joy swelled in her heart and she smiled. He had said he loved her.

Then her happiness fell. What if those were words a man just said when he was in the throes of passion? What if they meant nothing else? Suddenly, she felt like crying.

I can't cry, she told herself, swallowing back her tears. She eased herself away from him. "I think I need a bath," she said, grabbing the shirt and scrambling to her feet. "There's a warm water pool inside the cave," she chatted, suddenly self-conscious, more from the fact that she had taken it seriously when he'd said he loved her than from her nakedness. "It must be fed by a hot spring, and the water is fresh and clean."

Brand came up behind her and slid his arms around her waist, pulling her to him so she could feel his manhood pressing against her back. "What is it, honey? Why did you pull away?"

"It's nothing. I just want a bath. I watched for intruders while Flame took hers. Then we started talking and I never got mine. That's all."

"Don't shut me out, Rainy. Not now," he urged, bending his head to rub her cheek with his unshaven chin. "Are you embarrassed that we made love here?"

"No! It's not that." She relaxed her head back on his shoulder, luxuriating in the feel of his rough beard against her softer, more sensitive skin that bore the chafed pinkness left by his kisses. "It's just that . . ."

"What?" he asked, nuzzling her ear.

"It's just that I . . ." She hesitated, wanting to ask him about what he'd said. But she couldn't bring herself to do it. ". . . want a bath. That's all."

"In that case," he suggested playfully, reaching around her and taking the shirt from where she held it in front of her. With a gallant gesture, he swept her into his arms and started toward the cave. "M'lady's bath awaits!"

Setting her down beside the cave pool, he picked up a washcloth that had been left on a rock to dry. He dipped the cloth in the warm water and doused her body with scintillating rivulets that seemed to burn as they trickled over her feverish skin.

Slowly, carefully, gently, Brand washed their mingled perspiration from her body—her neck, her arms, her flat belly, and her full breasts. Then, when LaRaine's body heat had risen to a point where the warm bath water on her skin was the only thing keeping her internal temperature from bursting into flame, Brand slid his hands between her soft thighs to wash away the evidence of their lovemaking.

"Let me take care of you and protect you, Rainy," he said, lowering himself into the pool and holding out his hand for her to join him.

She didn't immediately take his hand. "Before, when you said . . ." Unable to look at him, she twisted her hands nervously. "I mean, just because we make . . ." She took a deep breath and tried again. "I just want you to know you don't have to feel obligated to say . . . uh . . . to say you love me," she said in a rush of words.

"Is that why you told me you love me?" he asked. "Because you felt obligated?"

Surprised he could even think such a thing, her head snapped up in denial. "Of course not!"

"Then why did you say it?"

"Because I lo—Why did you?"

"Because it's true," he said softly. "I love you, Rainy."

Her eyes widened. "You love me?"

Brand smiled. "How many times do I have to say it? I love you. Come, let me show you how much."

Her heart soaring, she took his hand and stepped into the pool with him, gliding into his arms. There was no further need for words. Their bodies were speaking, saying everything that needed to be said.

Brand's lips descended on LaRaine's, and she rose up to accept his kiss eagerly, wending her arms around his strong neck and pressing her breasts against his chest. The kiss was gentle, asking for and granting forgiveness for past differences. It was worshipful and loving, making a pledge more binding than any words either could have spoken.

Keeping his mouth fastened to her lips, he lowered her to a shelf on the edge of the pool that was only an inch deep in water. Her arms lingered around his neck, drawing his head down to her breast. Her nipples were tender and responded immediately to his sucking pressure as he drew on first one peak, then the other.

Slipping his hand into the glorious swell of her desire, he was met by gyrating, pulsing motion. Her body begged, pleaded to be united with his again. And Brand could not deny her the resplendent reward for which she appealed.

His entry was swift and sure, and her reception was just as certain, just as eager. Two bodies rising and falling in passionate harmony, her pain-driven ecstasy matched his thrusting urgency. Entwining her legs around his hips, she held him deep within the warmth of her, molding her hot, pliant flesh to his desire and greedily engulfing him within her raging core.

"Oh, Brand." Arching her body against his in a final burst of mind-shattering passion, she caressed his back and buttocks with urgency. Digging her nails into his corded muscles in wild demand, she burst in an eruption of sensuous feeling as his strength exploded within her.

Brand fell on her with a final shudder, his breathing still labored and irregular. "My sweet, sweet love," he panted against her ear. "I do love you."

"And I love you," she sighed, refusing to let this moment of happiness be spoiled by the sudden feeling that no matter how much they loved each other, this might be all they would ever have.

The more LaRaine saw of the heavily forested Ozark Mountains during the following two days, the more she could see how easy it would be for a person to just disappear into the landscape and never be heard of again. According to Brand, the Ozarks encompassed over fifty thousand square miles of the most rugged terrain between the Great Rockies and the Appalachians, and it stretched from St. Louis in the north to the Arkansas River in the south, and from Illinois in the east to Kansas in the west.

"There's a town two or three miles in that direction," Brand told her as they came to a road that crossed the path Flame's trail had led them along.

"I doubt she went that way. So far, she's skirted every other town."

Before he could answer, they were interrupted by the sound of galloping horses coming toward them from the town.

"Quick," Brand shouted, acting instinctively. "Get back." He slapped her horse's bottom and sent the animal scrambling into the brush.

"Why are we hiding?" LaRaine whispered when they reached safety in the shadowy woods and dismounted.

Brand held his finger to his lips. "Don't forget who you look like, Rainy," he said just as six fast-moving riders appeared in their sights.

LaRaine opened her mouth to speak, but Brand gave her a stern shake of his head and placed a steadying hand on her arm.

"She might've turned off along here," one of the riders shouted, slowing his heavily breathing horse to a walk and pointing at the path Brand and LaRaine had been on only moments before.

LaRaine snapped her head toward Brand, her eyes wide with fright. Though she said nothing, her mind raced with questions.

"Well, she won't get far," another rider answered, joining the first at the place the narrow trail intersected the road. "I'm sure I winged her."

A gasp of alarm escaped through LaRaine's lips before she could stop it. Clapping her hand over her mouth, she shifted her frightened gaze to Brand, certain she knew who the "she" was the man referred to.

His attention on the ground, a third man left the road and followed the trail several yards into the woods. Dismounting, he squatted down and wiped at something on the ground with his middle and index fingers. Holding them up to examine the tips, he nodded and lifted them for the others to see. "Fresh blood," he announced.

"Oh, Brand! They shot her. We've got to do something!"

"We don't know it's her they're after," he said softly, barely moving his lips. His eyes never leaving the riders, he placed his hand on his gun.

Accepting the blood as the proof he needed that their prey had left the road here, the searcher remounted and led the others up the trail, moving more cautiously in the hope they would find more clues.

Hardly daring to breathe, Brand and LaRaine

stayed hidden until they were certain the men were out of hearing. "Okay, they're gone."

"What are we going to do? They're going to hunt her down and kill her like an animal!"

"First of all, you don't know they're looking for Flame. It could be a wounded bobcat they're after. Or a wolf."

"Bobcats and wolves don't follow trails," LaRaine argued, the panic in her eyes wild. "They go through the woods."

"There's only one way to find out what's going on," Brand said, leading her and the horses in the opposite direction from the one the men had taken and parallel to the road. "I'm going to town and ask."

"That's a good idea!" LaRaine mounted her horse. "Let's go."

"It's too dangerous. You might be spotted. You'd better wait here." He scanned the area for a safe hiding place for her.

LaRaine looked around nervously, not a bit happy about the idea of staying here alone. "No one will see me if I keep my hair covered and my face hidden."

Brand shook his head. "We can't take the chance. If Flame is the one who's got them so riled up, no one's going to believe me when I tell them the truth about you—Pinkerton agent or not."

Spotting an outcropping of rocks ahead, he said, "I won't be gone more than a couple of hours. You'll be safe if you just keep out of sight."

LaRaine looked over her shoulder. "What about those men? What if they come back?"

A wave of foreboding swelled in Brand's chest. He'd feel better if he could take her with him. But he just couldn't risk it. If anything went wrong, they could find themselves in the midst of an angry mob—if what he suspected was true. And if she was spotted, he would automatically be taken for one of Flame's gang, and he would be in no position to protect her at all.

No. He had to go alone. It was the only way. He would slip into town unnoticed and find out what was happening, then come right back here. "It'll be dark soon. They'll probably camp along the trail they're following. You'll be okay," he promised, leading her and her horse between the tall rocks to a hollowed-out shelter at the bottom of a small cliff. "This is perfect. No one can see you unless they're right here. And if anyone approaches, you'll hear them coming. We'd better check your pistols before I leave," he said, taking a revolver from her holster.

Telling herself he was probably right, LaRaine allowed him to settle her in the cozy hideaway. "You'll hurry, won't you?" she asked.

Brand gathered her into his arms and laid her head on his chest. "I'll be back before you know it. And when I get here, I won't leave you again. Try to get a little rest while I'm gone. It'll make the time go faster."

Fighting the tears that threatened to expose her weakness, LaRaine listened to the steady thump of his heart against her ear and drew strength from it. "Tell me one more time that you love me," she asked.

"Can you doubt it? You're my heart, my very soul. Until you came into my life, I was only an empty shell of a man. I moved through the days and nights like a puppet, doing the job I was trained for, but never allowing myself to know anyone or for them to know me. But you've changed all that. Suddenly, because of you, everything I do, every

302

breath I take, has meaning. You've given me life. Yes, I love you, my sweet girl. Don't ever doubt it."

"Brand, I'm afraid," she admitted, her sense of dread only intensified by his words.

"Of what?"

"I love you so much, and I'm afraid if you leave me now, you won't be back."

A surge of fear like nothing he'd ever felt—even during the war—rose in him, and he tightened his hold on her. "I'll be back, Rainy. The devil himself won't stop me from coming for you!"

Part Three - The Journey's End

"Loving means to love that which is unlovable; and forgiving means to pardon the unpardonable."

—G. K. Chesterton

Chapter Nineteen

"Papa, why didn't you tell me before?" LaRaine asked her dying father, the shock almost tangible on her lightly freckled face. "Why didn't you tell me before now that I have a twin sister?"

"I couldn't. I just couldn't," Thomas Ashby said weakly, using his last bit of strength to confess his duplicity to his daughter, the daughter he had loved as his own, the daughter who had thought she was his natural child until only a few minutes before.

Thomas turned his head away from the bright, redheaded girl who was the light of his life, the hurt in her expression too much for the dying man to bear. "Oh, honey, I wanted to. Every day since that night I brought you home with me, I've wanted to tell you. But how could I? It would have killed your mama, and I didn't dare take that chance. She loved you so," he choked, his tears blinding him to all but his own guilt and loneliness. "She always believed you were hers." He swallowed, his voice growing softer by the word, so soft that LaRaine had to lean over him to hear what he was saying.

"But, Papa! Mama's been gone for six years. Why didn't you tell me about my sister after she died?" she asked the man whose health was deteriorating

307

before her eyes.

"I was afraid you'd hate me for what I did, Daughter. I still am, but I can't leave this world without having you know the truth."

"Oh, Papa, I would never hate you!" LaRaine cried, unmindful of the tears running down her cheeks as she grasped the man's face in her hands and forced him to look at her. "I love you, Papa! You've got to believe that!"

"But I left that poor little baby in a filthy shack with her pitiful, beaten mother and vile father." Clutching LaRaine's arm frantically, Thomas suddenly rose up in his bed, showing a desperate surge of energy. "I tried, LaRaine! I tried to think of something I could do for that poor baby!"

Allowing LaRaine to lower him back to his pillow, he went on speaking, the self-contempt harsh in his gravelly voice. "But I didn't try hard enough, did I? I didn't really try at all." He seemed to speak more to himself than to his daughter. "I was too afraid."

"Shh, Papa. Sleep now. We'll talk later."

"What was I thinking?" he went on as if she hadn't spoken. "Your mother would have taken that baby to her breast just like she did you. She never turned down anyone who needed her."

His tone growing more urgent, he tried to explain. "But I didn't realize it then! We'd been married such a short time, and she was so young and so frail. I was afraid she would insist on having another baby if she learned hers had died. And the doctor said she wouldn't survive another pregnancy. He said it was only a miracle she didn't die with her first one. So I left one tiny baby there and took only one. It was in my power to save you both, but I was afraid that saving her would kill your mother," he groaned, closing his eyes as if to sleep. "I just rode away and left her to live a miserable life."

"Papa, you sleep now. We'll talk later. You need your rest," she soothed, patting the gnarled hand that still gripped hers anxiously.

"Find her, LaRaine," Thomas rasped urgently, though he continued to keep his eyes closed tight, as if trying to blot out the memories. "Find your sister and ask her to forgive me! Make her understand," he pleaded pitifully.

"I'll try, Papa. I'll try," she murmured.

"Promise me, Daughter. Give me your word that you'll find her and make up to her for the wrong I did her."

"I promise, Papa," LaRaine cried. "I'll find her and help her no matter what it takes."

"I promise, Papa! I promise!" LaRaine mumbled, tossing her head from side to side on the rocky ground. "No matter what it takes . . . No matter wha—"

She bolted upright, suddenly wide awake, her eyes wild with confusion. The dream had been so real, so vivid, that she halfway expected to find herself beside her father's bed in her home in Virginia.

Her rocky surroundings immediately jolted her back to the present, and she panicked. How long had she slept? It had been early dusk when she lay down and now it was almost dark. Should Brand be back by now?

Scrambling to her feet, she dug into her jacket pocket and pulled out her father's pocket watch. Disappointment rocked her. Brand hadn't been gone thirty minutes yet, and he'd said it would be a couple of hours. She hadn't meant to sleep when she lay down, only to rest for a few minutes, but she must have fallen asleep almost right after he left.

A breaking twig and the crackling whisper of

leaves being crushed broke into her thoughts. It sounded suspiciously like someone moving through the brush toward her. Jamming the watch back into her pocket, she drew her revolver and cautiously peeked out of her shelter.

"Flame!" she cried, holstering the gun and racing out to meet her sister. "Where did you come from? I've been so worried."

Flame, who was filthy and drawn looking, gave her sister a sarcastic grin. "Why's that? The day comes when I can't outsmart a posse, I'll turn in my guns for sure."

"So it *was* you they were after," LaRaine exclaimed. "What happened? One of them said he shot you!"

Glancing around nervously, Flame shrugged. "It's nothin'. Where's Colter?" she asked suspiciously.

"He went to town to find out who those men were chasing—and why." She put her arm around Flame's shoulders. "Come over here and rest. You look exhausted. Have you eaten?" She guided her back to the rock shelter and took the horse's reins from her. "I'll get you something."

Turning away from Flame, she dug in her own saddlebags for food. "Are you sure you're not hurt? They found blood."

Flame chuckled. "I know. I used a dead rabbit to leave them a trail that'll take them on a nice little trip. Then I doubled back on them."

"Here," LaRaine offered, handing Flame a piece of hardtack. "Eat this. And tell me what happened. Why were they chasing you?"

Flame bit into the biscuit hungrily. "As usual, you had all the luck."

"Me? What are you talking about?"

Flame shook her head in disgust. "When I realized you and that bloodhound, Colter, wasn't gonna give up, I come up with a plan to get rid of you both, permanent."

"What kind of plan?"

"I rode into town an' robbed the bank!" she announced.

"Why would you do something so stupid?"

Flame laughed at the stunned expression on LaRaine's face. "And to make sure they knew exactly who was robbin' them, I didn't wear my hat."

"But why?"

"Then I rode outta town the way I come in, leavin' them a trail a two-year-old could follow. I figgered to meet up with you an' Colter comin' toward me."

Confused, LaRaine stared openmouthed at her sister.

"I thought I'd leave the loot where you'd find it about the same time the posse got to where you were, but . . ."

LaRaine stiffened. "You were going to set me up to be arrested?"

A surge of shame tightened in Flame's chest, but her expression didn't give her away. "What'd ya expect? It was your own fault. If you'd left when I gave ya the chance . . ." Her voice broke. "I mean, what'd ya expect?"

"Well, what happened?" LaRaine asked, her hurt obvious. "Why didn't you go through with it?"

"Somewhere, maybe when I was leadin' the posse on their wild-goose chase through the woods, we musta crossed paths. Anyhow, I missed you. When I came across signs that you'd already been there," she went on, alternating between poor and proper grammer without realizing it. "I left a trail that made it look like I'd kept goin' in the other direction, then doubled back this way, thinkin' you'd probably run

311

into the posse anyway."

Standing up, LaRaine walked away from where her sister sat. "I'm sorry to disappoint you, Flame," she said evenly, clenching her fists so tightly that her fingernails dug into her palms. Never had she felt such hurt or such anger. What a fool she'd been to have thought Flame would automatically love her because they were twin sisters. "But as you can see, they didn't see us and I wasn't arrested—or hung, which really would have suited your purposes, wouldn't it?"

Unable to comprehend the feelings of shame that rocked over her, Flame stood up and walked over to her sister. "Why couldn't you just go back to where you came from and leave me alone?"

Wheeling on her sister, LaRaine cursed, "Dammit! Because I loved you! And because I thought you—" She stopped herself. "Never mind what I thought." She turned away from her twin and stared woodenly at the ground. "I think you'd better leave, Flame. You don't have to worry about me bothering you again."

Loneliness like she'd never felt before seized Flame, and she lifted a hand to place it on LaRaine's shoulder. Then she let it drop. "Yeah, you're right. I'd better go."

Taking up her horse's reins, she put a foot in the stirrup, then hesitated. "I'm sorry, LaRaine," she said hoarsely. "I wish it coulda turned out different for the two o' us."

"Just go, Flame," LaRaine ordered through teeth clamped together, her anger with herself as great as her anger with her sister. What a fool she'd been. How presumptuous of her to have assumed she could change Flame—or that Flame would even want to change. "Just go."

LaRaine heard a soft moan, then a thud as something hit the ground, then nothing. Bewildered, she turned around.

"Flame!" she cried, rushing to where her sister lay on the ground beside her horse. "What is it?" she asked, her vow to have nothing more to do with Flame forgotten.

Flame opened her eyes and frowned sheepishly. "I guess I passed out," she slurred, explaining the obvious. "I'm okay now." She started to get up.

Helping her to sit up, LaRaine's hand touched something warm and sticky on Flame's arm. "You're bleeding!" she accused. "You have been shot, haven't you?"

"Just a nick. Nothin' serious. The bullet went clean through. It didn't hit the bone."

"Let me look at it," LaRaine demanded, tearing Flame's jacket and shirt back to expose her upper arm before Flame could stop her.

"It'll be fine!" Flame said, shaking off LaRaine's hands. "I gotta get goin'."

"Not yet, you're not. Not until I clean and bandage that arm of yours. You stay right where you are and I'll go find some water to clean it. There ought to be a stream nearby."

As soon as LaRaine was out of sight, Flame dragged herself to her feet and started to mount her horse.

"Hold it right there, lady," a gravelly voice ordered from the shadows.

Damn! she swore, whirling around to face the voice. *There's only two of 'em,* she thought, her hand immediately dropping to her holstered gun. But her wound made her slow, and before she could touch the gun, she heard the click of two gun hammers being pulled back.

313

"Don't try it."

Flame raised her hands.

"Well, I'll be goddamned!" another voice said. "Are you who I think you are?"

"That depends on who you think I am, mister," Flame answered evenly, nothing in her voice betraying the tremor within.

"Whoee, it's you all right!" the man laughed, approaching Flame from the darkness. He was young and skinny, with raw, acne-ravaged skin. "Can you believe our luck? We was gonna jest pick us up a coupla exter hosses 'n mebbe a lil cash, and we done stumbled onta Flame Rider! What ya worth now, Flame? 'Bout two, three thousand?"

"I think you gentlemen have mistaken me for someone else," Flame said, experimenting with pretending to be LaRaine. "My name is LaRaine Ashby," she told them.

"Listen at 'er talk. Hell, I bet with that fancy way o' talkin' she'd be able ta talk to the President o' the U.S. o' A!" the older man laughed loudly.

"Where'd ya learn ta talk like that, Flame?"

"I told you, I'm not Flame Rider."

"Well, whoever ya are, yer prettier'n anythin' we seen in a hellova long time," the younger man said, reaching out to grab a fistful of Flame's long russet hair, which had fallen out of her hat when she had passed out. "Mmm-mmm," he grunted, licking his lips voraciously. "Will ya look't all that hair? Whadda ya say we have us a lil fun, Flame? B'fore we take ya in ta collect our reward money?"

"I have no intention of having any fun, as you put it, with the likes of you."

"Sure ya do, Flame," the older man said with a leer, coming toward her with a rope tied in a lynching knot. His smell was vile and his face covered

314

with a straggly, untrimmed gray beard.

Hitting her in the middle of her chest with the heel of his hand, he knocked her into a helpless sprawl on the ground. "Put the noose 'round 'er neck, and t'other end over that branch, boy."

"We ain't gonna hang 'er, are we?" the pimply-faced younger man worried, but he did as he had been told all the same.

"She's worth jest 's much dead 's 'live, 'n she'll be a hellova lot easier to handle that way. But we'll wait till we've had some fun with 'er first. How long's it been since ya had a man, Flame?" he said, fumbling with his urine-stained fly.

"Not long enough," Flame said, feeling the strain on her neck where the boy had stretched the rope taut over the tree limb. Bending her knees, she sat up and grabbed at the rope, scooting back toward the tree trunk, but the boy tightened the rope the closer she got. Trying not to think about the noose, she searched the clearing for a way out of her predicament, but at no time did it occur to her to be afraid—or that she might die. She was mad, but refused to be afraid!

Flame was mad all right—madder than hell! Mad at the two who thought they were men enough to take in Flame Rider. Mad at herself for being taken off guard. And most of all, mad at her sister who had left her to face them alone—again. Just the way she had left her to be abused by Cutter Doyle and his sons. She struggled to her knees.

"Get back down there, whore," the old man ordered, kicking her on the chin and tumbling her down into the dirt.

Standing over Flame, his legs straddling her hips, the old man bent over to unfasten her breeches. "Don't you touch me, you filthy bastard!" she

315

screamed, bending her knees to bring her feet up between the man's legs in a violent thrust.

"Eieee," the man yowled, grabbing himself and falling away from her. "That does it! She hangs," he grunted, giving the rope a purposeful yank and pulling Flame's head a few inches off the ground, stretching her neck painfully. Already finding it impossible to breathe, Flame forgot everything but saving herself. Now, she was afraid.

"Okay, okay," she rasped breathlessly. "Just let up on the rope!"

"Too late, sweetheart. The boy here is gonna have his fun 'n then we're gonna watch ya dangle. In the meantime, yer gonna stay like ya are, gittin' jest 'nuff air ta stay awake, and knowin' all the time the end is comin'," he gloated, gripping his injured pride with one hand. "Git on 'er, boy,"

His eyes glistening, the boy grinned and dropped his trousers around his ankles. Flopping on Flame's prostrate form, he fumbled with her pants, finally opening them and tearing them up the middle to expose the target of his lust.

"You gawdamned scum," Flame hissed, biting the boy's lip when he tried to claim her mouth with his own. "The only way you're gonna stick me is if I'm dead, so ya'd better git on with the hangin'," she laughed, sinking the long knife she had secretly taken from her boot into the boy's left side and twisting it cruelly.

The boy raised up and looked into Flame's face, even more shocked by her smile than by the fact of his own death. He gasped and rolled off her body to lie jerking and twitching convulsively, even after his heart ceased to beat.

"Ya witch! Ya whore o' Satan!" the older man screeched wildly, yanking the rope and snapping

316

Flame's head back, hauling her first to a sitting position, then kneeling, then standing, then nothing. She lost consciousness.

She didn't hear the primitive cry that resounded piercingly across the dark clearing from the direction where LaRaine had vanished. She didn't hear the gun shots that echoed in the night. Nor did she see the self-appointed hangman double in half with the force of five bullets that penetrated his chest one after the other, coming so fast they had the eerie sound of one continuous shot. She would have been amazed to realize that the man continued to stand through the whole barrage, though each perfectly aimed shot forced him backward and was enough to guarantee his death. But still he stood, until the sixth bullet was fired into his head. At last he lost his hold on the strangling rope, toppling over onto his face—dead.

"Flame, Flame," LaRaine screamed, running toward her sister, who seemed to be dissolving before her eyes, her knees and body folding baroquely into a crumpled heap on the ground. "Don't be dead. You can't be dead. I won't allow you to die!" she cried, her hands frantically loosening the noose around her sister's neck.

Reaching down to feel for a pulse and finding none, she shook Flame violently. "No, damn you! You're not dead! You're not!" Refusing to accept her sister's death, she opened her own mouth over Flame's and tried to force life back into her limp body.

"Breathe, dammit! Breathe!" she demanded over and over again between breaths.

Suddenly, a soft moan against her mouth answered her prayers. "You're alive! My God! You're alive!" she cried, almost blinded by the torrent of tears coursing down her cheeks.

"Are you cryin'?" Flame croaked hoarsely. "Why?"

LaRaine nodded her head tearfully. "Because I'm happy. I thought I had lost you for good this time."

"Is that what a lady does? Cry when she's happy? Sounds dumb to me," Flame coughed, attempting to rise up, but finding the effort too much and letting her head drop back to the comfort and security of LaRaine's lap.

"Yes, it is," LaRaine agreed, and cried all the more.

"My throat hurts." Flame sounded like a sick child talking to her mother.

"I know it does. But everything will be all right now. I'm never going to let anyone hurt you again," she promised, clutching Flame's weak body to her breast. "They won't hurt you again," she crooned softly. "Never again." Her voice was like a stranger's. Her expression was primitive, yet her arms were gentle around her twin sister. "I'm going to protect you from now on. I won't leave you again."

She knew now that she would never be able to turn her sister over to the law. No matter what Flame had done in the past, LaRaine knew she couldn't play a part in anything that might result in her sister being hung. She couldn't take that chance.

Wiping her hand across Flame's forehead, LaRaine asked, "Can you travel? We've got to leave before someone comes in response to the gunfire."

"I'm okay," Flame answered hoarsely, studying LaRaine, her expression confused. No one had ever cried for Flame before, and she was touched by something so comforting, so warm, that she didn't try to understand what it was.

"Good." LaRaine stood up and drew Flame to her

feet. "Let's get you some different clothes and leave before someone comes."

"What happened?" Flame asked, her puzzled eyes traveling to where the slain men lay in pools of blood and dirt. "I 'member killin' the young one, but I don't recall anything else. Did I kill him, too?" she asked intently, pointing to the other man.

"No. It wasn't you," LaRaine said with finality.

"Then who?" The light dawned in Flame's eyes. "You? Was it you?"

"Yes," LaRaine confirmed, surprised that she only felt mild regret. "Don't think about them. Have a drink of water and we'll leave." She held the cup under Flame's lips.

"I could use a whiskey." She reached up to run her fingers over the ugly red rope burn around her neck.

"Water's all you'll get from me. No whiskey," La-Raine answered sternly.

"Now this is what we'll do," LaRaine started, handing Flame the cup and going to her saddlebags. "First of all, I'm going to write a note and stuff it into one of their pockets." LaRaine tilted her head in the direction of the dead bodies. "It's going to tell the world that those two lynched the famous Flame Rider and that her men found out and retaliated by killing the lynchers. We'll say they've taken Flame's body home to bury. Then we'll disguise ourselves and head west to start a new life as two new people. What do you think?" she asked anxiously, certain that Flame had reached a point where she would go along with her plans. What other choice did she have? What choice did either of them have?

Flame said nothing. She only stared incredulously at her sister.

"Well, do you have a better idea?" LaRaine huffed, the desperateness of their situation beginning to tell on her patience.

"You really think anyone's gonna believe a note sayin' I'm dead?" Flame asked, her husky voice still not her own.

"Why wouldn't they believe it? Especially if Flame Rider disappears off the face of the earth?"

"I thought you were gonna turn me in," Flame said warily.

"I can see now that the risk would be too great. Even after what you tried to do to me, I can't take the chance that you'll be found guilty and hung. So, are you willing to try this, or do we keep on our original course?"

"I guess it's worth a try," Flame cracked roughly. *I couldn't go through with my other plan now. Not when you saved my life. Not when you cried for me.* "Like you said, what other choice do I have? 'Cause, I promise you, I don't ever want to feel a rope around my neck again!"

"Fine. Then let's go." Doing her best to ignore the unbearable pang of desolation that gripped her, she took out paper and pencil from her saddlebags. Then, with businesslike motions, she sat down to write the note that would mark the end of her hopes for a future with Brand Colter.

"DER MARSHEL," it began in her roughest, most childish scrawl. "THES HER TOO SCONDRILS DON LYNCHED AR FREIND FLAME RIDER, SO WE DON THEM IN. WE TUK FLAME HOM TOO BE BARRYED NEX TO HER MA. FLAMES FREINDS."

"That ought to do it, don't you think?" LaRaine said, showing her handiwork to her sister.

"Looks good," Flame acknowledged, not admitting that she couldn't read the words on the page.

"All right, that's all done," LaRaine said, forcing

herself not to gag while cramming the note inside the vest of one of the dead men. "Let's go. We need to be gone before Brand gets back." She pushed her own hair up under her hat, then turned to help Flame cover hers.

"He's gonna come after us, you know."

LaRaine's bottom lips trembled and she turned away from Flame. There was no time now to mourn what might have been. She had a responsibility to Flame and to her father's memory. "He'll think I'm dead and he'll . . ."

As an afterthought, she reached under her hat and withdrew a strand of hair from her own head. Her face twisted with distaste, she entangled the red strands into the lynch rope left on the ground, then pried open one of the men's fists and wrapped hair around it. "That ought to convince him," she said, her heart breaking into tiny pieces inside her chest.

"Why're you doin' this for me, LaRaine?" Flame asked, puzzled by her sister's unselfish actions. Almost as puzzled as she was by her own confused feelings for the twin sister she had sworn to hate, but didn't, couldn't.

Her eyes glistening with tears, LaRaine smiled sadly and shook her head.

"Why, LaRaine?"

Boosting Flame onto her horse, she said, "That's what sisters do, Flame. They love each other and stand together, no matter what the cost."

Chapter Twenty

By the time LaRaine and Flame arrived in Galveston a month and a half later, there was little about either sister that would have suggested to anyone that the notorious Flame Rider was in their midst. Copper-colored hair had been darkened to brown and pulled back into severe chignons; rough men's clothing had been replaced with modest, decidedly feminine attire; and their recognizable horses had been traded for a pair of matched blacks with a buggy. Though they both had weapons secreted in their reticules and dress pockets, as far as the world was concerned, they were exactly what they seemed to be—twin sisters who had lost their parents on the way to Galveston from their ancestral home in Kentucky.

Once they had made the decision to go south instead of west because of the approaching winter, their long trip from Missouri seemed to pass quickly. Every waking hour, both in camp and on the trail, had been spent perfecting Flame's manners and grammar, as well as creating new identities—down to the slightest detail. Since it was not known that Flame Rider had a twin sister, LaRaine had suggested they play the fact that they were identical twins—dressing alike, wearing their hair alike, moving alike, talking alike, actually drawing attention to themselves rather than hiding the fact. They adopted similar mannerisms, speech patterns, and by the time they checked into Mrs. Flanagan's Boarding House for Single Ladies, they were confident no one would be able to tell them apart. And hopefully, no one would believe they could possibly be criminals.

"Oh, Mrs. Flanagan," LaRaine smiled bravely. "I don't know what we would have done if you hadn't had rooms for us."

"Ah, ye poor brave lasses," the rotund Irish woman responded, tears of sympathy gushing down her round red cheeks. "Ta think what ye've been through, and then ta arrive in Galveston and find that yer own dear uncle has left the city, leavin' ye not only parentless but without a place to lay yer dear heads."

"We were fortunate to find you," Flame added slowly, taking care that her articulation and grammar were perfect. "To think what might have happened to us if we hadn't spotted your lovely establishment when coming from our uncle's abandoned home."

Mrs. Flanagan smiled, pleased but embarrassed, her pudgy face growing redder by the moment. "I shudder ta think about it," she agreed, jiggling all of her portly flesh comically as she demonstrated. "Will ye be stayin' in Galveston? Or do ye think ye'll be goin' back ta Kentucky—now that ye've no one here?"

"Oh, we plan to stay here," LaRaine answered quickly. They had already decided to settle in Galveston, comfortable with the fact that if they had to get away in a hurry, they could leave for California, the East Coast, or even Europe, at a moment's notice. "There's no longer anything for us in Kentucky," she added dramatically. "Our home was ravaged and destroyed by the Yankees. Papa was bringing us to Galveston for a new start."

"But how will ye live?" the landlady asked bluntly. These hardly seemed like young women who would be able to take care of themselves, much less earn a living. In fact, she wouldn't have been surprised to discover that neither of them had ever done a day's work in her life.

"We haven't had a chance to make plans that far ahead," LaRaine said. "You must remember we have only known about our uncle for a few hours. We do have a small amount of money that Papa left us. It should take care of us until we can find work."

"Work!" the landlady hooted. "Sure and what would sweet young angels like yerselves do fer work? No, we'd better be findin' ye husbands. Rich husbands. And fast! Shouldn't be too hard, not when yer such lovely lasses."

"That won't be necessary, Mrs. Flanagan," Flame interjected anxiously.

"But we do appreciate your concern," LaRaine coughed, holding a handkerchief to her eyes, seeming to be trying to restrain her tears. "We do have enough money to tide us over, and even enough to invest in a small business of some sort—perhaps a small restaurant or a dress shop." She and Flame had decided they would use the stolen money from Flame's last robbery to finance their new start, but that eventually it, as well as everything else she had stolen, would be paid back to the banks from which it had come.

"Well, I suppose that sounds all right. I just couldn't see the two o' ye takin' in washin' or cleanin' other people's houses. Ye'd better be puttin' yer money in the bank right away though, before someone steals it from ye. And don't be tellin' no one else 'bout the money yer dear deceased da left ye. There's wicked ones in this city who'll be doin' anythin' ta steal a person's valuables," she warned ominously.

"We've already taken care of that, Mrs. Flanagan," Flame assured the woman. "But we will be careful and watch out for those evil people. We're very fortunate that we found Mrs. Flanagan, aren't we, Beth?" Flame said to LaRaine.

"Yes, Faith, we are. It's quite comforting to know there are still a few kind, unselfish people in the world," LaRaine said, really meaning her words and unable to stop the single tear that trickled down the smooth, lightly freckled skin of her cheek.

"Oh, darlin', don't ye be cryin' no more," Mrs. Flanagan said, unable to control the flow of her own tears as she hugged LaRaine to her large bosom. "Mabel Flanagan won't be lettin' nothin' else bad happen ta ye. Ye can count on that."

"You're too kind," LaRaine replied, feeling badly for deceiving the generous landlady.

"Now, let me take ye ta yer rooms. Yer real lucky, since right now two o' me best are vacant. And they're right next ta each other. With a connectin' door in between—just like they have at the Tremont Hotel!" she added proudly. "Me late husband, Harold, God rest his soul, put it in fer me. Most o' the time it stays locked though, so I'll be glad it'll be gettin' a bit o' use fer once."

Mrs. Flanagan continued her cheerful chatter all

the way up the narrow staircase and down the long hall leading to the two rooms of which she spoke. Taking them into the first room at the end of the hall, she stepped back to let them admire her handiwork. Though the room was small, it was sparkling clean and gay, with a ruffled yellow spread on the narrow bed and matching window curtains that fluttered in the afternoon breeze.

"And over here's the other room," Mrs. Flanagan announced grandly, swinging open the connecting door to reveal the pale-green counterpart of the room in which the three women were standing.

"They're lovely, Mrs. Flanagan," LaRaine said, the pleasure obvious on her travel-weary face. How long had it been since she had slept in a real bed?

A long time, she thought. *Not since Brand and I . . .* LaRaine closed her eyes for a moment, trying to gather her strength, trying to forget memories the bed had brought to mind, trying not to think about Brand Colter or the feel of his body pushing hers into the softness of the mattress. *How long until I forget? Will I ever stop longing for the feel of him, the smell of him, the taste of him?*

"Beth, are you listening to me?" Flame giggled, touching LaRaine's arm to remind her where she was.

"Of course, I am," LaRaine smiled, placing a hand affectionately over the fingers on her arm. "What is it?"

"The yellow room. Can I have the yellow room?" Flame pressed excitedly, almost jumping up and down like a little girl.

"Of course, you can. The green will be perfect for me." Flame's eagerness eased some of her personal pain. "Mrs. Flanagan, the rooms are lovely, so, if you don't mind, I think my sister and I could use some time to ourselves—to rest and to talk about what we're going to do. You understand, don't you?"

"Of course I do. So don't ye be worryin' yerself 'bout it. I won't be botherin' ye again till suppertime—we eat at five o'clock sharp. I'll have me nephew, Patrick, bring up yer things before he takes yer buggy 'round back and beds yer horses down fer the night."

"Thank you," Flame called cheerfully after the retreating landlady, then ran to flop herself in the middle of the yellow-covered bed in her room. "Isn't it beautiful, LaRaine? I mean, *Beth!* Isn't it the most beautiful room you've ever seen in your whole life?"

"Yes, it's beautiful," LaRaine replied, wondering again about the deprived life her sister had led before their meeting. "And so are you," she added, realizing again how Flame's very being seemed to have changed. It wasn't just her speech, her hair, her clothing, or her manners. It was something else. It was as if a tiny light inside her, never permitted to shine before, was at last free to cast its beam all around her. She was like a child discovering something new and wonderful every day, every waking moment. In fact, that's how LaRaine thought of her—as a child. A child to be nurtured, protected and loved. The child of her own she would never have.

"Am I? Am I really beautiful?" Flame asked in astonishment. "No one ever told me that before."

"That's because you were around fools too blind to see true beauty." With a teasing gleam in her eyes, LaRaine added, "And I wouldn't be surprised if your old ways scared off more than a few admirers along the way."

"I've never had a room of my own. Did you know that? I never even had my own bed—not a real one anyway." Flame's expression took on the look of sadness that LaRaine had come to recognize as a sign she was thinking of her terrible childhood.

"Well, you've got one now. And so do I. Why don't we both lie down on our very own beds and see if we can take a little nap before Mrs. Flanagan calls us to supper," LaRaine suggested, again talking to Flame as if she were her daughter rather than her sister.

LaRaine couldn't put her finger on the exact moment when their relationship had changed from wary opponents, to trusting friends, to loving sisters, to what they had now; but she was aware that Flame's dependence on her had increased daily since the hanging.

"Can we leave the door open?" Flame asked, totally unaware of how she had changed on the inside. Her laugh was embarrassed. "Just until I get used to the room," she added.

"We'll leave it open as long as you like. I'll ask Mrs. Flanagan to take it off the hinges altogether, if that's what you want," LaRaine offered teasingly.

"Would you really? Would you have the door taken down if I wanted?" This was all so new to Flame. In all her life there had never been one person who had loved her, who had cared what she wanted, who had asked nothing in return. Oh, there had been her mother. But she'd been so abused and overworked herself that she'd had little time to display love for anyone. And after her mother had died, there had been no one—no one to love her even a little bit.

Now there was LaRaine—LaRaine, who thought she was beautiful; LaRaine, who loved her in spite of the terrible things she had done in the past; LaRaine, who protected her; LaRaine who didn't stop caring for her if she accidentally said ain't instead of isn't, or forgot and used an unacceptable expletive when she was angry; LaRaine, who had saved her from being arrested and from the scavengers who had tried to hang her; and LaRaine, who had given up the man she loved for her.

"I'd ask her," LaRaine confirmed, eyes twinkling mischievously. "Of course, the late Harold Flanagan, God rest his soul," she quoted Mrs. Flanagan and rolled her eyes heavenward, "just might turn over in his grave!"

"I wouldn't want that to happen. I'll just leave it open and put something against it," Flame said, shoving her room's only chair over to hold the door. She lay down on her bed and looked through the open doorway where she could see that LaRaine had already taken off her bonnet and was lying back on a green sham-covered pillow. "Are we really going to open a restaurant or dress shop? I'm not much of a cook or seamstress, you know."

"I know," LaRaine said with a tired yawn. "We'll talk about it later, when we're both not so exhausted," she mumbled, drifting into a fitful slumber, filled with jumbled visions of trains, Brand Colter, Whit and Slidell Ruston, hundreds of redheaded women hanging from wooden gallows, and horrible, faceless men carrying enormous ropes tied in nooses.

In the end, LaRaine and Flame, calling themselves Beth and Faith Morgan, decided to open a dress shop that dealt exclusively in fine, ready-made garments imported from Europe. When they considered their other alternatives, they still felt Galveston was as safe as any United States city would be. But as far as choosing between a restaurant and a dress shop, they decided that an elegant shop would attract only rich women, women who had probably never heard of Flame Rider or seen a poster bearing her likeness—while a restaurant would serve all sorts of people, including lawmen, outlaws, and bounty hunters who might see through their disguises.

It had been six months since the exclusive House of Fashion had opened its doors on Avenue D in the heart of Galveston, and business had continued to increase rapidly. Word had quickly spread of the chic, one-of-a-kind garments the shop offered, and it was no time at all before the city's most influential wives were competing to be the first to pay outlandish prices for the latest extravagant styles imported from Europe by the Morgan sisters. In fact, it became the fashion for the rich women to try to outdo one another with the amount they paid for their *Paris-designed* garments. Imitations and copies would not do, so these special gowns had to come from the House of Fashion—no other shop.

LaRaine and Flame had quickly settled into a quiet life of hard work and complacent privacy. Under the pretense of being in mourning, they did not socialize, despite the fact that some of their wealthy patrons had sons they tried to introduce to the beautiful, brown-haired twins, who were obviously of excellent background. No one ever attempted to confirm or refute the story the reclusive sisters had told when they first arrived in the city in December. Obviously, it was true. Just look at their manners, their soft-spoken ways, the tasteful way they dressed, *and* the amount of money they had deposited in the bank as soon as they arrived in Galveston. Yes, there was no doubt these were women of breeding whose pride would not allow them to rely on their beauty to snare rich husbands to care for them. Instead, they had chosen to earn their own way, and could only be admired for it.

Though they had lived with Mrs. Flanagan for a few weeks, they had moved into a compact, three-room flat above their store as soon as it opened. There had simply been too many evenings when it was necessary for them to work late into the night, and it was too dangerous to travel the distance to Mrs. Flanagan's after dark. However, they did continue their close friendship with the motherly landlady and visited her each Tuesday evening for supper, no matter what demands their business put upon them.

It was one of those Tuesdays when Flame went to the post office with an envelope addressed to their Toronto solicitor. Though the sisters had been forced to use the stolen money to make their initial investment and pay their living expenses until their first shipment of merchandise could be imported from France, they had almost immediately been able to pay all of their personal and business expenses out of their incoming profits, as well as send an increasingly sizable check to the trusted solicitor in Canada every month.

Surprisingly, Flame had kept an accurate mental log of every bank she had robbed and the amount of each haul, and it was to these banks that the lawyer, a lifelong friend of Thomas Ashby's, would send the funds until all had been repaid. The payments were supposedly from a relative of Flame Rider's, a Timothy Doyle of Ireland, who had heard of his relative's crimes and wouldn't rest until he had made amends for the scandalous blemish on the name of Doyle.

Leaving the post office, Flame dashed along Avenue E with a new lightness in her step that couldn't be held back even by the foggy, gray morning air. The constant humidity in Galveston was a problem, but Flame and LaRaine had adjusted to it easily, to the point that Flame hardly noticed the weather at all, even though here was a thin coat of chilling mist on her cape.

Nor did she notice the man who had followed her the three blocks from Twentieth. But when she turned to head up Twenty-third, she suddenly became aware of a tall, black-clad figure coming up behind her.

When first coming to Galveston, Flame had found it difficult to muster the courage to go out alone, always fearing she would be recognized by someone on the street. Now the old fear was back—the feeling that she was being stared at, that someone knew who she really was.

Her step quickened, and she looked from side to side to see if there was anywhere she could go to escape her pursuer. *Not now! Not after all this time. I've been a good girl. Beth said it's all in the past. I've paid!* she cried silently to herself, wondering if she should break into a run and try to lose the man following her. *No, then he'd know I'm afraid.*

The man was drawing alongside her, and there was nothing she could do to escape his nearness. There was nowhere to go! Maybe, he would move right past her. Perhaps she was only imagining that he was following her. But in that horrifying moment, Flame knew this was not the case.

"Hello, Flame," he said, grasping her arm with strong fingers and bringing her to a halt.

The cry that rose in her throat was stifled by her own hand over her mouth. "I beg your pardon," she stammered, daring to look up into the man's dark, angry face.

Her eyes widened in horror, the enlarged pupils darkening her eyes almost to the point of eradicating the marble irises. *Brand Colter!* her mind screamed.

"I — You've made a mistake," she managed to say. "My name's not Flame." She was thankful for the full cape wrapped around her, since she was certain her heart was beating so hard he would have been able to see it throbbing and know she was lying.

Brand stared at her upturned face long and hard, startled by the girl's resemblance to LaRaine. Different hair, different eyes, no peculiar little brown speck in her left eye, a nose that turned up a little more, lips less full. Her voice even had a hoarseness to it that LaRaine's clear tones had never contained. But, God, how she reminded him of her. And how it made his heart ache to remember that if he had listened to her and taken her with him that last time he saw her, she would be alive today. But he hadn't, and she'd died a terrible death because of him.

"No, I guess you're not her," he sighed, releasing her arm. "I'm sorry if I frightened you. It's just that you look like someone I knew," he explained stiffly.

Not even taking the time to answer him, Flame broke into a run and left him. She didn't dare to look back for fear he would follow.

Of course it wasn't Flame, Brand scolded himself, staring after the frightened girl. *If I'd grabbed Flame like that, she would have pulled a gun on me, not just stand there and quake like that poor frightened sparrow did.*

He watched as the girl made her way up the street, wondering if he was ever going to be able to give up his search for Flame Rider and get on with his life. It he hadn't found her in six months, he probably never would.

Besides, what was the point? Finding Flame and seeing that she was brought to justice wasn't going to bring LaRaine back to him. And it wasn't going to rid him of this dead, hollow feeling that had consumed him ever since he'd found those two drifters' bodies where he'd left LaRaine all those months before.

The girl he was watching turned onto Avenue D and disappeared from his sight, and suddenly he was overwhelmed by the need to see her again. Obviously she wasn't Flame Rider, but her resemblance to LaRaine and Flame was so uncanny, that he just wanted one more look. Besides, he told himself as he started after her, he really ought to apologize for frightening her so badly.

His face wrinkled with pain, he dashed after the fleeing young woman, refusing to listen to the inner voice that warned him that he was only adding to his own torture by pursuing LaRaine's lookalike.

Her escape a panicked run, the girl vanished into a dress shop in the middle of the block just as he rounded the corner.

Seeing her slip out of sight, he suddenly grasped the futility of what he was doing and came to an abrupt stop. *I already scared the poor girl to death.*

All she needs is for me to burst into that shop after her. Face it, Colter, Rainy's dead, and you're never going to see her again.

Turning around and retracing the route to the post office where he had left his carriage, Brand morosely relived the moment he had learned of La-Raine's death. He had taken off like a madman, following the trail the posse had taken after Flame. He had been determined to find LaRaine's sister and make her pay for what had happened. But after five months of following every lead, he had finally admitted to himself that he was running in circles and that Flame had obviously evaded him.

He'd been in Galveston for two weeks now, having dragged himself home to heal and to regain his will to live. But though it made him feel good to see how glad his parents were to have him with them after so many years, he felt guilty for what he was putting them through with his depressed, almost lethargic actions. Yet, no matter how he tried, he couldn't shake himself out of the melancholia he had suffered since he lost LaRaine.

"Damn it! Why'd I have to see that girl? One more minute and I'd have already pulled away from the curb," he muttered furiously, stepping into his carriage and snapping the reins. "Seeing her made it all worse. This has got to stop! I can't go around accosting young women on the street. She's dead! And finding Flame won't bring her back. That's all there is to it. I've searched and mourned long enough. I've got to start living again," he scolded himself mercilessly. With concentrated determination, he turned his carriage toward Madame Belle's place on Post Office Street. *There's always someone there to help a man forget,* he remembered, thinking of the many bordellos in the notorious prostitution district.

"Maybe I'll just spend the next few days in bed with every whore I can find." *Maybe that'll erase her memory,* he prayed, knowing it wouldn't—knowing nothing could.

But now it was even worse. Now he had the memory of a second face that kept returning to his mind, the face of a dark-haired girl who looked more like LaRaine than any he had seen!

Chapter Twenty-one

"What's the matter?" LaRaine exclaimed when Flame came running into the shop, her breathing ragged and irregular as she gasped for air. Seeing her sister's face was red and damp with perspiration though it was cool outside, she hurried to meet her, certain she must be feverish. "You look as if you've seen a ghost! What is it? Are you ill?"

Guiding her to a chair and removing the damp cape, LaRaine quickly ascertained that Flame's skin was not only cool to the touch, but was actually cold and clammy. "Tell me what it is, Faith," she insisted. They had gotten into the habit of calling each other by their assumed names even when they were alone, as they were now.

Flame looked blankly at LaRaine, searching her own frantic mind for the words to explain her agitated state. What should she say? She couldn't tell her sister she had seen Brand Colter! Though LaRaine had never admitted it, Flame knew she still thought of him. She was certain that if they ever met, LaRaine wouldn't give him up again. And Flame knew she couldn't risk that. She couldn't let Brand Colter destroy her.

When Flame still didn't speak, LaRaine grew more worried. Shaking the breathless girl, she sternly ordered, "Tell me what it is, Faith. I can't help if I don't know what's troubling you."

"It's nothing. There's nothing troubling me," Flame answered haltingly, sucking in huge gulps of air with each word.

"Nothing!?! You come in here like the devil himself is chasing you and then expect me to believe nothing's wrong? Now, what is it?"

"I tell you, it's nothing!" Flame insisted, gathering her determination, speaking again when her heart had slowed to a more normal beat and her lungs finally were able to take in enough air. "I was just so excited about being able to make such a substantial payment that I ran all the way from the post office. I got winded, I guess," she explained weakly.

"You ran all the way from the post office? That's five and a half blocks away. That's the silliest thing I've ever heard of. Why would you do that? Are you certain it's nothing other than excitement?" she emphasized, one eyebrow raised suspiciously.

"That's it," Flame shrugged, hoping she seemed believable. "Actually, I had an idea and couldn't wait to tell it to you," she added quickly, forcing her facial expression to be excited and not desperate.

"Well, what is this idea that's so wonderful? It had better be good, to have you risk slipping on damp pavement and breaking your foolish neck," LaRaine said with a good-natured smile. She never could stay angry with Flame for long.

"Since business has been so good, can't we take our trip to Europe right away? We've always said we'd go when we could afford it. We could close the shop for a while—or get Patrick Flanagan's wife, Margie, to run things until we return. And our patrons won't mind waiting if they know we're buying more wonderful and extravagant gowns for them than ever before," she pushed eagerly.

"I suppose we can think about it. It would be nice to see more than a fashion doll or a plate of the dresses we have shipped in. Goodness knows, we pay enough for them that way. I doubt if it would be much more expensive to go to Paris and place our orders directly. Maybe we could make arrangements to go in August," LaRaine mused, immediately warming to the idea. It was something they had often talked of, but it had always been in the future. When their bills were paid.

"Not August," Flame protested ardently, her voice rising hysterically. "I meant right away before the weather gets too hot. In fact, tomorrow wouldn't be too soon," she added, forcing a laugh in an attempt to cover her skittishness. "I mean, aren't you tired of working so hard? Don't you think we deserve a rest? Please don't make me wait until August," she whined childishly.

"I just don't think we can go any sooner, love," LaRaine said, wondering why the girl was in such a hurry. But then, wasn't she always? Patience definitely wasn't one of Flame's virtues.

LaRaine knew it was her own fault her sister insisted on having everything "right this minute." Hadn't she been the one who had spoiled her dreadfully? In an attempt to ease her own feelings of responsibility for the terrible childhood her sister had lived, she had allowed, almost encouraged, Flame to become the child she'd always wanted, since she had vowed never to marry and leave her sister alone again.

Flame dropped her head in disappointment, frantically trying to figure another way to keep Brand Colter from finding LaRaine. "It was silly of me to suggest it, wasn't it?"

"No, not silly. It's a very good idea. A good businesslike idea—if we take our time and make all the plans in a sensible, adult fashion. We'll need to contact all of our clients and tell them we're going. They'll have certain things they'll want us to look for. In fact, the more I think about it, the more I think it could be a very profitable trip if we take our time and do it correctly."

"But we don't have to wait until August, do we?" Flame asked, the childish impatience in her voice attacking LaRaine's resistance.

"I suppose we could go a bit sooner. We could possibly have things in order by mid-July. Does that sound any better?"

"It would sound even better if you said the first of July," Flame teased coyly, looking pleadingly into LaRaine's eyes in a valiant effort to push the date even closer to the present. "Please."

"What am I going to do with you?" LaRaine laughed with all the warmth of an overly indulgent parent who has inexcusably spoiled a favorite child and knows it. "All right. We'll aim for the first week in July, but don't try to hold me to it. I'm not making any promises. If we can't be ready by then, it will simply have to be later in the month.

Is that understood?"

"Yes!" Flame cried, throwing her arms around LaRaine and hugging her excitedly. "We'll get everything done. You'll see," she promised, snatching up her cape and dashing up the stairs with all the energy of a ten-year-old. Now, all she had to do was keep Brand and LaRaine from finding out about each other for two more weeks.

The afternoon passed quickly, with Flame's needle moving more enthusiastically than ever before—making alterations and sewing special imported buttons and laces on dresses which were not lavish or unique enough for the shop's particular customers. She was determined to be on a ship bound for France on the first day of July!

The Morgan sisters closed their shop at six o'clock each evening, with the exception of Tuesday, when they pulled down the blind on the front door at four-thirty so they could drive to Mrs. Flanagan's on Avenue H for their weekly supper. As far as LaRaine was concerned, this night would be no different—trip or no trip.

"I'm not going to disappoint her, Faith. And that's that. We're going. Now, get your cape and hat and lock up while I see to the buggy and horses."

"She'll understand if we miss one Tuesday," Flame said. "I don't feel like going out. The weather's all foul and wet, and there's still so much to be done here. I hate to leave it. I won't be able to concentrate on another thing if I know it's here waiting for us when we get home," she reasoned, trying to sound terribly conscientious.

LaRaine stared at Flame, who stayed stubbornly

seated on her chair, her needle continuing to slip in and out of the material in her lap.

Listen to me giving her orders—as if I'm the parent and she's the child. I have to remember I'm not her mother. I'm her sister. And she's not really a child, no matter how much she seems like one to me. She's an adult. I've got to start letting her make her own decisions. What difference does it make if she doesn't want to go tonight? Mrs. Flanagan will certainly understand. Anyway, it might do us both good to have some time apart. We're probably together too much. Maybe if she had a suitor. Surely enough time has passed since Flame Rider made her torrid ride through Missouri. No one is going to even remember her name after all this time. Yes, that's it. I'll speak to some of our patrons about introducing her to a suitable young man. Mrs. Williams told me just the other day that Mrs. Colterelli has a handsome unmarried son who had just returned to Galveston. I'll see about getting him introduced to her.

It never occurred to LaRaine as odd that she gave no thought to finding a *suitable young man* for herself. That was just the way things were. As far as she was concerned, she had already had her chance at love and had given it up. Now she was destined to spend her life alone, with only the memories of a brief time spent with a tall, dark-haired man whose piercing blue eyes still haunted her dreams.

Ten minutes later, when LaRaine reentered the back room of the shop, she smiled to see that Flame hadn't budged and continued to concentrate on sewing a particularly large glittery button on a purple velvet hat. *Well, that's what I want, isn't it? She needs to be more independent. I've taught her what I know about the proper way to behave. Now I simply have to trust her to know what she wants to do.*

"Are you certain you don't want to come along? We'll miss your company."

"No, I'd rather stay here." Flame felt ashamed of her stubbornness, but she couldn't bear the idea of stepping outside the safe shop. She wished she could keep LaRaine inside, too—until they left for Europe.

"All right then," LaRaine said. "Be sure and lock the front door and don't open it for anyone." *Darn! There I go again. It's a good thing I'm not really a mother. I'd smother a child to death with my protectiveness,* she laughed at herself, feeling the pains of letting go as acutely as any real parent ever did. *Maybe it's the other way around. Maybe I'm the one who depends on her. Maybe I'm afraid she'll find out she doesn't need me as much as she thinks. Otherwise, why would I be so worried about leaving her for two hours?* "I'll tell Mrs. Flanagan that you send your love."

"Please do," Flame said, keeping her eyes on the work in her lap so LaRaine wouldn't sense the worry in her expression. "Drive carefully, and don't get to talking and stay out too late. You know I'll worry. Do you have your pistol?"

Who's the one who thinks she's the mother here, anyway? LaRaine asked herself silently.

"Yes, I have it, and I'll tell Mrs. Flanagan that I hate to eat and run but that I must get home because my sister doesn't want me to stay out late."

"Just be careful," Flame cautioned, waving her hand with forced casualness.

"You, too, sweet girl," LaRaine returned, hugging Flame's shoulders.

"I love you," Flame said suddenly, holding back tears that welled behind her blue-green eyes.

LaRaine swallowed the lump in her throat brought on by Flame's words. "And I love you—with all my heart," she said, embracing her sister one last time. That dear, unsolicited confession made it all worthwhile—the sacrifices, the loneliness, the hiding, the fear. "I won't be late," she promised, and dashed out of the room.

Flame didn't know how long she sat staring at the garish hat in her lap after LaRaine left, but suddenly she realized it was nearing six o'clock and she hadn't locked the front door. Just as she was putting her work down, she heard the bell over the entrance announce a late customer.

"I'm sorry, the shop is closed," she said, coming out from behind the curtain that separated the tastefully decorated shop from the back workroom. Her mouth dropped open in shock when she saw the latecomer was none other than Brand Colter.

Seeing the look of terror on her face, Brand assumed the girl thought he had come into the shop for some nefarious purpose, and he felt ashamed all over again. Why would she think anything else? Hadn't he accosted her in the street that morning? And now, here he was in her shop, obviously having followed her.

"I'm sorry," he responded, somewhat at a loss for words now that he was face-to-face with the timid, brown-haired girl. "I didn't know. There was no sign and the door was unlocked. I'll leave."

"What do you want? Why did you follow me here? I told you I'm not who you thought I was." Her husky voice trembled and her fingers closed over the pistol secreted in her pocket, the *old* Flame's instinct for survival very near the surface.

Brand found himself wanting to assure her that he meant her no harm. "I only wanted to see if the proprietress would tell me how to meet you formally. I wanted to ask you to dinner to make up for frightening you this morning. Now, it looks like I've a need to make amends doubly." He smiled apologetically.

"There's no need to make amends," Flame answered in the haughty, dismissing tone she had heard LaRaine use. "Now, if you'll excuse me, I must ask you to leave." She tried to direct him to the door, but his tall frame stayed where it was.

"Who should I speak to about calling on you?" he asked suddenly, admiring the girl's spunk, despite the fact that she was visibly terrified.

"No one!" she answered, a little too quickly. Thinking he might be suspicious, she explained, "I'm engaged to be married. Seeing you or any other man would be impossible."

"I see," he answered, seeming disappointed, but really relieved. This girl was nothing like LaRaine, and the fact that she looked so much like her made it even more difficult to be in the same room with her. He'd been a fool to come. But after the fiasco of his visit to Belle's on Post Office Street, he'd been drawn back here in spite of reason.

Looking curiously around the shop on his way to the door, he commented, "Nice place. It's gone in

345

since I was last in Galveston. Yours? Or do you just work here?"

"Neither!" Flame said definitely, following him—not too close behind—to the door. "I'm watching it for the owner while she does an errand. She'll be right back. The shop's doing my wedding trousseau," she added as an afterthought. "Now, if you don't mind," she said, almost shoving Brand out the door.

She breathed only a little easier after she had bolted the door behind him and pulled down the shade.

Leaning against the doorframe, she listened for the sound of his retreating footsteps. Instead, she heard the rap of knuckles on the door glass. Afraid to even peek out from behind the blind because she knew who it was, she didn't answer, but stood crying, praying he would leave. Finally, when she could bear the sound of the insistent knocking no longer, she cried out loud, "Go away! I don't want anything to do with you! I'm engaged. Can't you leave me alone?"

"I just wanted to know your name."

"Well, I don't want to know yours! I want you to go away and never come back!"

"I'm sorry I frightened you. Please believe that," he said sincerely, and turned to walk back to his waiting carriage.

"Leave me alone!" she was yelling hysterically, just as LaRaine came through the back door. Hearing Flame's screams, she rushed into the shop and was shocked to find her sister huddled in a corner and sobbing—her terror-filled eyes fixed on the front door.

346

Tossing her cape and purse onto the counter, she sped to Flame. "What is it?"

Flame looked beseechingly into LaRaine's concerned face. "Why now? After all this time? I've been a good girl. Haven't I been good?"

"What?" LaRaine asked, knowing the one thing that still frightened Flame—the fear of being recognized.

"A man. I think he knows who I am!" Flame replied, grasping LaRaine's arm with a deathlike grip. "We've got to leave, Beth. Tonight!"

LaRaine forced herself to remain calm—despite the frightening thoughts racing wildly through her mind. Was it possible? Had Flame been recognized? When? How? "What man?"

"He talked to me this morning and said he knew me," she confessed. "I told him he was mistaken, and he said he could see that he was. But tonight, while you were gone, he came here. To the shop! Beth, don't you understand? He followed me here! He must've waited until he thought I was alone!"

"How did he get in?"

"I forgot to lock the door," Flame admitted with a cringe, as if she expected to be struck for her mistake.

"What did he say when he came in?" LaRaine asked, the dread in her heart growing painfully.

"He said he was sorry he frightened me this morning and that he wanted to make up for it by taking me to dinner."

"Maybe that's all he wanted," LaRaine thought aloud, saying a silent prayer that he had been telling the truth. "What did you say to that?"

"I said I was engaged and couldn't see him, and

347

to leave me alone. But he wouldn't go away."

"Perhaps he was just an enamored young man who found you attractive. It's only a matter of time before you'll want to start meeting men. They're not all bad," LaRaine consoled, drawing Flame to her feet and holding her in her arms.

Flame tore herself from LaRaine's embrace to stare wild-eyed at her disbelieving sister. "I tell you, he recognized me! We've got to leave!"

"But we can't leave just like that. What were this man's exact words? Could you be imagining things? Did he actually say he knew you were Flame Rider? Was he rude? Did he hurt you?"

"No," Flame had to admit. "He didn't say anything. He was very polite. He wanted to know who he should talk to about calling on me. But he didn't fool me. It was a trick! He knows. Please, let's leave right away. That's why we came to Galveston—so we could leave in a hurry if we had to!"

"I think you're overreacting. Honey, this sort of thing happens to beautiful young women all the time. And using the excuse of having met before is one of the most common ploys an interested man uses on a woman he wants to know."

"I don't want to meet any men. I never want to have anything to do with another man. I hate them all. They're all lying bastards!"

"Faith Morgan!" LaRaine laughed in surprise. "That sounds like something someone I used to know would have said."

"I don't care," Flame spat defiantly. "I don't want any men in my life—ever! And I don't want them using their slimy tricks to meet me."

"Well, I suppose we could shave your head and put a false mustache and beard on you. That might keep them away," LaRaine teased, feeling more confident by the minute that Flame was placing more importance on the incident than it warranted.

"You don't understand. We've got to leave here right away—maybe never come back! We've got enough money to start over somewhere else, don't we?"

"I suppose we do, but we've been so happy here, and until today, you've felt safe, haven't you?"

"Yes," Flame whimpered, her lower lip quivering pitifully, hopelessly.

"Then let's sleep on it tonight. If you're still afraid in the morning, we'll talk about it some more. I'm not going to let anyone hurt you. You believe that, don't you?"

Flame nodded her head. "But you won't be able to stop him if we stay here."

"Just you watch me," LaRaine promised, guiding the shivering girl up the stairs.

"Are all the doors locked?" Flame asked when LaRaine had helped her undress and into bed.

"I'll recheck them. You just go to sleep," she chided, kissing Flame's forehead before blowing out the lamp on the table beside her bed.

While LaRaine inspected the front and back doors, as well as the windows, she reviewed what Flame had told her. Of course, it was the girl's imagination playing tricks on her. After all, what had the determined swain actually done to indicate that he recognized her as Flame Rider?

Still, they couldn't be too careful. And they had always planned the trip to Europe. Why not push the date up? If only to put Flame's mind at rest. It was on that thought that LaRaine laid her own weary body down to sleep.

Pouring himself another drink from the bottle, Brand tried to ignore the incessant pounding in his head. It was so loud, it seemed to shake the shadowy bedroom in his parents' house where he had been holed up since Tuesday night when he'd made a fool of himself at the little dress shop on Avenue D. He downed the numbing liquid and reached for another. "Leave me 'lone. I don't wanna talk to anybody."

"Dino Colterelli," a woman's voice called from the other side of the door. "I've put up with all of this childish behavior I'm going to. Either you open this door right this minute, or I'm going to have Joshua open it for me!"

Brand lifted his head and stared at the door. His mother's voice sounded as if she was a long way off, but it forced itself obtrusively, irritatingly, into the alcoholic fog enveloping Brand.

"Go 'way," he slurred, concentrating all his effort on splashing more whiskey into his glass. "Don' wanna shee anyone."

"Since when is your mother just 'anyone'? Now, open the door and tell me what's wrong. Let me help you, Son."

His elbow propped on the table, his forehead pressed against the heel of his hand, Brand blinked his bloodshot eyes slowly and tried to focus on the door to the room. "There's nothing you can do, Mother. Nothin' anyone can do."

"We won't know until you tell me what it is that's bothering you. Maybe just talking about it will help. But you can't go on like this. You've been in there for two days and it's time you came out. Now, are you going to open the door or shall I call Joshua?"

Brand staggered to his feet and crossed the room. Opening the door, he weaved drunkenly, his large frame bumping one side of the doorjamb, then the other. Feeling like a naughty little boy, he winced under his mother's fiery glare.

Kathleen Colterelli, the Irish colleen who had come to America when she was twelve years old and married the Italian emigrant, Giacomo Colterelli when she was fifteen, had changed little over the years. She still had her youthful figure, and though her dark, reddish-brown hair now had traces of gray, and there were fine lines on her face that hadn't been there the last time he had seen her, her blue eyes still sparkled with vitality and stubbornness.

"Now, what's this all about?" she asked, brushing past him, determined not to give away that her heart was breaking with sympathy for her son.

"I've made a mess of everything, Mother," he grumbled, staggering back to the whiskey-bottle-littered table.

Kathleen expressed no shock at the way he looked, though inside she ached with the pain she saw in her only child's eyes. "Tell me what it is, Dino. Let me help."

"It's too late, Mother," he answered, falling back on the bed and covering his eyes with a forearm. "It's just too late."

351

Gazing down at her son, Kathleen fought the desire to gather her twenty-eight-year-old son into her arms and hug him. Though he was over six feet tall, taller even than his father, he was still her baby, and she wanted to take away all his pain. But she couldn't.

Although Giacomo Colterelli was a successful merchant and banker in Galveston, it had been apparent almost from the beginning that his son's interests lay in directions other than business. So, at fifteen, young Brandino Colterelli, already six feet tall and calling himself Brand Colter by then, had kissed them goodbye and set out to seek his own fortune and adventure, only returning home a few times during the following thirteen years, though he had written frequently.

After working off and on for five years as a cowhand and stagecoach guard, two years laying railroad track, and six months as a Pony Express rider, Brand had finally made his way to Chicago in search of work. It was there he had met Allan Pinkerton, founder of the newly famous detective agency. Pinkerton, who bragged about his knack for hiring only the most skillful, honest men for his agency, had taken an instant liking to the strapping six-foot-two-inch twenty-two-year-old, and had convinced Brand he was cut out to be a private investigator; and Brand had liked the idea that the agency's guidelines specified the Pinkerton Agency would always be on the side of the law. So he had taken to the pursuit of criminals as if it were what he had been meant to do.

Though he had been with Pinkerton for six years now, and according to his letters had lived through some dangerous and heartbreaking experiences, Kathleen knew that whatever had happened to him this time could easily be the thing that would destroy him. And she didn't intend to let that happen. Not as long as she had a breath left in her body.

"Please, let me help, Dino."

He lowered his arm from his eyes and stared into his mother's concerned face. "Don't you see, Mother. It's too late. She's dead. And it's my fault. I killed her."

Chapter Twenty-two

The next few days passed quickly, and as word of the Morgan sisters' buying trip spread, their wealthy patrons rushed to the House of Fashion to be certain Beth and Faith knew what essentials were missing from their otherwise fabulous wardrobes — a lavender ball gown for Mrs. Beissner, a dust-rose traveling costume for Miss Alice Ricker, a mauve riding habit for Mrs. Austin.

On Friday evening, when LaRaine had written down the specific bidding of the day's last customer, and after Flame had gone upstairs to prepare their supper, LaRaine turned her attention to the display of special laces, ribbons, and buttons on the back wall of the shop, planning to begin her inventory and make her own shopping list for Paris.

"I'll be with you in a minute," she called pleasantly in answer to the tinkle of the doorbell. She made a last quick notation, then laid her pad and pencil down and turned to wait on her late customer.

She was surprised to see that it was a man, a very tall man with his back to her and his head hidden behind one of the House of Fashion's two mannequins that decorated the front of the store. He was inquisitively studying the skirt of the yellow organza gown on the model. She shrugged and took a step toward him. After all, he wasn't the first man to come into the shop looking for a special gift for his wife or daughter—or even for his mistress. "May I—" she started.

"My name's Colterelli," the man interrupted gruffly, not bothering to turn around.

LaRaine's heart did an excited flip. Colterelli! She'd met Mrs. Colterelli's husband, and this wasn't him. That had to mean this was the son she'd heard so much about, the man she'd been thinking about finding a way for Flame to meet. And now here he was.

She shot a nervous glance toward the back room, wishing her sister hadn't already gone upstairs. "How may I help you, Mr. Colterelli?" If only she could think of a way to get Flame back downstairs without being too obvious.

Brand's posture tensed and he whirled around. It was her! The girl from the post office. She was in the darker part of the store and looking over her shoulder at something behind her so he could only see her in one-quarter profile. But he had no doubt. It was the same girl, though her voice was no longer hoarse as it had been the day they met earlier in the week. And he was amazed to realize that she sounded even more like LaRaine than before. "I thought you didn't work here."

The familiar sound of Mrs. Colterelli's son's voice scored into LaRaine's spine, sending chills of trepidation and longing exploding over her flesh.

355

"Of course I work here," she said, turning to face the man who sounded so much like Brand that she halfway expected to find him standing there. "I own—Oh, my God! It's you!"

Her heart telling her to run into his arms, her brain telling her to get away from there as fast and as far as she could, she stood frozen to the spot. Colter? Colterelli? They were the same man.

Unable to further analyze how Brand came to be standing in her shop at that moment, LaRaine greedily devoured him with her eyes. He looked thinner than she remembered him, and there were dark shadows beneath his blue eyes, blue eyes that had gleamed with life before, but now looked pale and empty, as though he'd been sick for a long time. She longed to run to him, but something held her back.

"I'm sorry I keep frightening you," he apologized, taking a step toward her. "My mother asked me to pick up a dress for her," he explained. "If you give it to me I'll leave and won't bother you again."

He doesn't know it's me! LaRaine realized, hurt beyond understanding. She shrank farther into the shadows. Of course her hair wasn't red anymore and the place she was standing wasn't very well lit, but how could he not know her? She would have known him in total darkness or if he'd had purple hair.

Tears blurring her vision, she spun around and disappeared between the curtains to the work room. "I'll get Mrs. Colterelli's package," she said hoarsely.

Safely hidden in the back room, she braced herself on stiff arms and fists pressed to the work table. She sucked in a deep, shuddering breath. *Of course, it's for the best,* she tried to tell herself, reaching for Kathleen Colterelli's package.

"Why did you tell me you didn't work here when I asked the other night?" Brand said from behind her as he separated the curtains and followed her into the tiny room.

The package she was holding literally flew out of her hands as she jumped. Her back to him, she dropped to her knees to retrieve the dressmaking supplies which had been knocked to the floor by the falling package. "Look what you've done!"

"Let me help," he offered, bending to pick up scattered swatches of material, colorful strips of lace, and dress sketches.

"Please, just take your package and leave," La-Raine pleaded, pointing shakily at the fallen bundle. "I don't want your help."

Stunned, Brand took his mother's package and started to rise, but he didn't. Something about the frightened girl huddled there in the middle of her dressmaking supplies called out to him to stay. It was more than her resemblance to LaRaine, which he wasn't sure he could bear to be near another moment. But he couldn't just leave her there alone with her pain. He had to do something. He had to help her, the way his mother had helped him start his journey back from the hell he'd been in for six months. At least he had to try.

Despite common sense, which told him to just get up and leave, he reached out and touched her shoulder.

"Don't," she moaned, bolting to her feet. But

she couldn't run. She was trapped between Brand and the table, and she knew if he touched her again, she wouldn't have the strength to hide her identity from him another minute.

"Won't you let me help you?" he asked, standing up.

Please, Lord. Why are you doing this to me? Didn't I suffer enough when I gave him up before? Don't make me choose again! I don't think I have the strength to give him up again! "I don't want your help, Brand. I just want you to leave!"

"What are you so afr—?" Brand! She called him Brand! Not Mr. Colterelli! But Brand!

Dropping his package, he grabbed her shoulders and spun her around to face him. "Oh, my God," he groaned, "it is you. "But I thought . . ." His voice broke and his eyes filled with tears. "How . . . ? They hung you!"

LaRaine wanted to speak, knew she had to explain, but she couldn't. She looked up into his intense blue eyes, examining every feature, devouring the very essence of him. This was the moment she had dreamed of and fantasized about for six months. But she had never believed it would happen. Now it was here, and she didn't know what to say or do. Would he be able to forgive her? Did he hate her for what she had done to him?

"It can't be true," Brand rasped, certain his mind was playing tricks on him. He must have let his mother convince him to emerge from his self-imposed solitude too soon. His mind was cracking at last.

No longer able to pretend, LaRaine lifted her hand and laid her palm against his hollowed cheek.

"Hello, Brand."

Brand expelled the breath he had unconsciously held while waiting for her answer. All he knew was relief and joy. If this was a dream, or if he had finally gone mad, he didn't care. All he knew was that he had her back and that he would never let her go again.

He squeezed her to him tightly, so tightly she could scarcely breathe, and covered her face with kisses. "Rainy, Rainy. I thought you were dead," he babbled, his anguished words of love and relief almost incoherent against the wetness of her cheek. Clutching her hard to his chest, he deliberately closed his mind to the possibility that she had left him by choice.

She placed her hands on either side of his tortured face, her thumbs gently wiping away the tears streaming unabashedly down his cheeks. "Leaving you was the hardest thing I've ever done," she said huskily. "It was like ripping my heart out of my breast and leaving it behind."

"You mean you . . ." he started, choking on bitter realization. It was true. LaRaine was alive. But he didn't know her. "You let me think you were dead!" he accused, his features filling with loathing. "What kind of witch are you? You made me think I had killed you!"

"Don't hate me, Brand," she begged. "I didn't have a choice."

"No choice?" he shouted in her face. "Why didn't you just shoot me? At least it would have been quick and merciful that way. Instead of what you put me through."

LaRaine winced under the disgust she saw in his

eyes. "It was the only choice I could make. Can you possibly understand?"

"Yeah, I understand," he spit out harshly, the disillusionment evident in his contorted features. For a moment, he had harbored the hope that La-Raine had in some mysterious way been forced to leave him. But she was telling him it had been her decision all along. "You played me for a fool. All your talk about loving me and working together to bring Flame Rider to justice was a lie, wasn't it? You were just waiting for the right time, weren't you?"

"I didn't lie to you, Brand. I loved you with all my heart. I still do," she confessed. "But my sister needed me," she tried to explain, despite his withdrawal. "She never had anyone. No one, Brand. No one until me! She was like an innocent babe raised in the woods by rabid wolves. The only example she ever had was them. She had *animals* to teach her, Brand.

"No one to love her. No one to tell her she was good. No one to teach her right from wrong. No one to do all the things for her that I had always taken for granted, had actually had in abundance. She only had vicious beasts to teach her. She had no choice about the way her life was lived.

"But I had a choice. I could either turn my back on her and stay with you, or I could take care of her, love her, cherish her—the way someone should have done all along. She's my sister, part of me. I couldn't leave her to be devoured the rest of the way by the savage creatures. I had to take what was left of her and run. I'm sorry you can't understand, because it had nothing to do with my love

360

or you."

"Don't make me laugh. She's a murderer who deserved to be hung!"

"Brand, she's not a murderer. She's a child who survived in a cruel, brutal world the only way she could. Believe me, she's paid for any wrong she ever did. As for being hung, they did hang her, Brand!"

Confusion fleeted across his face, then all the pieces to the puzzle seemed to fall into place at once. The timid little mouse he'd talked to the other day, the one who looked so much like La-Raine, yet didn't, was Flame. The whole thing had been an act, and he had fallen for it completely.

Brand's lip curled and he glared at LaRaine as if he were seeing her for the first time. "It won't do any good to lie anymore, LaRaine. I know the truth. Flame isn't dead either. The hanging was just a story you two concocted to cover for her after she killed those two men, wasn't it?" He studied her face. The only thing keeping him from venting his entire rage on her was the fact that he was in a numbed state of shock.

LaRaine took a deep breath. She had to make him understand. Not only was she fighting for Flame's survival, but for her own.

"You're wrong, Brand. They did hang her. She killed one of them as she fought them off when they tried to rape her, but she couldn't stop the second one, and he hung her. By the time I got the rope off her neck, she wasn't breathing."

A feeling of panic rocked Brand as a bizarre thought occurred to him. "How'd the other man die?"

361

Tears running down her face, her mouth quirked in a hopeless half-smile. "I shot him."

"You?"

She nodded her head, her expression begging for understanding. "Don't you see? He was killing my sister. I had to stop him."

He could almost believe her. Almost, but not quite. "Forget it, LaRaine. I know she's not dead. I saw her the other day. I talked to her!"

So Brand was who had scared Flame so badly on Tuesday. No wonder she'd been so hysterical. She must have thought he was here to destroy her. "It was a miracle when she started to breathe again. If you talked to her, you noticed the hoarseness in her voice. The rope did permanent damage to her vocal chords, not to mention wounds you can't see. She's never been the same since that night. It's almost as if Flame Rider actually died at the hands of those lynchers, and Faith Morgan was born."

Taking a quick breath, LaRaine went on speaking before Brand could voice his disbelief. "Did you know that we're paying back all the banks she and her gang robbed? Every penny. Not just the share she got, but the entire amounts that were taken!"

"That doesn't change anything, LaRaine. She's still wanted for murder."

"Flame Rider is wanted, Brand! Not Faith Morgan. Flame is dead! Faith is alive. Give her a chance. I beg of you!"

"Do you expect me to ignore what's happened in the past," he asked, torn in spite of what he knew was the right thing to do. If he persisted in bringing Flame to justice he would destroy LaRaine at

362

the same time. And no matter what she had put him through, he wasn't sure he could do it.

"I wouldn't ask you to go against what you believe is right. But before you do anything, would you just talk to some of the people in Galveston—including your own mother—who have come to know her as Faith Morgan. They'll all tell you she's a sweet, shy, insecure girl who works from morning to night in a dress shop she owns with her twin sister."

"To give you time to run away from me again?" he asked with a sneer.

"Just give us a week," she petitioned beseechingly. "If at the end of the week you're not convinced that no purpose will be served by putting my sister in jail, then turn her in. I give you my word, we won't leave town. But while you're turning her in, you'll have to turn me in, too. Not only for harboring a criminal, but for killing one of the men who was hanging her. I'd have killed fifty of them if I'd found it necessary. Doesn't that make me a murderer, too?"

"That's different."

"Of course it was. I was defending my sister. There were extenuating circumstances," she said before swallowing her pride and making a final plea.

"Give her a chance, Brand. Just get to know her. You'll see she's changed. She's my family, Brand. My only family. She's part of me. Don't you see that but for a quirk of fate, her fortune would have been mine?" she implored emotionally.

"And if your fates had been reversed, do you think she would have come for you? Would she have been willing to give up her home, her name,

363

even her beautiful red hair, to protect you?" he pondered, catching a strand of hair that had worked its way out of the prim net at the nape of her neck. Hypnotized, he wrapped the loose brown curl around his forefinger and rubbed his thumb over it.

"I think she would have—if she'd known about me."

Despising himself for even considering going along with her suggestion, he shook his head doubtfully and dropped his hold on her hair. "Okay, I'll give you one week. If you can show me in the next seven days that Flame Rider is no longer a threat to society, I'll reconsider turning her in."

A spark of relief ignited in LaRaine's heart. "Oh, thank you!" she cried, throwing her arms around him in gratitude. "I promise you won't be sorry."

Peeling her arms from his neck, he took a step back and glowered down at her. "That remains to be seen," he ground out roughly. "But I'm warning you. I'm going to be watching you both like a hawk. And if either of you makes the slightest move like you're going to disappear on me again, I'll have you both in jail so fast it will make your head spin. Have you got that?"

Crushed by the distrust she heard in his voice, but knowing she deserved it for the way she had destroyed him, LaRaine nodded her head. "I've got it."

"Well, shall we begin?" he asked. "Take me to see this 'miracle' sister of yours."

LaRaine smiled weakly, the dread obvious in her eyes. "Faith has already started supper. Would you like to eat with us? It'll give you a chance to know the real her," she suggested optimistically.

Brand hesitated, not sure he wouldn't rather wait until tomorrow to confront the new Flame. It was one thing to say he'd give her a chance to prove that she'd changed, but quite another to come face to face with her.

"Wait here. Give me a few minutes to prepare her, then come up. It'll be fine. I promise," she assured him, and herself.

Approaching the narrow staircase that led to their apartment, LaRaine didn't notice the soft rustle of skirts swishing through the door at the top of the stairs. She was too intent on what she would say, how she would convince Flame that Brand wouldn't harm her.

But when she entered the second-floor sitting room, she immediately sensed that something wasn't right. Though the table was set, and dinner was ready, Flame was nowhere to be seen. "Faith, are you here?" Why hadn't she come down to say supper was on the table, as she usually did?

Suddenly she realized what had probably happened. Flame must have come down for her and seen her talking to Brand. "Honey, are you in there?" she called, knocking anxiously on the closed door to Flame's room. "I have to talk to you."

"Go away. I don't want to talk to you," the small, childish voice whimpered spitefully.

"You don't mean that. Faith, I know what you saw, and what you must have thought it meant, but you're wrong."

"You love him, don't you?" the hurt voice behind the door accused. "You love that bounty hunger. You never really loved me."

"You know that's not true. I love you and always will. No one can ever replace you in my heart."

"But you love him! I could see it by the way you looked at him. You're going to let him turn Flame Rider in so the two of you can go away together, aren't you?"

"I've promised to always be here for you, haven't I?"

"Yes" was the pitiful, frightened reply.

"Have I ever lied to you before?"

"No" was even more heartrending.

"You're my family. I'll always be here for you — as long as you need me. I'll never let anyone hurt you."

"But you love him!" Flame insisted. "How could you? How could you, after what he did to me?"

"You know he never did anything to you, and he's promised me that he wants to get to know you — the real you. I explained to him how none of the past was your fault, how you've paid for your mistakes. He understands. Give him a chance, honey. He's a good man. Let him know the sweet girl I know and love."

"But I don't want him to take you away from me." The little-girl voice was close to the door now, as if she must be just on the other side.

"I don't know what else to say to you to prove it," LaRaine said, sounding like an irritated parent who has finally tired of arguing with a willful child. "I've told you he won't, and all you can do is trust me or not trust me. I've invited him for supper, and he'll be wondering what's taking me so

366

long. Do you want to come out and meet him, or do you want to spend the evening locked in your room? The decision is yours."

LaRaine breathed a sigh of relief when she heard the bolt in the door slide open. "There's my good girl," she said, fighting her own tears with the knowledge that Flame might never grow up. Could Brand really understand how the girl he saw today was the little girl who had gone into hiding behind Flame Rider's rough exterior so many years before and was just now starting to emerge. Could he see how a beautiful, intelligent woman was locked into the emotions of an eight-year-old girl? Did she herself even understand? Or was she only fooling herself to think anybody could?

All we can do is try, she told herself hopefully. She hugged Flame and smiled. "You wait right here. You look beautiful in this light," she crooned, kissing Flame's wet cheek. "Dinner smells delicious," she added over her shoulder and disappeared down the stairs.

Flame waited exactly where she had been told to wait, because she really did want to be a good girl, really did want to do the right thing, really didn't want to do anything to make LaRaine stop loving her.

Brand allowed himself to be led upstairs by the hand, though he didn't know what to expect and dreaded meeting LaRaine's sister again. He had seen her and still couldn't believe the frightened girl on the street was Flame Rider. It had to be an act!

When Brand entered the apartment and saw Flame again, he saw the fear in her eyes and didn't

367

doubt that it was real. But seeing her waiting like an obedient child where her sister had left her, eyes still wet from crying, lips trembling, he had a hard time convincing himself that she was acting. He almost wanted to reach out to her, to assure her, to tell her he was no threat, but he caught himself in time.

He gave his head a hard shake. What he was seeing couldn't be real. It couldn't. It had to be a trick! No one could change so completely.

"Miss Faith Morgan, may I introduce Mr. Brandino Colterelli?" LaRaine said warmly. "Mr. Colterelli, I'd like for you to meet my sister, Miss Morgan."

"How do you do," Flame answered shyly, extending her hand the way LaRaine had taught her to do.

Drawn into the charade in spite of his misgivings, Brand looked askance at LaRaine, then took Flame's shaking hand. "Miss Morgan. I'm glad that we finally meet formally. I felt badly about frightening you the other day. I hope that I'm forgiven."

"Nonsense," Flame flushed, just as she had done millions of times in her daydreams when a handsome man had taken her hand. "There is nothing to forgive. It was an honest mistake."

A flicker of uncertainty flashed in Brand's blue eyes. What the hell was he supposed to say now?

"I've invited Mr. Colterelli to eat supper with us, Faith," LaRaine announced, easing the moment.

"In that case, I'd better put it on the table. Beth, will you seat Mr. Colterelli?" Flame suggested in her most grown-up voice, the voice she used when she played lady in her imagination. "I'll set another place."

During the course of the evening, Brand fought to keep from being charmed by Faith Morgan, and he had to keep reminding himself who she was. In fact, he found her to be intelligent, funny, a good cook, eager to please, and very much a lady.

"Well, what do you think?" LaRaine asked him anxiously at the front door of the darkened shop when he was leaving.

"I still don't believe she's not acting. But if you've really brought about this change, I think you're a miracle worker."

"But it wasn't me. Faith was there all along — buried deep inside of Flame. Only no one ever bothered to find her before. Now you can see that no purpose would be served by bringing her to the authorities, can't you?" she asked urgently. Her entire future depended on his answer. "For things she did when she really didn't know any better?"

"I'm not ready to make that decision yet," Brand replied, unable to ignore the disquieting feelings he had about Flame. As much as he hated to admit it, she seemed to be truly changed, and it was clear that she adored LaRaine. But the premonition that she was more dangerous than ever before nagged irritatingly at him. No, he had no intention of letting one pleasant evening sway him.

"You haven't changed your mind about giving us a chance to prove she's changed, have you?" she asked, her eyes wide with fear.

"No, I haven't changed my mind," he said, suddenly unable to deny himself the feel of his mouth pressed against hers any longer. Maybe he was a fool. And maybe the whole thing with Flame was a trick, but right now he didn't care.

Driven by his longing, Brand grabbed her by the upper arms and hauled her against him, opening his lips over her soft, pliable mouth with a need that surprised even him. The kiss was at once angry and loving, leaving them both craving more. His tongue filled her mouth, and she met its delectable invasion with a seductive sucking, pulling it farther into the sweet cavern.

Threading her fingers through his thick hair, she pulled herself upward, moving sensuously against his hard male body in a rhythmic dance of love as their mouths met with equal hunger, seeking an end to the famine their separation had caused.

Brand's lips moved from her demanding mouth to burn hot, moist kisses along her cheek and ear with a velvet-rough tongue. His teeth tugged gently on the fleshy lobe of her ear, further igniting the fire already raging violently through her veins.

LaRaine's hands roved greedily over the hard muscles of Brand's shoulders and back as his searching lips skimmed along her arched neck. She cried his name softly, totally having forgotten where they were, only knowing the agony of the restricting clothing that kept their flesh from mingling.

"Oh, Brand. I've dreamed of this moment so long. I don't ever want to be away from you again. I love you."

Her words struck a discordant alarm in Brand's mind. She had said she loved him before, and then she had gone off and left him to live in hell.

He pushed her away from him. "I'm warning

you, Rainy. The next time you say those words to me, be prepared to stand behind them. I won't take second place in your life again!"

She opened her mouth to protest, to tell him there was room in her heart for more than one person.

He covered her mouth with his fingers. "Don't say anything now, Rainy. Just think about what I said. And at the end of our week, when I give you my decision about your sister, you give me yours."

He turned and left without kissing her again.

From the curtained doorway at the back of the shop, marbled eyes watched as LaRaine closed and locked the front door behind Brand Colter. Bright with the crazed look of a trapped animal, they narrowed and turned agate hard, then disappeared.

Chapter Twenty-three

LaRaine listened until she heard Brand's buggy drive off, then hurried upstairs to check on her sister. To her surprise, Flame was not only cheerfully cleaning up the supper dishes, but she was humming to herself.

"Well, what did I tell you?" LaRaine asked, doing her best to put Brand's unspoken ultimatum from her mind. She caught her sister around the waist and twirled her on the imaginary dance floor. "Was there anything to be afraid of?"

"You were right, Beth. I like Mr. Colterelli much better than I did when he was Brand Colter. I think he liked me, too, don't you?"

LaRaine felt she could wait to tell Flame that he still went by the name of Brand Colter. "I do. I think he was captivated by your charming and stimulating conversation, your clever wit, your delicious cooking, and your exquisite beauty," LaRaine agreed, not sensing the way Flame's eyes narrowed in her direction for the barest instant.

"Captivated?" Flame asked in her youngest voice.

Picking up a dish towel and a wet plate to help, LaRaine nodded her head. "I was very proud of you tonight. And you know, seeing what a lovely hostess you were makes me think that perhaps you should start going out more, perhaps even meeting some young men. What do you think?"

Flame ignored LaRaine's question and asked one of her own. "Do you think Mr. Colterelli is handsome, Beth?"

"Why, yes I do," LaRaine answered, confused by the peculiar expression on her sister's face. "Why do you ask?"

"No reason. I thought he was handsome, but I wanted another opinion. Do you think he'll come see me again?"

A warning light went on in LaRaine's brain, sending fire blazing alarmingly through her body. It had been easy to think of Flame as a child in an adult's body when it was just the two of them; but no matter how immature her emotions were, LaRaine must remember that Flame was a woman! A woman who could develop an attraction for a man—a man already loved by another. "Yes, I'm certain he'll come to see us again," she said, stressing the *us*.

"I'm glad," Flame sighed, assuming a dreamy look on her face and gliding off to her bedroom, leaving her sister to worry about something that hadn't occurred to her before.

The next morning when Flame pulled up the shade, signaling the opening of the shop for the day, she was surprised to see Brand Colter peering at her through the glass. Her nostrils showed her displeasure with just the tiniest flare. Then her face broke into a broad grin. "Mr. Colterelli!" she cried, opening the door.

Brand hesitated a second, his decision to give Flame a week to prove herself wavering seriously. His plan was to pretend he believed the change was real. That way, Flame would be caught off guard and might betray herself for LaRaine to see the truth. But seeing Flame today, he suddenly felt the danger of falling for her act as completely as LaRaine had.

"Good morning, Miss *Morgan*," he boomed, breezing into the shop, the tense edge to his greeting barely noticeable. "You're looking particularly chipper this morning," he said, producing a nosegay of flowers from behind his back. "And these are for the other Miss Morgan, wherever she might be," he announced, bringing forth a second bouquet.

"The *other* Miss Morgan is right here!" LaRaine called out, rushing across the shop to greet Brand, not a little concerned by the adoring way Flame was watching him. "What brings you out so early?" she asked, blushing when he kissed her lightly on the lips.

Neither of them noticed the flash of anger that crossed Flame's features for a brief instant before her expression resumed its happy smile.

Brand laughed and looked down at LaRaine pointedly. "I'm not interrupting anything, am I? Maybe a sudden trip out of town?" He gave her a pseudoinnocent smile that made no secret of the fact that he didn't trust her to not run away again. "I'd be pleased to escort you."

"No," she answered, her hurt obvious, "we

374

weren't going anywhere."

"In that case, *Miss Morgan*," he added, placing definite emphasis on the name, "I'd like to purchase a gift for my mother."

"Oh, I know just the thing, Mr. Colterelli!" Flame said enthusiastically, drawing Brand's attention to her own animated face. "We have a lovely embroidered shawl from India that will look marvelous with the beige silk she bought just last month!"

"The shawl would be perfect, Faith. Why don't you go get it for Mr. Colterelli," LaRaine suggested, knowing the shawl was in the back room.

"I'll be right back," Flame simpered. "Don't you go away."

"No, we won't," LaRaine called after her. Then, turning to Brand, she whispered tersely, "What's this all about? Why are you acting like this? You aren't planning to watch us every minute of the next week, are you?"

Brand gave her a sly grin. "You didn't think I was going to just disappear and come back in a week, did you? You haven't exactly proven yourself to be trustworthy in our past encounters, have you, LaRaine? But putting all that aside, how else am I going to see that Flame has changed if I don't watch her firsthand?"

"Yes, of course, but . . ."

Before she could say more, Flame came running into the room, her face beaming. "Here it is!" she announced, holding the fringed shawl out for Brand's examination. "Isn't it lovely?"

"Yes, very," Brand acknowledged with a frown

375

on his handsome face. Damn, she was convincing! But sooner or later she would make a mistake and he intended to be there when she did. "I'll take it. That is, if you both agree that she'll like it."

"I think she will," LaRaine confirmed uneasily, not a bit happy she hadn't finished her conversation with Brand. He was obviously up to something. "It's a very good choice, Faith. I'm pleased that you thought of it," she complimented her sister.

"Well, now that that's taken care of, what about this evening?" Brand said with a mischievous gleam in his vivid blue eyes.

"What about this evening?" Flame asked excitedly, seemingly unaware of the becoming flush that glowed in her cheeks when she looked up at Brand Colter.

Brand automatically looked away from LaRaine to answer Flame's question. "I want you to come to a special birthday dinner for my mother in our home this very evening." Turning back to LaRaine, the look in his eyes threatening, he said, "I know you won't disappoint me, will you?"

"I don't know," LaRaine replied hesitantly. "We don't usually go out in the evening. There's so much work to do."

"Oh, Beth, you're such an old stay-at-home. Come on and go with us. We'd love for you to go with us," Flame said, hooking her arm in Brand's and effectively hiding her misgivings. They had never gone to a social function in Galveston. In fact, she had never been to one anywhere—except in her imagination. "There won't be a lot of people there, will there?"

"No, only my parents," Brand answered. "What do you say?" he asked LaRaine, wishing he could shake Flame off his arm and take the woman he loved in his arms and kiss away the unhappy expression on her sweet face. "Do you come to dinner, or do I . . ."

"I suppose we can close up early this evening," LaRaine cut him off, not wanting her sister to know about the bargain with Brand.

"Good, I'll pick you up at seven. I'll get the shawl then—if you'll be so kind as to wrap it up for me."

"But, Brand!" LaRaine protested, making faces indicating how important it was that she speak to him alone.

He smiled and kissed her cheek. "Tonight," he whispered. "Tonight."

"What about me?" Flame interrupted petulantly. "Don't I get a goodbye kiss, too?"

Brand frowned his puzzlement and shot an uneasy glance in LaRaine's direction. Then he regathered his composure and threw himself back into his act. "Of course you do. Wouldn't want to leave without giving you both a kiss," he announced, bestowing a brotherly buss on Flame's forehead. "Tonight," he called over his shoulder as he made a dash from the shop.

"I think you're just jealous," Flame told her sister as LaRaine styled her hair for her. "I don't know why. Just because he asked me to come to his mother's birthday party first. What are you so upset about? He asked you, too."

LaRaine closed her eyes and took a deep breath. This had gone on all day. Flame actually seemed to think Brand was interested in her. "Honey, please try to understand. I'm not upset because he asked you to come to his mother's party. I'm concerned that you seem to be imagining something other than a simple gesture of friendliness in his invitation. He's the first man who's ever treated you like a lady, so it's perfectly logical and normal that his attention could cause you to develop a little infatuation with him. But you mustn't think it's more than that. I don't want to see you hurt."

"I think it's you you're worrying about, Beth. Not me!" Flame said haughtily, poking her lip out to pout. "You're afraid he'll like me better than you."

"Faith, if I honestly thought he wanted you and you wanted him, I'd do everything in my power to make it happen. You know there's nothing I wouldn't give you if I could. But that's just not the way things are. I can't give you another human being. And the truth is, he's only . . ."

LaRaine caught herself. She couldn't tell her sister that Brand Colter was just testing her so he could decide if he was going to turn her over to the law or not.

"We'll see," Flame said, her natural tendency to fight for what she wanted now surfacing in full strength.

Knowing it was futile to argue any further, LaRaine put the final touches on her own hairdo and surveyed their reflections in the mirror. Both sisters wore high-necked lace and velvet, one in ice blue and one in mint green; and neither could ignore the fact that together they were a splendid vision. But that fact did nothing to raise LaRaine's mood as they descended the stairs to await Brand's arrival.

He was exactly on time and seemed in even merrier spirits than he had been that morning. Again he had flowers for each twin, white gardenias, and again he said all the right things to fan Flame's growing interest in him—and to add to LaRaine's intensifying sense of peril.

Sitting between LaRaine and Flame all the way to his parents' house, Brand realized that Flame was pressing her leg against his. He couldn't be certain that it was intentional. Surely not! After all, the bumps and ruts in the road could account for a certain amount of jostling and physical contact. But just the same, he moved closer to LaRaine.

The expression on Flame's face remained open and friendly, nothing more. There! That proved it was only his imagination. Then the increasing pressure against his leg began again. She had moved over closer to him!

His tension rose to the point of desperation when he felt the touch of Flame's hand resting lightly on his thigh—high on his thigh. What was she doing? What could she be thinking?

Brand glanced nervously at LaRaine, then back to Flame, who smiled sweetly at him, then back to LaRaine, who was oblivious to what her sister was doing. Brand didn't know what to do. He had never been in such a ridiculously awkward predicament before.

Fortunately, the driver pulled up in front of the Colterellis' home at that moment, and Brand was saved from the embarrassingly insistent advances. *How'd I get myself into this mess? How am I supposed to tell LaRaine her sister's trying to molest me?* he joked with himself. Anyway, if Flame was as changed as LaRaine believed she was, it *had* to be his imagination, he decided as he helped the sisters from the carriage.

Kathleen Colterelli, a spry, bright-eyed woman in her late forties, met her guests at the door, eagerly embracing first LaRaine and then Flame, before taking their wraps and handing them to a butler who stood silently in the background.

"When Dino told me he was bringing the lovely Morgan twins to dinner, I was thrilled. I've always worried that you two would be snatched up off the available market before he would have a chance to meet you. There are so few really lovely girls in the city," she chattered gaily, not at all embarrassed to admit that she had planned on doing a little matchmaking for her handsome son.

"Then, when he came home for the first time in years, and you were both still single, my plans were thrown awry by his terrible mood. Honestly, he's been such a dreadful bore to be around," she complained, her adoring smile beaming indulgently at her only child. "I couldn't have introduced him to anyone!"

"Have I been that bad, Mother?" Brand asked,

knowing he had and asking for forgiveness with his smile.

"You know you've been impossible," Kathleen scolded with a laugh. "Come, ladies, I want you to meet my husband and the father of this impudent son of ours."

She stepped between LaRaine and Flame and took their arms, guiding them through wide doors leading into an enormous library which was furnished with heavy leather furniture. Despite its large size, the room was made warm and cozy with its giant fireplace, Persian rug, soft lighting, and intimate seating arrangements of stuffed chairs.

"Gia, they're here!" Kathleen announced, crossing the room proudly with LaRaine and Flame. "You remember Beth and Faith Morgan, from the House of Fashion, don't you?" she said, looking from LaRaine to Flame. "Or Faith and Beth," she laughed happily. "I never can remember who's who."

Although the years had been more than generous with Giocomo Colterelli's waistline, he was still a handsome man. Only half an inch shorter than Brand, he was quite imposing with his bushy side whiskers, stylish mustache, and head of thick silver hair.

"Ladies, it's my pleasure," he said with just a trace of his native Italy in his accent. Bending to kiss each of their hands, he winked at Brand, making certain that everyone saw the mischievous flash in his eye. "Tell me, boy, how do you tell them apart? Or do you?" he teased.

Brand stepped forward, having enjoyed standing

back and watching his affectionate parents fuss over LaRaine and Flame. He slipped his arm around LaRaine's shoulders and squeezed her tenderly. "I guess it's all in the chemistry," he laughed, glancing down at LaRaine's blushing cheeks and loving her more than ever—despite the fact that he still couldn't quite trust her.

Kathleen studied Flame for a moment. She could have sworn she had seen the other twin's eyes narrow threateningly when Brand had singled her sister out for his attention. *I hope I'm wrong,* she thought, sensing a terrible problem if both twins were interested in her son.

Kathleen looked more closely at Flame. Her eyes were wide with excitement, nothing more. There was no ominous glare in them, and Kathleen felt foolish for letting her imagination conjure up a romantic triangle. She shook her head and forced her attention back to her son and the girl he was holding.

"But since you don't possess the secret formula, Father, I'll give you a tip," Brand teased. "Rainy . . ." He made a face at the slip of his tongue. "I mean Beth . . . Beth's wearing the green dress and Faith is wearing blue," he went on.

"Why did you call Beth, Rainy?" Brand's mother blurted out, not stopping to think that Rainy might be the name of an old girlfriend her son would prefer not to discuss.

Brand looked nervously from LaRaine to his mother and back again. "We met a while back and I called her Rainy then. I just can't break the habit, I guess," he explained lamely.

"Why would you call someone named Beth, Rainy?" his mother persisted.

"It was raining when we met, Mrs. Colterelli," LaRaine interjected quickly, hoping to allay the woman's questions. "And it seemed as if every time we saw each other after that it was raining, so he called me Rainy. He said I must have brought the rain. Silly, isn't it?" she smiled, not certain Mrs. Colterelli believed her hurried fabrication.

"Where did you meet?" Brand's father asked.

"In Kentucky!" LaRaine volunteered before Brand could say something else. "Brand had business with our father."

"And what did he call your sister? Or did he only have a nickname for you?" Kathleen persevered, already having noticed that her son only had eyes for one of the lovely twins.

"I didn't kn—" Brand started, planning to say he hadn't known Flame as well as her sister, but Flame interrupted.

"Oh, he called me *Sunny!*" she announced. "He said my smile reminded him of the sun on gloomy days." She looked worshipfully up at Brand and took his arm. She seemed unaware that Brand and LaRaine both stared dumbfoundedly at her as she blessed the group with one of her *sunny* smiles. However, Brand's mother didn't miss the strange interplay.

Brand's eyes narrowed visibly, but he said nothing—out loud. *What in the hell are you up to, Flame? Don't you think LaRaine can see that you're making a play for me?*

Deliberately separating himself from the clinging

383

sister, Brand walked to an elaborate oak bar and announced with more enthusiasm than he felt, "I'm fixing drinks. Anyone interested?" *I sure as hell am! I've got to get her aside and make it clear that she'd better stop, or I'm not going to wait a week to turn her in.*

"Where are you, Son?" Giacomo Colterelli's booming Italian accent broke into Brand's troubled thoughts.

"I beg your pardon. What did you say?" he asked, downing a swallow of whiskey and forcing himself to concentrate on what was happening around him.

"I said, I'd like a brandy, and the ladies all want sherry," Gio stressed, his heavy white brows knitted close together and showing his concern with his son's strange behavior.

"Oh, I almost forgot. Happy birthday, Mrs. Colterelli!" Flame congratulated Brand's mother.

Kathleen gave Flame a bewildered stare. "It's not my birthday," she said plainly, wondering where the girl could have gotten such a foolish idea.

Flame seemed to wilt before her eyes, and Kathleen was amazed to see how quickly her sister stepped in to defend her.

Putting her arm around Flame's shoulders and patting her encouragingly, LaRaine said, "Brand told us it was your birthday. Didn't you tell us this was a birthday dinner, Brand?" she asked, her eyes threatening. It was quite obvious, anything that hurt her sister hurt her.

"I did," Brand answered, fighting the queasy premonition he felt when he saw how protective La-

Raine was of Flame. He was certain she would never believe anything bad about her. How was he going to compete with that? "I wasn't here for Mother's last few birthdays," he explained hurriedly. "So I decided we would celebrate them all tonight. It's a surprise party! Cook's making a special cake, and I have a present," he said, his voice falsely gay.

"Well, for your information, young man, I quit having birthdays years ago. You'd know that—if you hadn't been gallivanting all over the United States and Canada," Kathleen scolded. "However," she added with an impish grin, "although I've given up birthdays, I haven't given up presents—especially receiving them. Where is it? I want it now!" she squealed enthusiastically, relaxing everyone in the room and making it possible to resume the congenial atmosphere that had prevailed before Flame had been embarrassed.

"I'll get it," Brand answered, relieved. He dashed out into the foyer to fetch the gift, leaving his father to serve the ladies.

"I don't know what's gotten into that boy," the older Colterelli grumbled, pouring the three glasses of sherry. "For days he mopes around here like he's come from his best friend's funeral, and now he's jumping around like a dog with fleas."

Hoping she knew the answer to her son's strange behavior, Kathleen smiled in LaRaine's direction. "I don't suppose you'd know why Brand's acting so oddly, would you, Beth?"

"Who me?" LaRaine asked with a nervous laugh as she accepted the sherry glass from Gio. "Why would I know—Oh! Here's Brand now with his present for you!" she exclaimed with relief, and a smile that was desperate.

Mrs. Colterelli loved her new shawl and happily draped it around her shoulders before they went in for dinner. LaRaine was pleased to see her so happy, because she found she genuinely liked Brand's parents, with their easygoing manners and honest way of saying what was on their minds. There was no pretentiousness or self-importance in anything they said or did. Even if she hadn't been in love with their son, she would have wanted the Colterellis to like her.

During dinner, Brand's mother became increasingly aware of her son's discomfort, seat as he was between the two Morgan sisters, but she couldn't determine the reason for his uneasiness. "What is it, Dino?" Kathleen asked. "You've barely touched your pheasant."

"I've been on the road so long, I guess I'm not used to such rich food," he said haltingly, unable to tell anyone that during the soup course Flame had resumed the assault she had begun in the carriage. And now during the main course, she was growing bolder by the minute.

"Is there something wrong with it?" Kathleen asked anxiously, looking at her own plate as if she would find the answer there. "Let me have Cook fix you something else. What would you like?" She was already standing and reaching for his plate.

"No, Mother," Brand answered irritably. "It's fine! I'm just not that hungry. Remember, I'm not a growing boy anymore," he pointed out.

"We can thank God for that!" Giacomo teased, rolling his eyes heavenward. "Leave the boy alone, Kathy. Can't you see he's got enough to keep him happy sitting between that pair of beauties," he laughed loudly before stuffing a large bite of potato into his mouth and chewing it enthusiastically.

"I see their beauty has done nothing to your appetite," Kathleen commented frostily before breaking into a delighted, high-pitched laugh.

"That's because I've only got eyes for one beauty, my love." Giacomo Colterelli's voice contained enough passion to make his wife lower her head in embarrassment. She was blushing. She was pleased, but still she blushed like a young girl receiving attention from her sweetheart.

LaRaine didn't realize how intently she had been watching the interchange between the two who were obviously still lovers after thirty-two years of marriage—not until she realized the long sigh she heard had come from her own throat. That broke the spell, and everyone laughed, including LaRaine.

Even Brand chuckled, able to forget for a moment the small foot that had constantly rubbed the back of his calf throughout dinner.

"I know another way to tell you girls apart," Kathleen announced proudly. "See if you can spot it, Gia," she challenged saucily.

Mr. Colterelli studied the sisters long and hard before he conceded. "I give up." He wouldn't have ruined his wife's discovery, even if he could see what she had noticed. "How else can we tell them apart?"

"Look!" she said, obviously pleased with herself.

387

"Beth is *left-handed* and Faith is *right-handed!*" She looked smugly at her husband for acknowledgment of her clever observation.

"You're right," Gio agreed. "How clever of you to notice."

No wonder Flame eats with her right hand. Her left hand is on my leg, Brand thought with disgust, deliberately covering the forward girl's hand with his own and putting it back in her own lap for what he hoped was the final time.

"We'll have our coffee and brandy in the library with the men," Kathleen announced, folding her napkin neatly and placing it beside her plate. The others did the same. "Since Gio and Dino don't smoke those nasty cigars, we dispense with the custom of the men being separated from the women after dinner—at least when it's just family," she added, smiling at LaRaine.

LaRaine was touched by the fact that Mrs. Colterelli wanted to consider them part of her family, and she knew for certain there was nothing she wanted more. *But it's too late now. Brand will never be able to understand how I feel about my sister.*

She felt tears welling in her eyes, dangerously close to the surface, causing her to feel foolish beyond belief. She hadn't realized how much she had missed being a member of a regular family. "Is there somewhere I can freshen up?" she asked Kathleen, hoping the older woman didn't notice her watery eyes.

"Of course, dear," Kathleen responded, patting her arm lovingly. "Let me show you the way. If you will excuse us," she added, smiling at the others before leading LaRaine out of the room and up the winding stairs.

"I hate to take you away from the others," La-Raine protested when she realized LaRaine's mother was going to go with her into the large bedroom at the top of the stairs. "I'll be fine," she stressed.

"Oh, they won't miss me. Besides, this will give us a chance to talk. If you're going to be my daughter-in-law, I think it would be nice if we knew each other a little better, don't you?"

Chapter Twenty-four

LaRaine stared incredulously at Kathleen Colterelli.

"Brand has asked you to marry him, hasn't he?" Kathleen insisted.

"Why would you think that?"

Kathleen patted LaRaine's hand and smiled. "Well, if he hasn't, it's only a matter of time until he does. You love him, don't you?"

"Yes, but I . . ." LaRaine began.

"And he loves you. I knew it the minute I saw you two together. It's written all over his face. I'm so happy I could burst!" she squealed, hugging LaRaine to her. "You're the girl he thought he had lost, aren't you?"

"I think you've misunderstood." LaRaine wished she could tell Kathleen Colterelli the whole story, but of course she couldn't. "Maybe if things were different, Brand and I could have married. But I hurt him terribly and I don't see how he can ever forgive me for it."

"Forgive you? How silly. Obviously he's already

done that. Why else would he have brought you to meet his parents?"

"Because he . . . Well, there are other reasons," she added, her voice an aching whisper.

"Would you like to talk about them?" Kathleen asked, deliberately ignoring LaRaine's protest that Brand didn't want to marry her.

"That would be nice," LaRaine sighed, feeling comforted by the thought of having another woman to talk to. Of course there was always Flame, but with Flame, she always had to be the strong one. And right now, the thought of being able to pour out her troubles to someone else was very appealing.

"I'm all ears." Kathleen sat on the large bed and patted the mattress beside her. "Come here and tell me all about it. You know, I always wanted a daughter, so I've had almost fifty years to prepare myself for giving a little motherly advice."

Her abundance of affection flowed over and enveloped LaRaine like loving arms, giving her the confidence to speak. "For one thing," she began, taking a seat on the bed beside Mrs. Colterelli. "I haven't seen Brand for a long time."

"And . . . ?

"People change, Mrs. Colterelli. Things change, situations change. Nothing remains the same."

"For instance?"

For the first time, she considered sharing her misgivings about her relationship with Flame. "It's my sister. She's very dependent on me and terribly afraid of having me leave her alone. I'm not really free as long as she needs me, and Brand can't

391

understand that."

"Maybe we could find your sister a young man of her own," Kathleen suggested, her mind already racing to come up with a list of suitable suitors for Faith Morgan.

"There's another problem." LaRaine raised her eyebrows, showing her hesitation to voice her dilemma aloud. "I think she's developed a crush on Brand. She thinks he's interested in *her*. So you can see, she would feel doubly betrayed if Brand and I . . ."

"She'll survive," Mrs. Colterelli assured LaRaine. "She seems strong enough to understand that if you and Brand love each other, you will want to be together. Just tell her right out."

"I know she seems strong and grown-up, Mrs. Colterelli, but it's only a part she plays. Actually, her emotions are very fragile, like those of a child."

A spoiled child, if you ask me, Kathleen thought, but couldn't say. "Don't you think you're being overly protective?" she suggested, her words more tactful than her thoughts. She wondered why the intelligent young woman her son obviously cared for would consider giving up her own happiness for her sister. Would Faith do the same if the shoe were on the other foot? Somehow, she doubted it.

"Faith is afraid of men. Brand is the first man she's ever been interested in. Can you imagine what it would do to her to have him reject her and choose me, the sister she thinks was always the one who had everything good happen to her?

392

She's certain that I was even loved better by our father and mother."

And she uses that against you, doesn't she, child? She uses your guilt to keep you under her control. Can't you see that you only think you're the one making all the decisions? Can't you see how she uses you? No, I suppose you can't. You're too sweet, too full of love, too full of giving to see what your sister is doing to you.

"Then what do you plan to do? Let life and love pass you by while you take care of her?"

"Actually, I had resigned myself to a life without marriage. We have the shop and a good income. Then Brand found me and changed everything. Mrs. Colterelli, I don't know what to do. I may have to choose between them. But how can I do that? I love them both so much. Even if Brand could ever forgive me for hurting him so badly, I can never marry him if it means my sister will suffer."

"I see," Kathleen mused aloud. *She's really got you where she wants you, doesn't she?* "Why don't you give her a chance?" Kathleen said suddenly. "She just might surprise you. I think she's stronger than you give her credit for being. Perhaps she's always taken the role of the weaker twin because that's where you put her. Why don't you go downstairs right this minute and tell Brand *and* Faith that you love him. She'll live through it. She really will," she encouraged.

"If I admit to her that I still care about Brand she might . . ."

"That's the girl. There's no way you can make

her first crush any less painful, but perhaps you can shorten it by showing her that you and Brand will still love her after you're married."

"But Brand hasn't said he still loves me, much less that he wants to marry me."

Kathleen grinned. "He will. You just prepare your sister."

"I'll do it, Mrs. Colterelli, but in private. I'll talk to her when we get home," LaRaine said with optimistic resolution.

"Then we'd better return to the others, or they may think we've gotten lost up here." Kathleen gave LaRaine a warm, motherly hug. "Thank you for letting me have a daughter for once in my life. I can barely wait until it's permanent."

LaRaine embraced Brand's mother tightly and sighed, "No, it is I who should thank you."

Together they went back into the library, holding hands. They were surprised, however, to find Giacomo Colterelli sitting alone in the room, his nodding white head resting on his chest, the drink in his limp hand precariously close to dropping onto the valuable rug.

Taking the glass from her husband's hand, Kathleen smiled indulgently. "He must've talked Dino into taking Faith for a little stroll in the garden so he could steal a few winks. The old devil does like his after-dinner snooze," she explained, giving her sleeping spouse an indulgent look of devotion.

"Let's not disturb him," LaRaine murmured, loving Brand's parents all the more.

"We can go outside and walk with the others,"

Kathleen decided, opening the large French doors onto the terrace. "Oooh, it's a bit chilly out here," she said with a shiver. "I'll get our wraps. Wait right here. I'll be back in a minute." She scurried back through the doorway, leaving LaRaine to gaze out into the garden from the edge of the terrace.

Looking into the darkness, LaRaine breathed in deeply. The salty smell of the night air was intoxicating and invigorating, and for the first time since Brand had come into her shop, she felt optimistic.

Her attention suddenly diverted by the sound of muffled voices, she leaned over the terrace railing, trying to determine where they came from. In the distance, she spotted two figures standing beside a luxurious hedge of oleander bushes. It was Flame and Brand, and they seemed to be having an animated conversation. LaRaine squinted her eyes and tried to hear what they were saying, but it was impossible. They were too far away.

She started to call out to them and lifted her hand to wave. But before she could get their attention, the two figures in the garden melted into one, turning the scene before her into a nightmare. Freezing with shock, she watched as Flame's arms went around Brand's neck and the couple kissed.

All she could think of was getting away before they saw her. Wheeling about, she blindly ran back to the house, colliding into Mrs. Colterelli.

Recognizing LaRaine's upset state, Kathleen asked, "What is it, dear? Are you cold? You should have waited inside. I'm sorry I took so long."

"No, it's just that I don't feel like a stroll after all. I think I need to go home. Can you possibly have one of your people take me?"

"Now? Without your sister?" What could have happened in the space of the three or four minutes since she had left the girl? The worried frown harsh on her pretty face, she looked out into the garden, but saw nothing out of the ordinary.

"Brand can bring her home later. I hate to spoil her evening just because I'm feeling a little tired. Please, Mrs. Colterelli," LaRaine insisted desperately. She couldn't face Brand and Flame. Not yet. "I must leave."

"Just wait a minute, and I'll have Dino take you both," the older woman suggested.

"No!" LaRaine spouted nervously. "I prefer to go by myself. I need to be alone for a while."

"Very well. I'll call Simpson. If you're certain," Kathleen said, taking one more puzzled glance into the dark garden.

"I'm certain. Very certain!" LaRaine answered, hating Brand for taking advantage of Flame's infatuation with him, and hating herself for getting caught up in Mrs. Colterelli's fantasy and believing Brand might still love her.

Though Brand hadn't seen LaRaine standing on the lighted terrace, Flame had been very aware that her sister had spotted them. It was the moment she had waited for, had hoped for, since Gio Colterelli had first suggested Brand take her for a stroll in the garden.

One way or the other, she intended to convince LaRaine that Brand Colter wasn't what she wanted. And she was sure her sister wouldn't want anything to do with him if she thought he had other women—but especially not if he gave his unfaithful attentions to her own sister! Once she made LaRaine angry with Brand, the field would be clear for her to make sure once and for all that LaRaine never married Brand Colter.

"Why in the hell did you do that?" He roughly disengaged Flame's arms from around his neck and stepped back into the shadows. "Haven't you been listening to what I've been telling you? I'm not interested in you. If you weren't Rainy's sister, and if I hadn't given her my word that I'd give you a chance to prove you've really changed, you wouldn't even be here."

"But you were so nice to me," Flame said, tilting her head away from him so she could be sure no one had witnessed anything past the kiss. "I thought you . . ." Her bottom lip trembled effectively.

Torn between feeling guilty for how bluntly he had spoken to her, and angry with her for being so damned convincing, Brand ran his fingers through his hair. "Look, Flame—I mean Faith—if anything like this happens again, I'll be forced to tell Rainy!"

"She won't believe you. In fact, she'll probably hate you for maligning me," Flame said spitefully.

"Well, I don't want to tell her because it will hurt her; and you've already caused us both enough unhappiness. But if it happens again, you can be damned sure I'll make her believe me. Have you got that?"

"Yes, Brand. I understand," Flame nodded pitifully, deliberately making certain he saw the tears trickling down her cheeks.

"Look, I don't want to be enemies. And I really want to believe you've changed. But you've got to understand that I love Rainy; and I'm going to marry her," he said a little more gently, placing his hand in the small of Flame's back and guiding her along the path toward the house. He didn't notice the involuntary jump his touch on her back caused.

Like hell you'll marry her, Brand Colter! Just don't count on it!

"What do you mean she left?" Brand bellowed moments later when his mother informed him of LaRaine's hasty departure.

"She just left! One minute we were going to join you in the garden, and the next she wanted to leave. She was perfectly happy on the terrace when I left her to get our wraps. Then, when I came back she was dashing into the house, insisting she had to leave immediately."

Brand glowered down at Flame. He knew exactly what had caused LaRaine to leave, what it was that had hurt her so terribly that she had needed to rush home alone.

"Do you have any idea why she would behave so strangely?" Kathleen asked Flame.

"I haven't a clue, Mrs. Colterelli," Flame exclaimed, her open-eyed innocence *almost* hiding the triumphant grin that slithered across her face.

"I'll talk to her," Flame urged, barring the door with her body when Brand started to follow her into the dress shop. "It was my fault. I'll tell her you were innocent, and that I threw myself at you," she offered, seeming on the verge of tears with shame for what she had done.

"Spare me the act, *Faith*. I'm talking to her tonight!" he persisted, pushing his way inside and slamming the shop's glass door behind him. He crossed to the back in long, angry strides, taking the stairs to the apartment two at a time. Bursting into the upstairs living room, he was surprised to find it dark.

"Rainy, are you here? I want to talk to you!" he demanded.

Flame entered the room behind him. "She must be asleep already." She laid a hand on his sleeve. "Maybe this should wait until tomorrow."

Snatching his arm from Flame's touch as if it burned through his clothing, he warned her, "You're not going to win this time, Flame. I'm not leaving until I talk to her. Which room is hers?" he asked, already starting for LaRaine's door.

"That one," Flame answered softly, wondering desperately how she could stop him from going in. She needed to talk to LaRaine before he did. "I really think you should wait," she tried again.

"I don't care what you think! This whole mess

is going to be straightened out tonight!"

Standing outside the door to LaRaine's room, Brand took a deep breath and tapped on the wood. "Rainy, open the door. We've got to talk whether you like it or not."

Still fully dressed, LaRaine lay on her bed examining the cracks in the ceiling by the light of the pale moon that beamed in through her window. She couldn't answer Brand. There was nothing to say. Obviously, Flame had been right when she had thought he was interested in her. Well, was it such a bad match? Before she had known that Mrs. Colterelli's son was Brand, she had planned to arrange an introduction to him for Flame. Maybe they belonged together. And maybe she shouldn't have dared to think of another life other than the one she had planned and worked for since they had come to Galveston.

There were worse things than being unmarried and alone—there was poor health, no roof over your head, being cold in the winter, hunger, no income, being forced to do work that you hated. Yes, she could be much worse off. She still had her shop, a very successful shop at that. Or if she found it too difficult seeing Flame and Brand together, she could always go back to Virginia. Then Flame would have a husband to care for her, and LaRaine would be free to take back her own name. She idly fingered a tassel of fringe on the window curtain that hung by her bed.

"Rainy, if you don't open this door, I'm going to force it open," Brand threatened.

"I don't want to talk tonight, Brand. I'm already

in bed," she finally answered, her voice stiff and weary.

"Well, that's just too damn bad," he roared, trying the doorknob and experiencing a surprise with the discovery that it wasn't even locked. He opened it slowly, peeking in tentatively, almost as if he expected to be attacked.

"I said I didn't want to talk to you, Brand," she said woodenly, unable to tear her eyes from the contorted expression of anger that consumed his handsome face. "We'll talk tomorrow, or the next day," she went on calmly, finally returning her gaze to the cracked ceiling.

"You don't have to talk, but by God, you're going to listen," he rasped harshly, placing his hands on her shoulders and roughly pulling her to a sitting position. If he noticed she was still dressed in green velvet and lace and not in bed clothes, he gave no sign. "You're going to hear me out while I explain what you saw."

"There's no need to explain," she insisted, dry-eyed and calm, allowing herself to be held up and arranged like a rag doll.

"Your sister kissed me. I didn't kiss her. I give you my word I didn't lure her out to the garden to seduce her. I took her there to explain to her that I wanted to give her a chance to prove she had changed and that I was going to marry you. She just suddenly kissed me—maybe to congratulate me. I don't know. But that's all it was." He didn't have the heart to tell her how Flame had thrown herself at him all evening. LaRaine would feel even more betrayed than she did now if she realized what her sister had tried to do.

Why don't you tell her the truth, Brand? Flame asked silently, hidden in the shadows outside the door to LaRaine's room. *Tell her how I forced myself on you? Why don't you tell her that part?* She smiled to herself, satisfied that she knew the answers to her questions. *No, you won't tell her because you know she won't believe you. She'll think you did something to lead me on. No matter which way you turn, Brand Colter, you're going to lose. You lose and I win!*

"Is that true?" LaRaine asked, studying Brand's anguished face intently. "I want to believe you, but I can't be sure."

"You're the only woman I love—or will ever love. Since the moment I first saw you, I've loved only you." The look on his dark face was so anguished that LaRaine began to soften.

Brand stood up and crossed to the door. Reaching around the corner, where he knew Flame had been eavesdropping, he clutched her arm tightly and pulled her into LaRaine's room. "Tell her, Flame. Tell your sister that I didn't make a pass at you. Tell her how you were just 'congratulating' me when you kissed me." The threat in his voice was harsh and violent.

"Yes, I kissed him," Flame said, her voice small and irritatingly childlike. She sounded like a little girl being forced to admit a wrongdoing that would result in some terrible punishment. "I didn't mean to hurt you, Beth. I love you too much." Now she was crying, the tears gushing profusely down her cheeks and her loud sniffles racking through the room.

"Oh, baby, you didn't do anything wrong. It was my fault for jumping to conclusions," LaRaine insisted, rushing to take her sister into the protective circle of her arms, leaving Brand standing to the side—alone.

Damn! he thought in frustration. *How can she fall for that crap? I'm the injured party here, and she's consoling that cross between a helpless infant and a scheming bitch. Now, even if I tell her what Flame did, she'll insist Flame didn't mean any harm. Hell, maybe she didn't. But what good does that do me?*

"Rainy?" Brand said over the annoying wails of LaRaine's twin sister. "When can we talk?"

Flame cried louder, bemoaning the fact that she was a terrible person who had hurt her beloved sister.

"Tomorrow," LaRaine mouthed over her shoulder as she guided her sobbing sister through the sitting room to her own bedroom. "I don't want to leave Faith alone tonight. She's too upset," LaRaine explained, as if that said it all.

Poor little Faith. She's upset. What about poor little Brand? He's more than upset. "When, La-Raine? When tomorrow?" His voice forced a casualness he certainly didn't feel. What he really wanted to do was throw the wailing Flame out of LaRaine's arms and show the woman he loved what real need was.

"I'll be here all day, except when I go to the bank. Come by any time," she said, still too concerned with how badly Flame felt to notice the

403

clenching of Brand's fists and jaw.

"Tomorrow then," he said, and turned angrily on his heel, leaving LaRaine to care for her weeping charge.

When LaRaine heard the front door click shut, she excused herself from Flame — whose tears had suddenly subsided to an occasional sniff — and hurried downstairs to make sure the lock was in place. Then she ran back up to Flame.

Knowing how young and helpless she looked in her flannel gown and with her hair down, Flame quickly dressed for bed and then waited for her sister to come to her. "Are you certain you forgive me, Beth?" she whimpered, peeking out from under long, wet lashes.

"Darling, there's nothing to forgive. You were only responding to Brand's news like a warm loving sister should. I'm mad at myself for acting so foolishly. What will Mrs. Colterelli think of me?"

"You were right about me, Beth," Flame admitted, making a great show of baring her soul. "I did think he was interested in me. I guess I imagined the way his hand kept brushing my lap under the table at dinner and in the carriage. Oh, I feel so foolish, so ashamed," she moaned dramatically.

"Things always seem the worst at night, love. You'll find a wonderful man of your own one of these days, and then you'll look back on tonight and laugh at how you felt. I promise."

"I don't think so, Beth," Flame said forlornly, with heartbreaking finality.

"Yes, you will. Mark my words," LaRaine promised supportively. "Now, let's get some sleep. We've got some busy days ahead of us if we're going to leave for Europe on the first."

"You mean we're still going?"

"Of course we are. If we don't go as we promised, the women of Galveston will tar and feather us before they hang us up by our thumbs!"

"But what about . . . *him?* Aren't you going to marry him?"

"He hasn't really asked me yet."

"But you're going to do it when he asks you, aren't you?" Flame asked, her tone full of accusation. She burst into a new attack of crying. "I knew it! You're going to leave me!"

LaRaine hugged her. "Don't cry, honey. I'm not going to leave you. And I'm certainly not going to get married anytime soon. At least not before we get back from Paris. That's for certain. And maybe in the meantime, we'll find a handsome husband for you. Maybe a European prince! Now, go to sleep, and I'll see you in the morning."

She bent to kiss her sister's cheek and hug her. It was obvious to LaRaine that Flame was scared to death at the prospect of having her sister marry; and she felt doubly guilty for even considering the idea.

You'd do it, wouldn't you? You'd marry that man and leave me. Well, not while I still have a breath in my body, Flame swore silently. "Good night, Beth. I love you," she mumbled sleepily in her little-girl voice and snuggled down into her bed, curling herself into a ball.

"I love you too, baby," LaRaine returned softly,

blowing out the lamp on the table before returning to her own room to spend a long night tossing and turning—only to awaken the following morning even more tired than when she had gone to bed.

Chapter Twenty-five

The next day, every time the bell over the door jingled to announce a visitor, both LaRaine and Flame jerked their heads up from whatever they were doing. Though neither sister mentioned Brand or anything that had happened the evening before, it was obvious his next visit was the prominent thought on both their minds.

However, business was hectic so it kept their minds occupied most of the time. Even with Mrs. Flanagan's niece Margie helping out, there was little time to dwell on personal problems. In fact, it was nearly one o'clock before LaRaine was able to get away to go to the bank. And even then, she hesitated to go, thinking she might miss Brand. But she had no choice.

"While I'm out, I'm going to make a dash by the market and the shipping office to make our final arrangements," she told Flame and Margie as she left the busy shop. "Can you handle things while I'm gone?"

"Just don't be too long. You know how I worry," Flame said, following her to the door and using the excuse to look up and down the street for Brand's buggy. If he came now and missed LaRaine, maybe she could put him off for another day. She would tell him LaRaine needed time to think, that she wasn't certain she wanted to marry him yet. *Good, he's not here. Now, if he'll just come before she gets back, everything will go according to my plan.*

Around the corner from the shop, Brand slouched back against a brick wall and crossed his ankles restlessly. He had been there much of the day—waiting for LaRaine to pass by. It had been the only way he could think of to see her alone—without her clinging sister to interrupt them.

At last his patience was rewarded. As she turned onto Twenty-fourth where he'd stationed himself, he leaped into his buggy to follow her up the street, hoping no one—Flame in particular—spotted him crossing Avenue D.

Pulling alongside LaRaine's hurrying figure, he flashed her a bright smile and tipped his hat. "Want a ride?"

LaRaine gasped in surprise, aware of the excited flutter deep in the pit of her stomach she never failed to have when she saw him unexpectedly. "What are you doing here?" she asked warmly, really needing no answer. She could see it in his eyes.

"Following you," he responded mischievously, the twinkle in his blue eyes almost hiding the frustration that lurked behind them. "Where have you been? I almost froze to death waiting for you to come by," he exaggerated theatrically.

"I was in my shop waiting for you to come in," she scolded. "Where have *you* been? I couldn't let my banking wait any longer, so I finally had to give up. I was certain you'd arrive right after I left and I would miss you."

"Hey, fella!" a loud male voice yelled belligerently. "Ya wanna move that rig outta the way?"

"Sorry," Brand hollered over his shoulder to the impatient man. "Get in." He reached out a strong hand and pulled LaRaine into the seat beside him, without giving her a chance to protest. Not that she would have. She found she was very anxious to spend some time alone with Brand.

There were so many things to say to each other, so many questions to be answered. What had he decided about Flame? Did he plan to turn her over to the law or did he believe her? Flame, who had worked so hard to become the person she thought LaRaine wanted her to be; Flame, who depended on her for almost every decision; Flame, whom she felt she owed something that could not be repaid in a thousand lifetimes. Even if Brand decided at the end of the week to forget Flame's past, could she make the choice Brand was obviously expecting her to make?

If she and Brand married, what would become of Flame? She couldn't live with them. La Raine knew without asking that Brand wouldn't hear of that.

What it all came down to was that she probably shouldn't have allowed Brand Colter to step back into her life. She should have taken Flame and run the first time she had seen him, because now she wasn't sure she was strong enough to give him up again if she had to.

"We're going to work this thing out, Rainy," he said, covering her small hand with his, knowing instinctively what she was thinking.

LaRaine's yellow-green eyes searched deep into Brand's intense look of love, and her heart began to beat faster in anticipation of what it meant to have a man gaze at a woman the way he was looking at her. Her eyes glistened with tears of love, magnifying the tiny brown speck in the pigment of her left eye.

His hand burned its impression through the smooth kidskin glove that had so effectively protected her fingers from the cold in the winter, and her worried frown of concentration was replaced with a shy smile, a trusting reflection of the love she saw in his expression. Yes, they would work it out. They had to!

"Where are we going?" she asked, all thought of banking, marketing, or travel arrangements driven from her mind. Even the matter of Flame didn't seem quite so urgent. Not when he looked at her like that.

Right now, nothing mattered but the moment, a moment when there was no one but the two of them in the world. As far as she was concerned, they were alone. There were no other carriages on the street and no people on the sidewalks. The world had stopped revolving and clocks had ceased their ticking. It was just them. This was their moment in time, meant to be shared with no one else.

Everything had come to an abrupt halt. Everything but the sound of the horse's hooves clicking on the pavement in the same staccato rhythm that LaRaine's heart pounded out its lonely call to Brand.

"Here we are," he announced, turning his concentration away from LaRaine to drive his buggy into a small carriage house behind a neat two-story home on Avenue I.

"Where is here?" She laughed, realizing she had no idea where they were. North, south, east, or west. It didn't matter. They could be in another city, another state—even on another planet. "Whose house is this?" she inquired curiously, forcing herself to tear her eyes from Brand's smiling face to look at the back of the comfortable but modest white house.

"It's mine," he answered, grinning secretly as he reached up and circled her waist to lift her down from the buggy.

"Don't you live with your parents?" she asked, weak with the realization that his hands remained resting at the curve of her slender waist longer than necessary.

"Yes." He chuckled for no reason at all. Just from the sheer delight of being with her. With LaRaine finally there, looking up at him with her strange, inquisitive eyes, it was as if the last six months had never happened. He felt there was no problem too large or insurmountable for them to overcome. They would be together—no matter what obstacles they encountered.

"This was my grandmother's house. She left it to me," he said, denying them the kiss his mouth ached to experience. He knew that once their lips met, he wouldn't be able to stop kissing her. Not ever.

"No one lives in it anymore," he explained, slipping her hand into the crook of his arm and escorting her along the walk toward the house. "I had planned to sell it since I've been in Galveston so rarely the last few years. But now I don't know," he said thoughtfully. "I really hate to part with it. It holds lots of good memories."

"I see that it does," LaRaine said, her voice filled with love for the tall man who at that moment looked like an excited little boy, despite the weathered lines on his face. "I can see it in your expression when you talk about it."

They walked around the house slowly, leisurely, as if they had all the time in the world and as if they had made the same walk hundreds of times before.

When they finally ascended to the front porch, Brand produced a key and let them into a dark foyer that had a narrow stairwell at one side. The house smelled musty, and the sheet-covered furniture in the living room gave the place a ghostly look. Yet, despite the gloom, the house emitted a feeling of warmth and love.

"It doesn't look like much now. It's been closed up a long time," Brand apologized, glancing self-consciously around in the half-light that filtered through the window blinds and the front door.

"I think it's lovely. I can almost picture this room with its furniture all dusted and aired, the sunshine streaming through sparkling windows, fresh flowers from the garden on the table, your grandmother doing embroidery over there—while a dark-haired little boy ran up and down the stairs making all sorts of peculiar sounds—sounds that only boys can make," she laughed.

Brand gave LaRaine a look of absolute astonishment. She had unknowingly described the scene that had taken place in this room so many times in the past. "How did you know? Are you really a witch after all?"

"Mere deduction, my love." She smiled, letting Brand wonder only a moment longer. "There's the stitching frame over there. I can tell by its shape under the sheet. All children like to play on stairs, and all boys make those funny little-boy noises. Girls don't make them. They just giggle. And I doubt this place would have held happy memories for you if you hadn't been able to make those noises. Am I right?"

Brand answered by circling her waist with his hands and picking her up off the floor. Making a whistling, whirling sound as he had so many years before, he swung her in a wide circle. He never wanted to let her go.

When at last he stopped turning, he didn't put her down, but held her above him, his arms tight around her waist, her hands balanced on his shoulders, his chin at her midriff. There were no more giggles, no more whistling, whirling sounds, only the sound of breathing, already growing ragged with desire. He let her slide down his chest until her face was even with his, her arms around his neck.

They stayed like that, mouths almost touching, eyes locked in common desire. And when Brand sucked in an agonizing breath, LaRaine knew it was her breath, her scent, her soul he inhaled. A spiral of fire deep within her ignited explosively.

Slowly, he expelled the breath he had taken from her, and she drew it back into her own lungs, taking the entire essence of him into her heart.

At last, when she had almost given up hope that he would ever kiss her, his mouth brushed hers with a feathery kiss, then another, and another. Still they watched each other silently.

The light kisses grew more insistent, more frequent, his lips lingering slightly longer with each delightful contact, the pressure more intense, the need more agonizing.

Threading her fingers through wavy black hair, she held his head still, wanting to stop his teasing kisses, wanting to feel his mouth pressing against hers, crushing her lips against her teeth.

Then it was happening. No longer was Brand's mouth soft or playful. No longer was LaRaine the passive recipient of his light kisses. This kiss was long and deep, each of them giving, each of them taking. Tongues caressing tongues and lips, mating in an urgent rhythm of feral desire. Hands caressing bodies so close together that each could feel the burning languor that swirled wildly through the other, making their desire one.

Continuing to search the warmth of her mouth with his tongue, Brand allowed LaRaine to slip farther down his lean, hard frame, until she was standing on her toes, her arms still clinging desperately to his neck.

"I'll never let you get away from me again," he moaned. Keeping her hips molded to his, he drew his upper torso back so that he could watch the beautiful expression of rapture on her face, the face he had dreamed of for so long. Running his strong hands up over her arms, along her shoulders to her neck, Brand held LaRaine's head while his callused thumbs made disturbing circular motions around and into the shells of her ears.

LaRaine didn't know when Brand removed the pins holding her hair in its prim chignon, but suddenly they were gone, and her hair was tumbling free down her back in a glorious cloud of sweet-smelling silk. He buried his face in a handful of thick tresses, dragging a deep breath of its fragrance into his lungs. He slowly released it in a warm puff that wafted deliciously over the sensitive flesh of her neck.

Unfastening her warm cape, which had suddenly become an irritating hindrance to him, Brand slid it from her shoulders, allowing it to fall to the floor in a dark puddle of wool at their feet. He drew her hips hard against his rotating pelvis as he bent to kiss each of her closed eyes, her nose, her cheeks, the corners of her mouth, her chin, then her open, waiting lips.

"I'd given up the hope that I'd ever know this

perfection again, Rainy." His voice was a tortured confession of desire.

Awkwardly, almost bashfully, he fumbled with the tiny buttons down the front of her tight-fitting brown bodice. After several attempts to unhook the small fasteners, he grew frustrated with his shaking hands. "Damn!" he laughed self-consciously. "I'm as nervous as a kid."

During the moments while Brand had concentrated on the buttons, LaRaine was able to come to her senses. Covering his trembling hands with her own, she held them still against her breast. "Maybe it's because you know we shouldn't be here," she suggested, her voice low.

"Don't say that!" he ordered, forgetting the bodice and embracing LaRaine so tightly that the breath was squeezed out of her lungs. His mouth descended on her protest in a searing kiss, driving all thought of self-denial out of her mind, branding her his for all time.

Lifting his head to look down into her worried eyes, he shook his head, the hunger in his eyes imploring. "Don't stop me, Rainy," he said softly.

"Brand, you have no idea how much I want to be with you." She cupped his cheek in her hand. "But there are just so many things we need to work out first," she said, her voice evidencing a calm the telltale pulse in her neck belied.

He lowered his head to kiss the rapid flutter. "We'll talk, Rainy. We have our whole lives to talk. But right now I don't want to think about anything but loving you. Just let me love you."

The need in his eyes, more black than blue in

the half-light of the dusky foyer, stoked the growing flame inside her—which was fast approaching the point of uncontrolled lust.

Deeming herself a fool with her last rational thought, LaRaine surrendered her remaining ounce of resistance with a yielding moan as she leaned into his embrace. "Yes, love, me, Brand. Please love me," she cried against his neck.

In one lithe motion, Brand swept her slender body into his arms. Taking the stairs two at a time, he carried her to an upstairs hallway with two doorways on the left. Opening the door at the end of the narrow passageway, he took her into a neat, pale-blue room which had obviously been readied for someone. There was none of the musty gloom that permeated the downstairs rooms, and it had been cleaned and aired. There were even fresh flowers on the table beside the blue quilt-covered four-poster bed.

"Who did all of this?" she asked, peering happily around the gay room.

"Shh." Brand laid her back on the bed, not wanting anything to spoil the moment. Slowly, as if sculpting a work of art, he again began unbuttoning the front of her dress.

LaRaine watched him, loving the way he bit the side of his bottom lip as he concentrated seriously on what he was doing.

When the final button was at last undone, Brand trembled a deep, rasping breath and slid his hands inside the bodice to open her dress front.

"You're so lovely," he murmured, his questing

eyes taking in the rise and fall of her breasts, their rosy centers visible through the opaque chemise that covered them. Dragging the tip of his tongue along his bottom lip, he anticipated the taste of those glorious peaks, already hardening and thrusting upward under his gaze.

LaRaine reached out to caress his shoulders, wanting to feel his mouth on hers again, needing to feel his weight on her. But he resisted.

Lifting her to a sitting position, he slipped her arms out of the bodice so that it fell down around her waist, leaving her upper body clad in nothing but the thin chemise. Only then did he kiss her mouth, just before burning a trail of hot kisses down her throat and over her shoulder to nudge a lacy strap off one shoulder, then the other. When both shoulders were bared, he returned to the sweet hollow at the base of her throat.

When he had thoroughly kissed the arching paleness of her neck, he began his descent to the tiny blue ribbon that secured her chemise over her breasts, already so swollen with the need for his touch that she had no control over the way they thrust forward, begging him to caress and love their fullness.

Standing beside the bed, he held his hands out to her. She took them readily and rose to face him. Quickly finishing the task of opening her dress, he slid everything—bodice, skirt, chemise, and drawers—down over her hips until she stood before him naked, each nerve cell in her body quivering for the merging of their flesh.

Remaining perfectly still, LaRaine shuddered as she felt his ravenous gaze glide over her, burning her flesh as she basked in the light from his eyes.

Quickly divesting himself of his own clothing, Brand was thrilled when she watched him undress with unabashed curiosity and desire.

Passion shivered demandingly through her as his nakedness was revealed to her, and she reached out a tentative hand to touch the taut, hair-covered skin of his muscular chest with her fingertips.

Now it was his turn to give her time to explore him with her eyes, and she did just that. Glancing up at his handsome face, she returned his loving smile, then allowed her voracious gaze to travel lazily, hungrily, to his broad shoulders, to the crisp black hair curling across his chest, narrowing to a pencil-slim line over the flat plane of his stomach, his narrow hips, and at last to the proud seat of his manhood, rigid with passion.

Taking a step forward, Brand's hands spread around LaRaine's waist and pulled her against him. Her eyes closed, she went willingly, anxiously. Using his splayed hands to caress her back, buttocks, and thighs, he lowered his head to explore her face once more with his lips.

He laid her gently onto the bed, his kiss on her mouth providing even more fuel for the already burning volcano threatening to erupt inside her. His lips slid from her mouth, along the softness of her cheek, to the curve of her neck, and the heat from his touch raced through her like wildfire.

He stretched out beside her, nuzzling and nibbling at her skin as his hand began a delightful, bone-melting exploration of her breasts. His touch brought her apricot nipples to aching peaks of longing, arching and pushing against his palm, needing — no — demanding the blissful torment of his kiss.

Continuing to tease and massage one breast with expert fingers, he kissed a hot, wet trail along the valley between the two glorious mounds, finally sucking a swollen tip deep into the warm moistness of his mouth. She moaned with delight and desperately gripped his head to her. His tongue was liquid fire as it crossed to the other breast to give it his special attention.

She was burning, her whole body aflame with longing. Her hips arched and gyrated in animal anticipation, and heat radiated violently from the center of her body to every extremity. But Brand was not to be hurried. He had waited too long for this moment to rush it. He was going to prolong it, savor it.

Extending his excursion down her satiny skin, his lips followed in the blissful wake of his hand. He slid his fingers over the downy portal that guarded her femininity and into the moist center of her sexuality to quickly bring her to an unexpected climax.

As she shuddered and moved against his hand, she tried to draw him up over her, wanting to feel his strength inside her. She was adamant. She needed him in her — but still he resisted her demands.

Her eyes were closed, her fingers tangled in his thick hair, when she felt the warm stirring of his breath on the smooth skin of her belly. He was kissing her stomach, her hips, her thighs, licking the delectable flesh hungrily, worshiping her with his tongue. LaRaine was certain she would die, but she couldn't help lifting her hips upward, begging for his touch.

On his knees between her legs, Brand moved his mouth over the soft enclave of coppery hair. She could feel his breath moving the fine curls, already moist with her need, and her hips rose of their own accord to meet his lips and tongue.

Cupping her buttocks with his hands and pressing her thighs farther apart, he brought her upward to bury his kisses in the center of her longing.

Almost immediately, she was flung to wild fulfillment by the unyielding caress of his tongue on the sensitive pearl of her womanhood, leaving her gasping for air and begging for mercy.

When Brand could no longer withstand the agony of waiting, he entered her, meeting her arching hips with deep, penetrating strokes as she surrounded his hardness with the willing flesh of her trembling interior.

With frenzied movement and a feral sense of urgency, they carried out the wondrous ritual of mating, until together they were hurled violently, spasmodically, to the pinnacle of fulfillment.

"Brand!" LaRaine cried out in the aftermath of the explosion, her voice hoarse, her breathing ragged and shallow.

"Tell me you love me, Rainy," he breathed heavily into her ear. "I want to hear you say you love me."

"I love you, Brand," she said. "I love you," she said louder. "I love you, Brand Colter. With all my heart!" she cried with even more volume, her smile ecstatic as she held him closer to her with her arms. "I love you," she shouted, still intoxicated with their lovemaking. "I want the whole world to know I love Brand Colter," she yelled happily, squeezing his perspiration-soaked body to her own by wrapping her legs more securely around his hips, ensuring that he wouldn't, couldn't, roll away from her.

"Will you marry me?" he asked simply, instinctively dreading her answer.

Brand's question brought back all LaRaine's misgivings, and a wave of reality ruptured her mood. "It's too soon, Brand," she murmured, aware that his body had grown tense and was already withdrawing from hers. She wanted to cry, despite the fact that she continued to cling desperately to him.

"It's been six months, LaRaine," he said coldly, deliberately not calling her Rainy. "When will it not be too soon?"

"Please don't be angry. I love you. I do! But Brand, even though it's been a long time since we first met, we really don't know each other. I didn't even know your real name until a few days ago. We've spent such a short time together," she said, trying to sound sensible, knowing she was only making excuses. He knew, too, and her heart went out to him, sitting on the edge of the bed, his back to her.

"Is there someone else?" he asked bluntly through clenched teeth.

"No!" she responded, startled he should even consider such a possibility after what they had just shared. "Not if you mean another man. You're the only man I'll ever love. But I can't marry you. Not yet. Maybe never."

"Why?" He looked over his shoulder at her, his blue eyes growing hard. "Why not, Rainy?"

"You know why, Brand," she sighed.

"Say it. I want to hear you say the words!" he ordered, his lip curled bitterly.

"All right!" she cried. "It's Faith. I can't make the 'choice' you want me to make! Is that what you wanted me to say?"

Brand's expression grew hard with her answer, even though he'd known what it would be. In a way, he wished it had been another man. That he could have fought. But this! How was he supposed to fight this. "You 'can't' or you 'won't'?" he asked bitterly.

LaRaine's heart felt as if it was splintering in her chest. Regaining some control, she lowered her voice. "She needs me, Brand. And until she doesn't, I have to be there for her. I owe her that much."

"Do you owe her your life, Rainy? My life?" he asked, still unable to fathom the fact that she actually believed she had a debt to Flame Rider! "It's the other way around. She owes you. Can't you see that? She would have died at the end of a rope if it weren't for you! You gave her a new life. What the hell do you owe her? You've paid any imagined debts you have to her!"

"It's not that easy, Brand. There are scars on her soul that will never heal, scars so deep and ugly that she'll never fully recover from the abuse she suffered at the hands of our natural father."

LaRaine tried to explain, wishing the stinging tears she felt in her eyes could be stopped. She told him how Flame's father had raped her repeatedly from the time she was eight years old.

"But it wasn't your fault, Rainy. Can't you see that? You're the one who helped her. You didn't scar her."

"Yes, I did. I left her behind to suffer alone. I wasn't there when she needed me."

"Do you mean to tell me a person of your intelligence thinks she's responsible for something that happened a few hours after you were born? You didn't even know about her, Rainy. The fact that you went and she stayed was not of your doing." His voice was rife with incapacitating frustration. "It was just luck. Nothing more!"

"But she knew about me and always believed I'd come and save her. I never did and Mary Doyle died inside. They killed her in little bits and pieces, Brand. When I found her, Mary no longer existed. She had become Flame Rider, an empty shell that only resembled a human being on the outside. You've seen what miracles being loved has brought about in her. That little girl who disappeared so long ago has been reborn. But I can't ever forget how little it would take to

424

force her into hiding again. I know in my mind that what happened to her wasn't my fault. But in my heart . . . In my heart, I still feel responsible."

She looked at him beseechingly, her lips trembling as she fought her tears. "I just feel responsible. And I can never leave her. Whatever becomes of her would be my fault, and I won't take the risk."

"So you plan to give up your own happiness to coddle her?"

"I don't expect you to understand. It was foolish of me to think you could," she added, admitting her defeat and rising to pick up her clothing. She began dressing, her actions wooden. "I promised her I'd never let her be hurt again. And I won't, Brand. No matter how much I love you, and no matter what I have to give up, I'm going to always be here for my sister as long as she needs me."

"What if she meets someone and leaves you?"

"I'd marry you without a moment's hesitation — if you still wanted me," she sighed, walking over to the window. "But I can't ask you to wait that long, Brand. What if she never meets anyone?" LaRaine's voice was saturated with hopelessness.

"Rainy, Rainy." He slid his arms around her from behind and rested his chin on the top of her mussed hair. "Can't you see what she's doing? She's punishing you for what happened to her as a little girl. She's forced you to give up your individuality, a life of your own, your name, even your beautiful red hair. All for her! When will

425

you have given enough? When will the price of her love be too great! When will your guilt be assuaged!"

"Never," LaRaine answered quietly, knowing the truth in his words, but also knowing that her choice had been made, and that she had to stand by it.

"I need to go home. Faith will be worried," she said, not looking at him as she busied her hands with the buttons on her bodice. Her trembling fingers were no better equipped to manipulate them than Brand's had been earlier.

"No, we can't let 'Faith' worry, can we?" Brand responded, dropping his hands from her waist and turning to finish his own dressing.

Chapter Twenty-six

When Flame realized that Brand and LaRaine must be together, she decided it was time to take more drastic measures if she wanted to end the relationship before it resulted in marriage and destroyed her. It would have been so much easier if Brand had chosen her when she had given him the opportunity. But now she would have to make the choice for him.

Her anger seething and festering like a boil, she left the shop in the care of Margie and stormed out to her buggy. First, she went to the bank to make a withdrawal, then to the steamship office to confirm their passage to Europe.

Stuffing her money into her purse along with her pistol, she drove to the docks where unemployed seamen loafed while waiting to hire on one of the many ships that sailed in and out of the Galveston harbor every day. There, she quickly chose three particularly tough-looking seamen to approach with her proposition.

"I have a job that needs three good men," she

said, drawing her buggy up beside them. "The pa[y]
is good, and I'm looking for men who can b[e]
trusted to complete the task and then leave Galve[s]ton. Do any of you know someone who would b[e]
interested?"

A large, cocky sailor in a striped shirt an[d]
heavy coat sauntered up to Flame's buggy, h[is]
half-lidded eyes studying her cloaked figure, tryin[g]
to make out her features through the heavy blac[k]
veil over her face. "Whadda ya got in min[d,]
sugar?" he drawled, his voice thick with sexu[al]
overtones.

"Your name is . . . ?" Flame said, glaring dow[n]
at him through the thick covering that she ha[d]
worn to obscure her features. The veil didn't hid[e]
the cold, frightening glint in her eyes, and th[e]
man shuddered apprehensively. He didn't kno[w]
what it was about her that was so threatening, bu[t]
he knew she wasn't a lady to cross.

"Tom Smith," he answered sheepishly, obviousl[y]
showing more respect than he had at first. "What['s]
the job, ma'am?"

"Are you gentlemen in, or do I need to loo[k]
further?" she asked the two who continued t[o]
gawk at the way she had made the bigger ma[n]
cower.

"Oh, yes, ma'am, we're in," they eagerly agreed[,]
the thought of extra spending money overcomin[g]
their curiosity about the mysterious woman wh[o]
talked like a lady but had a voice as hard as stee[l.]

Flame quickly outlined her proposal to the thre[e]
eager ruffians—fifty dollars each up front, anothe[r]
fifty when they carried out the job, and a fina[l]

428

one hundred to each of them when they hired on the first available freighter out of Galveston.

After making certain they understood what she expected of them, Flame paid the men and left, promising to meet them the following morning with the second payment — assuming, of course, that everything went as she had outlined.

Long after closing time, when LaRaine hurried into the House of Fashion, she wasn't surprised to find a worried and frantic Flame waiting for her. She rushed to explain. "I ran into Brand and we just lost track of time. I'm so sorry. I hope you didn't worry," she apologized breathlessly.

That son of a bitch. He's not going to get away with doing this to me, Flame swore as she surveyed her sister's blushing cheeks, swollen lips, and rumpled clothing. LaRaine's customary chignon had obviously been pinned hastily into place, but Flame didn't need to see her sister's tousled hair to know that she had done more than just talk to Brand Colter, and she made no attempt to hide her contempt for what she saw.

"I take it you didn't manage to make it to the bank or to the market," Flame commented sarcastically. "And what about our travel arrangements? I don't suppose you found the time to take care of them, either. No, of course you didn't," she answered her own question. "You had more important things on your mind, didn't you, Beth?"

Now there were angry tears coursing hotly down the enraged twin's face, and LaRaine felt totally responsible. "Don't do this to me," she pleaded, reaching out to embrace Flame.

"Don't do this to *you?*" Flame shrieked, her voice high and hysterical as she pulled violently away from LaRaine's touch. "What have I done to you, Beth? Tell me! I'd really like to know! Was it me who left you here alone all afternoon to worry that something dreadful had happened? Though, I don't know why I concerned myself so. I can see by the disgusting look on your face that you thought it was anything but dreadful."

LaRaine tried to protest, but Flame went on cruelly. "And was it me who couldn't wait to sneak out and spread my legs for some man to hop on top of me? How many others have there been before this? Or is it just this one man whose bed you couldn't wait to get into?" she sneered spitefully.

"It wasn't like that, and you know it," LaRaine gasped, horrified by the way her sister was acting and talking. "You know there's been no one else. Brand and I love each other. We always have. You've known that all along!"

"Love!" Flame spat distastefully. "What about me? You said you loved me. How could you betray me like this if you really did? Was it all lies, Beth? Lies to make me behave the way you thought your sister should act? Did it embarrass you so much to have Flame Rider for a sister that you set out to reform me, only to turn on me when you were finished making me over?"

"This is ridiculous, and you know it!" LaRaine said, her voice quivering with frustration and hurt.

"One love has nothing to do with the other. There's enough love in my heart for more than one person. Especially when it's two different kinds of love. I can't stop loving Brand because I have a sister I love, too. Don't you see how foolish you're being? This isn't a contest. I can't just stop loving him. No more than I could stop loving you."

Flame wrapped her arms around her own waist and hugged herself in a gesture of withdrawing into herself. "Is that why you're rubbing your dirty little 'affair' in my face? Because you love me so much? Is that why you made a scandalous spectacle of yourself by coming home looking like a well-used *whore?*"

The only sound in the shop was the stunned hiss of LaRaine sucking air in through her teeth, followed by the stinging slap of her open hand on her sister's cheek. Flame's head snapped back with the blow, and LaRaine stared at her in horrified amazement. She had never even raised her voice to Flame, and here she was being provoked into hitting her.

Holding her hand to her burning face, Flame stared incredulously at LaRaine. "Is that what he's done to us, Beth? Turned us against each other? Has he come between us?" she whimpered, the tears in her eyes very real.

"No! No!" LaRaine insisted tearfully, hugging Flame's unresisting body to her and petting her hair soothingly. "I'm so sorry I did that. I didn't mean it. I don't know what got into me. Please forgive me," she implored, trying to put Flame's cruel words out of her mind.

"I'm sorry, too," Flame cried against LaRaine's shoulder. "I was just so afraid something had happened to you. I would die if I lost you," she stressed. "And then when you came home looking like you do, I just couldn't stand it."

"We both said and did things we didn't mean," LaRaine consoled, the unutterable weariness heavy in her tone.

"Are you going to marry him?" Flame asked.

LaRaine's muscles tensed. "I told him I couldn't. Not if it would cause you to be unhappy," she answered dispiritedly.

A jolt of triumph bolted through Flame's blood, but it wasn't enough. "What did he say to that?" she asked, drawing back to watch her sister's pain-racked face. She hated to see the unhappiness in her expression, but this was a battle for her very own existence, and she couldn't let sympathy get in her way.

"He didn't understand," LaRaine answered simply, turning to go upstairs, using every modicum of control not to cry.

"What about me? Is he going to tell the sheriff about me now that you've told him you won't marry him?"

"I think he's convinced nothing will be gained by sending you to jail."

"Did he actually tell you that?"

"No, but I'm sure he's no threat to you now."

Maybe not as long as Mr. Brand Colter thinks there's a chance you'll change your mind and marry him, Flame said silently. *But he's not fool-*

ing me. I know what he's thinking. He'll keep coming back until he wears you down and gets you to marry him. Then, once he's got you in his trap, he'll turn me in. You say you won't let it happen, but sooner or later you'll give in. You won't be able to resist him. I can see it in your eyes. But I'm not going to let that happen.

Flame smiled to herself as she watched her naïve sister enter her bedroom and take off her cape. Right now she thought she couldn't live without Brand Colter, but she could and she would once and for all—with her sister to help her get over him.

Brand and LaRaine wouldn't see each other again, and Flame breathed a sigh of relief at the thought. If the three men she had hired had carried out their end of the bargain, the deed was probably already done.

Flame would have indeed been pleased if she had known how well her plans were being carried out. The men she had hired had already done her bidding and were at that very moment delivering their prisoner to a deserted building on the wharf. It had been no easy task for the three to disable the strong man, but after a lengthy scuffle Tom had finally managed to sink a knife into Brand's ribs.

Brand had been so shocked at being injured that he had instinctively looked down at the spreading stain of blood on his shirt and didn't see the other man's boot as it came up and kicked his chin.

"Ya damned fool! Ya know what she said. She said she wouldn't pay nuthin' fer a damned corpse. We can't kill 'im till we git out ta sea. She don't want his body found nowhere on the island," Billy scolded the others.

"Hell, he ain't dead," Tom snorted, slipping a burly arm around Brand's limp body and holding the half-conscious man in a standing position. "Get on t'other side o' 'im. If'n anybody asks, our buddy here's jest had a bit too much ta drink."

"He better not die," Billy grumbled, helping hold Brand upright. "I'm gonna be real mad if'n I don't git the rest o' that money! I'm holdin' ya responsible, Tom," he said threateningly.

"Quit yer bitchin'. We're gonna collect all what's comin' ta us. One way or t'other," the third man, Harry, chuckled knowingly, slipping Brand's wallet and gold watch into his own pocket, unnoticed by his partners.

"Should we jest lay 'im there in the corner fer now?" Tom asked Harry, who was older and smarter than his two companions. "Do ya think we need ta tie 'im up er what?" When it came to thinking, Tom and Billy needed to rely on the older man.

"O' course," Harry nodded, pointing to a rope in the corner of the dingy room. "Sometimes I git real worried 'bout you two. If'n somethin' ever happened ta me, there wouldn't be no one ta tell ya when ta take a pee. What were ya plannin' on doin' with 'im? Givin' 'im free run o' the place? Mebbe invitin' 'im ta join us in a little card game? Tie 'im up!"

434

"I jest meant since he's sleepin', he can't cause too much trouble," Tom defended himself.

"I know what ya meant. Jest what did ya think was gonna happen when he wakes up? Tie the bastard up an' quit yer yappin'. Then pour some o' that sleepin' potion she gave us down his throat so he don't wake up anytime too soon."

"I wonder what he done ta make 'er so mad at 'im," Tom pondered as he helped Billy tie Brand's hands and feet.

"I'm gonna check that there hole ya put in 'im," Billy said, opening Brand's coat and examining the slowly spreading red stain on his white shirt. "It don't look real bad. Looks like ya stuck the knife in here and it come out there," he commented, pointing at two oozing wounds. "Probably didn't hurt nuthin' 'portant. Looks like it jest grazed the ribs," he decided, and closed Brand's coat over the blood, certain the man would live at least long enough for them to collect their money.

When Brand regained consciousness some hours later, it took him a while to remember what had happened. He lay in a groggy daze for several minutes before it all came crowding back into his head at once—the men jumping into his buggy as he had pulled away from LaRaine's shop, the fight when they had pulled him from the moving vehicle, his horses running haphazardly down the dark street, the burning heat of the knife as it had entered his flesh, and the boot against his chin.

He opened his eyes slowly, realizing that one of them was swollen almost shut. *Why didn't they just rob me and leave me? Why'd they bring me here?* he asked himself, in spite of the pain that thinking caused. Using his one good eye to peer curiously around the dark building, he realized he was alone. Tied up, wounded, and alone. Flexing his hands, he tried to work them out of the tight ropes, but it was no use. The bindings were secure.

Swallowing in an effort to make his dry mouth moist, Brand tasted blood. He tried to move his jaw, cringing at the pain that shot up the left side of his face. Running his tongue along the inside of his teeth, he surmised that he must have bitten his tongue when the thug had kicked him. He opened and shut his mouth cautiously. Though he could feel what seemed to be a loose tooth, he was relatively certain that his jaw was not broken. *Thank God for small favors.*

"But what good does that do if I lie here and bleed to death?" he asked aloud. Raising his head to see if the ache in his ribs was as serious as it felt, he found the effort was too much for him and he lost consciousness again.

The next time he awoke, Brand realized that it was no longer dark. There were dancing beams of sunlight glittering through cracks and knotholes in the ramshackle building where he had been dumped. He could taste the caked blood on his dry, cracked lips, and the hot sticky wound in his side was the source of grueling pain that pulsated cruelly throughout his arms and legs, as well as his chest.

He was only vaguely conscious of the sound of the sea washing against the wooden pilings of the pier, only slightly aware of the dingy building where he lay, already feverish. He couldn't focus on a plan for escape, nor did he wonder what would become of him. He could only think of LaRaine, how beautiful she was, how much he loved her, the feel of her in his arms.

Nothing else was of any importance—not the pain, the numbness in his hands and feet, the terrible thirst. Nothing. Not even living if he had to live without LaRaine. "Rainy, Rainy," he croaked pitifully.

Then suddenly she was there, bending over him, touching his burning brow with her cool hand, opening his coat to examine the painful wound in his side. He tried to sit up, viewing her through swollen, bloodshot eyes. Then he slumped weakly against her breast. "Rainy, is it really you? I knew you'd come."

"Shh," she whispered. "I'll take care of you now, Brand."

"How did you find me, Rainy," he asked, his words almost incoherent. "You have to be careful. They might come back. You shouldn't have come alone. It's too dangerous. Leave me here and go for help. Don't let them find you with me. Rainy. Rainy, are you listening to me? You must do what I say," he ranted on. "Rainy, I love you, I love you," he babbled, gripping her soft, soothing hand with desperation.

"Drink this," she said, lifting his shivering shoulders and holding a cup of water to his lips. "This will make you feel much better," she promised, forcing the cup between his parched lips and making him drink the cool liquid.

"Get help, Rainy," he slurred, relaxing against her and allowing himself to be lowered to the floor again, sleeping heavily.

When Flame was certain Brand was beyond hearing, she turned to the three who watched her care for the wounded man on the floor. "You fools! I told you I wanted him alive!"

"He's alive," Tom said sullenly, knowing that his partners were blaming him for the woman's anger.

"Barely," she snarled, standing to glower at the trio.

"But alive," Harry smiled, showing a mouthful of yellowed, rotten teeth. "Ya owe us some money, lady."

"Here!" she hollered, digging into her purse and handing them the bills they were expecting. "Have you made the other arrangements? Or did you botch them, too? How soon will you and our friend be able to leave?"

"The three o' us're signed on the *Galveston Queen,* leavin' fer San Francisco on Tuesday. We booked 'im a cabin like ya told us ta do," Harry announced proudly. "We're s'posed ta board by sundown on Monday night. When can we 'spect the rest o' our money?"

Flame studied the man, her mouth set in an expression of disgust. God, how she hated dealing with this scum. She had been forced to be around their type all her life and had hoped that she was through with them forever. Maybe after she finished this job she could at last turn her back on her past once and for all. "I'll meet you here at six o'clock on Monday afternoon. You have him alive, cleaned up, and on his feet. I'll have your money then," she promised.

"Ya don't think he'll git hisself on board willin'ly, do ya? Look't all the trouble we had jest gettin' 'im in here," Billy protested. "He's gonna make a turrible ruckus when he figgers out what's happenin'."

"Oh, he'll be willing. You just leave that part to me. All you have to do is get him ready and help me get him to the ship." It would be a tight squeeze, but if everything went as Flame planned, she could make it work with time to spare. She and LaRaine were scheduled to board the ship for France by five that same evening.

"Whatever ya say, lady," Harry said, his head shaking doubtfully after taking one more quick glance at the unconscious man in the corner. "It's yore money. We'll do it any way ya want."

"That's right, and don't you forget it. I won't pay for a dead man or one that's filthy. He'll need a shave. And get his suit cleaned and pressed," she ordered, dismissing the men with a wave of her hand which sent them outside.

Returning to Brand's side, she spoke softly, so softly that the usual hoarseness in her voice was undetectable. "Brand, darling. I must leave you now. I'm going for help. Can you hear me?" The flutter of his eyes told her that he was trying to focus on her and what she was saying. "I'll be back, and then you and I will go away together. No one will ever come between us again," she vowed earnestly. "Will you be all right until I

439

come for you?" The concern in her voice was genuine.

"Mmm," he nodded weakly, licking his lips. "Be fine." Closing his eyes, he drifted back into his drugged sleep.

"Good." She smiled, giving him a kiss on the brow to make him feel confident. "It won't be long before all our dreams will come true." She breathed a relieved sigh and rose to go. *At least mine will come true!*

Minutes later, she took her leave of the seamen, reminding them once more that she wanted Brand to board the ship under his own steam. He couldn't be dead—although drunk would be permissible, even preferable.

While Flame was busying carrying out her furtive early-morning dealings, LaRaine was coming to some decisions of her own. Brand was right. She hadn't been at fault for the misfortunes that had been dealt her sister in the past. If Flame really loved her, as LaRaine knew she did, she should want her to be happy. *I've taught her to be on her own. She'll be just fine.*

"I'm going to marry Brand," she resolved, swinging her feet out of the warm bed onto the cold floor. She was not even aware of the shudder that ran through her at the chilly contact. *I've given up enough. I'm not going to lose him again,* she thought, finger-combing her long brown hair as she padded across the room to call Flame.

"Time to get up," she sang out, not really concerned about the time. She had made a decision, and she suddenly felt the weight of the world

440

lifted off her shoulders. *It'll work out. It's not as if I'm leaving her alone. I'll always be nearby. And I'll still come to the shop every day.* "Faith, are you awake?" she called again, wondering why she didn't hear her moving around in her room. "Come on, sleepyhead. Wake up," she repeated, crossing the living room to open her sister's door.

A bolt of alarm cut a jagged course through her. The bed was made up and her sister was nowhere to be found. Racing to the head of the stairs, she listened for a sign of activity coming from downstairs. Nothing. "Faith, where are you?" she appealed, the panic rising suffocatingly in her voice. "Are you down there?"

Where can she be? She was so upset last night. Did I drive her away? I'll never forgive myself if I did. What if she goes back to the life she had before? What have I done to her? LaRaine's mind was flooded mercilessly with thoughts of self-chastisement and guilt. *Why didn't I realize what she was feeling? If anything has happened to her, it's my fault.*

LaRaine was frantically dressing herself, wondering where she should begin her search, when she heard a door open and shut downstairs. "Is that you, Faith?" she shrieked, running back to the head of the stairs.

"Of course it's me," Flame answered dejectedly. "Who did you think it would be?" she laughed uneasily, her expression masked.

"Where have you been?" LaRaine cried, racing down the stairs to embrace Flame. "I've been frantic with worry. I woke up and you were gone. I couldn't imagine what had happened to you. I was scared to death," she confessed, only now getting control over her rapidly beating heart.

"Well, nothing happened to me, as you can see. I'm sorry I worried you," Flame said woodenly, giving LaRaine a strange look of pity.

But when LaRaine noticed the peculiar expression, Flame made a show of looking away, as if she were hiding something.

"What kind of errand did you have to take care of this early in the morning?" LaRaine asked suspiciously, leading her sister up to the apartment.

"Nothing important," Flame said, her response quick and tinged with shame.

"Tell me! It must have been something to leave you with that sad expression on your sweet face. Nothing could be that bad," she insisted cheerfully, lifting Flame's downcast chin to look into her eyes.

Flame stared at LaRaine. She seemed to be on the verge of speaking but holding back. She bit her lip to keep from crying and LaRaine's heart went out to her. "What is it? What happened?"

"Oh, Beth! It was so terrible!" she blurted out, burying her weeping face against LaRaine's shoulder. "I can't bear to think about it."

"What?" LaRaine insisted, her voice rife with fear that Flame had been recognized. "Tell me, honey. Let me help you."

Instinctively realizing what her sister was thinking, Flame shook her head. "It's not that, Beth. No one recognized me. It's worse. Much worse!" she wailed loudly, desperately.

"What could be worse, Faith? You've got to tell me," she demanded, gripping Flame's stooped shoulders and shaking her. "What is it? Tell me right this minute!"

"It's Brand," Flame sobbed hysterically.

"Brand?!?" LaRaine gasped in horror, her heart rate leaping sporadically. "What about Brand? Has something happened to him? Oh, my God! He's dead, isn't he?"

"No, he's not dead," Flame said, the animosity in her voice vicious. "But I wish he were after what he's done!"

LaRaine was becoming exasperated with the confusing conversation. If he wasn't dead, wasn't injured, what could he have possibly done? "What are you talking about, Faith? If he's all right, what in heaven's name has happened?" she breathed impatiently, aware that the erratic beat of her heart had slowed to a more normal pace. As long as Brand was alive LaRaine was sure she could handle almost anything.

"I can't tell you," Flame whimpered.

"What do you mean, you can't tell me?" LaRaine shouted. "You've scared me to death by running off and not letting me know where you were going. Then you come in here like a crazy person babbling about something terrible happening with Brand. And now you say you can't tell me. You listen here, miss. You tell me what's going on, right this minute! I'm tired of this foolishness. If you've got something to say, say it!"

"Promise you won't be mad at me," Flame begged childishly, tugging on LaRaine's dress

443

sleeve.

"I won't be mad," LaRaine vowed impatiently. "Now, what is it?"

"I went to see him this morning," Flame confessed, cringing as she spoke.

"Why?" LaRaine choked, flabbergasted. Had Flame actually gone to Brand to tell him she was interested in him, maybe hoping to seduce him into making love to her? Certainly the little infatuation she'd noticed hadn't gone that far!

"After the way I acted last night, I felt so terrible I wanted to make up to you for it. I only went to tell him I couldn't bear to see you unhappy and that I wouldn't stand in your way if you wanted to marry him. I wanted to tell him that your happiness was more important to me than anything in the world and that I wouldn't do anything to interfere with your marriage. Are you angry with me?"

"Of course not," LaRaine breathed with relief, and not a little self-dislike for thinking Flame would have tried to seduce the man her sister loved. "Why would I be mad? It was a sweet, selfless gesture. I know how hard it must have been for you to do."

"I didn't know what else to do, Beth. You were so unhappy last night. I can't bear to have you be sad. I couldn't let you give him up because of me. I knew I had to do something. It was all I could think of to make things right for you," she said gallantly.

"I told you I'm not angry, silly girl. You don't have to keep apologizing. I'm touched that you care so much. What did Brand say? Did you see him at his parents' house?"

"No," Flame said defensively. "I went there first, but the butler said Brand keeps a room at the Tremont Hotel and that he must have spent the night there."

"The Tremont Hotel? He never mentioned a room at the Tremont."

Flame released a snide grunt. "It's no wonder."

"Go on," LaRaine said, the apprehension in her voice suddenly strangling.

Chapter Twenty-seven

Flame watched LaRaine, her expression filled with pity. Then she looked down at her hands twisting nervously at the edge of her cape. "You know I would never want to hurt you, don't you? And I swear to you, if I didn't know I'll be stopping you from making a terrible mistake, I would go to my grave with the secret of what happened this morning. But . . ."

LaRaine grabbed Flame's arms and turned her to face her. "Just tell me what happened."

Flame closed her eyes and drew in a deep, fortifying breath. "As I told you, the butler said Brand was probably at the Tremont Hotel, so I went there and asked the desk clerk. The man at the desk directed me to Brand's room—after giving me a rude wink and calling me *sweetheart*." There was just the right amount of indignation in Flame's quaking tone.

"Go on," LaRaine prodded, her dread building to explosive proportions.

"When I knocked on the door, a man's voice called out for me to come in. It was Brand, Beth! And he was in the bed with a woman! And they were both naked!"

A sharp, jabbing pain gripped LaRaine, feeling as if a giant claw were ripping her heart out of her breast. "No! There must be some mistake!"

Flame shook her head. "I'd give anything to have that be true," she said, her tone convincingly sincere. "But it was him."

"Nooo," LaRaine wailed, turning away from Flame and burying her face in her hands. "It can't be true. There has to be a logical explanation. What did you do?"

"I wanted to turn and run—away from the room, away from the hotel, and forget what I had seen, but I just stood there frozen to that spot. Beth, I couldn't move! I couldn't even say anything!"

"Brand with another woman?" The intense ache in her chest spread to all her vital organs, cutting them to shreds. "Please, God, let me be having a nightmare. Don't let this be true."

"Beth, he wasn't even embarrassed to have me find him like that. When I finally found my voice, I asked him how he could do something like that to you. He told me that what you didn't know wouldn't hurt you. I threatened to tell you, and he just laughed. He told me if I said anything to you, then it would be my fault if you got hurt. Is it, Beth? Is it my fault?"

"No, it's not your fault," LaRaine answered numbly, her vision glazed and blurred. "You were

447

right to tell me."

"Then he, then he—" Flame buried her face in her hands, as if she might not be able to go on. But somewhere she found the strength and continued. "He—he told me to close the door and take off my clothes and *join them*!"

LaRaine spun around to face her sister again, her expression sick and horrified. "What?"

"He wanted me to get into bed with him and that naked woman who kept rubbing and kissing all over his body the whole time I was there. He said he'd heard I had been a 'pretty hot number' before I let you turn me into such a prude. I wanted to be sick. I didn't know what to do or say. I thought I'd faint. And the entire time he was talking to me that vile woman kept touching and kissing him—as if I weren't standing there in an open doorway. When I didn't do as he suggested, he laughed and said he just might go have a little talk with the police when he was through there. That's when I finally managed to run out of the room. But I could hear the two of them laughing behind me. I can still hear them. I don't think I'll ever be able to forget that horrible sound!"

LaRaine didn't speak until Flame finished her outrageous tale. She continued to watch her sister's lips moving, her own mouth open in a silent scream, her eyes overflowing with tears. "Why did he ask me to marry him if he didn't care any more for me than that?"

"He said it was to appease his parents. He wanted to get them off his back, and you were the type of wife they thought he should have. He said it didn't make much difference to him since he didn't plan on being around long after the wedding."

"But I thought he really loved me! How could I be so wrong?" LaRaine begged.

"I know, I know," Flame consoled, her own eyes now suspiciously dry and showing a strength she hadn't displayed before. "I thought he did, too. He was very convincing."

Viewing the look of betrayal on LaRaine's tear-stained face, and knowing she was responsible for it, Flame felt a pang of guilt for what she was doing to her sister. But she had no choice. It wasn't enough for Brand Colter to simply disappear from LaRaine's life. She had to hate him enough that she would never want to see him again. Nothing short of that would do.

"I'm sorry I had to be the one to tell you this. I'd give anything if I could have spared you," she said, really meaning her words. "There, there," she soothed, wrapping her arm around LaRaine's shaking shoulders and drawing her sobbing head to her own shoulder. "You still have me. I'll take care of you. I'll always be here for you. I promise."

"Yes, I still have you," LaRaine wept. "What would I do without you?"

"Well, you won't ever have to find out," Flame promised. "I'll always be here." *Always. I'm never going to let anything come between us, Beth. No one will ever take you away from me!*

* * *

The next three days went by in a haze for La-Raine. She didn't hear from Brand, not that she expected to or even wanted to. She had allowed herself one good cry the morning she discovered what kind of man he really was, and then she had refused to indulge herself with any further outward display of her grief. No matter how she was aching inside, she resisted the temptation to give in to her emotions and allow anyone to see how she was suffering. But anyone who knew Beth Morgan couldn't help but notice the change in the usually outgoing girl.

Though she tried not to think of Brand Colter at all, telling herself that she had gotten over him once before and that she could certainly do it again, she was unable to put him out of her mind. But she vowed the next time he tried to step in and disrupt her life he wouldn't find it so easy. Never again would he be able to hurt her. This time she would get over him for good. She would write him out of her life forever.

But for all her stubborn determination and iron will, there was nothing she had been able to do to make herself stop thinking of him. Over and over, she had relived every wonderful—and not so wonderful—moment they had ever spent together, searching her mind for a clue, any clue, that would have indicated that he could be the type of man to so blatantly betray her trust and love.

Of course she had told him she couldn't marry him. Had that been the reason for his terrible actions? Could he have been so distraught that he'd turned to another woman to heal his broken heart? If only she could believe such a romantic assumption. It would have made her pain much easier to bear. Unfortunately, she was too intelligent to swallow such a convenient excuse for his unpardonable behavior.

No, there was no doubt in LaRaine's mind. He had either thought Flame wouldn't tell her, because she wouldn't want to hurt her sister, or he hadn't even cared enough to try and hide his real personality from her any longer.

LaRaine had barely noticed the many last minute details to be taken care of before Monday afternoon when they boarded the ship bound for France. She was just relieved that her sister had been able to move their departure date up and was handling everything. In fact, if LaRaine hadn't just been going through the motions of living, she would have been amazed at the way her twin had assumed the confident authority to handle not only the shop's business, but all their packing and travel arrangements, too. All she cared about was that her sister was making it possible for her to put Galveston—and Brand Colter—behind her.

Boarding the Europe-bound *La Cygne* on Monday afternoon, LaRaine still could muster no enthusiasm for the trip that should have been the highlight of her young life. But she didn't feel very young anymore. She felt old—very old and tired.

Standing at the rail, with red-rimmed eyes, the skin beneath them dark with shadows caused by sleepless nights, she surveyed the busy activity that surrounded her. As exhausted and broken as she felt, she wasn't able to stop herself from searching

451

the crowd of well-wishers and passengers milling about the deck of the French ship. Of course, he wouldn't be there—and she didn't want him to be. But still she studied every man who boarded, unable to extinguish the stubborn spark of hope in her heart that he would miraculously appear and be able to explain what had happened.

"Why don't I go with you to our cabin and get you settled in? Then I'll take the buggy to Mrs. Flanagan's for Patrick and Margie to use while we're gone," Flame said gently, breaking into LaRaine's thoughts as she had so many times during the past three days.

"That'll be fine," LaRaine said absently, then added as an afterthought, "Why didn't we just have Patrick bring us to the dock? I know I asked before, but I can't remember what you said. I guess I'm getting a little forgetful in my old age," she laughed softly, her smile empty of all humor.

"I told you," Flame said patiently, trying to guide LaRaine toward their cabin. "There wouldn't have been room for all our luggage, plus the two of us and Patrick. This way, he and Maggie will both be able to come down and see us off. You remember how she was looking forward to that, don't you?"

Suddenly turning about, LaRaine started back toward the ship's railing. "I think I'll wait for you on deck, Faith. I don't feel like being cooped up in the cabin just yet."

"He isn't coming, Beth," Flame said harshly, the impatience obvious in her voice. "You can stand up here and hope all you want, but sooner or later you've got to face the facts. He's a contempt-ible womanizer, and by now he must have figured out that I wouldn't let you remain in the dark about his loathsome character. Forget him, Beth. He's a despicable cur, and you don't need him," she said with avid contempt.

"I know that, Faith. And that's not why I don't want to go to the cabin yet. It's just that I like watching the people board. I enjoy seeing the beautiful dresses on the ladies. That's all I want to do, just watch the people as they come on board. I'm not looking for . . . him. Really, I'm not. I never want to see Brand Colter again."

"I'll never forgive him for what he's done to you, Beth," Flame said sincerely, giving her sister a warm hug. "I'd better go now or I won't be back in time. Promise me you'll keep your cape up around your face, and that you'll go to the cabin if the sun gets too warm. We can't have you get-ting ill on our trip, can we?"

"There's a nice breeze. I'll be fine," LaRaine promised, finding herself a place beside the rail where she could see. "You just go and don't worry about me. Take the buggy to Patrick and I'll wait right here for you."

"Unless it gets hot. Then you'll go below. Prom-ise me," Flame scolded.

"I promise," LaRaine laughed. "I'll go below if I get hot. Now, stop your fussing and go on. I'll be fine," she vowed, touched by the concern Flame had shown for her sorrow. She didn't know what she would have done if she hadn't had her sister to lean on the past few days. "Thank you for being here, Faith." Taking care that her twin didn't see the tears that were welling in her eyes, she hugged Flame.

"I'll always be here, Beth. I'll never leave you." Flame left a quick kiss on LaRaine's cheek and turned to go.

The twinge of guilt that had nagged at her for days now squeezed at Flame's heart as she glanced back at LaRaine. *She'll get over him,* she assured herself. *Once we get out to sea and she starts to relax, she'll realize how much better off she is without him. She'll be herself again in no time.*

Minutes later, Flame stood outside the dilapidated shack where Brand had been kept a prisoner since Friday evening. Glancing around apprehensively to be certain no one was witness to her visit, she adjusted the thick veil over her face and entered the dark, one-room building.

"Rainy? Is it you?" Brand rasped from the corner where he was bound and sitting in a chair. Though he could barely hold his head up, he looked much better than he had the last time she'd seen him. The seamen had been true to their word and had cleaned him up to the point where he was halfway presentable. She breathed a sigh of relief. Now, if he just wouldn't realize who she really was.

"Yes, darling, it's me," she whispered, rushing to his side and untying the ropes at his hands and feet. "I'm sorry it took me so long, but now I've come to help you. We're going away together, Brand. No one will ever come between us again," she promised, gently rubbing the circulation into his hands and feet.

"I knew you'd come, Rainy," he said drunkenly, obviously under the influence of the drug the seamen had been giving him. "Where're we going?"

"We're going to San Francisco. How does that sound? Just you and me in San Francisco! I've already talked to the captain about marrying us on board," she told him excitedly. "You do still want to marry me, don't you?"

Nodding his head and looking around groggily, he tried to stand up for the first time in days. "But what about Flame? Are you leaving her behind, or are you planning to take her with us?"

"No, we're not taking Flame. Just you and I are going," she said, wrapping her arm around his back and encouraging him to lean on her shoulder. "Now, come on, or we'll miss our ship."

"I don't understand. Where is she? Why're you suddenly willing to leave her?" he insisted, sensing even in his narcotic haze that something wasn't quite right.

Knowing she wouldn't be able to make him move until she gave him a plausible answer, Flame spoke hesitantly. "She betrayed me, Brand. It was Flame who had you brought here by those terrible men. She told them to kill you, but I paid them off to keep you hidden until I could make arrangements to take you to safety. She thinks you're already dead, or she would have come here looking for you."

"I don't understand," he groaned, the pain in his side bothering him again.

"She didn't want you to marry me, so she tried

455

to kill you. That's why we have to leave here. I don't ever want to see her again."

"Where is she now? Does she know you found out what she tried to do?" he argued, his concern with time unimportant.

"No, she doesn't know, but we have the rest of our lives to talk about it and figure out why she did this evil thing. Right now, the important thing is to get you on that ship and in a bed where you can recuperate," she said gently, at the same time firmly prodding him toward the doorway, determined not to let him delay any further.

Brand didn't argue anymore and took hesitant steps, knowing that freedom and a life with La-Raine were at last within his reach.

Using all his concentration to keep standing, he leaned on her for support and started walking. They moved forward slowly, each step laborious, his legs trembling and weak from the days of inactivity, as well as the opiate he'd been forced to drink. He was unaware that the three men who had held him captive followed close behind, ready to help Flame if he gave her any trouble.

Inhaling the fresh evening air, tangy with the salty smell of the sea, Brand could feel his strength returning as they made their way to the buggy. Suddenly he found he was starting to think clearly for the first time in days. And with the partial unclouding of his hazy mind, a tiny seed of suspicion began to grow in his subconscious.

A tremor of fear swept throughout his battered body.

Holding him as she was, Flame felt Brand's

body shiver and assumed it must be from the drug, nothing more. "We'll have you comfortable in just a few minutes," she soothed softly. "Just get in the buggy, and we'll be there right away. Our ship's berthed nearby. Are you going to be able to make it?"

Why was she whispering? he wondered, but something told him not to act as if he thought anything was unusual. Besides, he wasn't certain he could trust his instincts right now. He had been drugged and tied up for days. His mind was no doubt having a strange reaction to the fresh air, nothing more. "As long as I have you, I can do anything," he coughed, pulling himself into the waiting buggy.

He must have dozed during the short trip to the San Francisco-bound freighter, because he couldn't recall anything about it. He only remembered closing his eyes to rest them, then opening them again to find himself being helped up a gangway by La-Raine.

He looked around to take in his surroundings. The short nap seemed to have cleared his mind even more, though things were still annoyingly fuzzy.

He held onto LaRaine even harder, letting her support a great deal of his weight. Odd, he didn't seem too heavy for her. *She seems stronger than I thought she was,* he noticed, glancing down at her, his expression puzzled. *And taller.*

Frowning, he tried to focus on her face, but it was impossible to see through the thick netting she wore. Besides, even if she took off the veil, her

features would still be blurred like everything els
he saw. The drugs were just playing tricks on hi
senses. She wasn't any taller than before, n
stronger. He was just weaker. He'd probably eve
lost some weight.

It was too much for Brand to fathom, and h
shook his head, doubting his intelligence. *Once
get to a bed and sleep off the effects of whateve
it was they gave me, I'll be able to figure this a
out,* he told himself repeatedly, trying to force th
nagging thoughts of mistrust from his mind as h
entered the cabin.

"Here, Brand. Drink this. It will make you fee
better," she told him once they were in their cabin
picking up a glass and handing it to him.

Brand took the glass she offered him and held i
to his lips. He was thirsty. But he didn't drink
The liquid smelled and looked like the same thin;
the kidnappers had given him! Why would La
Raine be trying to drug him? "What is this?"

"It's for your pain," she explained in a husk·
whisper.

Of course that was it. She was helping him. Bu
no matter how it would ease the pain in his hea(
and side, he wanted to stay alert. He'd bee
drugged too long already. Knowing LaRain
wouldn't take no for an answer, he pretended t(
sip at the drink.

"Drink it all down now," Flame urged as sh(
guided him to the bed. "I'll go and make arrange
ments for the horse and buggy to be returned t(
the stables, and then I'll be back. Will you be al
right until I return?"

458

"I'll be fine, but I'll miss you," he answered, trying to sound as if he felt better than he did. He kept trying to put the nagging question of why she was still whispering from his mind. He would ask when his head cleared. Right now, nothing seemed to make any sense.

"I'll miss you, too, but I can't just leave the horses deserted on the docks. You try to get some sleep and I'll be here when you wake. I promise. Now, are you going to finish your drink?" she coaxed, pushing his hand holding the cup toward his mouth.

"I'll finish it in a minute," he promised, putting the drink down. "But right now I need something else to make me feel better. Kiss me, Rainy. Just one kiss before you leave me," he said, reaching for the veil that hid her face from his eyes.

Shooing his hand away from her face, Flame laughed nervously. "We don't have time for that sort of thing now, Brand. Let me take care of the horses. Then we'll have the rest of our lives to kiss each other all we want," she whispered.

"We have time for one kiss, Rainy," he insisted, grabbing her wrist with a strength she didn't expect and pulling her against him.

"All right, but remember you promised only one kiss, and then you'll drink your medicine all down and I'll take care of our other business," she teased, raising the veil slightly. Knowing Brand was the one person in the world who could tell her from her sister on first sight, she tensed, tempted to go ahead and tell him who she was and be done with it. But still, her whole plan would be

459

carried out much more inconspicuously if he were cooperative, and that meant convincing him that she was LaRaine for a while longer. The cabin was dimly lit, and he was drugged. It shouldn't be too hard to fool him through one kiss.

Not giving him a chance to get a good look at her face, Flame threw back the veil and wrapped her arms around his neck in one swift motion, kissing him long and hard. She felt his hands move hungrily over her bottom and back; and from the urgent way he was responding to her kiss, she was certain she had him fooled.

Brand's kiss was deep, thorough, and Flame was seized by the unexpected desire to lean farther into his embrace. Repulsed by her reaction, she cringed. What was she thinking of? She hated men, and this man above all others. He had tried to destroy her, tried to take Beth away from her. She detested him. How could she want the kiss to go on?

Frightened by her response, she tore her mouth free. "You don't act like a man who's been wounded and ill for the past few days," she whispered breathlessly, looking up into his eyes a moment before remembering to turn her face away.

What the hell?!? You're not LaRaine! Suddenly, his mind cleared and some of the pieces to the puzzle slapped into place. No wonder he had felt there was something different about her. It had been her conniving twin sister all along!

Flame was so shocked by her reaction to Brand Colter's kiss that she didn't notice the strange look he gave her, before he was able to mask it behind the confused look of a drugged man.

"Is that better?" she asked, turning away from him.

Brand glared at her back. *I'd take you on right now, Flame, but something tells me your three goons are outside this door.* "Maybe I'm not as strong as I thought," he said, staggering clumsily to the bed, pretending to be weaker than he was. "Another kiss like that one, and I'll collapse."

"Good," Flame said, lowering her veil before he could get a better look at her. "I won't be too long," she promised, picking up the glass again and handing it to him.

"I'll finish it. I promise. You don't have to stand over me like a mother hen." He effectively disguised his anger with a false laugh.

"All right then," she said hesitantly. "I'll go on." *Why was she putting off leaving? Obviously he was on the verge of passing out already, and as soon as he finished the drug, he'd be dead to the world for hours. She was sure he would finish drinking it. After all, his precious "Rainy" had told him to. And I can't waste any more time standing here waiting for him to get through. He might start suspecting something if I push him too hard. He'll be fine,* she thought with satisfaction.

"I'll be right back," she vowed sweetly, and stepped into the corridor. "You just try to get some sleep."

"Mmm," he hummed, taking the glass to his lips as if to drink from it.

Satisfied, Flame left. Closing the door behind her, she met Harry, Billy, and Tom, whose beam-

461

ing faces reminded her of the depths to which she had found it necessary to sink to protect what was hers.

"Well," Tom said, grinning proudly, obviously anxious to get his hands on the rest of his money. "We done it, didn't we!" he announced, sounding like a child expecting a compliment.

"Yes, it's done," she agreed irritably, looking at the closed door behind her. "Here's the rest of your money." She handed them each a hundred dollars. "But remember, your job's not done until he goes overboard when you're out to sea," she added, her tone threatening. "He should sleep for a long time — at least until you're out of the port — but I want one of you to stay outside his door all the time. Harry, you're the one I'm trusting to decide when the time is right for him to go overboard." She bestowed a rare smile on the older man.

"Yes'm, ya can depend on, ol' Harry and the boys ta finish the job."

"I know I can," she said, knowing that a little flirting would help to ensure that the three would continue to do her bidding, even though they had already received the rest of their money. "And if I'm ever in San Francisco and need a job to be done, I know who I'm going to look up to do it," she promised.

Flame hurried off the ship, taking care that she stayed in the shadows and saw no one who might recognize her. Applying the whip to the backs of her horses, she drove quickly to Mrs. Flanagan's to get Patrick. *Beth is in such a daze, I hope she* won't realize how long I've been gone. Of course, once we set sail, I'm not going to put up with any more of this moping about. But until then, it's just as well she isn't aware of what's going on around her.

Chapter Twenty-eight

When the tall, thin man first glanced at her, LaRaine turned her head away, thinking he was no doubt some shipboard Romeo who made it a point to meet young women who were traveling alone. She gave her full attention to a wooden crate that dangled precariously above her as a crane swung it from the dock toward the ship's hold. But she couldn't escape the feel of eyes boring into her back.

Daring a peek back over her shoulder, she was alarmed to realize the man was still staring at her, blatantly. There was something compelling about the way he was watching her, something deadly in his expression, and LaRaine shuddered involuntarily, unable to ignore the feeling of danger his nearness evoked.

He could be considered handsome by some standards — tanned skin, blond hair, and dark, penetrating eyes shining with an expression LaRaine couldn't discern. Was it lust? No, not really. It was more a look of familiarity, as if he already knew her, knew all there was to know about her.

But of course, that's impossible. He doesn't know me. I've never seen him before. How could he know me? He's flirting, that's all, she told herself unconvincingly.

Yet, there was something so frightening, so violent about the way the man watched her that the uneasiness pumping through her veins escalated to panic. She tried to tell herself she was being foolish, but still she was unable to escape the burning heat of his eyes as they bored intrusively into her back.

He looks as if he hates me, she realized. Spinning away from the rail, she made a dash for the stairs.

By the time she reached the door to her cabin, she was breathing so heavily and shaking so much that her fingers wouldn't obey her commands, and she couldn't fit the key into the lock.

"Allow me," a male voice offered as a warm, tanned hand covered hers and removed the key from it.

Releasing a startled gasp, LaRaine jerked back her hand and looked up into the cold dark eyes of the man from the deck.

"I can do it myself," she stuttered, realizing the man's hand had not moved and continued to hold hers in a deathlike grip.

"Ya always could, couldn't ya, Flame?" the man said, his words more statement than question. "Ain't ya gonna say hello?" He grinned, showing crooked, tobacco-stained teeth. "Ya ain't bein' very friendly," he went on when LaRaine continued to look at him dumbly, obviously not recognizing him. But Roy Benton didn't see the lack of recognition in her expression. He had waited too long for this moment.

Finally LaRaine spoke. She had to straighten this out before Flame came back on board. This man, whoever he was, couldn't see the real Flame. She drew on all the strength and aplomb she could muster. "You must have made a mistake, sir."

"I knew ya weren't dead. When they tole me ya was, I tole 'em it was a trick. I jest been bidin' my time till you'n me could meet up agin. I guess today's my lucky day. Ain't ya gonna 'vite me in?" he asked, pushing her into her cabin and following close behind.

"You can't come in here!" LaRaine gasped, stumbling forward with the force of a hard shove in the small of her back. "I don't know who you think I am, but you're wrong. My name's Beth Morgan, and I've never seen you in my life." Breathing heavily, she turned on him, making ready to defend herself.

"Yeah, I can see ya done real good fer yerself, Flame." Roy surveyed the plush cabin she had been able to afford and all the luggage she had with her. "An' I ain't gonna do nuthin' ta ruin it fer ya. Not if you'n me can strike up a little bargain." He smiled, lowering his gaze to her heaving breasts. Seeing the fear in her eyes was what he had waited over six months for, and this was

466

even better than he had envisioned.

"What kind of bargain?" Maybe he would take money to go away and never bother them again. It would be worth it to protect Flame from having to meet him face to face.

"Why, the same kind o' bargain we had b'fore, 'cept this time I'll be callin' the shots!" he said, reaching for her and pulling her against his chest.

LaRaine looked up at him, her eyes wide, his glistening with revenge. "Please, I'm not who you think I am!" she pleaded uselessly.

Yanking her bonnet off and throwing it to the floor, Roy grabbed a fistful of her hair and jerked LaRaine's head backwards exposing her vulnerable throat to the knife that suddenly appeared in his other hand.

"Did ya think a little thing like changin' the color o' yer hair could make me fergit the way ya treated me when I was s'posed ta be yer man?" he said, drawing the point of the knife slowly over the delicate lines of her pale neck.

LaRaine tried to speak, but only a choking sound came out. She needed to swallow, but she was afraid the movement the natural reflex would make against the knife point would be just enough to cause the pressure to break the skin.

"No, it'd take a lot more'n that ta make me fergit ya, Flame. I'll never fergit the way ya made me feel like half a man. I was crazy 'bout ya, Flame, 'n ya treated me like scum, makin' me look weak in front o' that boy. No, the only way I'm gonna fergit yer purty face is ta give ya a little bit o' what ya gave out," he said, his voice

467

threatening.

The grip on her hair arched her back even more, forcing her hips against his swelling manhood. She felt as if she were going to break in half, but she managed to work a hand into her dress pocket where she always carried a pistol.

My God! I didn't put it there when I changed clothes for the trip, she realized, her heart exploding with hysterical panic.

Roy noticed the increased speed of the pulse in her unprotected neck, and he laughed, pressing the blade of the knife against the jumping pulse beneath her delicate skin. "Ya ain't skeered, are ya, Flame? I ain't never seen ya skeered b'fore."

"Yes," LaRaine admitted. "I am afraid. I don't know what you want of me. I'm not Flame. You've got to believe me!" she insisted hoarsely, barely moving her lips when she spoke.

"I told ya, honey. I jest wanna take up where we left off. Only this time, you're gonna follow through on those promises ya used ta make to keep me in line. I'm gonna screw ya, Flame. That's all I want," he sneered, slipping his knife into the neckline of her bodice and slicing downward through all the layers of her clothing.

LaRaine cried out and tried to pull the edges of her dress together to cover herself.

Roy dropped his hold on her hair and grabbed her wrists, wrenching her arms behind her. Holding her wrists with one hand, he opened her dress. "Oooee," he yelled delightedly as he took in the expanse of milky white flesh his knife had presented for his avid scrutiny. "Ya look even better'n I remembered," he exclaimed, his eyes voraciously devouring her exposed breasts and belly. "You always had the best tits I ever seen, but I do believe they're even bigger now," he said, cupping a breast roughly in his hand.

She was helpless to protect herself, and she was so frightened, so mortified, she didn't even notice the sting of the thin red line that ran the length of her torso where his knife point had drawn a fine trickle of blood.

Bringing the knife around to the front of her trembling body, Roy trailed the point along the narrow red line that ran between her breasts and shook his head. "Damn shame ta scar up somethin' so nice lookin'," he sighed, the evil smile on his face telling LaRaine that the sight of her blood was exciting to him. "Maybe I won't have ta put no more cuts on that purty skin. Not if yer a good girl an' behave," he promised huskily, his mouth coming down hard on hers to fill it with his tongue.

He tasted like stale tobacco and alcohol. The contents of her stomach rose in her throat, but she knew if she got sick, he would kill her. She would have to pretend she didn't mind his kisses until he moved the knife away from her skin. There was nothing she could do to defend herself, not if she wanted to avoid the feel of his knife sinking into her and killing her. She forced herself to relax and suffer his kiss, allowing herself no reaction whatsoever.

When the repulsive kiss ended, Roy looked deep into her eyes. She wasn't resisting him. She wasn't responding to him, but she was no longer resisting. "What is this, Flame? Some kind o' trick?" he asked the woman who was practically limp in his arms and staring woodenly at him.

She forced herself to remain silent, hoping her best resistance was no resistance at all. Roy pushed the steel blade deeper into the soft flesh of a breast, hoping to evoke a response from her, but she maintained her cool facade and didn't even flinch.

"What're you tryin' ta prove?" he asked, burying his face in the curve of her shoulder and biting her hard enough to leave red teeth marks in her skin. She said nothing, did nothing. "Well, we'll jest see 'bout this," he threatened, determined to force a response from her. He wanted her begging and crawling. Like he had imagined for so long. He didn't want her like this.

Holding LaRaine away from him, her hands still secured behind her back, Roy unfastened his trousers and let them drop to the floor. "Now, let's jest see if this don't wake ya up some," he chuckled wickedly, forcing her to her knees in front of him.

Burrowing his fingers into her hair, he pulled her against him, thrusting himself toward her at the same time. She was able to turn her face to the side just in time, and the side of her head took the full force of his assault. It sent her head reeling backward, but it was no use. He still had his tight grip on her hair and turned her around to face him. She closed her eyes tight, clenched her lips together, and tried to struggle.

470

"It ain't no use, Flame. I'm gonna stick this whole damn thing in yer mouth, so ya might as well get used ta the idea, 'cause there ain't nuthin' ya can do 'bout it, if you wanna come out 'o this here cabin alive. So go on and open up," he said, pushing himself against her cheek, trying to force her.

"Beth, I'm back," Flame bubbled excitedly, bursting through the door to be assaulted by a sight worse than any she could imagine. "Roy!" she gasped, unable to stop her reaction.

"What the hell?" Roy yelled, his head swinging around to take in the unbelievable sight of an identical duplicate of the woman he had before him on the floor. "I'll be goddamned! What the hell's goin' on?" He jerked LaRaine to her feet and held her in front of him.

Stepping warily to the side, Flame ignored his question and looked at LaRaine, her fright hooded behind her eyes. "Are you all right, Beth? Did he hurt you?" she asked, her hand already in her pocket and fingering her pistol. All she had to do was get him to step aside for a minute. Just one minute. That's all she would need to shoot him dead for what he had put LaRaine through.

"He was going to m-m-make me . . ." LaRaine couldn't finish saying it.

Roy pressed the point of his knife against the soft tissue beneath her chin. "Shut up!" he ordered, grabbing an exposed and bruised breast with his free hand.

You just signed your death warrant, Benton,

471

Flame told him silently, her eyes narrowing with purpose, her fingers tightening on the gun in her pocket. "What're you doing here, Roy?" she asked, her voice soft, deadly. "How'd you find me?"

"So, she was tellin' the truth. She ain't Flame Rider. Then who the hell is she?" he asked, running a thumb harshly back and forth over La-Raine's nipple and squeezing the mound of flesh cruelly. "She sure has got great tits," he said, enjoying how much Flame was being hurt by his treatment of the other girl. "Answer me, Flame. Who is she?" He poked the knife harder into La-Raine's chin, forcing her head back and arching her spine awkwardly. "Is she the gal who you was so hot to go after back in Missouri?"

"If you've hurt her, Roy, so help me I'll . . ." Flame warned through clenched teeth, warily eyeing him as she waited for a chance to draw on him.

"I said who is she, Flame? If ya don't want ta see 'er blood spillin' all over this here floor, ya better start talkin'," he threatened, drawing a trickle of red where his knife punctured LaRaine's tender skin.

"She's my sister!" Flame shrieked, feeling La-Raine's pain as if it were her own. "Don't hurt her! It's me you came for, not her. She hasn't done anything to you. Let her go!" she begged, willing to do anything to save her twin.

"Sissy 'n me was jest startin' ta get acquainted," he smiled, sticking his tongue in LaRaine's ear and forcing a rough hand down between her

472

ighs. "She feels real nice, Flame. I don't wanna
t go o' 'er fer a while yet. In fact, I might jest
pend the whole trip in this here cabin servicin'
oth o' ya. Never had me no twins b'fore," he
dded, tightening his intimate hold on her.

Cringing at his touch, LaRaine folded in half.
Her sudden motion caught Roy off guard, and
hen she doubled over, his knife sliced along the
ide of her neck below her ear.

"Stop it!" Flame cried out, beside herself with
ear at the sight of more of LaRaine's blood
taining her skin. She couldn't let Roy hurt her
nymore. She had to stop him!

Then she changed her tone of voice from desperation to seduction. "Come on, lover. You've
had your joke now. Why don't you let her go,
and let's you and me have some real fun. We can
have a real good time together," she promised,
using one hand to unbutton her own bodice.

"Faith, don't!" LaRaine pleaded, unable to bear
the thought that her sister was going to sacrifice
herself to the animal who was holding her captive. "You don't have to do this, not for me."

"Honey, I'm doin' it for myself. It's been too
long since I had a good lay, and Roy was about
the best I ever had," she said, smiling into the
man's brown eyes. "What do you say, Roy? Don't
you want a real woman right now? Not some
scared little girl who doesn't know how to please
a man."

"What would you know 'bout pleasin' a man,
Flame. 'S I recall, ya always took time ta please
yerself, and that's 'bout it. The worse ya made

me feel, the more ya liked it. I don't 'member never doin' nuthin' ta please nobody 'cept ye self."

"But I've changed since then, Roy," Flame sai not allowing his words to dissuade her from h purpose. Opening her blouse and pulling her ch mise down below her breasts, she smiled sugge tively. "But I guess you're never going to find o what I've learned if you keep on with her. Con on, lover. I've missed you real bad," she smiled stepping out of the rest of her clothing an standing before him naked and available.

LaRaine could feel the building pressure c Roy's swollen manhood mashing against her back and she tried to pull away from him, but hi hand between her legs and the knife at her nec made it impossible to move.

"What's it going to be, Roy? Her or me? Flame challenged, her own hands caressing he body in a way that drew his attention to all th right parts of her anatomy.

"Why should I choose?" Roy answered. "I'n gonna have ya both all I want ta, 'n there ain' nuthin' ya can do but 'blige me," he sneered, al ready planning ways to make Flame Rider craw at his feet. "Tell 'er she ain't got no choice, sissy,' he said to LaRaine, bringing a hand up to pinch a breast.

"It's no use, Faith," LaRaine said, steeling her self for what would come next.

"Listen ta yer sissy, Flame. She know's what she's talkin' 'bout. Now, git over on the bed 'n watch while I give this little gal here a taste o' a

al man." Laughing at the double meaning to his
words, he dug his fingers into LaRaine's shoulder
and forced her to her knees again.

" 'Member, Flame," he warned. "Ya don't do
what I tell ya 'n sissy here gits cut up real bad.
'd be a shame ta mess up this purty hide o'
ers," he said, enjoying the suffering in Flame's
ace. To emphasize his threat, he drew the blade
f his knife down the length of LaRaine's up-
urned face to prolong Flame's agony.

"Okay, okay, I'm going," Flame said, stooping
o pick up her clothing and make her way toward
he bed. With her back turned to LaRaine and
Roy, she eased the pistol from her skirt pocket.

She had tried to catch him off guard by getting
his attention away from LaRaine, but that hadn't
worked. As out of practice as she was, the only
option left was to trust her aim with the pistol.
She knew she couldn't let him do what he was
planning to do to LaRaine. An ordinary rape
would be more than LaRaine could bear, but
what Roy had in mind was much worse. And
Flame knew if he carried out his plan, LaRaine
would never survive the shock. It would kill her
to be taken that way. Flame had to stop him.

With LaRaine on the floor in front of Roy, his
upper body was an ideal target. Flame was certain she couldn't miss at the close range, but if
she did, she realized she might hit LaRaine. However, it was a risk she had to take, knowing without a doubt LaRaine would prefer death to Roy's
evil use of her body.

Damn, I was crazy to think we could ever es-

cape the past. I really thought we could go aw
and live happily ever after. I should have kno
better. I wasn't ever meant to have anythi
good. But LaRaine was. If I never do anythi
else, I've got to save her from him.

"Come on, Flame," Roy goaded loudly, holdi
LaRaine by the hair on either side of her he
and forcing her to face him.

Wheeling around to face the revolting sight
her beloved sister on her knees before Ro
Flame's face was a study in maniacal retaliatio
and it was a brief instant before the man cou
comprehend what was happening.

Wild with fury, Flame's marble-blue eyes he
Roy's stare captive for the split second it took t
aim and fire her weapon, not once, but twice
into his chest.

LaRaine's head was held in a such a way sh
couldn't see what was happening, but she sense
a tightening in the grip the man had on her hai
and a straightening of his posture. Then, as i
things were happening in a dream, LaRaine hear
a gunshot, then another, each followed by th
sound of a bullet whizzing past her head and en
tering Roy's chest with a soft sucking sound. Sh
was only slightly aware that his hold on her hai
loosened seconds before she felt herself falling t
the floor, to be held there by a suffocating dea
weight.

Lying with the full weight of the dead man
over her body, LaRaine was too stunned to move.
She couldn't find the strength to struggle to free
herself. For that matter, being free now seemed

important. Maybe she was dead. Perhaps that was why she felt nothing, heard nothing, saw nothing.

She had an eerie sense of floating and was oblivious to the constricting heaviness on her chest, the difficulty she was having breathing, the warm sticky blood that pumped out of Roy's wound to cover her torso.

As the seconds ticked away, LaRaine had a strange impression of a hysterical animal scream echoing piercingly through the void where she had been hurled. The sound was so primitive, so afraid, so forlorn, that it tore at LaRaine's sensibilities as no words could have done. She knitted her brow in concentration, and forced herself to think about helping the poor tortured creature she heard.

It was then she realized it was a woman's voice. Not an animal at all, but a woman. Who was she? Why was she so upset? She was calling a name. What was the name?

Beth! The woman was screaming the name Beth! That was her. Someone was calling for her.

LaRaine struggled to sit up, frantic to help the screaming woman. She had to make her understand that there was nothing to be afraid of now. Suddenly the weight which had held her pinned to the floor was lifted off her, and the numbness engulfing her faded mercifully.

She opened her eyes and glanced sleepily around. Her vision was assaulted by a grotesque portrait of horror. Flame was kneeling beside her, her naked, blood-spattered body shaking visibly.

Unmindful of her own nudity, Flame was dabbi
the blood from LaRaine's breasts.

Attempting to cover her sister by pulling t
edges of her torn bodice over the bruised flesh
her breasts, Flame cried at the sight of the ug
blue marks on LaRaine's skin.

"How could this have happened to you? It's a
my fault. I never should have left you," Flam
wept, continuing to hold LaRaine in her arm
and talk.

Seeing her sister so miserable brought LaRain
to the present with a jolting realization of wha
had happened. It had been Flame she had hear
screaming. It was Flame she had to console. .
was Flame who needed her.

Placing a hand on the hand that tenderly wipe
her face in a useless attempt to clean it, LaRain
smiled. "It's all right now, love. He didn't hur
me. You came in time," she comforted the youn
woman who held her in her arms. "We're both
going to be all right," she promised adamantly
reaching up to touch the tears on her sister's face

Flame stared incredulously at LaRaine. She had
been afraid she had shot her when she had fired
the pistol. "I thought I'd killed you," Flame wept,
the relief tangible in her trembling tone.

Rapid knocking on the cabin door broke into
their stunned rejoicing. "What's going on in
there?" a man's voice shouted from the hallway.

"I heard shots," a woman's voice squealed.

"Are you all right, Miss Morgan?"

"Break the door down!"

LaRaine and Flame watched as the door

ashed into the room, exposing them to the hor-
fied stares of the ship's first mate and several
assengers. "Oh, my God!" the officer exclaimed,
king in the bloody scene before him.

LaRaine and Flame lay in the bunks of the new
abin they and their trunks had been moved to as
oon as they'd been treated by the ship's doctor,
nd the captain had ruled they'd been the victims
f a madman and not responsible for Roy Ben-
on's death.

"We should have accepted the doctor's offer of
sedative," LaRaine said woodenly, her shock
still so great that she couldn't muster the strength
o move.

"I've done a terrible thing, Beth," Flame said
suddenly, her voice even more husky than usual.

LaRaine rolled over onto her side and faced her
sister. "You didn't do anything wrong! You heard
what the captain said. If you hadn't killed him,
he would have . . ." Her voice broke and she
couldn't finish. "I owe you my life, Faith."

"You don't owe me anything."

She sounded so despondent that LaRaine felt a
sudden surge of apprehension. She propped herself up on her elbow and studied Flame. "Of
course I do. If it hadn't been for you I would
have—"

"I did it for us, Beth! For you and me!" Flame
said, sitting up in the bed, her gaze shifting nervously from side to side. She felt like a frightened
animal seeking an escape.

"I know you did. Now you need to put it o of your mind. Don't think about it anymore. Ju think about the future."

"Everything I did was because I love yo Beth," she went on as if LaRaine hadn't spoke "Don't you see? You're the only one who ev loved me. I couldn't let him take you away fro me!" she went on anxiously. "I didn't know wh else to do!" she defended herself.

LaRaine watched her sister, hating the terribl dread that was beginning to gnaw at her min She tried to ignore it. Flame loved her. Sh wouldn't have deliberately done anything to hu her. "What happened wasn't your fault," sh stressed. "You couldn't have know that ma would attack me."

"Everything I did, I did because I love you, Flame said again. "He couldn't love you as muc as I do. And I needed you. He didn't. There ar other women for a man like him," she said, he voice pleading for understanding. "He was going to take you away from me. I couldn't let tha happen. You understand, don't you, Beth? I couldn't let him take you from me," she murmured with finality, as if she had just reached a grave decision and was finding solace in her choice. "I'm sorry."

Her heart racing with concern for the way Flame seemed to be obsessed with guilt, LaRaine crossed the cabin to the other bunk and sat down. She wrapped her arms around her sister and pulled her head to her shoulder. "There, there, Faith. There's nothing to be sorry for."

"You don't understand. I hired three men to ill him," she admitted, her words muffled gainst LaRaine's shoulder.

LaRaine caught Flame's chin in her fingers and fted her face. "What did you say?"

"I hired men to kill him, Beth. I hired them to nake sure Brand Colter could never bother us again."

Chapter Twenty-nine

A feeling of numbness descended onto LaRaine and she stared helplessly at Flame. "I must have misunderstood. I thought I heard you say . . ."

Flame shook her head. "You didn't misunderstand. I hired men to—"

LaRaine leaped to her feet and stared down at Flame, the impact of her shock the only thing keeping her from shattering into a billion pieces. "Are you telling me Brand is dead and that you . . . ? No!" She clamped her hands over her ears and wheeled away from the sight of Flame. "I don't believe it!"

"It's true," Flame insisted. "Brand didn't really do all those terrible things I told you he did. I had him kept prisoner until I could get him on a ship out of Galveston. I thought if he was out of the way, you and I could go back to the life we had before. I'm sorry I hurt you. I never meant to."

LaRaine pivoted back to face Flame and forced her to her feet. "Why are you doing this to me?"

he shrieked, shaking her. "Why?"

Flame didn't resist her sister's attack. "I didn't want to lose you. And he wouldn't go away. I just wanted him to go away."

"Stop it! Brand's not dead. If he were dead, I would have known. Surely his parents would have sent word! Why are you making this up. Tell me Brand's not dead!"

"He will be in a matter of hours," Flame said dejectedly.

"A matter of hours? Is he alive or not?"

"He should still be alive, but . . ." Flame broke into hysterics, her sobs filled with self-punishment and excuses for what she had done.

Growing more and more afraid that Flame wasn't lying, LaRaine knew she had to calm her down enough to get the truth from her. If Brand was supposed to die in a few hours, she had to find out where he was and go to him.

Putting her arm around Flame's shaking shoulders, she guided her back to the bed and forced her own voice to reflect a calm she didn't feel. "Just tell me what you did and why you think Brand is going to die in a few hours."

"Promise you won't be mad at me," Flame whimpered, the efficient young woman of the past few days gone, leaving the frightened eight-year-old in her place.

LaRaine took a deep breath, forcing herself to appear natural. "I won't be mad."

When Flame had finally spilled the entire plot, she collapsed back on her bunk, sobbing. "I'm so sorry, Beth. Can you ever forgive me?"

"I don't know," LaRaine answered, unable deny the truth any longer. She snatched up he cloak and wrenched open the cabin door, the turned back to Flame, her expression betrayed an desolate. "We could have worked it out, Faith. I you had just had a little trust. I loved you with al my heart, and I was willing to give you everything I had to give. But it wasn't enough, was it? Now I only wish I never had to see your face again But as it is, for the rest of my life, every time see my own reflection in the mirror, I'm going to be reminded of you and how you've repaid my love."

Brand stood behind the door of his dark cabin, his ears alert to every sound. He had waited to make his move until he was steadier on his feet and the effects of being drugged had worn off some more, but he knew he had to act now. Even though his head wasn't completely cleared, and he was still very weak, he was sure he had a better chance of escaping if he avoided a direct confrontation with his captors by leaving while most of the passengers and crew were still asleep.

"Oooh," he moaned, making sure he was louder than the snores he heard outside the door. "Someone help me."

The snoring stopped, followed by a grunt and the scrape of a chair on the wooden deck. "Jest when I was gettin' to sleep," the guard grumbled.

Brand tensed as he heard the key click into the lock. *This is it. It's now or never.* "Help me. I'm ick," he wailed.

"All right, I'm comin'," the guard growled, pushing the door open. "What's all the complainin' abou—"

Brand brought the heavy chair down on Billy's skull with a loud crack. Dropping to his knees as the man slumped to the floor, he hurriedly bound his wrists and ankles with strips of sheeting, then dragged him to the bunk. "This ought to hold you," he grunted, heaving his prisoner onto the bed. He quickly stabbed Billy's gun into his own waistband and drew a blanket up over the unconscious form.

Stooping to retrieve the key Billy had dropped, he crossed to the door and pressed his ear to the wood. When he heard no other sounds, he cracked the door slightly and peered out into the dark passageway.

Relieved to find it unoccupied, he tugged on Billy's knit cap and opened the door enough to slip out of the cabin, locking it behind him. He hesitated a moment, concentrating on remembering the way he'd been brought down to the cabin. Making his decision, he took off at a crouched run in the direction he thought the stairs should be. Nearing the end of the passageway, he saw the exit he'd been looking for and breathed a sigh of relief.

As he started up, he heard voices from above and stopped short. *Damn!* he cursed to himself, making a frantic check of the dark stairwell for somewhere to hide. Realizing the only place he might go undetected would be under the open staircase, he dashed back down and dove out of sight just as the door from the upper deck opened.

"I don't know what you're so worried 'bout, Harry," the voice Brand recognized as belonging to one of his captors complained.

"It's jest a uneasy feelin' I got," Harry said, lighting the stairwell with the lantern he held out in front of him.

"You know you can trust Billy."

"It ain't Billy I'm worried 'bout, Tommy. He's too dumb not to do what he's told. It's that feller in the cabin I don't trust."

"Hell, he ain't goin' nowhere. He's dead to the world."

"Yeah, I know. But this whole job's gone too easy. I jest ain't gonna feel right 'bout it till he goes over the side tomorrow night."

In the gray light of predawn, the San Francisco-bound freighter loomed in front of LaRaine like a giant gargoyle come to life as it rocked and groaned with the tide. Squinting, she raked her gaze over the decks.

Only one man on guard—as far as she could see. He shouldn't be too difficult to get past, she assured herself. Taking a deep breath, she adjusted Flame's hat on her head and pulled the veil over her face. "Just act as if you've every right to be here," she told herself. Stiffening her spine, she stepped out of the shadows and glided up the gangplank.

" 'Old on there, miss. Whar ya think yer goin'?"

he sailor shouted.

"To my cabin, of course. Aren't we due to sail with the tide?" she answered indignantly, though her insides were quivering.

"All the passengers was s'posed ta come on board last evenin'. What're ya doin' out alone this time o' night?"

LaRaine drew close to the cautious sailor. "My luggage and my husband came on board last evening, but I made arrangements with the captain to spend most of the night on shore with my family and to board now. You may check the roster if you like—Mr. and Mrs. B. Carter," she said, using the name Flame had given her.

The night guard looked over his shoulder as if he were considering what to do.

"Perhaps we should awaken the captain and ask him," LaRaine suggested, her tone a challenge.

"Uh . . . no. I don't guess we gotta do that. You go on down to your cabin. Can you find it? I can't leave my watch to take you."

"I know the way," she answered, praying the directions she'd gotten from her sister were accurate. "I would appreciate the use of a lantern though."

His nerves stretched to the point of snapping, Brand waited uneasily as the two men made their way down the passageway to the cabin he had just left.

"That's what I was afraid of," Harry muttered as he examined the empty chair Billy should have been occupying.

"Maybe he's inside checkin' on our man," To suggested defensively.

"I told him to stay out here." Harry tried the door and found it locked. He fished a key out of his pocket. "Hold that light up," he ordered, bending to fit the key into the lock.

His hand on the revolver in his belt, and his eyes on the two men as they entered the cabin, Brand bounded out from beneath the stairs and started toward the upper deck. However, as his foot touched the first step, the door at the top of the stairs opened, revealing the figure of a woman in the lantern light.

Damn! Diving for his hiding place again, he waited as the woman descended the stairs.

Watching as she hurried down the passageway, holding her light up to the number on each cabin door, Brand inched his way out of his hiding place. If she would just keep her back to him long enough for him to get up the stairs, he'd be clear.

"I don't want none o' your excuses!" an angry male voice shouted as the woman neared the door of the cabin where he'd been a prisoner. She stopped in her tracks and turned to the side, raising her lamp higher to confirm the cabin number.

Flame! Brand recognized, as the light of the lantern exposed her profile through the veil.

"You'd jest better find him if ya know what's good for ya!" the voice from the cabin threatened.

"I can't see it makes no diff'rence," a second voice whined as the door latch clicked. "We already been pa—"

"Miss!" Harry gasped as the door swung open

reveal the woman to the three men. "What're ya
in' here?" he asked, hurriedly slamming the
bin door behind him. "Don't tell me ya don't
st us."

Aghast, LaRaine stared at the three in the door-
ay. Her first impulse was to turn and run. But
e couldn't. She had to get to Brand. And if
ame was telling her the truth, he was on the
her side of this door. Thank goodness her face
as hidden behind the thick veil, because they'd
now in an instant how terrified she was if they
uld see her face.

"Uh . . ." She cleared her throat and tightened
er grip on the revolver hidden under her cape.
've come to check on . . . uh . . . him," she
xplained, nodding toward the door with her head.
Is he still alive?"

"He's jest fine," Billy said, stepping between her
nd the door. "Sleepin' like a baby!"

"Stand aside. I want to see for myself," she
aid, barely able to recognize the hoarse, shaky
oice as her own.

Brand peered down the passageway at the group
gathered in front of the cabin door. They were all
so occupied with their conversation that he could
probably just stroll up the stairs and off the ship
without being noticed. But something about seeing
the four culprits responsible for his ordeal all in
one place, and so conveniently vulnerable in the
lantern light, gave him the sudden impulse to toss
common sense to the wind. He held up the gun
he'd taken from Billy and spun the cylinder to
count the bullets.

"Isn't this a cozy sight," he said from the d end of the passageway when he was confident revolver had no empty chambers.

Tom and Harry reached for their guns, and Raine wheeled to to face him. "Brand!" she cri

"Drop them, boys!" he snarled, his voice st ping the two in mid-action. "I'm just looking an excuse to fill all four of you with lead!" guns clattered to the floor and all three men rai their hands.

"You, too, Flame!" he ordered, walking towa them, knowing that the lanterns highlighting group had made it almost impossible for them see him in the darker end of the hall.

Stunned by the bitterness she heard in his voi LaRaine raised her hands too. "Brand, it's m—

"Spare me the talk, Flame," he growled. "To that extra key over here, old man."

Harry lowered one hand cautiously and dug in his coat pocket. Holding up the key for Brand see, he pitched it toward him.

"Good boy. Now, all four of you get back in t cabin," he said, drawing close enough to step in the circle of lantern light.

It was then that LaRaine saw how bad looked. His eyes were deep in their sockets, and obvious weight loss had sunk his cheeks, leavi him gaunt and unhealthy looking. And she shuc dered with guilt to think what he'd been p through because of her blind love for her siste "Oh, Brand," she cried, "I'm so sorry. I had n idea it would go so far."

"You're a little late with the apologies, Flame,

490

said with a bitter laugh, nodding his head to-
ard the cabin. "All I want from you now is to
now where Rainy is. Then you and your pals here
e going to have a nice long rest in jail. Now get
side."

Harry, Billy, and Tom bounded into the cabin
head of LaRaine. They hadn't been paid enough
stare down the barrel of a revolver held in the
aking hand of a mad man.

"Go on, Flame."

LaRaine started to follow, then stopped on the
reshold. "Brand," she said, tearing off the hat
nd turning to face him. "I'm not Flame."

"Rainy?" he asked, his voice cracking and his
ision blurring with heartbreaking recognition. He
taggered back, this blow more than his limited
trength could handle. "Oh, my God! You were in
n it with them?"

"No!" she protested.

Seeing their chance, Billy and Tom and Harry
olted from the cabin, shoving past LaRaine, and
itting Brand with a united force as they made the
lash for the stairs.

Brand fell back, crashing into the wall and tumbling to the floor.

"Stop, or I'll shoot!" LaRaine ordered, whipping
her revolver out from under her cape and aiming
at the fleeing men.

Recognizing the real threat in her tone, all three
came to an abrupt halt and raised their hands.

"What's going on down here?" an authoritative
voice asked from the stairs.

LaRaine and her prisoners looked up to see the

491

captain and his first mate coming toward them

"These men are criminals, sir!" she accuse "They were going to murder this man and du his body overboard once you were out to sea.

As soon as the officers, backed by two bu seaman, took the protesting hoodlums into c tody, LaRaine dropped her pistol and fell to knees beside Brand's half-conscious body. "Bran she wept, taking his head into her lap. "Plea forgive me. I thought she was telling me the tru when she told me those terrible things about yo I didn't want to believe her, but when you did come to see me again, I had to. How could I ha known what she was capable of doing to keep n to herself?"

"You couldn't have known, Rainy," Brand sa sluggishly, knowing now that it was truly over ar that LaRaine was his. "It's not in your nature doubt anyone. You're always able to see the goo ness in people, and for the most part your tru makes others want to prove to you that you we right about them. Look how your faith in Flan changed her. If I hadn't come back into the pi ture, she might never have shown that other sid of her personality."

"But I'm still responsible for what happened t you. I should have been able to see what she wa doing, and I didn't. I should have tried to fin you and confront you with what she had told me If I hadn't taken her lies as truth, I could hav saved you from all this."

"There was nothing you could have done. Some times we have no choice but to go along with

492

ings the best way we know how," he sighed, oking deep into LaRaine's marble-green eyes and ondering if he would ever see them happy again.

"But you still haven't told me how you escaped ose terrible men," she said, caressing an errant ack curl off his forehead. It was a useless ges- re, because the lock of hair seemed to be deter- ined to spend its existence out of place.

Brand shook his head weakly, trying to sit up. Ordinarily, I wouldn't have been able to cut but- r in the shape I was in. My legs were shaking nd my vision was blurred. I could barely hold yself upright. But I knew I had to get to you, nd if the only way to do it was through them, hen somehow I'd do it. To be truthful, I think I ad some outside help," he smiled, rolling his eyes pward.

"You've lost so much weight," she said, smooth- ng her palm over his forehead. "I'll never forgive myself for putting you through this. And I swear I'm going to spend the rest of my life making it up to you—that is, if you still want me."

"What about Flame?" he asked.

LaRaine's eyes clouded and she shook her head. After all she had done, it still hurt LaRaine to think of Flame as a lost cause. "I left her on the ship for Paris. You can have her arrested now. I won't fight you anymore."

Brand staggered to his feet and started toward the upper deck. "Is that what you want?"

LaRaine frowned, unable to toss off the guilt she felt for her sister's behavior. "Isn't it what *you* want? I mean, it's what you've said we should do

493

all along. After what she's done to you, I wo
never ask you to look the other way again."

"You didn't say how you found me, LaRain

"Flame admitted to me what she'd done. S
couldn't go through with her plan. She knew s
was wrong. But that doesn't mean anything n
She still needs to pay for what she's done." S
looked up at him, her gaze beseeching. "Does
she?"

Brand nodded his head. "On the other hand,
telling you where I was, she may have saved r
life; and that deserves some consideration." Lea
ing on LaRaine, he started up the stairs.

A frisson of optimism curled up her spin
"You know, she told me where you were of h
own free will. She didn't have to. I didn't suspe
anything. A person who's really bad wouldn't ha
done that."

"No, I don't think so," Brand said with a smi
as they opened the door onto the deck above.

It was dawn, and the sunshine made everythin
they saw glisten with the gold of a new day.

"I still don't believe she's really bad, Brand," L
Raine sighed, gazing toward the sea. "She jus
doesn't know how to love or be loved. She though
that if I loved you I would stop loving her, so sh
fought to keep that from happening the only wa
she knew how. I tried to make her understand tha
loving is giving and sharing. But I failed.
couldn't overcome the past. By the time I foun
her, it was already too late to teach her to under
stand love."

"Maybe not," Brand said, wrapping his arms

494

ound her, feeling stronger as he breathed in the
isp morning air.

LaRaine looked at him quizzically. "What do
ou mean?"

"Maybe she understood after all. Maybe in those
ast minutes when she knew she couldn't go
hrough with having me killed, she finally under-
tood."

She stared at him for a few minutes, absorbing
what he had said. "She gave up the thing that
meant the most to her for my happiness." Her
tone was amazed, relieved.

As if in response to her revelation, the horn of
a tugboat sounded loudly. They looked up in time
to see the sturdy little vessel towing a much larger
ship out to the Gulf of Mexico.

"It's the *La Cygne!*" LaRaine cried, immediately
recognizing the lone cloaked figure on the deck as
her sister. She looked at Brand questioningly. "We
can have the captain signal to stop the ship and
have her taken into custody."

Brand smiled and pulled LaRaine closer into his
arms. "I think Faith Morgan has been punished
enough for the past, don't you?"

"Thank you, Brand!" She turned in his arms
and leaned her head back on his chest, covering
his hands at her waist with her own. *And thank
you, Faith. May the future finally bring you
peace, my sister. I'll always love you.*

"Do I what?" LaRaine asked a week later, feeling like a lighthearted girl for the first time in

what seemed like years. Maybe for the first ti
in her life. She could actually feel the guilt th
had consumed her for so long slipping away, me
ing into the past where it belonged.

"Do you love me?" Brand laughed, gloryin
the change in her.

"Haven't I told you?" she asked innocently.

"Not lately."

"Well, I do!" she sighed helplessly, tiring of th
game and wanting to be kissed, wanting to se
their love with the union of their mouths. "I lov
you with all my heart! I always have," she cor
fessed. Then she thought better of their first day
together and amended her words. "Well, almost a
ways."

"Where do we go from here?" he asked softly
studying her small hand in his, idly comparing th
textures, colors, shapes, and sizes. "Are you read
to think about the future?"

"The future is all I want to think about," sh
assured him. "As a matter of fact, I've given it
lot of thought."

"And—"

"What would you think if I told you I've always
had a dream of going out West?"

Brand's face broke into a smile. "What about
your dress shop?"

"I'll sell it. I think Margie would take it over. I
can't stay here anymore. There are too many re-
minders."

"What about Virginia? I thought you always
planned to go back there some day."

"Virginia's in my past, Brand. I don't want to

496

back. I want to go forward. And the more I read about the West, the more I feel that's where my future is."

"And is there room for a second person in this future of yours?" Brand asked.

"Are you sure you want to be part of my future—after all that's happened?"

"Don't you know you're my future, Rainy? How does California sound?"

LaRaine's eyes filled with tears. "It sounds wonderful." Anywhere would be heaven as long as they were together.

"Will you marry me, LaRaine Ashby? Will you be my future?"

"Just try and stop me!"

He hauled her to him and covered her lips with his, filling her mouth and her very soul with the essence of his love as his tongue raked in and out of the delectable hollow. He devoured her hungrily, and LaRaine returned his kiss just as greedily.

She knew she would die if she were suddenly denied his wonderful, life-supporting presence. Just like air and water, she now knew she could only live if she had Brand Colter in her life.

"I love you, Brand," LaRaine said against his mouth. "I'll never love another. Wherever you want to live, wherever you want to work, I want to be with you. I'll follow you to the ends of the earth if that's the only way I can have you."

"I don't think it will get down to that," Brand said, finally beginning to believe that what he had waited for so long was going to come true. "But it's nice to know—just in case I get an assignment at the end of the earth!"

And they kissed again, this time not stoppi
until they had shown each other with their bodi
how real their love was.

Epilogue

"Good morning, Mrs. Colter," Brand whispered into LaRaine's ear as he nibbled at the tender flesh along the column of her neck. "It's time to get up," he coaxed, sliding his hand between her thighs.

"Good morning, Mr. Colter," she answered sleepily, her marble-green eyes glittering with love. This was her favorite time of the day. Early morning, when there was no one in the world but the two of them, and they were free to love or talk—or both—without interruptions. "Did you sleep well last night?" she asked, arching her hips against his hand, which had begun to move over her stomach in slow circular motions.

"Mmm," he mumbled, kissing his way from the scented hollow at the base of her throat to the deep valley between her breasts. "But the best part about sleeping is waking up," he teased, opening his mouth over a rosy nipple and pulling gently on

499

it with his teeth. "You taste extra good in t
morning," he said, sucking the entire swollen t
into his mouth and bringing his hand up to cu
the underside of her lush breast and massage i
"Like warm, sweet cream."

LaRaine felt the familiar tightening deep insic
her belly, as if there were an invisible cord fror
her breast to her womb and it was being draw
deliciously taut by Brand's mouth. She sighed, giv
ing herself over to the feeling as she wrapped he
arms around his head and pulled him close
against her.

"I never get tired of waking up with you besid
me," he said against the softly rounded flesh o
her stomach, where his mouth had leisurely
traveled.

"That's good." Her words were breathless, his
mouth and tongue already setting her body afire,
as if it were the first time they had ever made
love. "Because you're stuck with me," she said, her
husky voice playfully threatening.

"I can't think of anywhere I'd rather be stuck,"
he said, meaning the double entendre as he nuz-
zled the coppery mound at the top of her long
slender legs. Separating her thighs, he dipped into
the warm flesh that arched against his mouth.

Lazily exploring the hills and valleys of her femininity, he left none of her unlaved by his hot
tongue, none of her secrets uncovered; and she
was immediately hurled over the precipice of sen-
suality with a vibrating, shuddering climax.

Then she was pulling on his hair, his ears, his
head, insisting that he enter her immediately, while

he threshold of her desire was quivering to be filled only by him.

He came willingly, covering her body with his and filling her mouth with his tongue. Suddenly she knew she had to taste him as he had her. Laying a palm against his shoulder, she rolled him over onto his back and buried her face in the forest of wiry black hair that covered his muscular chest.

Pulling at the curls with her lips, she worked her way across the muscled wall of his flat stomach, over the powerful sinew that covered his ribs, to pull a turgid, brown male nipple into her mouth. She sucked it long and hard, her tongue making agonizing circles around the tiny nub until she had worked it into a hard pebble and she could feel him writhing beneath her.

He tried to roll her over onto her back, but she wasn't ready yet. Lying atop the man she loved more than life itself, she slid downward, biting, kissing, and tasting his golden-tanned body until she was lying between his legs, his manhood before her.

Taking the hard male column in her hand, she caressed him slowly before bringing the love-moistened tip of his sex into the warmth of her mouth to know every bit of him as he knew her.

"Rainy, Rainy," he groaned, his head tossing helplessly from side to side until he could tolerate no more of the blessed torture. Unable to wait any longer before he entered her, he roughly pulled her up over his body to straddle him. With hands splayed against taut pectoral muscles, LaRaine held

herself above Brand's raised hips only an insta
before she allowed her full weight to settle ov
him, around him, the tight folds of her body pul
ing him deep into her warmth. Grinding her ow
hips against his gyrating pelvis, she rejoiced in th
glorious sense of oneness. She now felt complet
Had she ever before been so whole? So alive?

Raising and lowering herself on the swolle
maleness of him, LaRaine was flung wildly int
space, where she viewed the dawn of a new da
from astral heights. Her surroundings seemed t
be brightly illuminated in rich colored arcs, band
and streamers, and she cried out at the beauty o
the moment, only to cry out a second time wher
Brand gave a final thrust and emptied his showe
of life into her.

"Oh," she laughed breathlessly, falling on his
chest and taking a playful bite of his neck. "That
was wonderful," she murmured, tightening the
muscles of her womanhood around his shaft and
making him twitch involuntarily. "What will I do
if you ever get tired of me?" she groaned wistfully.

"By then, we'll both be dead. I can see it now."
His voice was husky and still shaky from their
strenuous lovemaking. "We'll have to be buried in
the same coffin—you know, in case there's 'life'
after death," he teased, pinching her bottom.

"You're terrible," LaRaine laughed throatily. "I
don't know what I'm going to do with you."

"Just what you've been doing. You do it so
well," he teased, slipping his hands beneath her
underarms and pulling her upward to run his
tongue over her perspiration-misted breasts.

"Mama! Daddy!" a little voice cut into their private world from outside their bedroom door. "Is it Christmas yet?"

"Yes, it's Christmas, Son," Brand answered, winking at LaRaine and allowing her to roll over and pull the covers up over both of them. "Come on in. I was just thinking about giving Mama her present." He slanted a sly grin toward his wife and shrugged his shoulders.

The invitation was all the small boy needed, and he came bursting through the door to leap on the bed and sit between his parents. "What are you going to give her? Can I see?"

"Sure you can," Brand said, looking mischievously at his wife.

LaRaine raised her eyebrows in pretended disapproval and clutched the blanket tighter to her bosom.

Grinning, Brand reached into the drawer of the bedside table. He produced a small gift-wrapped box and handed it to the redheaded, freckled four-year-old. "Here, Son. Give this to your mama."

The excited tot grabbed the package anxiously and started to hand it to his mother, but thought better of it. "Want me to open it for you, Mama," he offered, already untying the satin ribbon.

"Would you please, love? I'm too tired to do anything too strenuous this morning," she said, smiling at her husband with secret meaning.

Tommy didn't wait for LaRaine to finish speaking before he tore into the box. "Hey! It's a marble," he said disgustedly. "Mamas don't play marbles!"

503

"But this is a special marble, Tommy. It's not play with," Brand explained, taking the yellow a green and blue agate from its box. "See? It's necklace for Mama to wear. Mamas don't usual play with marbles, but there's nothing to say th can't wear them," he teased his son, allowing th marble to dangle in front of the boy's blue eye "Look at it very closely and tell me what you see.

"Just a marble!" the boy said, tired of tha present. "Can we go downstairs now and open th good presents?" he asked, kissing his mother o the cheek and bounding off the bed to hurry hi parents up.

"Just a marble?" Brand reached out and grabbed the boy around the waist and hauled him onto his chest, tickling him. "That marble wa: mine when I was about your age, and it looks jus like your mama's eyes. I bet Mama doesn't think it's *just a marble*, do you, Mama?" he asked, grinning expectantly at LaRaine, seeing her answer in her eyes.

"No, it's not 'just a marble.' Anyone can see it's the most wonderful marble in the world. I'll treasure it all my life," she promised, tears blurring her vision as she watched her husband and son wrestle on the bed.

Taking a swipe at the tears that coursed down her cheeks, LaRaine swatted Tommy on the bottom and scooted him off the bed. "Go see if the girls are awake while Daddy and I dress. Then we'll all go downstairs together to see what Santa Claus brought to good little children."

"Do *they* have to come, too?" Tommy whined,

504

noyed at the thought of sharing Christmas with
s younger sisters. "They'll just tear everything
," he groaned disgustedly, then ran out of the
om to noisily waken the two-year-old twins.

"So much for brotherly love," Brand laughed,
vinging his feet to the floor and reaching for his
obe.

"He'll appreciate them more when they get a
ttle bigger," she defended her son, knowing the
oy loved his sisters a great deal, but that they
vere active enough to try the patience of Job,
nuch less a four-year-old boy who hated having
nyone disturb his belongings. "You have to ad-
nit, one two-year-old in a house was trying, and
wo are more than twice the trouble. You're not
sorry, are you?" she asked, dragging the brush
through her long hair, once again its natural copper color.

Coming up behind her, Brand took the brush
from her hand and ran it lovingly through the
waves that cascaded down her back. "No, I'm not
sorry. I can't bear to think of life without any one
of them. In fact, I wouldn't mind having a few
more—though our son might have something to
say about that."

"You really would want more children?"

"As long as they're yours," he said smiling at
her in the mirror. "You know how much I like
making them," he reminded her with a mischievous
wink.

"In that case, I think I'll give you your Christmas present early, too. At least I'll give you a
hint. I won't be able to have the actual item deliv-

ered for about six months. I think you can ex[
it around the middle of June," she said casua
studying his surprised expression in the mirror a
loving the happiness she saw there.

"You mean we're going to have another bab
he shouted, slamming down the brush and lift
LaRaine in his arms to whirl her around. "Wl
did it happen? How?" he asked numbly.

"Don't tell me you still don't know the answ
to those questions," LaRaine giggled, wrapping l
arms around her husband's neck and kissing
mouth long and hard.

Brand smiled sheepishly. "Yeah, I guess I do

"Do you know what would make today perfect
she asked, suddenly pensive.

"What?"

"I wish my sister could see our beautiful ch
dren."

"You still miss her, don't you?"

LaRaine's eyes filled with tears and she nodde
"I can't help worrying about her. Her letters a
some comfort. At least I know she's alive ar
making a new life for herself in Paris. But
would be so nice to see her after all this time. D
you think we . . ."

"Tell you what, why don't I write and invite he
for a visit? Maybe if the invitation came fro
me . . ."

"Oh, Brand!" LaRaine cried, throwing her arm
around his neck. "Would you really do that fo
me?"

Brand hugged her tighter. "Like you said, it
been a long time. It's about time we put the pa[

hind us once and for all and concentrated on e future." He gave her stomach an affectionate t.

"Mama, Daddy. They're up! Let's go!" the little >y's voice announced as he rounded the corner in eir doorway. Seeing his parents kissing, he smiled ppily and energetically threw himself across the ace that separated him from them and hugged em. He was only slightly disgruntled when his vo raven-haired sisters toddled in and pushed eir way into the family embrace.

LaRaine and Brand stooped down to encompass neir babies in their embrace and smiled at each ther over the tiny heads. "Are you sure?" she nouthed silently.

"I'm sure," he mouthed in return. Gathering all hree wriggling, giggling children in his arms, Brand stood up and started out of the room. "Let's go see if Santa Claus brought me anything," ne teased, leaving LaRaine to run after her family as they descended the staircase.

"Santa Claus doesn't bring presents to grownups," Tommy argued, happy in his father's arms, even if he had to share the moment with his little sisters.

Brand poked out his lip. "He doesn't?" Wheeling about, he started back up the stairs—to the horrified dismay of his son and to the childish giggles of his daughters.

"Quit torturing your son," LaRaine chuckled, turning her husband around and heading him in the right direction. "Santa brought you something, Daddy. Go on downstairs,"

"Yes, he brought me something. And every y
it gets better and better," Brand said, leaning b
to kiss his wife's cheek.

"Come on, Daddy!" the boy's high-pitched vc
insisted.

"Yes, Son. I wouldn't miss this for the worl

"Neither would I," LaRaine crooned into Bran
ear, from the stair behind him. "Neither would